"An absolute triumph of a book. Propulsive and
to the book, a heartbroken rage that threads th
—Cassandra Khaw, bestselling author

"This book will mess you up, and you'll be glad. ping horror with heart (and viscera) in spades."

—Kiersten White, #1 *New York Times* bestselling author of *Hide*

"Nat Cassidy has written a creepy page-turner where the scariest things of all are what reside in the human (or inhuman) heart."

—Paul Tremblay, author of *The Cabin at the End of the World* and *A Head Full of Ghosts*

"Delectably dark, gorgeously gory, and hypnotically engrossing. With its strong *Rosemary's Baby* vibe and contemporary sensibilities, *Nestlings* brings the Manhattan gothic to a triumphant new level."

—Zoje Stage, bestselling author of *Baby Teeth* and *Mothered*

"A fresh take on an old monster, *Nestlings* is an absolutely horrifying tale. Just remember: When you're reading into the wee hours, turn on all the lights in the house. It helps. A little." —Andy Davidson, author of *The Hollow Kind*

"Told with the same verve and sharpness of classic 1980s literary horror blockbusters penned by Stephen King or Robert R. McCammon, *Nestlings* is a modern, dread-filled masterpiece."

—Eric LaRocca, author of *Things Have Gotten Worse Since We Last Spoke*

"*Nestlings* slides beneath the itchy flesh and burrows, tick-like, into your heart. . . . It will flood your senses with the sweet calling of the dark. But worry not, because Cassidy leaves a pinprick of light within reach, a distant beacon that feels like hope." —Philip Fracassi, author of *Boys in the Valley*

"Surprising and mysterious. *Nestlings* is rich in the ominous discomfort of a prize that's too good to be true. This book sticks to your skin."

—Hailey Piper, Bram Stoker Award–winning author of *Queen of Teeth*

"Like *The Shining* meets *The Changeling*. . . . I think people are going to lose their minds over this book. Like *Mary,* it has all the makings of a classic."

—Rachel Harrison, bestselling author of *Cackle* and *Such Sharp Teeth*

"Couldn't put it down." —Clay McLeod Chapman, author of *The Remaking*

NIGHTFIRE BOOKS BY NAT CASSIDY

*Mary: An Awakening of Terror*

# NESTLINGS

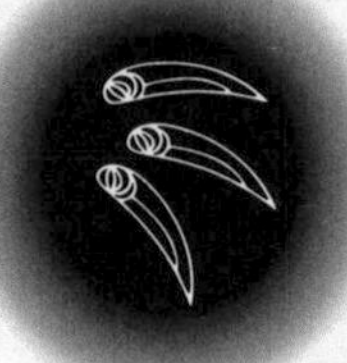

NAT CASSIDY

TOR PUBLISHING GROUP
NEW YORK

NESTLINGS



A Nightfire Book
Published by Tom Doherty Associates / Tor Publishing Group
120 Broadway
New York, NY 10271

www.tornightfire.com



The Library of Congress Cataloging-in-Publication Data is available upon request.

ISBN 978-1-250-26525-8 (trade paperback)
ISBN 978-1-250-26524-1 (ebook)



First Edition: 2023

Printed in the United States of America

0 9 8 7 6

*For Asta, Leonard, and Hailey.*
*And for Kelley, the strongest human I know.*

# NOTE

A quick heads-up about the content of this book. You're going to find marriage troubles, parental trauma, child endangerment, talk/images of infanticide, postpartum depression, suicidal ideation, bodily harm, ableism (internalized and externalized), anti-Semitism (internalized and externalized), claustrophobia, some gaslighting, and a whole lotta bug stuff. There's also a character who's a real racist, sexist piece of shit.

Look beyond the broken bottles
Past the rotting wooden stairs
Root out the wine-dark honeyed center
Not everyone can live like millionaires

Look through the air-thin walls
Tear up the floorboards, strip the paint
Go over every inch of space with the patience of a saint
Grab your hat, get your coat
The cellar door is an open throat

—The Mountain Goats, "The House That Dripped Blood"

I am gonna make it through this year if it kills me.

—The Mountain Goats, "This Year"

# PART ONE

## OUTSIDERS

# WALK-THROUGH

## 1

*We don't belong here.*

That thought, quiet but insistent—like a best friend tugging on her sleeve, trying to pull her out of an embarrassing, maybe even dangerous, situation. *Get out, hurry, before anyone notices.*

Ana did her best to ignore it.

She looked out the huge living room window, where wintry green-and-white Central Park spread out beneath her. She could see all the way across Manhattan to the East River from this vacant, top-floor apartment.

Reid and the broker, Vera, were in the second bedroom. Vera—(*was* she a broker? It suddenly occurred to Ana they had no idea what the woman's official job was)—could be heard delighting Reid with trivia about the building. Reid could be heard delighting Vera with videos of their almost-one-year-old daughter, Charlie.

Ana, not delighted, remained alone with her thoughts.

*We don't belong here.*

*We don't belong here.*

*We—*

Eventually, Vera and Reid came back into the living room. Vera explained how the same man who'd designed Central Park, Frederick Olmsted, had also designed the Deptford's courtyard—something of a visual joke, but also an appeal to Olmsted's vanity, because now tenants could reflect on his genius whether they looked inward or out.

Reid's vanity also appeared piqued. Ana had never seen him hang on someone's every word like this. *He needs this,* she thought.

"I can't get over how green the courtyard is!" he exclaimed. "I mean, it's January!"

"Hardy plants from the mother country," Vera said—though, where was she from, Long Island? "Hey, show me another video of your little one! I can't get over that noise she makes! She's like a baby bird."

"That's what we call her!" Reid eagerly dug out his phone.

Ana excused herself with a tight smile. Wrapped up in their enthusiasm, Reid and Vera barely registered it. Although, Reid brushed a hand against Ana's shoulders as she passed between them.

The second bedroom was just like the rest of the apartment: perfect.

This would obviously be Charlie's room. If they lived here, Charlie would grow up looking down ( . . . down . . . down) at the aforementioned courtyard.

At the center of the huge courtyard was a massive, wild-looking forest—it *was* shockingly green and vibrant. Hardy plants, indeed. In the middle of the foliage lay a flat, tamed rectangle of grass. From this high up, Ana got the so-called visual joke right away: all those wild trees were buildings, skyscrapers, and the flat grass was Central Park in miniature.

*We don't belong here.*

From the other room, Vera cooed rapturously over another video.

What a bizarre woman. Twitchy. Off-putting. Ana sensed something like desperation in her, which was laughable because . . . why would anyone showing off a luxury apartment at the Deptford to a couple of lower-middle-class nobodies like Ana and Reid feel desperate? It's not like anyone in the history of ever would say no, right?

Ana leaned her head against the cool glass of the window. She could almost feel the building swaying in the winter wind—but that had to be her imagination.

Technically, this floor, the top floor, was the eighteenth, but because of the duplexes and triplexes beneath them—the apartments inhabited by the movie stars, financial moguls, famous musicians, maybe even, God help us, some unholy combination of all three—they were something like twenty-five stories high. Maybe even thirty, it was impossible to really say.

Ana and Reid had entered the housing lottery for the Deptford Apartment as a joke when they first started looking for a place together a little over a decade ago. Why had they won it *now*? It was so fucking unfair.

*You have to tell him.*

That made her feel slightly nauseous. She closed her eyes.

When she opened them, she noticed a gnarled, twisted face staring back at her.

Across the courtyard, just above her line of sight, under the peaked gables of the roof.

A pug-nosed, leering creature with its stony mouth pulled into a comical pout.

When they'd been notified about their names coming up in the housing lottery yesterday, Ana googled the building, curious what insider info she could find. She came up surprisingly short. Plenty of surface appreciation, but, despite being one of New York's most famous apartment buildings, no movies had ever been shot inside, no photographers had ever been allowed in for so much as a *Vanity Fair* spread, no tell-all books had hit the bestseller lists. No previous lottery winners had started so much as a blog. New York City seemed to enjoy keeping intimate details about the Deptford a secret.

Except for its gargoyles.

Besides the Chrysler Building and maybe the Woolworth Building or City College, the Deptford had some of the city's most famous gargoyles. Vera had pointed them out when she met Ana and Reid on the street half an hour ago.

"Even when the Deptford was only three stories tall, those gargoyles have been in place. Rumor has it they were fashioned out of the stones of an ancient Valland graveyard where Thomas Emile Janebridge's earliest traceable relatives were buried. They protect the building. And after a hundred and forty-four years, I think we can assume they work, huh?"

Ana and Reid had craned their necks upward to see them, looking like any of the other clustered tourists holding up pedestrian traffic on Eighty-Second Street, gaping and gawking in front of the black-and-gold iron gates surrounding the building. The building was used to gapers and gawkers. It was the Deptford, after all. The kind of building that makes you stop and say, *Wow, what a city. Maybe one day I'll live in a place like—*

A hand fell on her shoulder. She jumped in her seat.

"So? What do you think?" It was Reid. Eyes wide, tone hushed. Giddy.

"It's . . . it's a lot."

He squatted down to her eye level. "I know," he said. "But . . . Maybe this is finally a lot in a good way? I mean, I looked around and the entire apartment is . . ."

"Perfect."

"That's the only word for it! Even the doorways are wide enough! And Vera said they'd be able to lower some countertops and install everything in the bathroom for us!"

"Right. But . . ." She trailed off, hoping he'd know where she was going with the thought.

"What?"

"Reid." Dull embarrassment pulsed through her, followed, as usual, by a humming, intensifying anger. Why was he making her say it?

"What?"

"Notice anything else about that courtyard?"

He went to the window. "I mean, Charlie's gonna love this view. Did you notice how there's that little patch of green in the middle down there? It's like the wild trees are buildings and then there's a little Central Park. Vera was just saying how it can almost make you feel like you're even higher up because—oh."

He finally looked at her.

Then he looked at her wheelchair.

She watched his face as it registered what he should have known all along.

"Fuck."

## 2

They kept their voices low.

"What if there's a fire? What if the elevator breaks down? I just—how can I feel safe—?"

"No," he said, "no, you're right. One hundred percent. Fuck. We need to say no, right?"

To his credit, he didn't hesitate. All the same, she wished he hadn't phrased it as a question. She wished he'd just made the horrific decision for her, taken any responsibility off her so she could resent him and be thankful in equal measure. She didn't *want* to say no. She wanted to say yes to this more than she'd wanted to say yes to anything in her life.

"I fucking hate this," she said, feeling the prick of tears, craving permission to hit something, him, herself, the handles of her goddamn off-the-rack, piece-of-shit wheelchair, anything. "Why does it have to be the top fucking floor?!"

All they'd been told was that their name had been pulled in the housing lottery. Vera hadn't even mentioned the apartment number when she took them inside the building; Ana and Reid had to piece it together, floor by floor, in that cramped, deco-style elevator that didn't stop going up . . .

And up . . .

And up . . .

As if feeding off their increasing dismay, it was during that elevator ride that Vera had asked, "Have you always . . . ?" Her expression twitched toward Ana's wheelchair as effectively as a hand gesture.

"No," Ana said quietly, dreading how much higher they could possibly go. "Just a little under a year."

"But it's not forever!" Reid blurted.

"We don't know that," Ana said as if apologizing for an embarrassing outburst.

Up . . . and up . . .

Vera was undeterred, fascinated. "Was there an accident?"

An incredibly rude question, but Ana almost appreciated its naked rubbernecking.

"Sort of." She could have left it there, but dreadful silence unspooled as the elevator crept impossibly, horribly upward. "We were really stubborn about wanting to avoid a C-section, but it was a long labor and the epidural kept me from feeling how badly the position I was in was actually hurting me." The lithotomy position, legs spread as far as they could go, which she indicated with her hands in her lap. "I had an old dance injury in just the right spot. Wound up causing a hemorrhage in my spinal column. I didn't know how bad it was until I tried to get out of bed the next day."

"Goodness," Vera said. "Is that common?"

Ana remembered the neurologist she'd been referred to, shaking his head and sighing (while making eye contact mostly with Reid): *You have to understand, this sort of injury is a million to one . . . billion to one, even . . .*

"Nope!" Ana tried to sound upbeat. "Super rare. Billion to one."

"Goodness," Vera repeated, not without sympathy. "I guess you've won all sorts of lotteries lately, haven't you?"

That's when the elevator gently bumped to a stop at their floor and the silent, practically invisible elevator operator who'd been lurking in the corner this entire time pulled an almost-maritime lever to open the gate.

Now, in the second bedroom, Reid stroked Ana's arm.

"I know you do," he said. He kissed her hand. "It's okay. We'll just say no. Easy as that. The timing isn't right, and, y'know . . . it happens." He almost sounded like he meant it. "It's too small for us anyway. Where are we gonna put your voice-over booth? It'd have to go in the living room, and then furniture would be all crazy around it. And Charlie would outgrow this room quick."

"But . . . people do this all the time, right?" Now she was desperate for a reason not to say no. It wasn't fair. If their names had been pulled at any other point in their lives, jumping at this opportunity would've been a no-brainer! Why did it have to be an any-kind-of-brainer now?

*You've won all sorts of lotteries lately, haven't you . . .*

"Do what?"

"Move to such high floors when they're . . ." She gestured to her wheelchair: a cheap, Medline Basic Lightweight.

"I don't know," he said genuinely. There was so much they were still learning. Then: "I mean, maybe once we're in the building for a little while, we could get priority to transfer to another apartment? I don't know."

They sat in silence for a moment, Ana in her chair, Reid crouching next to her.

Ana found herself looking at her hands. She spoke in an embarrassed, confessional whisper.

"I can't stop thinking . . . we don't belong here. Like . . . places like this just aren't meant for people like us."

"What do you mean? They've got these lottery units for a reason—"

"No. Not that. I mean people like *us.* Cursed people. Luckless people."

"Honey," he sighed. "Come on. Cursed? We're not—"

"Then why is this happening? Right *now*?"

He took her hand. It was sweaty, the calluses from eleven months in her chair already prominent.

"Why does *anything* happen? Maybe this is just a sign that, I don't know, it's time to start looking for a new place anyway. Turn a page, start fresh after the year we've had. Somewhere *actually* perfect. That's big enough, and still in our price range, and on a first floor, and, best of all—"

"No Frank?"

"Exactly."

"Does a place like that exist?"

He shrugged. "Only one way to find out."

But melancholy had crept into his voice. The reality of saying goodbye to this apartment was beginning to sink in, she could tell.

They gave themselves one final moment in the room. Then Reid said:

"Thanks for coming with me to check it out. I know you hate coming into the city." He kissed her forehead, then leaned his own against hers. "I love you."

"You don't have to," she said.

"Tell it to my heeaaart." He'd flipped his voice into a soft falsetto, sounding more like a cartoon chicken than the soulful '90s R&B crooner he was trying to mimic.

It got a smile from her all the same. "You're disgusting."

"Should we get going? Relieve the DelGrossos from baby duty?" Their trip back to Ditmas would be long and annoying—more so than it used to be on account of now having to find the right chair-accessible stations and buses. Maybe they'd throw caution to the wind and spring for a cab, assuming it didn't take forever to flag down the right kind. It's not like they'd be paying for movers now.

Ana gave his hand a squeeze. "Yeah."

He got behind her chair to help push her out to the living room. Sometimes she hated when he did that. Not this time.

## 3

"Well," Vera said. "What do we think? Perfect for baby, isn't it?"

She'd been leaning against the kitchen counter when Ana and Reid had come out of the bedroom. For the briefest of moments, it looked as if she'd been in a light doze. Her face twitched . . . and her hands stayed pressed primly in front of her like a kindergarten teacher.

"Perfect," Ana said. She wheeled herself away, back toward the living room window overlooking the park, while Reid delivered the bad news.

They were twenty-something stories up. Up against the bedroom window, the drop had been dizzying . . . but from here, the city stretched out as if promising to catch them. God, it was hard, almost impossible, to imagine seeing a view like this every day and not feeling capable of doing anything.

It was all about perspective, Ana realized.

And hadn't they fallen off higher cliffs than this and survived?

*You've won all sorts of lotteries lately, haven't you?* That was certainly true. Billion-to-one shots, left and right. Dark ones like her injury, her lack of progress in PT. Bright ones like meeting each other in the first place. Or winning an apartment at the Deptford.

They'd made it this far. If anyone shouldn't be daunted by a precipice, it was them.

What was one more? Why *couldn't* they belong here?

"Unfortunately," Reid was saying to Vera, "we've hit a pretty big snag."

"Oh?" Vera asked, blinking and twitching at the unimaginable, unprecedented taste of rejection. Her hands stayed clasped in front of her.

"Yeah," Reid began. He swallowed, cleared his throat. "Yeah, I just don't think we—"

"—have the right furniture for this layout," Ana cut in, bright and loud and confident. She stared out the window. "So we're gonna have to buy some new pieces. But we can figure that out after we move in."

Reid looked down at her in surprise. Ana met his eyes with hers, a gesture that might as well have been two hands linking before leaping together, and smiled.

## 4

With the couple gone, Vera the broker-not-broker exhaled. They would work.

Disappointing that they hadn't brought the baby with them—it would've been nice to see her in person—but the vetting had been thorough, and the husband had been more than happy to show photos and videos.

A beautiful child.

The mother's disability was an asset, too.

In a word, they were *perfect.*

Envy rocketed through her, as it often did when she met lucky new tenants of the Deptford.

Then she remembered what she was holding on to. She looked down, wondering if the couple had thought it odd she hadn't shaken their hands as they left.

No, probably not. They had their own issues to discuss.

The roach continued to squirm against her palms.

Vera carefully opened her hands, then plucked the roach up by its back. Its legs kicked helplessly.

She'd caught it scurrying across the kitchen counter while the couple talked in the second bedroom. It was quick, but not quick enough.

"You don't belong here," she reprimanded with a grin, an actual, genuine grin.

Roaches were common enough in any building—and this particular apartment had sat empty for a few months now—but she couldn't help feeling a sense of . . . holy confirmation finding one at this exact moment. This building teemed with life, after all. Its new tenants were about to discover just what that could mean.

Here came that envy again. They were so *lucky*. Vera wished she could experience what the young couple was about to experience. What their baby would get to experience.

Vera settled for the closest thing.

She popped the shiny, brownish-black insect into her mouth. It scrambled impotently against her teeth, her palate, until that oh-so-satisfying crunch bathed her tongue and flooded her senses.

Vera closed her eyes and swallowed slowly, savoring all she could of the warm, bitter, sweetly delicious taste of life.

# RIPTIDE

## 1

Because life was bitter *and* sweet, wasn't it? Like that Joni Mitchell song about holy wine.

Or, no—

Reid came to an abrupt stop on the semi-crowded sidewalk on Fifty-Ninth Street. He paused the music in his earbuds, just in time to hear someone seethe as they veered around him—"*Good job, asshole!*" Reid didn't care; he was too busy chasing the thought.

No, the better analogy was . . . life was like Joni Mitchell's entire catalog. Increasingly complex and difficult to understand but still full of face-smacking beauty if you were willing to forgo expectations and *listen.*

Yeah. He liked that. There was even a possible song here. "A Song for Joni," or something.

Lyrics were never his strong suit—melodic hooks came so much easier—and writing an homage to one of the greatest lyricists of all time would be a hell of a presumption. Still. He hadn't written a new song in months. Hadn't even had an idea for one.

What an unexpected gift, today of all days, when he was so exhausted he could barely think straight.

*I bet Joni feels like this from time to time, too.*

> *Oh, Joni, I feel a lot like you*
> *But I could never do the things you do.*

Smiling a private smile, he pulled out his phone and wrote the lines down in his notes app.

That done, he blinked and looked around. It was a beautiful, temperate mid-January afternoon in Manhattan. The air felt crisp, but the sun kept it from being truly cold. The lunch-hour pedestrian rush filled the sidewalks, and somewhere, just far enough to sound like the air itself, someone was busking on a saxophone. It was exactly the kind of day made for being alive in New York City.

Reid was on his lunch break. He carried a small loaf of bread in a clear plastic bag, and he moved quickly, running errands before he had to be back at his desk—or at least, that had been the plan before he slammed on the brakes.

He felt like a man spat out after being dragged along by a riptide. Disoriented. Gasping.

But also somehow happier than he could remember feeling in a long, long time.

Bitter *and* sweet.

Had the events of the past week *actually* happened?

It had taken this moment—this random, arbitrary New York moment, occasioned by the barely articulated inspiration for a new song—to make him stop and take it all in.

Yesterday, they had moved into the Deptford.

## 2

It hadn't been easy—no wonder everything seemed a little blurry in retrospect.

After Ana and Reid had gotten back from their walk-through of the apartment, they'd discovered a voicemail on Reid's phone from an unknown number. There'd been no ring, no missed call.

A stranger's voice, flat and impersonal, informed them, "the Applicants," that if they were indeed interested in the apartment at the Deptford they now had, "as per the statutes and bylaws provided, seven days to move in." Failure to do so in the provided time would result "in our beginning the interview process with the next Applicants."

The voice added with ominous finality, "That process will not take long."

Seven fucking days. To pack up their entire apartment—or, more accurately, for *Reid* to pack up their entire apartment. Ana wasn't going to be able to be much help, as much as he hated to admit that to himself.

There'd also be the matter of Frank. Their belligerent, meddlesome, obnoxious, racist, please-God-soon-to-be-*former* landlord.

Frank would be furious at them for breaking their lease. He'd be outraged once he saw the private modifications they'd made to the apartment. And more than anything, he'd be insistent that he be involved in every step of the moving-out process. He'd want to oversee how they packed things up; he'd want to make sure they weren't scratching the floors; he'd want to offer Southern Comfort–scented monologues about all the things they were doing wrong, all the reasons they were idiots for wanting to move out of his apartment, and oh by the way, what kinda movers did you hire, did you see on *Tucker* about the latest horde of immigrants coming to sully our fair, white country? Parasites, they are, frickin' cock-a-roaches.

Listening to that voicemail from the Deptford, Reid had known immediately that their next week would be a nightmare.

And yet, he hadn't felt upset about it. Because he'd known, one way or another, he was going to *make* this move happen. All the ensuing sweat and sleep deprivation would be his down payment for their sweeter, less bitter life.

They'd waited until the night before to tell Frank, betting he wouldn't answer his phone during his so-called highball time. Their gamble paid off. They left a simple, vague message: so sorry, there's been another emergency, we're going to have to move in with Ana's mother in Connecticut. (The idea of moving in with Ana's mom was hilarious, but Frank had never bothered to ask about the intricacies of that particular relationship.)

For an exorbitant extra fee, they'd also arranged for movers to arrive a couple of hours before dawn. They loaded their stuff out under cover of night. Quick and dirty.

Ana sat with Charlie in the car they'd rented to move their most fragile and personal items while Reid directed the movers and tidied things up in their wake. When he finally joined his wife and baby daughter, he assured Ana that everything was in good order, and the three of them said goodbye to the first apartment they'd shared together as a family. Not the happiest of memories there, but an important locale all the same.

And if Reid left out a few details, like just how *exactly* the apartment looked when they left it? Hey, that's what security deposits were for. Besides, Frank had been a real piece of shit during their time there. Consider this his comment card.

They moved into the Deptford as the sun rose. A fitting image, all told.

By noon, the movers had gone, and they were finally, firmly in place in their nest.

Charlie was cranky, unsettled, and confused.

Ana was clearly nervous and conflicted.

Reid was exhausted and not thrilled that he had to go to work the next day.

But they were *in*.

## 3

He still hadn't moved from his spot on Fifty-Ninth Street. Not yet.

He reached into the clear plastic bag he carried and tore off a hunk of bread. Challah, courtesy of the Chabad Lubavitchers who parked their Mitzvah Tank nearby and surveyed his office building every week to ask each Jewish person they could find if they wanted to hear a Torah portion and/or wrap themselves with some tefillin. Reid always passed on those last parts, but he appreciated the bread—it made for a good lunch when he was trying to pinch pennies.

He was going to get walking again in a minute. Ana's voice-over booth had gotten messed up during the move, and she needed Reid to pick up some parts from the Home Depot on Lexington.

But first, Reid realized there'd been another reason he stopped, not just the sudden lyrical inspiration.

He turned around and, farther back up the block, he saw the building he'd passed while he'd been lost in thought.

The Argosy Book Store. One of the few remaining bookstores in this neighborhood—one that, as far as Reid knew, specialized in old, random, out-of-print books.

In all his googling of the Deptford, he'd found only one book written about the building. A gossipy paperback written in the 1970s, out of print for decades. Amazon had some copies for sale, but they were going for more than he should spend on a book, and Ana was philosophically opposed to using Amazon if they could help it, so . . .

Was this bookstore worth a visit?

He chewed another hunk of bread. He always got indecisive when he was tired.

*How about we think of it as a little test?*

Nothing important, nothing that *means* anything. Just a fun little test to see if their luck really *had* turned around.

He walked back to the bookstore.

The Argosy overwhelmed him. It was one of those intimidating, old-timey bookstores that used to be all over the city, full of rich brown, wooden shelves and ladders and spines. You half expected to get chased out if you didn't know the right ISBN or Dewey decimal or whatever. Reid always felt stupid in bookstores like these. Among his many day jobs over the years, he'd even worked at Keats & Yeats, a bookstore in the Village, in his early twenties, but he'd been so obviously useless there, it was one of the only gigs he'd ever been straight fired from.

Near the front of the Argosy, troughs and bins held used books for a dollar. Reid looked there first, idly flipping through, not knowing where else to start, already certain this would be a waste of time and that he'd—

The book was in the very first trough.

## 4

There was a word Reid's mom used whenever she spoke of the early days, when she first met his dad—the happier times, before he'd revealed himself as a selfish, cowardly piece of shit capable of abandoning his family, never to be seen again. *Bashert.* In a romantic context, it meant "soulmate." More generally, it meant fate. Destiny. God's plan.

That word rang in Reid's ears as he stepped back into the January sun, laughing. Actually laughing. He looked at the old paperback in his hands. Holy shit, he couldn't believe it.

*Behind the Iron Gate: An Unauthorized History of the Deptford Apartment Building, New York's Most Mysterious Home,* by Preston Treadwell.

It was just *there.* Flipped through by how many hands, ignored by how many browsers?

Great condition.

Only a dollar.

They didn't even charge him tax.

*Bashert.*

He was hit by a sudden impulse to call his mom, tell her everything.

His laughter died.

For a moment, it all felt so overwhelming, he almost started crying.

He couldn't call his mom; she'd been dead for well over a year now. COVID had snuck into her nursing home and, to paraphrase Springsteen (a better lyricist than Reid could ever hope to be), that was all she wrote. A common enough tale these days. Even Ana's mom had caught it in her own assisted living facility around the same time—although, typical of Ana's mother's refusal to ever do what anyone wanted, she shook it off and survived.

The loss of his mom had been overshadowed by the rest of the chaos he and Ana had endured lately—the unpleasant, savings-draining fertility procedures, the pregnancy, the difficult labor, the paralysis, the compounding expenses, the loss of Ana's personal trainer income, the newborn . . . and, of course, that night with the knife . . .

Reid tried not to think about any of that. The way a tightrope walker tries not to think about the hard ground below.

He looked around at the block he stood on. Really looked at it.

It seemed like every other storefront was empty. Windows were papered over, or left vacant. Realtor signs were as common as people sleeping in doorways lately. New York had started to look like the caricature his mom had always feared: destitute, desperate. Broken.

The city had been through so goddamn much. Even beyond the baseline PTSD from that nightmarish, ambulance-scored spring of 2020. The mass graves, the portable morgues. Then came the economic contractions. The rise in anger, in violence. Not from the racist stock footage on the news but from the news viewers looking for someone to blame. Sooner or later, their sights always landed on the same group as the ultimate cause, didn't they? Swastika graffiti wasn't uncommon anymore, politicians (and even some celebrities) were trying on anti-Semitism like some vintage, tailored coat, and Reid was glad his mom wasn't alive to see all that.

His mood began to deflate—too much bitter creeping into the sweet.

Then he looked back down at the book he'd purchased. A beautiful building graced the cover. *His* building. His new home.

In the distance, the busking saxophonist began a new song.

Reid felt a curious sensation coming from a dozen blocks away, farther north, up along the park.

A pulse.

No. More like . . . a gentle tug. As ephemeral as the music.

Distance made it faint, but the direction was unmistakable.

The Deptford. It had been waiting for him as surely as the book in his hands.

His mom would be proud. Proud of him for finding this new apartment. For taking care of his wife and his daughter. For not letting grief break him down. For *surviving.*

The same could be said of his city, his chosen home.

Every person walking by—even the fuckface who'd cursed at him when he broke the cardinal rule of pedestrian traffic, or the goddamn bless-his-brass-blowing-heart saxophonist—they were all still going. And soon, Reid would have new music of his own to add to this joyful noise.

His heart swelled with love. There was no other way to describe it.

He *loved* this goddamn city.

And this bittersweetness? This holy wine? This is what it means to be a New Yorker.

They had been through hell. They still wore masks or walked around with them in their pockets just in case. They had the scars

(*Ana put the knife down*)

(*What were you doing?!*)

to prove they had made it through the worst years of their lives. But only survivors have scars in the first place.

Reid came to an abrupt decision: change of plans for the rest of today's lunch break.

He would find the nearest homeless person and give them the bread he was currently noshing on—they wouldn't be hard to find, and they needed it more than he did.

Next, he was going to buy himself a nice lunch, because he could afford it. He was going to eat that lunch in the goddamn sunshine, and he was going to start reading his new book.

After that, he'd still have time to stop by a hardware store. And if he didn't? Hey, he could do it on his walk home. He could *walk* home now. No more hours spent crammed in the subway on the interminable trek to South Brooklyn.

Then when he got home, he would kiss his wife and his daughter—the two jewels of his life (*and were they bittersweet sometimes? Sure. But he could push those feelings all the way down, press those grapes into holy wine, baby*)—and he was going to write a new song.

He *loved* this goddamn city.

But he didn't move from where he was standing. Not yet. For now, he wanted to relish this feeling.

After the past couple of years, he wanted to stay in this moment forever.

# LOOSE

## 1

"Whoa," Georgia said, standing in the living room and turning in a circle as if to take in as much of the apartment as she could. "This place *sucks*."

Ana nodded solemnly. "I know. We're the laughingstock of New York."

"We laugh so as to not cry for you poor, pathetic dum-dums."

Georgia stood five feet ten inches tall, with broad shoulders and a lean but muscular build. Even now, wearing blue-and-black exercise pants and an oversized, faux-vintage *ThunderCats* T-shirt, a winter coat draped over one arm, and her hair pulled back in a thoughtless ponytail, Ana thought Georgia looked like a comic book superheroine: unquestionably strong and effortlessly feminine. Which was weirdly appropriate considering her full name was Georgia O'Keefe.

"Don't let that fool you," she'd told Ana when they first met years ago. "I can't paint a tree to save my life, let alone a portrait of your lady bits. But my mama's mama was Georgia, and she died right before I was born. And nothing to be done about my daddy's last name, so. Coulda been worse: I went to high school with a girl named Holly Wood. Parents are monsters."

She still had a soft twang from her Midland, Texas, upbringing, as well as a dry, sarcastic wit that made Ana like her immediately. She was the sort of person you instantly wanted to impress, to try to get a reaction out of her usual deadpan demeanor. It was the perfect quality for a physical therapist.

But that's not why she was here today.

Georgia hung up her coat and popped a piece of gum in her mouth.

"Wanna show me the rest of this farthole before we get to work?"

## 2

The amenities impressed her. Texas girl or not, Georgia was New Yorker enough to know a miracle apartment when she saw one. The huge windows overlooking the park and the city. The dishwasher. The washer-dryer hidden in one of the numerous closets. The floors—in some rooms hardwood, in others marbled tile—that shone and sparkled no matter how many feet shuffled over them. But Georgia also thought of Ana as a client and a friend, so what she was *really* interested in was a different set of features.

Not everything passed muster. There were a few light switches that were a little too high. All the upper kitchen cabinets might as well have been on the moon. The bathroom sink used two handles instead of one. Little things like that. But overall, Georgia had to admit, they—whoever *they* were at the Deptford—had done an extraordinary job making the apartment more accessible. Countertops had been lowered in the kitchen (without sacrificing much storage space, hallelujah). The sink was low enough in the bathroom and the toilet had been raised. In fact, the whole bathroom was a marvel. There was a shower stall *and* a tub, and the shower had a seat *and* a rail.

"Okay, then," Georgia said, almost begrudgingly, as if she didn't want to be this impressed.

"Right?" Ana said. "I kinda can't believe they did all this just for me. And so *fast*."

"Well, a building full of ancient, rich muckety-mucks? I bet they've had to make these kinds of alterations before. They probably have a whole stash of shower seats in the basement next to the sidewalk salt."

"Good point."

"Besides, babe." Georgia smacked her gum and play-punched Ana's shoulder. "You're worth it."

"Shucks."

They spoke low. Down the hall, Charlie napped in her bedroom. After last night's on-again, off-again cry-fest, it was almost hard to imagine Charlie *could* sleep.

The tour completed, Ana and Georgia got to work. They only had an hour before Georgia had to run—less, if Charlie decided to wake up first.

They moved boxes around, organizing, putting like with like, making sure nothing was in the way so Ana would be able to start unpacking things on her own. Reid and the movers had done a decent job leaving space for her, but many of the box piles were randomly arranged.

At one point, Georgia discovered a particularly old-looking stack of boxes.

"That's all stuff from Reid's mom," Ana explained. "Reid still hasn't gone through all of it."

"Gee, that doesn't sound like him," Georgia mumbled sarcastically and shunted the boxes into a corner.

Also in a corner—neatly, as though it belonged there—was Ana's voice-over booth. Its door hung open.

"Of all the goddamn things for the movers to fuck up," Ana seethed. "They must have lifted it up by the door handle or something."

"Hmm." Georgia put her hand on the side of it. "You ever think of getting a bigger one? You know, one you can get into easier?"

"You wanna lend me some money for a bigger one? We barely paid *this* one off."

It was a single-occupant WhisperRoom—kind of like a heavily fortified black phone booth. Inside was just enough room for a shelf containing Ana's laptop, mic, and preamp, as well as a ratty old rolling desk chair. Definitely not ideal for a wheelchair user.

There *were* booths that could accommodate her chair, but in truth, even if they had the money Ana liked the challenge of getting in and out of this one—it became something of a ritual. Plus, getting a new booth to fit her wheelchair would feel like a concession. Another defeat.

Georgia tested the door. Sure enough, no satisfying *click*; the door just swung open again.

"And you can't record without it?"

"Well, I could try, but . . ."

As if on cue, another siren began wailing outside. Probably the fourth siren that afternoon. And, as seemed to be the rule, none of the other cars sounded very interested in letting the screeching vehicle past, so the siren just . . . kept . . . going. When it wasn't sirens, it was horns. Incessant. *Beep, beep, beeeeeeeep, me, me, meeee.*

"Manhattan is so *loud,*" Ana complained. "Have you noticed? It's so much louder than Brooklyn."

"I guess so. Or maybe you're just more aware of it?"

"Gosh, that's deep."

They fell into a short, if not somewhat uncomfortable silence. Then Georgia spoke up, tentatively:

"Hey, um . . . can I ask you something else? It's . . . kinda important."

Ana looked up from the box she was examining.

"Yeah? What's up?"

"Um . . ." Still fiddling with the broken door, Georgia looked away. "Shoot, I don't know how to put this, but . . ." She looked back at Ana. "Is Isobel ever going to hook up with Claudia or what?"

It was such an unexpected question that at first Ana barely understood the words in sequence. Then her eyes went wide and her cheeks flushed.

"Wait. You—?! How—?!"

A shit-eating grin spread across Georgia's usually deadpan face.

"I knew it!" she shouted, triumphant. "I *knew* it was you!"

"Baby!" Ana reminded her in a harsh whisper, pointing to the other room.

Georgia mouthed, "Sorry," while Ana looked for something to throw. Finding nothing suitable, Ana instead settled on two vehement middle fingers.

Claudia and Isobel were the names of the will-they/won't-they protagonists of a supernatural erotica book series, *Blood Rink*. The series, currently four volumes with a fifth on the way, detailed warring clans of immortal vampires whose members flirted and fought and fucked (and fucked and fucked) while also, naturally, playing on opposite teams on the Women's National Hockey League circuit.

The audiobooks for *Blood Rink* were narrated by a woman named Kay Dalton—a woman who'd been narrating erotica for a few years now and who'd begun to amass a pretty good portfolio of titles under her no doubt lacy belt.

"You asshole!" Ana whisper-yelled. "How long have you known that was me?"

"Honestly? Not until this exact moment for sure. Your narrator voice is just different enough, *Kay*. How many other fake names are you using?"

"I'm not telling!" In fact, Ana worked under several names, more for branding purposes than any sort of compunction with the material. Preventing friends or family from coming across some of her racier work had just been a bonus. Until now. "Ugh, Georgia! This is *weird*!"

"Why, because now you know I rub up against my stuffed animals while you talk dirty to me?"

"Oh my *God*."

"You shouldn't be ashamed—"

"I'm not ashamed! It's just weird! Now I know what you're . . . into."

"Oh, honey, I'm into much weirder stuff than that," Georgia said. "*Blood Rink* is like my cooldown."

Despite everything, Ana was smiling. She felt good. She was *doing* something. She'd been dreading this first day in this strange new apartment and found herself wishing Georgia could stay all day. She didn't look forward to the hours that would stretch before Reid got back from work.

Those hours that would leave her here, alone, with nothing but her thoughts . . . and the baby.

## 3

They managed to organize most of the living room and kitchen boxes by the time Georgia had to leave.

Ana followed her to the front door of the apartment.

"Thank you for your help. Seriously. This was above and beyond."

"That's how I do. And the sooner this place is cleared, the sooner we can have a proper session. Unless, of course . . . you want to come back to the clinic instead?"

Ana made a face. "Georgia."

"You know I'm right." This was the argument they always had, and it always ended in stalemate. After a beat: "You gonna be okay alone here?"

"Of course."

"Because the next couple weeks might . . . be weird. Adjusting and everything."

"Yeah. Sure." Ana felt herself growing hot and itchy, suddenly eager for Georgia to hit the road after all. She didn't know what Georgia planned to say next, but she knew she didn't want to hear it. It looked like it was going to be personal. Ana didn't like personal.

Georgia continued.

"Hey, um. When I was a kid, I had this book of 'amazing true stories.' Actually, it was my brother's book, but I was obsessed with it so I stole it and never gave it back."

"Monster."

"I know. But I just loved how each story was this little miracle—like, the guy who survived a giant nail through his head, or this dog who got lost during a move and walked cross the whole country just to find his owners again." Her Texas accent became thicker with the memory. "But there's one I've been thinking about lately because, well, it's about you a little bit."

*This is going to be some inspirational pablum about someone believing in herself and regaining the ability to walk, isn't it?* Ana thought.

"So, there was this stewardess in Russia in the 1970s, and someone put a bomb on her plane. There was some war going on, or terrorism, or I dunno. Anyway, the bomb ripped open the plane, everyone died either in the explosion or in the crash. Except for . . ."

"This stewardess?"

Georgia nodded. "She got sucked outta the plane midair and fell *six* miles down to the ground."

"And survived?" Ana didn't want to be interested, but she couldn't help herself.

"Pretty sure it's still the longest free fall with no parachute anyone's ever walked away from. Because, here's the thing. Apparently, she had a history of really low blood pressure, so when the cabin depressurized so fast, she passed right out, right as she was sucked through. She was just a rag doll. And that's the reason they say she survived the fall."

"You said 'walked away'—wasn't she—?"

"Oh, no, she was all kinds of messed up. Broke everything. Sorry, dumb figure of speech. That's not my point. I'm just saying: the only reason she *survived* in the first place is because . . . she stayed loose. I mean, sure, she was unconscious, but—sometimes bracing for impact, being all tense and holding on tight, hurts you more than just . . . staying loose. You get me?"

"I get you."

She stared at Ana for one suspicious beat too long. Finally, either deciding that she believed Ana or that her dead horse had been sufficiently whipped, she sighed. She looked around the apartment again. "I guess this place is okay." Her eyes landed on the giant windows overlooking the park. "I sure wish you could've gotten a lower floor, though."

"We're hoping we get priority for something lower once it opens up."

"Building full of old rich farts, they gotta drop dead at some point, right? Unless they're like Isobel and Claudia . . ." She pointed a reprimanding finger at Ana. "Get that booth fixed. Mama needs her smut."

"Goodbye, Georgia. See you next week."

"Later, gator." She stepped out into the hall. "Stay loose."

"Weird," Ana replied. "My mother always told me a lady does the opposite."

As she started down the hallway, Georgia groaned: "Womp-womp."

# 4

She was at a loss for what to do next. Georgia's diagnosis had gotten under her skin: Ana *did* feel tense, bracing for impact. All the same, what else could she do?

Right. *Stay loose.* So easy.

She needed activity. Distraction. She wanted to go for a jog, run along the park, sprint over to the Hudson, *move.* This injury could be so maddeningly boring. Just as new motherhood could be so maddeningly boring—even if she weren't in this damn chair, she had to stick around and wait for Charlie to wake up.

Ana wiped her sweating palms on her legs. She should capitalize on the remainder of Charlie's nap somehow, but the door to her anxieties kept swinging open like her busted booth.

She could climb into that booth now, try to get a tiny bit of work done—but, right on time, another siren, another flurry of horns. There'd be no reliable recording until they fixed that door.

She pulled out her phone. Hours to go before Reid got back. She could finally respond to some old text messages—if unanswered messages had physical mass, her phone would be dense as a dying star. Friends who'd reached out, checked in, asked if she wanted help or company or just to hang. Ana made an effort to respond for a little while after Charlie was born, but ultimately, she'd grown more and more comfortable leaving well-meaning messages unanswered, and soon enough . . . everyone stopped trying.

She wasn't much for social media, either. She lurked around Instagram, but hadn't posted in a year. She'd never shared anything about Charlie's birth, or any cute baby videos, no #newmomlife or even #wheelchairlife. She followed a host of people with all kinds of disabilities who made it their business to destigmatize and educate and inspire and show others in similar conditions they weren't alone. Social media wasn't all bad when it came to profiles like that, but . . .

*But that's not* me. *I'm in no position to be inspiring right now.*

Her eyes fell on Reid's mom's boxes, full of the religious knickknacks Reid's mom loved, and she thought, *What do you do when you've lost faith in everything? Even your own body?*

Charlie's first birthday loomed, and they were planning on inviting some friends over for a celebration/quasi-housewarming. It would be the first social thing Ana'd done since, well, everything—maybe she could work on planning Charlie's party?

*But you know why you don't want to start work on* that, *don't you, Ana?*

That was the voice of her own mother. Cathy, the Great and Sedentary Insult Queen. A cheap Don Rickles wannabe hurling judgments and insults from her Raymour & Flanigan throne. Who'd hectored her husband to an early grave when Ana was only seven.

Ana found herself moving through the apartment, looking for tasks—movement had always been her antidote to Cathyness. She navigated around the furniture and stacks of boxes in a herky-jerky zigzag. Even after Georgia's help, it was going to take a while to get used to this new space.

She ended up in Charlie's room.

Charlie was still asleep. Thank God for that; she must be as exhausted as Ana and Reid were. From the moment they'd all entered the Deptford yesterday, Charlie had been unsettled and fussy. Whining, squirming, crying. Up all night. No one had slept well.

Ana inched closer to the crib. She found herself avoiding looking directly at the baby, focusing instead on the blankets, the mobile, the crib, as if her gaze might nudge Charlie awake. But also because she hated looking down on Charlie like this. Bad memories of

*(Ana!)*

one awful night.

She turned her attentions to the window overlooking the courtyard. She quietly wheeled herself closer.

Yesterday, as they'd begun their attempts to get situated in the new place,

Ana had looked out this exact window and noticed a strange buildup of gunk in the corner of the windowsill. She hadn't noticed it during their walk-through the week before—but then, she'd been a little overwhelmed. Now that the place was theirs, Ana'd spotted it right away.

The gunk had been clear and lumpy, nowhere near as dry as its shape might have suggested. Probably a sealant of some kind, something to weatherize the window. But to be totally honest, it also looked kind of . . . organic. Like someone had spewed a glob of goo, either from their nose or some other orifice, onto the windowsill and forgotten about it. She'd cleaned the spot a half dozen times before the disgust went away.

Now the window, and its sill, were spotless. But something else bugged her about the view. What was it?

*The drop. You had nightmares last night, remember?*

True. But, no, she didn't think that's what bothered her. It was something specific, but she was too tired and frazzled to put her finger on it.

She leaned forward, forehead to the glass, as she had during their walk-through. Then she looked up at the dark, impenetrable windows of the other Deptford apartments—such a bummer she couldn't at least spy a little.

She closed her eyes. It felt nice. There was nothing to be anxious about. Everything was okay. She just had to be loose, right? Flop like a rag doll onto the hard, hard ground of their new life.

*And you'll plan Charlie's birthday party, and your friends will come here and coo in jealousy over how lucky you are. And they'll tell you they're proud of you and how far you've come. Not just because of the apartment but because you're making the best of a difficult situation. You're getting by and getting better.*

*And they never have to know the awful truth—*

A familiar sound made her turn in her seat.

Charlie sat up in her crib, blinking, face scrunched up in concentration, deliberating what kind of mood she was about to be in.

Then she made eye contact with her mother, and her face lit up. She babbled a little, then let out a short, high-pitched chirping noise. It was her signature sound—a bizarre, gleefully falsetto yip that sounded eerily like a birdcall. The first time she'd done it, Reid practically fell over himself in amazement, and Charlie had been chasing that reaction ever since. She might only be a couple of weeks shy of one year old, but Charlie already knew the value of making grownups happy.

"Hey," Ana said. "Look who's awake." She stretched herself over the bars to lift Charlie out, setting her on her lap. Charlie did a little more babbling, then, when she noticed Ana looking at her, chirped again.

"Trying to cheer us both up, huh, Baby Bird?"

Ana's thoughts continued in a poisonous whisper.

*The awful truth is that you hate your daughter and wish she'd never been born.*

Ana forced a smile.

"How about we go unpack some boxes, huh?"

# UCKIT EYE

## 1

"So!" Reid beamed from the doorway. "How was my girls' first day as residents of the historic Deptford Apartment Building?"

Ana, wrist-deep in another box, blew sweaty hair out of her face and looked back at him from the living room. A tower of empty boxes leaned precariously next to her. Charlie was in her playpen, crying.

"H'okay." Reid set his bag down by the door. "Lemme help."

## 2

Later, in the dining nook of their kitchen, they caught each other up—the nightly debrief that was an essential ritual of married life. While Ana worked on fitting pots and pans into the lower cabinets, she filled Reid in on what he'd missed at home. About Georgia. About Charlie, who'd continued to be fussy all day, but who was, for now, thank God, happily distracted by the arrival of her daddy.

Reid took care of feeding Charlie and bitching about work. He also showed Ana the book he'd found, which he'd managed to read a quarter of already. Halfway through his excited recounting, bubbling like a kid showing off the features of a toy he'd always wanted, he realized he'd forgotten something.

"Your booth! Home Depot—*fuck*!" He gave himself a smack on the forehead with the heel of his hand not currently holding Charlie's giant blue plastic spoon full of mashed potatoes. Dinner for the adults would be next; they'd yet to figure out what to cook for themselves.

"Uck!" Charlie echoed with glee, kicking one chubby leg. "Uck, uck!"

Ana and Reid shot each other a wide-eyed look.

"Reid, if that's her first word, I swear to *God* . . ."

"There was no *F,*" Reid said. "Doesn't count."

Ana wheeled herself closer to Reid to swat his arm playfully with a frying pan.

"No more swears around the Bird."

"Okay, okay!" He threw his hands up in surrender. "Not the pan!"

Charlie giggled at her parents' pantomime . . . then a cloud crossed her face. She blinked, like she just remembered something onerous she had to do. Tears usually followed this look, so Reid handed her a sliced strawberry, and that seemed to keep the storm at bay. For now. He turned back to Ana.

"I'm really sorry I forgot. I guess . . ." He laughed, embarrassed. "I guess I was just too excited to get home."

Ana rolled her eyes, smiling in spite of herself. She was relieved to have him home, too—more than she'd like to admit.

"Honestly? There's so much crap to unpack, and if Baby Bird stays miserable for the next few days, I probably won't be able to get much recording done anyway. But, please—*please*—can you pick the parts up sometime this week?"

"Totally." He faked eating a spoonful of potatoes, and Charlie squealed in delight, kicking her leg again.

"I really don't want to have to use Amazon, Reid. They're the devil. And I always order the wrong-sized stuff anyway . . ."

"I'm on it. Seriously."

She went back to the pots and pans. "It felt good to unpack a little. Feel a little more settled."

"You did a lot! I'm impressed."

She grunted. "There's just so much more to do. I hate it."

"Yeah . . ." His voice trailed off. "I've got something else you're going to hate."

"What . . . ?"

He pulled out his phone and played a voice message on speaker. A thick Noo Yawk accent, clearly six sheets to the wind, demanded Reid pick up, pick up, or, *fine, call me back, you left me holding my frickin' bag here, Reid, and I don't know what I'm gonna—*

"No! Reid! Turn it off—!"

Reid did so, laughing.

"He called me like three times today! Same message every time. Unbelievable."

Ana shuddered. "Even just hearing his voice—don't play me any of his messages again!"

"I just thought you'd get a kick out of how upset he is. 'Eyyyy, you left me holdin' the frickin' bag here!'"

Charlie giggled. Reid did a passable Frank impression, somewhere between Ray Romano and a drunk Muppet. Sometimes when Reid had to speak with Frank, his voice would even start to take on the sounds and shapes of that thick Brooklyn accent. Like they were just two guys from the block.

Ana knew Reid didn't like Frank—he was one of the most unlikable people they'd ever met—but even that little bit of empathy was a bridge too far for her. She *loathed* Frank.

"Sorry," Reid said. Then: "I just wish we'd set up a secret camera or something yesterday. You know? He probably had his little tool belt on. Probably all excited to tell us how stupid we were for leaving his apartment, *you look around, you tell me who else is gonna give you a home like I gave you a home*—"

"Probably excited to tell us what was wrong with the races of each one of our movers."

"Exactly. But then he gets there and—poof! We're gone! All our stuff! Just keys on the counter. Eyyy!"

"Eyy!" Charlie mimicked. Daddy's little best friend.

It should have been hilarious. It *was* hilarious. But also . . .

"I just don't want to hear that voice again, okay? You don't know what it was like, Reid. Especially after . . . after your paternity leave was up and I was stuck in that apartment alone . . . hearing him drunk and farting around in the basement with his tools all the time . . . dreading whenever he'd look into our windows or yell through the door to see if I was home . . . God, any time I even had a window open for some fresh air, he would stand there and just shout at me. His conspiracy theories, how he was so much smarter than everyone else on the block, his recaps of everything he saw on Fox and the dirty immigrants and the 'globalist cock-a-roaches' and, ugh, now even I'm starting to sound like him!"

"You sound much cuter than—"

"Do you think he even knew we were Jewish? All those times he stood outside, yelling through our window about George Soros and crap?"

"Would he have rented to us if he did?"

She didn't know. They weren't that demonstrable about their religion. They'd each been raised relatively observant, by two very different single moms, but these days considered themselves more culturally Jewish than anything (although Reid *had* become more stubborn in his Jewish identity post-Trump). They didn't practice most holidays. They didn't hang mezuzot. They had their own, nebulous, ever-changing ideas of God. But they'd had their ketubah displayed prominently on a wall inside, and Frank had been in dozens of times to check this pipe or that window. Sure, he probably didn't know what a Hebrew marriage contract looked like, but even he probably could recognize the foreign squiggles for what they were.

"I just felt so unsafe. God, the fact that *he* had to be our landlord while I was stuck at home, dealing with everything, it was so . . . unfair . . ."

"Hey." Reid came over and kissed her forehead. "Do not worry about him for a second. He'll get bored and stop calling soon. He's got his security deposit and, hell, as far as he knows, we moved to Connecticut, right? We're done with him. The time of Frank is over! Over!" He put his hands up in celebration, and Baby Bird copied the gesture. She let out a short chirp, and Reid cheered her.

"Yeah. Still." Ana pushed herself away from the counters and made her way to the fridge. She pulled out a can of seltzer (they'd made sure to bring all of the essentials from their Brooklyn fridge). "Fuck that guy."

"Uckit eye," Charlie pronounced in a determined, serious voice, examining another slice of strawberry in between her fingers. Reid shot Ana a look of triumph.

## 3

They decided they were too exhausted to cook.

"Let's just Seamless," Reid said. He had his guitar on his lap, and Charlie faced him in her Baby Einstein activity station: his favorite captive audience, her favorite command performer.

Ana worked on moving herself from her chair to the couch.

"Again? We got delivery last night."

"I know. We won't make a habit of it. Even though—"

"Yeah, yeah, even though our rent is cheaper now. It adds up, Reid."

"I know."

He pulled out his phone and went to the app. It had been an unexpected private thrill for him to change their home address yesterday—even more so than the USPS Change of Address form, updating their primary location in Seamless had felt like an official seal on their new identity.

Actually *receiving* their food had left a little to be desired. They'd ordered pizza (as per the rituals of moving day), but the delivery guy had refused to come up to their apartment. He'd made Reid come outside and cross the street to get his order.

They wouldn't be ordering from that place again. They'd find new favorite places. Reid might even ask his new neighbors for the inside scoop. He was an insider himself now, after all.

Tonight, they opted for Thai.

While they waited, Ana lurked on her phone and Reid noodled on the guitar. He sang a couple of Charlie's favorite songs, and Charlie joined along with little noises. She had surprisingly good relative pitch for a baby (Reid was convinced she'd grow up to become a musician like her old man; Ana couldn't carry a tune with a forklift). Then Reid started playing something unfamiliar. That was nice, Ana thought; she hadn't heard him work on a new song in a while.

Half an hour later, his phone rang.

"Yeah?" he answered. A moment. Then, somewhere between shocked and annoyed: *"Seriously?"* Another moment. "Just *come up*; it's fine, they'll let you in. We're floor—" Another moment. "You're just not gonna—come on, man, this is—ugh, fine! I'll be down in, I don't know, *minutes.*"

He hung up with a growl. Nothing was quite as anticlimactic as angrily ending a call on a touchscreen cell phone.

"Again?" Ana looked up.

"This better not become, like, a Thing," he grumbled. Although, if it was, what exactly could he do about it?

"Maybe they're just intimidated by how fancy we are."

"Yeah, right." He forced himself to cool down. He caught himself in a mirror. "Christ, another gray hair."

He threw on his jacket and shoes. Before he stepped out the door, he looked back at his wife and daughter.

They were both looking off into their own separate nowheres, brows knit. Though neither looked like they were exactly having pleasant thoughts, Reid couldn't help but chuckle.

"What?" Ana asked, coming out of her daze.

"Sometimes you both look so much alike it's a little creepy. You're like twins. Be right back."

# UNFAMILIAR SHAPES

## 1

She stared up at the ceiling and tried not to think. The trapeze handle that helped her sit up dangled over her side of the bed, casting unfamiliar shapes in this new space.

Even though they'd spent the previous night here, it was tonight, without the chaos of the move hanging over the day, that truly felt like their first night in the Deptford.

What was happening in her head was anything but unfamiliar.

Outside, the midnight city had quieted. Only the occasional honk or rattle of traffic. Twenty years ago, a clock might have ticked through the silence. Now: just the woolly, oppressive nothingness of the white noise from the baby monitor—itself, picking up the white noise machine in Charlie's room, compounding nothingness on nothingness, like a tide that never ebbed.

Ana couldn't get comfortable. The room was too hot. She tried to kick off the covers but, of course, that wasn't so simple anymore. She wanted to roll over on her side, but that was also complicated: lifting and tugging and pulling and shifting, possibly waking up Reid.

Her right leg, the one that still had a modicum of sensation and movement (not enough to support her, but enough to encourage her doctors that support would one day be possible), throbbed dully, restlessly.

She wished she could get up and get a glass of water, but that would require so many steps—(*Without a single step, har har*)—and she didn't feel comfortable enough in this new space to navigate in the dark.

More than anything, she needed her mind to quiet down. How was it she could spend her days so exhausted and nights so restless?

She'd always had this proclivity, even as a teenager. Nights were the worst. One of the many things she'd loved about dance early on was it left her tired enough that she could sleep soundly most nights. And if not, she always could run the choreography over in her head, a safe litany, until she dropped off. She didn't actually miss much about dancing anymore—her heart had been drifting even before the aches and pains started to collect—but she missed the clarity of purpose it gave her. Teaching lessons and then personal training had similar mental perks, but these days, she mostly just had PT exercises. She didn't like to think about those.

*Told you dancing wasn't a real life-plan,* she imagined her mother saying. *Shoulda gotten a desk job like me. You wouldn't be in this mess at all.*

But, no, that wasn't just her mother's voice. It was also Frank's. Reid playing that message had worked like an evil spell, conjuring forth Frank's voice, his proclamations, his dumb, pickled face. He and Cathy actually would've gotten along great—they could've both been the Smartest People in the World together. Great, now she was picturing them fucking. She searched her mind for something less nauseating. Something safe and boring. Something like Charlie's window, specifically what was bugging her about it.

But that was the wrong topic to think about. Because wasn't her inability to see what was wrong with that window a great metaphor for how useless she was as a mother, how fucking lost? Hadn't Cathy been right that she was endlessly stupid? Maybe that's why her life was full of know-it-alls like Cathy, like Frank. She attracted them. She *deserved* them. She also detested them. Then again, she detested *everyone.* Why was she so full of hate? She hated her mother for not providing a good mothering example she could draw on. She hated her baby for derailing her life and stealing her mobility. She hated her husband for somehow getting away unscathed. Suddenly, Ana would've given anything to take back every choice that had led here, all of it, to spare herself and to spare those around her from her monstrosity, because the nighttime is the right time to cruise the Panic Attack Expressway, baby, keep your useless foot on the gas and let's crash into that wall at the very end, the one where you start thinking of that awful night, you know the one, when you were so exhausted you grabbed a knife and *came so very, very close to—*

No more exit ramps, so she did the only thing she could; yank the wheel and pull over on the shoulder.

Reid's shoulder.

She grabbed it and shook.

## 2

Reid hadn't been asleep. He was also lying there, lost in thought. But his thoughts were far less personal.

He couldn't stop thinking about that book.

The few reviews on Amazon all agreed it was no great piece of literature. A real three-star consensus: gossipy and superficial. But the author boasted of "unprecedented insider information" and "diligent research," so whatever the book lacked in style, it wasn't boring.

It was structured chronologically, but each chapter was full of digressions, so, while Reid wasn't even halfway done, he'd already sampled a fair number of stories from various eras. Rumors of mysterious disappearances, of golden-era

Hollywood royalty attending parties in the Deptford, never to be seen again. Urban legends, like the 1930s blues musician who started out as a servant in one of the apartments, emerging from his employment with a prestigious recording contract, only to kill himself in the studio while he was laying down tracks—"slicing his throat with a broken bit of acetate," according to a source—an obvious riff on the Robert Johnson crossroads myth, Reid knew.

The grisliest, but most intriguing, episode got an offhand mention as "the Plummet of 1919." One afternoon in the early part of that year, no fewer than twenty people jumped off the roof of the Deptford in one go, shattering their bones and splattering their guts all over the very pavement tourists nowadays stood on to gawp up at the architecture.

Something about this stuck in Reid's brain. How had he never heard about it before? How had every New Yorker, by birth or adoption, not known about the Plummet of 1919?

Maybe Reid was so fascinated because of the way the author contextualized it. The Plummet occurred a few months after the end of World War I, while the country was still in the grips of the Spanish flu epidemic, so the Plummet was fairly under-covered. Having lived through the past couple of years, Reid knew something about how pandemics could suck up all the oxygen. That was if, in fact, the Plummet had even happened.

Reid found himself compelled: if he could prove or disprove the Plummet, it would go a long way toward proving or disproving the whole book—a prospect that filled him with a strange sort of sadness. Bloody as the history was, he wanted it to be true.

He'd already planned how he'd carry any further research out: on his lunch breaks, since YouTube and other fun sites like it were blocked by the law firm's firewalls. Can't have the drones enjoying their workday, can we? He suspected this was going to keep him busy for a while. The Deptford used to be quite a repository for the bloodiest kinds of city gossip.

He just hoped he didn't stumble over any horror stories that were more recent. His book was published in the late '70s, and even in its intro, the author noted that most of the really remarkable events of the Deptford predated the Robert Moses era. That was good—otherwise Reid might have to share some of this with Ana. He didn't want to do that. She was nervous enough about living here.

It was just as he was having this thought that she shook his shoulder. He almost yelped in surprise, but managed to keep it to a groggy, "Huh? What's—?"

"Sorry," she said in a raspy, hushed voice. "I'm . . . I'm having a bad night."

"Oh." Reid sighed, hoping he sounded sympathetic and not too disappointed. "Baby. What do you need?" This was a shorthand for them; they'd been here before. Sometimes she requested he sing to her. Other times she wanted—

"A story."

"Okay." He rolled over onto his back and racked his brain for a good story, something from his personal life he hadn't already told her during previous moments like this. "Did I ever tell you the time about *my* first panic attack?"

"Maybe?" She reached out and grabbed his hand. Her palm was clammy. "I don't remember."

So he told her. It had been the year leading up to his bar mitzvah and he'd gotten a taste for stealing toys from the supermarket around the corner from where he, his mother, and his brother lived. He turned out to have a talent for it, amassing quite a collection over those months. Then one night, a week before his ceremony, he lay in bed and suddenly couldn't breathe. He broke into a cold sweat; he felt like his heart was going to burst. He woke his mom and confessed everything. She took it in stride. She made him write a letter of confession to the store and then, at the reception for his bar mitzvah, THE social event for any Jewish kid that age, she made him organize a toy drive for all his friends to donate their old toys (including all Reid's ill-gotten gains) to kids in need. Lesson learned, mitzvot all around.

"Your mom was so cool," Ana said. "If that had been my mom, she would've held it against me for the rest of my life. She'd have called me the Toy Thief and yelled, 'Don't steal anything!' every time we walked into a store. She would have mentioned it at our fucking *wedding*."

"Yeah. Probably." Reid chuckled knowingly. "Feeling any better?"

"Yeah. Thank you."

"Of course, bab—"

"No, I mean it, Reid. Thank you. For listening. For talking me down. For . . . for moving us here. I know it wasn't easy. Thank you."

"Hey." He kissed her hand. "It was a team effort. Besides, I'm pretty sure it was your idea to enter the lottery in the first place, so thank *you*."

"God, we were so young and stupid then." They'd entered their names in a dozen affordable housing lotteries. They were both living with awful roommates and had just begun the process of looking for a place together. They figured, what's the worst that could happen? It's not like their names would ever get drawn.

"Sometimes young and stupid pays off, I guess. Eventually."

"I want to be grateful, Reid. I want to *stay* grateful. I really do. I don't want to be like *her*. Like Cathy. I'm so sorry I'm such a bummer all the time."

"You're not a bummer—"

"I'm *such* a bummer. I bum *myself* out. I'm sad. I'm angry. I'm embarrassed. I'm . . . scared. All the time. And I hate it."

"I know."

Silence spooled out. He felt like he should say something.

"Maybe . . . maybe you should look into going back to that support group?" he ventured. "The postpartum one? You liked that one, right?" He tried to keep his voice light, no pressure. "Or maybe the paraplegia group? Or the SCI one? Maybe Georgia has some ideas, too?"

"So many groups. I'm just so lucky." She went from sounding like she might consider his suggestion to annoyed. He'd overstepped.

"Sorry, I didn't mean—"

She turned her head to face him. Thanks to the muted glow of the city outside, he could see her clearly, as if she'd always been made out of shadows. "The thing is, Reid? No one in the postpartum group can't walk anymore. No one in the SCI group has postpartum. And no one in any of the groups has fucking Cathy in their heads all the time. I just, I don't . . . I don't belong anywhere."

"That's not true. You belong here. With us."

She snorted bitterly and looked up at the ceiling. "Cute."

"You're not alone, that's all I'm saying. At all. You've got so many people who care about you."

"What about *you*?" She turned to him again. She sounded interested now, as if this had never occurred to her.

"Of course I care about you! Honey! More than—"

"No. I mean . . . what about you? How are you so good at compartmentalizing everything? Don't you feel alone?"

For a moment, it all came back to him. The months of screams and wails. That horrible bubble of time after the birth and the injury, when he ran around like the proverbial headless chicken, taking care of a newborn baby and a desperate wife in physical and emotional agony. He'd never seen someone sob like Ana had, her nerves on fire, her entire life upended, begging him to let her die, let this all die, while Charlie wailed in the other room. He'd never felt so impotent, so miserable, so goddamn *stuck*—

He pushed those thoughts away.

"Sure," he said, "but it's not the same. It's . . ."

"Maybe you should talk to someone, too? There are groups for partners. I don't want you, like, repressing anything or burying resentments because I'm such a mess."

"You're not a mess, and I'm not repressing anything. But. Sure," he said. "Sure, if—" He almost said, *If that would make you feel better,* but he was smart enough to know that was the wrong thing to say. "After we get more settled in, I can . . . look around. That'd be nice."

"Thank you." She squeezed his hand.

"You're an amazing wife and you're an amazing mother, and you know what?"

"What?" She turned to him again. The nightglow caught the tears drying on her cheeks.

"If things were different, it wouldn't be us. I like us."

"I like us, too." Something in her voice changed. Like she was hearing herself for the first time. "I just want us to be happy," she whispered.

"Me, too."

"This is going to be a new start for us. I'm going to *make* it a new start."

"Okay," he said. "Me, too."

He leaned over her and kissed her. Softly, gently. Hoping she'd be able to sleep and that Charlie wouldn't choose this moment to wake up and need consoling, too.

Then Ana's hands slid up his cheeks, and she was kissing back, mouth open. The way they used to kiss.

There was a desperation to it. He was desperate, too. Between the exhaustion and the pain and the depression and the infant, it seemed like his sex life would be relegated to guilty bathroom visits after Ana had already gotten in bed for the foreseeable future. Eagerness aside, though, he didn't know how far she would take this tonight.

"Are you—?" he began to ask.

She kissed her assent.

They both slept relatively clothed in case of any midnight emergencies. He pulled her nightshirt over her head, and she did the same for him.

Time was short, because the baby could interrupt at any point, and also because he knew he was too excited to last long. Her vibrator was somewhere in a box (and probably without a charge anyway), but he was determined that she get hers first. He surprised her by tossing back the covers and kissing down her stomach, past her navel. Lower. Lower.

Sensing what he was about to do, she moaned in weak protest: "Reid, I haven't bathed in—"

"I don't care."

He positioned himself between her legs, spreading them apart himself, lovingly, gently, but without allowing for any debate.

He devoured her. He was ravenous.

She still had plenty of feeling where it counted for this sort of thing. Judging by the noises she tried to not make loudly, she'd forgotten what those nerves could do.

The lube was also stashed somewhere—neither had been optimistic they'd need it any time soon—but that proved to be no problem, either.

He was right about not lasting long. But that didn't matter; it was no less intense. He finished on her stomach—each of them experiencing a fleeting but powerful terror at the thought of another pregnancy—and after he cleaned her off with a T-shirt, they collapsed in each other's arms. This apartment got good heat during these winter months, and they'd worked up a sweat.

"Thank you," she said. It sounded like she might have resumed crying.

He kissed her chest, and as he felt himself beginning to drowse, he thought—or maybe said, "Thank *you*."

This was followed by something more inchoate. Something he didn't quite understand.

*The building will provide . . .*

Before he could either chase that thought or drift away, the sound they had momentarily forgotten to dread: Charlie, awake and crying in the other room.

Ana groaned weakly as Reid sat up.

"So much for hoping she'd sleep through the night," he half sighed, half chuckled. "Time to clock in."

"No," Ana said, stopping him. "Wait."

"But—"

"I might be able to fall asleep if you just hold me a little. Let's see if she settles down."

He waited. Charlie continued crying.

"It's okay," Ana said, her voice getting softer. She was falling asleep after all. "She has to learn how to self-soothe, right?"

Reid fully intended to give Ana a few more moments before he detached himself and saw to their daughter. But after the week they'd had, and the activities they'd just concluded, he, too, drifted off before he could help it.

He had time for one thought—*We belong right here*—before he followed his wife to sleep.

## 3

Their sleep was deep and pure. So much so that neither registered the noises coming from the baby monitor. Noises strange enough that they might not have even recognized them anyway.

The sound of heavy hands hitting the window glass outside Charlie's room.

The squeal as the window slid open.

The sigh of cool air puffing into the room.

On some level, though, they *did* register that Charlie abruptly stopped crying. Ana and Reid nestled further into each other and dove deeper into sleep.

# WIND

## 1

Ana dreamed she stood on the roof of the Deptford.

She was always still able to stand in her dreams. And walk. And run. And dance. Like some part of her brain refused to remember the realities of her waking life. Was that cruel or hopeful?

The freezing wind shrieked and moaned, almost blowing her over, pushing her closer and closer to the edge of the roof.

Worse, she realized she held Charlie in her arms.

Charlie screamed. High, miserable wails barely audible under the chilling shriek of spinning air.

It was too cold for a baby. It was too cold for either of them.

The strong wind made it hard to move anywhere other than closer . . . and closer . . . to the drop.

It wasn't just the wind she heard now. There was low rumbling underneath. It sounded almost like . . . growling. Snarling. Just underneath the angle of the roof. Something—some *things*—circling like sharks. Waiting for her.

Then from behind: the rattle of metal. Ana looked toward the door that led up onto the roof and saw her wheelchair, empty, quivering in the wind, approaching her. It stopped halfway across the roof. It seemed almost to be tsking her: *You forgot about me.* And didn't its imagined voice sound a little like a former landlord?

All at once, Ana realized she *couldn't* be standing here, holding Charlie. She *couldn't* be standing at all. Like a cartoon character realizing they'd already run off a cliff, her legs buckled.

She had time to look down at her baby once more, only to realize Charlie wasn't screaming. She stared up at Ana and laughed, open-mouthed and insane, the delighted glee of a spider finding a struggling insect in its web. Her eyes were alien, dark pools, shining like wet, open mouths, and Ana was appalled when twin tongues flicked out of the pupils, tasting the air, taunting her.

Ana hurled the baby out of her arms just as another gust of wind slammed into them. pitching them forward and off the roof.

## 2

When she woke, she didn't scream, but she did gasp quietly for air. Had Reid still been next to her and not already attending to Charlie, he likely wouldn't have even heard.

Faint, roseate light seeped in through the curtains. Dawn. A new day.

She closed her eyes again, not quite awake, trying to force her mind to reset. Certain details of what had happened next in her dream clung like an oily residue.

The feeling of free fall. Her guts suspended. The pavement rushing up to meet them.

She could also remember the snag as something grabbed her leg the instant before she hit the ground. A stony, clawed hand.

It wasn't a grace, though. It wasn't rescue. She'd understood immediately that she was being saved only to ensure she got to watch when Charlie hit the ground first, when her soft head exploded brains against the pavement and her viscera shot out of her toothless mouth and her blood splashed everywhere, hot and steaming against the winter pavement.

And the sound of her mother's voice from somewhere above her, asking, *Isn't this what you wanted?* as Charlie made her way down, down, down to the ground—

Suddenly, something occurred to Ana as she lay there, half-asleep, half-awake.

She finally realized what had been bugging her about the view from Charlie's window.

*No, that's impossible,* she thought. *I'm not remembering it right.*

But she knew she was.

Just as she knew, in that moment, they had to leave this place.

She thought about getting up to confirm her suspicions right away. What would happen next, she had no idea, but at least she could tell Reid, and they'd proceed from there.

But she was still so tired. She decided to try for another few minutes of sleep. It was okay. Reid had the baby. And it's not like she'd forget her epiphany. It was obvious. Unforgettable. Besides, today would be another long day—and she'd need her energy to tell Reid what she'd realized and come up with a plan—so grab sleep where you can.

By the time she woke up again, the thought had dissolved, the way most revelations do upon waking. She remembered the feeling, but not the reason why she had it.

For the rest of the day, she felt that maddening itch of something she needed to remember but couldn't.

Kind of fitting, in a way, since everything before the Deptford was already taking on the aspects of a dream. Details were fading, and there was a sort of illogic to everything that had brought them here . . . Such was the way of dreams, right?

Perhaps that's why later, when she would wonder at what point it had all become too late, she would find equal parts horror and comfort in the realization that she couldn't think of one particular moment.

Call it fate, or call it bad luck. Life had always been pushing them in this direction, it seemed. As merciless and inescapable as the wind.

# PART TWO

## INSIDERS

# ADJUSTMENTS

## 1

The next several days were a blur. There was the monotony of unpacking and organizing—what goes where, which space is defined by which person in the family (done with a bit more urgency than usual given the first birthday party for Charlie they were hoping to throw in a couple of weeks)—but that wasn't the main reason things started to feel so hazy.

Something was wrong with Charlie.

Not just in some anxiety nightmare; actually, *really* wrong.

A text, from Ana to Reid:

**Was BB weird with you on your walk this morning?**

A few minutes later, from Reid:

Seemed okay?

Started crying when we walked back inside but nothing awful. Y?

**She's been crying all day. Again. Getting worried.**

Hungry? Fever?

**Checked all that. No. Ugh. Can't get anything done.**

Ugh. Sorry you have to deal with that on your own.

Gotta go. Boss breathing down my neck.

Let me know how she's doing

**K**

I'm sure it's gotta be the move. Big change.

She'll be back to normal soon 🤞🤞🤞

## 2

Their pediatrician agreed.

His name was Dr. Bronson, and he was aptly named. Given he was six foot five inches and roughly the size and shape of a grizzly bear, he was somebody's brawn son, all right. Guy seemed like he'd be more at home hauling lumber than examining children. But his care and expertise were undeniable. He handled

Charlie with delicate consideration—so much so, in fact, that she seemed in better spirits in his examining room than she did in their apartment.

"That's messed up, right?" Ana exclaimed after pointing this out. "A kid more comfortable at the doctor's? That's, like, body snatcher weird!"

Dr. Bronson pouted. "I like to think I'm fun."

"Don't insult the physician, darling," Reid said with mock propriety. "We'll never get our lollipops."

"Thank you. I'm very sensitive," Bronson replied in his deep, rumbly voice. "And don't worry, Charlie will hate me soon enough, when I stick her full of needles at her yearly. Right, Charliegirl?" He gave Charlie a coochie-coo under her chin. Charlie, currently sitting on the exam table, acted like it was the funniest thing that had ever happened to her. "Anyway, I think your husband's right, Mrs. Greene: if it's not teething, it's probably just the stress of the move. Remember, it's not just all the boxes and the blank walls and all that. She's a little antenna. She picks up *everything*. That includes your own stress levels. Moving isn't easy on grown-ups, is it?"

Ana and Reid looked at each other, a score of shared, move-related freak-outs passing between them.

"They say moving is one of the most stressful things a person can go through," Reid graciously donated to the room. "Besides the death of a loved one."

*I can think of a few more stressful things,* Ana almost said.

"Exactly," Bronson agreed. "*They* are very wise sometimes, aren't They? Except when They are not." He moved over to his workstation and typed a few notes into his computer.

"I'm sorry we wasted your time," Ana said. Her cheeks burned. It had been her idea to rush Charlie to the doctor after yet another day of strange behavior.

Bronson looked over at her and smiled warmly. "No sorrys! Believe me, I have parents who bring their kids in for *every little thing*. You guys are just paying attention and taking changes seriously. That's good." Then he dropped his voice to a conspiratorial low. "Just try not to make too much of a habit of it. Remember, I'm very sensitive."

"We won't," Reid said. He began clipping on his BabyBjörn with practiced ease. "But we're still on the schedule for her one-year in a couple weeks, right?"

"You bet. Gotta make sure she's still human. Ain't that right, Charlie?" Another coochie-coo.

Charlie giggled and babbled an enthusiastic agreement as Reid slid her into her carrier. Then she made eye contact with Ana and gave one of her cheerful bird chirps.

"That's right!" Dr. Bronson said. "'Cheer up, Mama.'"

It did her parents' hearts a world of good to hear that noise again.

## 3

Until they got back to the Deptford.

The moment they passed into the building's mirrored front lobby, Charlie became a different baby. Miserable. Fussy. She squirmed and grunted the entire elevator ride up.

The elevator operator, a squat, gnomish-looking man whose eyes somehow burned too bright under the shade cast by his hat, didn't stop staring at her. Ana had been in the elevator only a couple of times since they moved in, and this guy was always there. He made her deeply uncomfortable. And, she thought, this time it sounded like he was maybe muttering something just under the rattle of the little golden box. Like a voice made inaudible by a high wind.

## 4

So it went for the rest of that week. The fussiness, the distractedness, the crankiness, the nonstop crying.

Worst of all was the lack of sleep.

Three, four, five, six times a night, Charlie woke up screaming. It wasn't hunger. She wasn't usually wet. She was just *upset.*

Sometimes it took her hours to fall back to sleep. Sometimes she fell asleep quickly but was up again barely any time later. It just didn't make sense. She had been such a good sleeper a week ago!

A familiar, specific exhaustion began to wrap itself over both adults in the household. Especially Reid, who tried to spring out of bed before Ana could wake up.

Bronson—and all the blogs—had warned of occasional periods of sleep regression. It was a natural part of development. Knowing didn't make it any easier, though.

This felt like regression in too many senses of the word.

Every time Reid snapped awake, the same thought echoed through his head: *No no no no, not again, I don't want to go back there again.*

Those Bad Old Days. That one awful night he and Ana had tacitly agreed to never acknowledge.

He was determined. He wouldn't *let* them regress.

Things would get better. This was just a temporary hiccup while they all adapted to this new place.

In the meantime, he did what he could to find happiness. Often that meant sitting up with Charlie in the living room of their new, beautiful apartment, looking out at the sleeping city sprawled beneath them, letting Ana get as much sleep as possible.

And he had his book. Sometimes he would even read it out loud. It didn't matter that Charlie couldn't understand. And it didn't matter that he'd already finished the book once.

When he got to the end, he went right back to the beginning and started it again.

# MAINTENANCE

## 1

"Oh, before we get started," Georgia said, setting down the heavy duffel bag full of equipment in the living room with as much effort as if it were an empty coffee cup. "Got you a little housewarming present."

She revealed in her hand a key.

Ana took it, confused. It looked like an apartment key, an almost identical cut to their own.

"Um—thanks?"

Georgia shrugged. "I found it out in the hall. Yours?"

"No." Ana examined the key as if it held any answers. "At least, I don't think so."

"Huh. Maybe one of your neighbors', then?"

"Maybe." Ana wheeled herself over to the small end table they used as a put-all and set the key down. Something about it made her feel uneasy; she couldn't say why.

"You met any of 'em yet? They nice?"

"No, not yet."

"Are you getting out much?" Georgia asked, her tone clearly implying she knew the answer.

Ana heaved a sigh, in no mood. "We're still unpacking. And Charlie's been—"

"Just busting your chops. I get it." She held up her hands in surrender and smiled. "Well, look, now you have an excuse to introduce yourself."

"Great."

"Where *is* Baby Bird, by the way?"

"Reid likes to take her on a morning walk before work. Now that his commute's so short, he can spend more time with her."

"Aw, that's nice."

Ana yawned her lukewarm agreement.

It was 7:30 a.m. Since she was fitting Ana around her schedule, sometimes Georgia's sessions came early in the morning like this.

After a quick trip to the bathroom, Georgia took a spin through the apartment to see the progress they'd made. The place was in better shape since the last time—now instead of the clutter of the just-moved-in, the place was full of the clutter of the just-unpacked. Collapsed boxes, tied up with twine, leaned up against every wall.

Since Charlie wasn't currently sleeping, Georgia also got to take a peek in her bedroom, which was the room in the best shape. Ana and Reid had tried to re-create her old room as best they could in the hopes that, if the room felt familiar and normal, it would help acclimate Charlie, settle her down. The mobile. The changing table and diaper caddy. The pictures of soft, pastel-colored birds singing on branches or flying across her walls.

From the doorway, Ana watched Georgia take in the room, and she felt that strange pang again. Something was off here. She thought of that morning a week ago when she woke up, certain of what it was, and how it had slipped away. She almost joined Georgia at the window just to have yet another look at the puzzle.

Instead, they went back to the living room and got to work.

## 2

There were only so many PT exercises a person with Ana's paraplegia could accomplish at home. As Georgia so often reminded her, these visits were just for maintenance. If Ana really wanted things to start improving, she'd have to come back to the clinic. And as Ana so often reminded *her*: Georgia didn't know *everything*.

They'd met at the gym where Ana worked as a personal trainer. (The same gym, in fact, where she'd met Reid a few years earlier, when he'd thought maybe getting a six-pack would help him land a record deal.) Georgia had joined the training staff, and she and Ana had worked side by side for a couple of years before Georgia started musing about studying physical therapy. "I think I'd rather work with people who need me," she'd said, "instead of people who ignore my calls a few weeks after New Year's."

After the hospital discharged Ana, she'd been given several options, none of which were realistic. Ideally, she should stay at an inpatient treatment center, followed by an intensive, regular at-home regimen once she'd made a certain amount of progress. But those plans were for people who didn't also have a newborn at home . . . and those plans were for people with the right kinds of insurance.

Ana and Reid had no at-home care in their insurance plan and, by that point, their premiums would have been through the roof if they'd signed up for some. They also made just enough money to not qualify for subsidies. It was one of those catch-22s that only something as cruel as the American insurance system could conjure: if Reid or Ana quit working, maybe they'd be able to get some financial assistance . . . while also not being able to afford anything else in their lives.

However, for three months immediately after her injury, Ana had been granted permission by the Great and Terrible Insurance Powers That Be to visit an outpatient rehab facility. It wound up being a horrible experience. Between juggling the newborn, lack of sleep, depression, having to learn how to navigate a city seemingly made only of stairs and broken sidewalks, flare-ups of nerve pain (which her doctors swore was a good thing, because it proved her nerves weren't totally dead), those months became a dizzying parade of agony. Hell, she was still also healing from goddamn childbirth during all this, which her doctors all seemed to forget. Maybe she could have thought it was all worth it if she'd started showing any real improvement, but that didn't happen. So once her three months were up, they were up.

There was one saving grace of the experience, though: Georgia. She was there as part of her studies. She hadn't been on Ana's regular PT squad at the clinic, but they'd run into each other enough times that she might as well have been. Ana had more or less avoided anyone from her gym days, but there was no avoiding Georgia, and having someone familiar and friendly to talk to at the clinic wound up being a blessing.

Now, Georgia came to Ana a couple of times a week, free of charge, each thinking they were helping the other out: Georgia got a little more extracurricular experience, and Ana got assistance with partner-based exercises. (Reid assisted the other days, although his support strengths were always more emotional than physical.)

Georgia was always keen to remind Ana, though: "This arrangement can't last forever, babe. Sooner or later, you're going to have to come back and try again."

Ana knew a thing or two about bodies. As with their yearslong, savings-draining experience with fertility treatments, she knew her body wasn't responding the way it was supposed to (and when *those* treatments finally worked, look how she paid for it). Going back to the clinic—even with its treadmills and exercise bikes and "functional electrical stimulations"—was just more pointless misery. She had blessings to count: she could still use the bathroom on her own, there were no major gynecological issues, her circulation was okay.

Something else kept her from truly, fully committing, too. Something inchoate and hard to articulate: as long as she kept the promise of improvement just a bit further off in the future, it couldn't devastate her if it never actually happened.

They'd just finished a set of side leg lifts with a resistance band on the floor, when Reid and Charlie came back in.

Reid was red-faced and excited. Charlie was whimpering and about to cry, which always seemed to be her expression whenever she came back into this apartment.

"I'm late!" Reid exclaimed, stomping his snowy boots in the doorway and kicking them off while trying to stay upright. "I gotta get going! Oh, hey, Georgia."

Georgia grunted a greeting while helping lift Ana up and put her back in her chair.

Meanwhile, Reid set to unfastening Charlie from the chest carrier. "Can I . . . ?" He gestured to Ana to see if he could hand off the baby, another lap in the infant relay race that was their lives.

Ana looked to Georgia. Georgia shrugged. "I guess we can take a break."

Reid set Charlie on Ana's lap.

"You've been late every day," Ana said to Reid while Charlie continued fussing, trying to squirm her way off her mother's lap, as if that would make her feel better somehow.

Reid tromped into the kitchen. It took him a moment to remember which cabinet contained their glasses, then he poured himself a cup of water.

"I'm 'adjusting to the new commute.' They don't care; they only notice me when I'm right in front of them." He gulped the water down. "I just found the coolest thing."

"In the park?" Ana disengaged Charlie's hand from her hair.

"No, when we got back. We were hanging around the lobby. I was trying to see if any of the doormen wanted to say hi to Charlie, which, you know, was like trying to get a reaction out of the potted plants."

"I mean, they're *working*," Georgia said. "They're not there to entertain you."

Reid looked at her. "Okay, thanks, Georgia." He tried to sound like his shock was jovial. There had always been a tension between the two of them. Ana assumed it was because Reid was the embodiment of those people who'd signed up at the gym only to ghost a few months later. Only, in his case, he'd managed to snag a girlfriend during his brief time there.

"They *are* pretty stoic," Ana said, coming to her husband's aid. "I've never really seen them react to anything."

"Right? It's *weird,*" Reid said, perhaps a bit too emphatically, still looking at Georgia. "It's like Buckingham Palace. Except for the concierge. Mr. Smiler."

"*That* guy's a bit much," Georgia admitted. "If he smiles any harder, his lips are gonna split."

Of all the new characters they'd met in this building, Ana thought the concierge—a.k.a. Smiler—was by far the most unsettling. The elevator gremlin was a close second. She didn't like feeling this way about any of the building's employees, but she just couldn't help it.

"Anyway," Reid continued, "you know how the elevator's kinda in the center, and the front desk is over on the right side, and the rest of the lobby is, like, mirrors and potted trees and stuff? Have you ever noticed that on the front desk side, behind the plants, there's a little hallway and the lobby actually keeps going? The mirrors and the plants kinda hide it, but . . . we waited until Smiler wasn't looking, and we snuck past."

"Reid," Ana warned. They'd just moved in; now wasn't the time to start getting on the building's bad side. He waved her away.

"There's a whole other lobby back there! It's not as big, but it's just as fancy. The walls are just regular walls, though, not mirrors, in a dark, dark red color—"

"Burgundy," Ana said.

"Whatever. They're the same color scheme as the main lobby. And there are all these really old, framed photos on the wall. I recognize some of them from that book I'm reading—photos of the building like a century ago. And there are also pictures of old, famous residents." He laughed, surprising himself. "It's a little like those dry cleaners that have, like, Al Pacino's and Billy Crystal's head shots from the eighties hung up on the wall? Except these are *old*. And, get this: there's another elevator."

"Okayyy . . . ?"

*"Where does it go?"* His eyes were wide. He sounded like the first man to notice the moon. "I don't see two elevator banks on this floor."

"Maybe it's a service elevator? Or, Reid, it probably goes to the apartments that have, like, private entrances or something. Like penthouses."

"I wanna know." He waggled his eyebrows.

"Reid."

"I've heard of buildings having a special entrance and elevator for the low-income tenants so the building doesn't have to be grossed out by the peasants, right? But this is the *opposite*."

"Reid—"

"It's not like anyone told me I couldn't be there—"

"Go get ready for work!" Ana yelled. "Stop planning trouble!"

She was right. He was late enough already. He deflated, a child told it was time for bed.

"Ugh, fuck that place." Reid's usual prework jingle. He disappeared into the bedroom to change.

# 3

Ana started crying a few minutes into their final set of core exercises. The tears came on like a spring rainstorm—first a trickle, then a sudden downpour.

She waved Georgia away, embarrassed and frustrated. Georgia knew Ana well enough to give her space, so she started packing her equipment, moving gently, unobtrusively. It was just the two of them now. Reid had snuck off to work, offering a quiet and desultory "Bye" under Ana's labored breathing as he slipped out of the apartment. Charlie sat off to the side in her little activity station, that bastard love child between a high chair and a hemorrhoid doughnut.

When Ana's tears subsided, Georgia came over and helped her up from her yoga mat. "Pain?"

Ana shook her head. "Not really." Although that dull ache of her body not doing what she wanted was always agonizing. She adjusted herself in her chair, moving her legs in place, and wiped her eyes. "I'm just . . ."

Charlie started crying, too. Ana rolled her eyes a little at the competition.

"Could you—?"

"On it." Georgia pulled Charlie out and handed her to Ana. Ana tried to calm Charlie while swallowing the dregs of her own tears.

"Hush, Baby Bird. It's okay. We're okay." She looked at Georgia. "We're just exhausted. This is as bad as it ever was. She hasn't slept through the night since we moved here."

"Oof," Georgia said. "Hey. I have some stuff this morning I can move around. Want me to hang for a bit? You can nap, or we can talk about dirty books or . . . whatever . . . ?"

Ana had the sudden, intense urge to say yes. She'd make coffee—or tea; she knew Georgia was anti-caffeine—and tell Georgia all about the horrible dreams she'd been having. Or maybe they could try to get to the bottom of what Ana thought was wrong with Charlie's bedroom together. Maybe she could even finally tell someone about that one awful night six months ago. That night she kept locked in a box in her brain, but which only grew stronger and angrier the more it rattled.

"I really should try to get some recording done," Ana said instead. "But that's very sweet of you to offer. I'm okay, I promise."

A suspicious beat. "Well. Tell you what. Why don't I come back tomorrow? I've got an extra opening up, and we can help get you back on track after taking time off. If you're ready."

"That would be great."

"Okay, then. You two—"

"Stay loose, right?"

"You know it."

After the door closed behind Georgia, Ana puzzled for a moment about why it felt so ominous that Georgia left without pressuring her to come back to the clinic for once.

# 4

She wasn't fibbing; she had some audio tracks to lay down: a couple of commercial auditions from her voice-over agent, and she really should get back into reading *Blood Rink* to stay on schedule.

Reid still hadn't picked up the parts to repair her booth. She made a mental note to remind him. Again. In the meantime, another solution occurred to her.

First, though, she had to wait until Charlie's crying gave way to telltale big yawns.

"Nap time, Baby Bird." Ana strapped the squirming infant into the padded band she wore around her waist. They had a variety of other baby carriers—the chest carriers, the ring sling—but Ana liked the LapBaby best for her days alone in the apartment with Charlie. It was quicker and easier to use (she often even forgot she was wearing it), and also . . . she didn't feel quite so suffocated by baby.

She wheeled them both to Charlie's bedroom. Charlie continued to fight a little, but eventually settled down in her crib, and soon after, her eyes closed.

Ana finished the lullaby she was only half-aware of singing and watched as Charlie's breathing slowed. Sometimes Charlie faked them out and woke up immediately after her parents left the room, so Ana stayed a few minutes longer.

She found herself looking at the window again, which she did practically every time she was in this room now. What was wrong with this view? The answer was so close . . . so obvious . . . and yet . . .

Once assured Charlie truly slept, she turned around and headed back to the living room. Not to the booth but to the closet they used for jackets and coats.

It was a big closet. Bigger than most she'd ever had in New York. She and Reid had been thrilled at the prospect of being able to put things away, out of sight, like civilized grown-ups. Besides their outerwear, the closet contained a number of things—boxes (of course), the vacuum, the foldable metal cart some New Yorkers called a *granny cart,* and of course, all the diapers, wipes, and other baby products that always seemed to be both stockpiled and in constant danger of running out.

Ana pulled everything out, one by one, and stacked them as neatly as possible in the living room.

Soon she'd cleared out enough for her to fit. Not the chair, though; she activated the brakes, eased herself onto the floor (left hand knuckles first, in the way that had become almost second nature now), and scooted into the closet. Yes. This would work. It was nice and quiet in here. Now she needed her equipment. She scooted back out, eased herself into the chair, undid the brakes, and wheeled herself over to the booth. God, but everything took so much longer these days. Like moving through molasses.

After a few trips, she had everything she needed. She'd made the house a mess, with wires trailing across the floor, over and through the stuff she'd pulled out of the closet, but would you look at that? She hadn't had a thought for a good several minutes. Her mind had been blessedly blank.

Her *body,* on the other hand, was pissed. All this work after a session of PT made her literally shake with effort. Reid would have to do everything with Charlie when he got home because she probably wouldn't be able to lift the damn baby. But this felt good. Worth it.

She lowered herself back down, scooted into the closet.

*Goodbye, prying eyes,* she thought as she reached for the door—then froze.

Suddenly, it came to her.

The thing that was wrong with Charlie's window.

Just like that.

"Noooo," she whispered. Not in horror, not in shock, just pure confusion. "No, that's . . ."

*Impossible.*

But she was certain.

She had to see for herself.

Getting back out of the closet and into her chair took agonizingly long. She was going to lose the opportunity to get any work done, wasn't she? Charlie would wake up any minute, and there'd go her chance at recording.

But Charlie remained asleep.

Ana wheeled closer to Charlie's window. As close as she could.

*Impossible,* she thought again.

She put her face fully against the glass and moved her head around.

During their walk-through, she could have sworn she'd seen a set of famous Deptford gargoyles festooning the interior upper walls of the courtyard. But now? Nothing. No gargoyles.

*That's* what seemed off about the view. The gargoyles—the gargoyles that she had *imagined* were there—had been just hard enough to see that the answer hadn't been obvious.

*How . . . ? Why did I imagine them? What does this mean?*

Maybe it was a simple mistake. She'd been so frightened, so anxious during that walk-through, that her memories of the whole ordeal weren't the most reliable. She definitely remembered seeing the gargoyles on the front of the building, even hearing a little spiel about them from Vera. Ana must have carried that memory inside and, in retrospect, overlaid it on her memory of looking out Charlie's window and being horrified at the drop.

That explanation made more sense than the other possibility—that maybe, during the week, the building had somehow removed the gargoyles or repositioned them somewhere else. They were historic stone statues, not LEGOs or Christmas decorations.

No. It had just been a false memory during a stressful time. Simple as that.

She forced herself to head back to the living room, to the closet.

*Or here's another answer for you,* her mother's voice whispered. *You're cracking up. Finally losing it.*

The evidence seemed to be on full display in the living room. The place was a disaster area.

"Shut up, Cathy," she muttered, trying to put all this out of her mind, to just accept what had happened and be loose. She had too much work to do.

Once more: the brakes. Once more: lowering herself onto the floor and scooting into the closet. Once more: praying to the Gods of Babies that Charlie didn't decide this very moment to wake up.

She turned the baby monitor in her hand to silent—its red light would tell her if there were any noises—then fired up her laptop, eased her microphone toward her, and put on her headphones.

The mic gain was set too high, but she'd stupidly put the preamp out of reach behind the laptop. She moved things away to reach the gain knob, then stopped. Turned the volume up instead.

This whole time, she'd been trying—and failing—to keep thoughts of vanishing gargoyles out of her mind. Now those thoughts evaporated. Because she was hearing something through her headphones.

The sound of a baby crying. For a moment, she thought it was Charlie. Two things quickly clarified that it wasn't.

The first was that it was obviously too far away, coming from another apartment, probably the one next door.

Second, it wasn't *just* a baby crying.

An adult was crying, too.

# NEIGHBORS

## 1

By the time the crying intensified to full-on wailing, Ana couldn't stop herself. Still holding the baby monitor, she worked herself back into her chair—again—and left the apartment, preemptively engaging the dead bolt to keep the door from locking.

She approached her neighbor's apartment door and pressed her ear to it. The sobs were muffled and distant . . . but *there.*

Ana wiped her sweating palms on her knees. For a moment, her fist hesitated above the dark mahogany of the door. Then she began to knock.

"Hello?" she called. "Everything . . . okay?"

She winced at her intrusion. She knew all too well what it was like to need a gut-cleansing weep-fest from time to time, and if anyone had ever bothered her while she was in the middle of one, she would've been mortified. There was something about this, though, that wasn't letting her be a good, invisible neighbor.

She knocked again.

In the high center of the door was a gold, art deco plate housing a small, dark peephole. Too high for Ana to look into, but a small rectangle jutted from the bottom of the plate: the doorbell. The kind that you punch inward with an old-timey *ka-chunk*.

A phrase Georgia sometimes said during their sessions popped into her head: *Motion is lotion.* She lifted herself up in her seat and tried the bell.

It made no noise, other than a faint rasp of metal sliding in and out. For some reason, though, it sent a shiver of revulsion through her. She felt as if she'd touched something organic, like a stranger's belly button or skin tag. It only lasted a moment, but still. Ugh.

She put her ear to the door again, feeling very conscious of how she must look right now, a mostly stranger to this building spying on her neighbor.

The sobbing continued, faint but unmistakable.

Ana realized what she was going to try next before she could stop herself.

## 2

It only took a moment for her to wheel back into her own apartment, grab the key that Georgia had found out in the hallway, and go back to the door. In that time, she had an insane idea.

*What if this key hadn't been dropped accidentally?*

*What if it had been, I don't know, slid out—like, the person inside that apartment was desperate for rescue, and they slid the key under the door in the hopes that someone would find and use it?*

Of course, that led to the obvious question: Why? Why would anyone do that? If they could slide the key out in the first place, why didn't they just, you know, leave?

Ana didn't know . . . but that didn't erase the feeling that maybe she was onto something. Those cries sounded too desperate, too forlorn.

This was all assuming the key even worked, of course.

*You've been reading too many bad erotica books. Too many plot jumps, too many contrivances. You should walk away and—whoops, wrong word choice, huh?*

"Shut up, Cathy."

Ana jammed the key into the lock.

It fit.

It turned.

The door to her neighbor's apartment swung inward, revealing an interior that was impressively dark. Impossibly dark.

"Hello?" Ana called from the hallway. "Is everything . . . okay?"

The sobbing stopped.

Silence.

Heavy, pulse-quickening silence.

Then a sound from somewhere inside the apartment that filled Ana's heart with ice water.

The increasingly loud thud-thud-*thud* of someone running toward her.

## 3

If the nightmare sound of someone rushing up from the throat of darkness made Ana's blood go cold, the figure who appeared moments later flash froze it. It was all Ana could do to keep her hands steady on the wheels of her chair and not shove herself back toward the relative safety of her own apartment.

The figure kept its distance on the other side of the apartment's entry hallway, bathed in darkness. It had rushed in from the other room, but now it was stock-still as if unsure what to do about this unexpected intruder. Or perhaps it was blinded by the light from the hallway.

*How is it so dark in there?* Ana wondered. *All the lights must be off, and all the curtains must be drawn.*

Just a shape, barely visible in the murk, but even its silhouette communicated great, glaring wrongness. The angles were wrong. The behavior was wrong. The whistling, panicky sound of its breath: wrong.

Ana assumed it was a woman, based on the cries she'd heard. It—she—had erratic, wild hair that reached out into the darkness in all directions like tendrils. She breathed in short, shallow, whistling gulps. A loosely cinched robe hung from her spindly frame, making her appear wraithlike.

"Are . . . are you okay?" Ana asked, trying to keep the fear from her voice. "I heard crying and, and, and . . ."

The woman began to walk toward Ana. Bare feet slapped against the polished surface of the floor. Even her steps were wrong. Tentative, unsure, clumsy.

"Was . . . Did . . . *My key?*"

Her voice was hoarse and rusted.

"I'm sorry," Ana babbled. "I wasn't sure, I just wanted to make sure you were okay, I didn't want to intrude, I'm sorry—"

*Don't apologize; get out of here! Go back to your own apartment and lock the door.*

But Ana stayed put.

As the woman approached, the light from the hallway spilled onto her.

Ana thought of movies where killers trapped women in basements, women who went insane in subterranean hells. Her neighbor looked worse than her silhouette suggested. Her hair was the kind of filthy only weeks of neglect could achieve. Her clothes—pajama bottoms and a robe—were stained and ragged and seemed almost to float *around* the woman rather than on her, she was so clearly starved. She wore no shirt, and one of her breasts hung out from the robe's opening, limp and deflated, calling more attention to the crenulated shadows of the rib cage just behind it.

But it was her face most of all. Wild, staring eyes rolling on top of deep-set bags. Flared nostrils. Cheeks reddened by crying—or perhaps by slaps and scratches. Snot bubbling out of her nose and down to her chin.

The woman stopped at the doorway. She looked at the threshold, up, over, down, as if she couldn't believe the door had simply opened. Ana caught a rancid, milky smell.

"You found my key," the woman said. "I didn't think anyone would try, but . . . but I heard new people and I had to. All I could think of."

"What do you need?" Ana heard herself asking. "How can I help?"

From inside the shadows of her apartment, the neighbor's baby began to wail again. Loud and outraged. *Come back and do my bidding.*

Ana expected her to look back, concerned and attentive. Instead the woman's worn-out face broke into a smile.

"Nope." She laughed quietly. "No, no, no. Fuck you." She put a grimy hand on Ana's shoulder, stepping over her, and stumbled through the doorway.

Ana did a double take, looking into the shadows, then back at the escaping woman. "But your—your baby—?"

"Ate," she heard the woman muttering. "Ater . . ."

Or was she saying *hate*? *Hate her?*

Before Ana could wrap her mind around what was happening, the woman broke into a run, bolting down the hallway, full tilt, heading for the elevator. Then, something made her skid to an abrupt halt. She turned, but tripped over herself and fell with a teeth-clattering thud onto the floor.

She picked herself up and started back toward Ana, moving in a limping trot, obviously hurt but having no time to register it. Blood dripped from her bottom lip, where she'd bit through in her fall.

Ana sat, watching this, stunned. What the fuck was happening?

In a moment, the woman limped past Ana and headed farther down the hallway. Ana gathered her wits and followed.

"Wait, stop," she said, but of course, the woman wasn't listening.

Eventually, though, she did stop. Ana pulled up behind her.

They were at the edge of the large, decorative staircase going down to the next floor.

The woman stood at the edge of the topmost step. For the moment, she didn't appear to be ready to move any farther. That was good. For obvious reasons, if she decided to start down these steps, Ana wouldn't be able to follow.

*But why are you following at all? You know the cardinal rule of this city: don't get involved with Crazy.*

"Your baby is crying," Ana said after a silence. Outraged peals of distress floated down the hallway. Were other neighbors hearing this? Was anyone else going to help? Or at least stick their heads out and tell them to shut the fuck up?

Then the woman spoke. A clear, complete, unmistakable sentence.

"She's killing me."

Ana blinked. She must have misheard. "What?"

"She's killing me."

"Your . . . *baby*?"

The woman didn't answer for a long time. She just kept staring down that long, winding staircase. Ana followed her gaze.

This was Ana's first real look at the stairs. She'd known they were here, but she'd avoided ever coming over and looking. No doubt there was also a smaller, enclosed set of fire stairs somewhere, but someone designed *these* to be seen.

They seemed dizzying, not owing to any particular height or steepness, rather they formed a repeating shape that became almost vertebral the farther down you looked. Each flight rounded in an arc of white and black, leading from one floor to the next in a half spiral of black-and-gold banisters. Picture windows looked toward the courtyard and ran along the wall with the stairs, and the winter light made every smooth surface shine and sparkle. It gave the impression of a slight wetness. Organic somehow.

"I can't do it anymore," Ana's neighbor said. She spoke softly, almost to herself, but another shriek floated out from deep inside her apartment as if in response. "I can't. I can't. I can't."

Just as Ana began to realize that maybe the woman hadn't come to this spot to simply walk down the steps, her neighbor climbed onto the railing of the staircase and swung one leg over.

"Ican'tIcan'tIcan'tIcan'tIcan't . . ."

*Holy shit, she's about to jump.*

"Hey!" Ana exclaimed, startled. She had to think fast, or she was going to witness at the very least an attempted suicide (a manic thought whipped through her mind: *She should go up to the roof—that's what I would do if I could*).

She reached out and grabbed one of the woman's hands. It was clammy, appallingly sticky. Ana didn't let that stop her.

The woman paused for a moment, and Ana debated what to do. Pull her back? Ana was strong—stronger than this emaciated wraith, for sure—but she had little doubt the woman would be able to squirm out of her grasp, and it's not like Ana would be able to get in her way. Worse, what if the woman managed to pull Ana over the edge with her?

Instead, Ana gave a gentle squeeze and said, as calmly as she could:

"Hey. I know how you feel."

The woman, who still straddled the railing, looked down at Ana, momentarily surprised.

"Y-you . . . do?" How long had it been since anyone had said something like that to this poor woman? What lonely hell was she dealing with?

"Yeah." Ana nodded with conviction. "I do. I know exactly what you mean."

The woman's eyes glistened. *Tell me,* they begged.

And just like that, Ana found herself telling this disheveled stranger everything.

# 4

Well. Almost everything.

More than she'd ever told anyone—even Reid. Once she started talking, it was hard to stop.

She told her neighbor all about the feelings she'd stuffed into a deep hole inside herself. Feelings of disconnect, of loathing. Of resentment. Of terror—for her baby, of her baby, for herself, of herself. The books called it *postpartum depression,* sure, how quaint and categorizable, how empirical. The lived reality, however, was something far more obscure, far more horrifying and disorienting. It didn't feel normal. It didn't feel diagnosable. It felt wrong. It felt unprecedented. No. It felt *damning.*

What made it worse was that Ana could distinctly remember *not* feeling this way immediately after Charlie's birth. When they'd first laid that squalling, naked little raisin of a human on her sweaty chest, Ana had felt a rush of giddiness. She had felt pride in herself, in her baby—they'd done it, they'd navigated the treacherous waters of pregnancy and birth together. Not every mother got to feel this, she knew; she tried to treasure it.

It wasn't until several hours later, pre-dawn of the next day. She'd woken up in her hospital bed feeling a strange restlessness. A painful tingling, mental as well as physical. And typical Ana—even after birth, after feeling like someone had just tenderized her with a baseball bat, she craved movement. She decided to see if she could handle walking to the bathroom.

Instead, she learned, with the help of gravity and the merciless hospital floor, that her legs no longer supported her weight.

Her life, as she knew it, had just changed in ways she had not signed up for.

A garden of resentment was sown that day. Its hideous plants bloomed at irregular, unpredictable intervals. A sprig of hate. A blossom of blame. Entire teeming hedgerows of depression and alienation. There were whole stretches of time when all she could do was look at her baby, her new, beautiful baby, and think, *This is your fucking fault. You did this to me.* Always in a voice that sounded like her mother's . . . but also unmistakably like her own.

Things got worse those first few months, when Charlie refused to sleep. The crying drilled into Ana's skull. On top of the excruciating nerve pain, the devastating first attempts at physical therapy, the dull, throbbing, ache in her breasts. *What exactly are* you *crying about, you fucking life-ruiner?*

Reid had made an almost superhuman effort to keep Ana from doing as little as possible so she could concentrate on healing, on adapting. He tried to be there for her as she broke down and sobbed, screamed, at the unfairness of it all. He tried to be her legs, her hands, her heart. But some things he couldn't do. Things only a mother could do. Things only a convalescent could do. Plus, he was as fallible and vulnerable as any other human body.

It culminated in a night about four months in, when Reid had been so exhausted Charlie's midnight cries simply didn't wake him. It wasn't his fault, Ana knew; it was the baby's. This monstrous, shrieking misery that had chewed its way into their lives like a cancer. Their own cells, gone rogue, trying to eat them up.

Ana, sleep-deprived herself, had somehow forgotten the inconvenient fact of her paralysis. In a horrible echo of that first morning, only this time underscored by the nearby sounds of their infant's shrieks, Ana tried to get out of bed to tend to the baby and plummeted straight over the side of the bed, slamming her head into the nightstand.

Blinking stars away, blood running down her temple and into her eyes, she managed to get herself into her chair and wheel over to the baby. She lifted Charlie up and discovered why she was crying. It wasn't hunger or fear. It was shit. Great jets of it. Up and down her back, the crib, in her hair. Industry-standard liquid infant shit. A *baccident,* the parenting blogs called it.

"Okay," Ana heard herself muttering, "okay, okay, okay."

Her own hands were now covered in shit. She left Charlie in her crib and tried to head to the kitchen to get a roll of paper towels.

If she'd been able to just walk, it would have been the simplest thing; she could have just kept her hands out and moved. Perhaps she should have just wiped her hands on her shirt or something, but she was so dazed from the abrupt waking, from the head injury, that that simple solution eluded her.

Instead, it was an awkward, excruciating process, trying to use her wrists to move her wheels, until finally giving up and gripping them with soiled hands, smearing shit across the rims and then across the floor as she proceeded.

At one point, she wiped the blood and sweat from her forehead and realized a few seconds later she had succeeded in smearing shit across her face, as well.

It could have been funny.

It should have been funny.

It wasn't.

"Okay," she kept reciting. "Okay, okay, okay."

That word. Her last toehold of sanity.

Okay. Okay. Okay.

She came back to Charlie, paper towels and wipes in her lap.

She didn't notice the knife in her hand until the moment before Reid turned on the light. Moonlight had glinted off the blade, and only then did her nerves register the handle's heaviness. It was the butcher knife they'd bought after their wedding. Bad luck to register for knives, they'd been told, so they got the knife set themselves, laughing at the superstition.

She couldn't remember bringing it from the kitchen. She held it over the crib, where Charlie sniffled and mewled. The stench of liquid shit covered the world, and she imagined running the blade into Charlie's soft belly and making this all go away.

Then the light clicked on. Reid's sleepy voice: "Ana?"

For the rest of her life, she would never forget that moment before her husband rushed over and pried the knife out of her grip. That realization: *Yes, I can do this, and then everything will be easier again.*

Ana and Reid never talked about it.

She held on to a dim hope that maybe Reid had forgotten it. Maybe his sleep deprivation had convinced him it was a horrible dream or something and they could just move beyond that unspeakably horrendous episode like a gory wreck passed on a highway. But there were moments when she caught him looking at her, or offering to do something, and she had no doubt whatsoever that he was thinking about that night. Asking himself, *Is she going to break again? How weak is this stranger I'm suddenly married to?*

Ana stopped going to support groups soon after that. She stopped talk therapy. She knew from books she'd read, movies she'd watched, that some monsters had to be invited in. She was never going to entertain that idea with *this* particular monster. It was almost beautiful in its simplicity: that horrible night, and all its ramifications, disappeared into an isolated prison cell, never to be let out. Unhealthy? Ill-advised? Maybe, but it also *worked.* Things became easier. At least, a little bit.

Until this moment in the hallway, looking up at her obviously deranged neighbor, who perched there covered in slime and filth, one tit hanging out, teetering on the brink of a swan dive down a marble staircase.

All these memories, all these feelings, came back as Ana held her neighbor's hand. A part of her even felt lighter, grateful . . . almost guilty for taking this moment of a stranger's misery to purge something of herself. It was a wonder all these feelings didn't shut her down. But mothers can handle a lot of sensations at once, can't they? It's part of the job: to be torn open and persevere.

## 5

The woman stared at her.

Ana squeezed her hand once more.

"Look, I'm sure you went through something different, something totally your own," Ana said. "All I'm trying to say is you're not alone. Okay? I'm here. I'm literally right next door. So . . . why don't you come down from there and we can talk about it."

"Talk about it."

"Yeah." Even though this woman looked like absolute hell, Ana suddenly felt hope in her own chest. Maybe this was a lucky break for both of them. Maybe they could help each other. "You could come over to my apartment, we could have some tea or, shit, we've got beers? Or we could both go over to your apartment first and maybe I could lend a hand with whatever you need? I could watch your baby while you get some sleep? You know, I've got one of my own and—"

The woman's face soured. "That's not my baby."

"Oh?" Ana wasn't sure what to say to that. Was she being literal? Was the baby adopted or a surrogate's, or was her neighbor being more metaphorical?

"That's *not* my baby," the woman repeated. She swallowed, and Ana heard how dry her throat was. "My baby was different."

An anxious tremor ran through Ana.

"Okay," she said. "That's okay. That's a normal feeling, I promise." Then, even though she of all people knew how these offers could land, she added, "If you want, I can give you the name of a support—"

The woman yanked her hand away, then leaned down to stare at Ana face-to-face. She still straddled the banister—in a way, she looked weirdly like a gargoyle herself, and for a flash, Ana thought about the one she'd imagined outside Charlie's window.

The woman's breath smelled sweet and rotten. When was the last time she'd brushed her teeth? It was such intense closeness that Ana couldn't help but break eye contact. The woman's robe had fallen open farther and Ana found herself looking down at her exposed chest. Between her breasts, Ana noticed what looked like a rash. Red welts, slick with what appeared to be pus, ringed in foamy, outraged flesh. She thought of brown recluse spider bites, the kind that dissolve a person's skin away like acid. Or leprosy.

The woman spoke vehemently, repeating herself, making this point very clear to Ana with trembling intensity.

"That's *not*. My baby. Anymore."

"Okay. I'm sorry. I believe—"

"You don't know *anything*." In her frustration, the woman brought her leg back over the railing and hopped down. "That thing *keeps* me here. It keeps me *stuck* so I can't leave. See?" She lifted one of her pant legs, revealing a skinny calf. More red, raw flesh, including a shallow crater where it looked like skin had been peeled off with an adhesive. Then she suddenly let out a loud, harsh laugh and looked around, as if she just realized she was on her feet again. "And maybe I can't leave! Ha! I didn't jump! Why didn't I jump?!" Next, her voice dropped into a speedy tumble. "I can't use the elevator, because they'll stop me. They'd catch me on the stairs. And now *you're* here. I thought you were going to help, but, no, you're not helping." She started laughing again, mad, insane barks of laughter.

"I want to help," Ana offered weakly, but the woman went on, tumbling again.

"They know I know, and so they lock my doors. Sometimes I think the doors lock on their own—but what do I know, I'm crazy, like my husband says, right? Said. Like he said. He doesn't talk to me anymore. But I heard voices, new voices, outside, and I put my key out there because—I don't even know now! So stupid! You can't help me! You're trying to stop me, just like them!"

Ana backed up, barely following this rambling, erratic monologue, but not liking how it swung from emotion to emotion. Worst of all was the laughing. It made her think wildly of the sort of laugh a cow might give once it realized there was no getting off the slaughterhouse conveyor belt.

Then the woman coughed. A wet sound. Something ripping inside her. She turned her face to look at Ana with a horrid smile. Fresh blood dripped from her lip. "I'm melting," she said. "Inside. It's *draining me dry*—"

Ana had her hands up, impotently trying to do something, offer something, stop this disturbing one-woman show.

"I'm sorry. Look, it's okay, it's okay, just calm down and let me—"

"Can I be of assistance, ladies?"

The voice made Ana jump in her seat. Her heart rocketed into her throat so hard that she actually wheeled backward a few inches.

A man in a rich, burgundy suit, artfully accented with black silk trim and gold fabric at the lapels and cuffs, capped off with a short black top hat that looked as if it had never seen a speck of dirt, appeared beside them. It was the concierge from the main lobby. Smiler. He must have come up in the elevator.

"I—we—" Ana stammered. She had the sudden, irrational sense memory of sneaking out with one of her friends to do something illicit in the school bathroom and being caught.

"Mrs. Jacobs?" the doorman asked, his sharp smile arcing upward, painfully, underneath his placid, patient eyes. The woman—Mrs. Jacobs—was still laughing, but her laughs were silent now, petering out. Her eyes had gone glassy at the sound of the concierge's voice. It was the look of exhaustion, defeat, complete dissociation.

"Oh no. She's having a difficult time, huh?" the concierge said to Ana.

"She's—yes, I—"

"It sounds like your baby's hungry, Mrs. Jacobs. We're getting complaints."

"Hungry." Another new phrase for Mrs. Jacobs to taste. Again, Ana heard the words *ate, ate,* or maybe *hate, hate,* echoing in her mind.

"Hungry." The concierge nodded. "Don't you hear him crying?"

"I . . ."

Ana burst in. "I'll go with her. She needs help, and I—"

"That's incredibly kind of you, Mrs. Greene. But Mrs. Jacobs is okay. Aren't you, Mrs. Jacobs?"

An expression of absurdity blossomed on the woman's face. Like she was about to start braying laughter again. "He's *hungry.* The baby's *hungry.*"

"That's right. He needs his mother. Mr. Jacobs can't do it alone. Here, let me—" The doorman reached over and closed Mrs. Jacobs's robe.

Ana felt anger flare. Who the fuck was this condescending prick to come up here and start manhandling this poor woman? He was a greeter, a glorified retiree standing in front of the world's fanciest Walmart.

Then again, what was *she* going to do, throw this woman on her lap and wheel her to safety? She also suddenly remembered the baby monitor in her own hand. Charlie. How long had they been out here?

Ana shook her head. "This doesn't feel right. Something is wrong."

The concierge beamed down at her.

"This isn't the first time this has happened. We're sorry it bothered you." He gestured for Mrs. Jacobs to follow him back to her apartment.

Ana's anger burned brighter. "Mrs. Jacobs, *are* you okay? Do you want to come back with me to my apartment?"

Mrs. Jacobs met Ana's gaze with wide, shining eyes. No longer wild and darting—they were fixed and horridly aware.

"I should've jumped," she said.

"No—"

"I should have jumped."

"You need some rest, Mrs. Jacobs." The concierge put his hands on her shoulders and began to guide her forward. "You need to be with your baby. It's going to be okay." The baby's wails continued, but as if the baby sensed his parent coming back, they began to abate a little.

Ana watched, feeling utterly powerless—and confused. She called after them, "I'll check on you tomorrow, okay? We'll . . . we'll talk!" What a stupid, facile thing to say, but she had to say something before this poor, broken woman disappeared.

Mrs. Jacobs looked back at Ana and offered an oppressively sad smile. "You don't know anything. But you will! If you're really here, if you're like the rest of us, you'll know everything soon! I think it's like music; once they really listen to it, they change! It's in the air, I think!"

Ana had no idea what she meant. "What?"

Mrs. Jacobs and the concierge reached her apartment. He worked on pushing, then pulling, her inside as gently as possible. Obviously, he could have been much more forceful if he'd wanted to—probably if Ana weren't there. "Don't start this again, Mrs. Jacobs; you know that's not true." He made eye contact with Ana and gave an apologetic smile. The baby continued crying.

"Who's 'they'?" Ana asked.

Suddenly, Mrs. Jacobs laughed again. "Babies! Hahaha! They're the reason why we got these apartments! They're the only reason why we're—"

The door closed on Mrs. Jacobs and the concierge before she could finish her sentence, but Ana was pretty sure what that final word was going to be.

*Here.*

*They're the only reason why we're here.*

## 6

Ana sat in the hallway for a good two minutes, waiting for the concierge to exit Mrs. Jacobs's apartment. She wanted to question him . . . and also see him leave. He never did. And then a curious, unpleasant thing: Ana began to feel the physical presence of the stairwell pressing on her back. Tempting her to come back and stare down its hypnotic depths. Maybe even climb onto its ledge like Mrs. Jacobs . . .

*You might become like her one day. Unless . . . you end it now . . .*

Ana quickly wheeled herself back into her own apartment, as if she'd been jolted by an exposed wire. She'd never had so sudden and strong an ideation like that before. It deeply disturbed her.

A lot of things deeply disturbed her, actually. She replayed every moment of the strange encounter. None of it made sense. All of it made sense. She knew better than anyone how badly an infant could fuck your mental health. The sleep deprivation, the stress, the hormones. She didn't know this woman; Mrs. Jacobs could've been in bad shape even before her screaming baby came along.

*But could that ever be me . . . ?*

It wasn't until Ana was back inside her own living room that she noticed the key to Mrs. Jacobs's apartment still tucked in her hand. She quickly ditched it into their key bowl like it was burning hot.

## 7

Charlie sat up in her crib, awake but unbothered, half waving, half throwing her stuffed rabbit around. It was a rag doll rabbit, given to them by Reid's mom before they'd gotten pregnant as a sort of good luck charm. Reid had one just like it when he was a baby. Ana's mom had commented to Ana later that she didn't like it; it was the sort of stuffed animal she imagined a "meth head baby would drag around its trailer park."

Ana watched Charlie from the doorway. She was so lost in thought it took a handful of seconds before she realized . . . the window was open. Cool air wafted into the room, rippling the curtains.

"Jesus. Did I leave that open?" Ana asked out loud as if her baby or the room could confirm. She must have. It's not like anyone else here could have done it. But, good lord, that was a hell of a thing to forget.

As she went to the window, it occurred to her: Shouldn't there be bars on these? Wasn't that a law? She'd have to look into that. They had plenty of time before Charlie would be able to pull herself up to the sill, let alone open the window—but still. Those skills would probably show up out of the blue and sooner than expected.

*Weird how they made all those alterations for my chair but not for the baby. They knew we had a—*

*(They're the only reason we're here!!)*

She reached out and closed the window, taking an extra moment to look around for any sign of the gargoyles she'd imagined. God, that discovery felt like a lifetime ago.

Then she heard the voice of Mrs. Jacobs again.

*I should have jumped*

*Sometimes I think the doors lock on their own*

*I'm crazy, like my husband says*

Charlie must have sensed Ana's pensiveness, because she made one of her precocious chirps. Ana looked over at her, but as she did, she noticed something on her own shoulder. She reached up and wiped it off—it must have come from Mrs. Jacobs's hand as she'd stepped over Ana to get out of her apartment.

Ana's hand came away covered in some sort of slimy, gooey gel. It was appallingly sticky. Like honeyed cement. Up close in the light, it looked like it squirmed on her fingertips and she thought of that ragged, peeled-away flesh on Mrs. Jacobs's leg.

"Be right back, Baby Bird," she muttered, wiping her hand on her shirt.

She went to get paper towels. For once, this task didn't make her think of that one awful night, when getting paper towels almost ended everything.

This time, she was too busy thinking how the stuff on her hand looked a lot like the stuff she'd scraped off the windowsill.

# HELP

## 1

Half an hour and a new shirt later, Ana sat in her booth, while Charlie babbled in her playpen just outside the booth's broken door.

Charlie seemed in better spirits than she'd been in days. Ana was glad at least someone was in a good mood—maybe they'd all actually get sleep tonight.

Ana didn't need to be in the booth right now, but it helped her feel grounded, like maybe if she went through the motions of having a productive day, one would materialize. Plus, the living room was still a mess from emptying out the closet, and this helped her avoid that particular chore for the time being.

She propped open the booth door with one of her weights and had her iPad so she could read through *Blood Rink V: Offsides* once again.

Unfortunately, her attention span wasn't cooperating. Before she realized it, she had her phone in her hand and googled the nearest police precinct. She could have called 911, but she didn't think this was an emergency per se—or, at least not the kind a person in her position could *prove* was an emergency.

Trouble was, she spent just enough mental energy gaming out who to call that she didn't plan out what to actually *say.* When a flat, nasal voice answered the phone at the precinct, asking her about the nature of her call, Ana stammered and said, "Um, hi, um, I'm worried about my neighbor?"

A pause.

"Worried how, ma'am?"

Ana floundered her way through an explanation. No, she didn't need someone dispatched. No, she wasn't calling to report a crime. Her neighbor was just acting strange. Scared. Dazed, almost drugged.

"Are you calling to report drug abuse?"

"No! Sorry, no, I just, I was calling to see if . . ." She let out a deep breath. "I guess I was just calling to see if there's anything I could do. Or should."

It wasn't until Ana gave their address that she received any hint of interest from the other voice.

"That's the Deptford, isn't it? What floor did you say?"

"The eighteenth." She almost added, *Although it's really more like the twentieth. Or maybe thirtieth. It's hard to tell some days.*

"One moment."

When a detective finally came on the line—a brusque, phlegmy voice belonging to "Detective Hauck"—he wasn't any more helpful. He told Ana that he appreciated the call and he'd made "a note of her complaint."

"A what?"

"A note. The complaint has been written down. On a piece of paper. Is there anything else y—"

"But I'm not complaining about anything; I'm—"

"We've added it to the list. Okay? We've dealt with this stuff before."

"What do you mean, this stuff? With the same apartment? Is this a pattern or something? Have they been living here long?"

"Ma'am, do you really think I can give that kinda information to a stranger over the phone?" He was losing patience.

"I'm sorry, it's just . . . I just moved in. I *live here* now. So I'm trying to . . ." She took a deep breath and asked the question she just now realized she had been skirting this entire time. "Is there something wrong with this place? You get these kinds of calls a lot?"

Another long pause. Longer than any of the previous, except for when she'd been put on hold. In the silence, she heard Mrs. Jacobs again: *I'm crazy, like my husband says . . .*

"Look. Miss Greene, right? All I can tell you is we get these kinds of calls from time to time. Okay? Not *all* the time, but . . . whenever we follow up, there's never anything. You understand?"

"What kind of calls, exactly?"

He sighed. "Strange noises. Strange feelings. People just get spooked. Some buildings just have a vibe, make people unsettled, I don't know. But again: we follow up, we check it out, and there's never anything wrong. Your neighbor wasn't the first. You're not the first. Whoever moves in next won't be the first, either. You're safe. Relax. Honestly, I bet it's got something to do with vibrations or something. Tall residential buildings are weird like that. Plus, I mean, hell, low-income units in a luxury building? Bound to be the occasional, y' know, mental problem. Maybe that's why some folks are low-income in the first place, I dunno. Shit. I shouldn't be saying that. Forget I said that." He cleared his throat again, then began speaking with a slightly more pronounced articulation as if he had put on a new, professional persona. "I have made the note. I have put it in the file. If the situation escalates or anything further happens to your neighbor, or to you, you can give me a call, and we will pay you all another visit. But. Like I said. Some buildings just have a vibe."

"I'm sorry to have wasted your time." She realized she'd said the same thing to Dr. Bronson and cringed.

Instead of telling her she hadn't wasted his time, that it was good she checked, that of course if she saw something she should say something, hadn't they been drilling that into everybody's heads for the last two decades and change, he said, "That's why we get the big bucks. You have a good day." And the line went dead.

## 2

She could still feel that gooey residue on her hand hours later. Scrubbing with soap and water couldn't make that sticky, crawling after-feeling go away. She didn't mention to Reid that it reminded her of the gunk from Charlie's windowsill. She left a lot of things out of her retelling, in fact, like the disappearing gargoyle she'd imagined or the fact that she told Mrs. Jacobs everything about that one awful night. She especially didn't mention that terrifying, suicidal siren call she'd felt coming from the staircase.

Reid seemed more delighted that they could spy on their neighbors if they hid in the closet and turned the mic up.

"That's what you're taking from this?"

"No, but . . ." He sighed. "Is there something you want us to do about it? I mean?"

It was a very Reid response. The idea that sometimes you just had to listen to a story, not treat it as a riddle that needed solving, always made him itchy. Plus, work always left him a little irritable, even if the day hadn't been particularly good or bad. He just hated that job.

"Yes, Reid, go over there and offer to sleep on her couch for a few nights. In fact, let's become a throuple and raise our children together."

"Cool. She sounds hot."

Reid grabbed a beer from the fridge while Ana worked on feeding Charlie. Charlie was back to being strangely fussy, rejecting her microwaved chicken tikka masala, which she normally loved. They'd prided themselves on raising a kid with a wide palate, but tonight Charlie seemed more interested in punishing her food against her high chair tray than eating.

"I wonder what she meant by 'babies are the reason we're here.'"

Reid shrugged. "Maternal mission statement? Or maybe she's a religious nut?"

"Or . . . maybe everyone on this floor has a baby?" Ana ventured, trying to sound bemused and ironic. "Maybe that's the real price of admission here?"

"Right." He rolled his eyes. "So where are the strollers? Where's the chorus of screams in the hallways?"

"Yeah . . ." Ana fell silent, trying to get Charlie to accept one more forkful of soft chicken. "Unless . . . maybe a lot of the other apartments are empty?

Maybe they only accept applicants with babies of a certain age, so their applicant pool is actually really limited? Maybe—"

She felt his eyes on her. Staring. Assessing. Again, Mrs. Jacobs's voice:

*I'm crazy, like my husband says.*

"I'm just kidding, Reid. Don't look at me like that."

A beat. "I know. I'm just . . . I'm not gonna lie, I'm not thrilled to be living next door to someone like that. She sounds super messed up." He took a swig of his beer, then stared into the bottle. "I hope she's not, like, a sanitation hazard. I hope we don't have to worry about bugs or something."

"Bugs?" Ana almost gagged. She paused in wiping down Charlie's face.

"Didn't you say she had bites all over?"

"More like welts. Or eczema. They weren't *bites.* At least . . . at least I'm pretty sure."

He grimaced. "A building like this probably has a pretty thorough extermination setup, right?"

"Yeah."

Neither sounded very sure. They each remembered their previous brush with bedbugs and suppressed a shudder. The plastic tubs. The multiple exterminator visits. The kids in the hallway telling them they lived in the bughouse . . . Whole lotta unwelcome memories coming up today.

"Well," Reid said, coming over to help clean up Charlie, "as my mom used to say, kaynahora, peh-peh-peh." He mimed spitting onto the floor three times.

Yiddish superstitions notwithstanding, though, the mood felt distinctly sour.

After Charlie was wiped down, Reid decided to order dinner again. Ana wanted to protest—they were ordering delivery too frequently—but decided to save that argument for another day.

Thirty minutes later, things had relaxed a little. Until Reid's phone rang.

"No, fucking *dammit*!" Reid seethed, looking at the number.

He stomped over to grab his jacket. He threw it on while he answered the phone and headed out the door in a huff. Ana could hear him as he made his way to the elevator.

"You seriously won't come up? I'm gonna cancel your tip, you know. I mean, *why* . . ." His voice faded away.

She looked down at Charlie, whose brow was knit in her recently ubiquitous expression of perturbed contemplation.

"We're all doing great today, huh?"

Charlie stopped chewing on a yellow plastic block to look up at her mother and give a desultory raspberry.

"Good idea," Ana said. "Let's figure out a way to cheer him up."

# 3

Reid had other reasons to be in a crappy mood—work had been annoying, and this nonsense with food delivery was infuriating—but he knew, in truth, it was because of Ana's story of the neighbor woman. It rattled him.

Goddamn, did he not want Ana to start finding things wrong with their new apartment already. He knew how her mind worked, obsessively finding something to pick at. He already wasn't mentioning the calls from Frank he still regularly ignored. Sometimes he felt like trying to keep Ana in a good mood was another full-time job.

Plus . . . well, there really *was* something so unpleasant about sharing a wall with the woman Ana described. Was that really their class of neighbor, even here?

He didn't like that kind of elitist thinking, but . . . news of a disgusting, crazy neighbor had broken a bit of the illusion of living here, hadn't it? All this talk of bugs and madness—it was too much like the worst parts of their past. They were supposed to be beyond that now.

He was so wrapped up in his thoughts that it wasn't until he stepped off the elevator that he realized this was the first time he'd ridden the entire way without being aware of the elevator operator—the one Ana had dubbed "the gremlin." Ignoring him made Reid feel even more elitist and gross. He had to make sure not to do that again.

He found the delivery guy across the street. Reid had to wade through several tourists taking photos in front of the Deptford's famous wrought iron gate. Reid felt their eyes, checking to see if he was recognizably famous. He tried to pay them no mind.

"You know," Reid said to the deliveryman, taking his food, "the whole point of delivery is that it's brought *to* you, right?"

The guy stared at him. He stood astride a little scooter, looking out from a thick black helmet with the visor up.

"Seriously," Reid continued. "There's a messenger entrance. I put it in the delivery notes. Why don't any of you come into the—?"

"No one goes in there, man. We all know better."

The guy drove off, the whine of his scooter sounding like a playground taunt.

What the hell did *that* mean?

Reid wanted to scream . . . but, no, people were watching. The price of celebrity. Or perceived celebrity, at any rate.

Instead, Reid huffed his way back into the building.

"Everything well, Mr. Greene?" The concierge smiled from behind the front desk.

"Great." Reid tried to match him with his own grin. How did the guy have a mouth like that? Did he have extra teeth or something? "Everything's great."

He began marching to the elevator when a woman came out of the hidden hallway, and he almost collided into her.

He managed to pull his bag of food out of the way, narrowly avoiding one disaster, then almost dropped the bag, causing another.

"Well," the woman said with impressed good humor. She was elderly, almost definitely in her late seventies, maybe even eighties, and radiant. Reid's breath stopped for a moment, as if the oxygen in the room rushed to her first.

He stammered. "I'm so—"

"Think nothing of it."

Suddenly, Smiler appeared, his concern an unnatural rictus. "Are you all right, Miss Varné?"

"Perfectly fine," the woman said, as unruffled as silk. "Just going for a stroll. Meeting neighbors."

She and the concierge exchanged a few more pleasantries, but Reid barely caught them. The blood in his ears swelled and it blotted out most of the world around him. His knees felt weak. This was, he realized, his first real moment in the presence of one of the building's *other* residents.

*Take that, crazy neighbor lady—we're all outclassed by someone.*

A few moments later, the woman—Miss Varné, even that name, like a string of jewels—disappeared out the front door . . . but not before her eyes flicked toward Reid. A smile crossed her lips, and she tipped him a wink. Then she was gone.

"Is there anything else, Mr. Greene?" the concierge asked.

"What? No. No. Sorry. I'm . . . Haven't eaten yet." He held up his delivery to explain further.

"Happens to the best of us."

"Right."

Reid stood at the elevator. His mind kept returning to that woman. *Miss Varné.*

When the elevator arrived, Reid paused before stepping in. A sudden wave of sadness hit him at returning upstairs to his stressful, broken little family. That wave was followed by intense disgust at himself for even thinking such a thing. *What the* fuck, *dude?*

"Forget something?" The frog-like voice of the elevator gremlin snapped him out of his thoughts.

"Just my head." Reid stepped in, blinking so much he looked like a man who'd been spritzed with a fine mist. What a weird night.

With a whir of metal, the doors closed.

## 4

He planned on looking up Miss Varné. What was her story? A movie star? Had to be. She was just too arresting to be anything else.

She hadn't been mentioned in Treadwell's book, but Reid knew he could probably find some trivia on IMDb, some clips on YouTube. He wanted to be an expert on this building. A dim part of himself realized it'd help him feel like he had something to contribute here.

Except he forgot all that the moment he got back to his apartment. When he opened the door, music blared back at him.

Curtis Mayfield. "So in Love."

The song he and Ana danced to at their wedding.

She waited for him inside, with Charlie on her lap. Charlie, of course, squirmed and whined, but not enough that Ana couldn't control her.

"I think we've all had a rough day," Ana said, smiling. "So . . ."

Reid, fighting his own smile, took her outstretched hand. There in the middle of their new apartment, the two of them slow danced together for the first time in over a year. Neither knew how to accommodate the chair or the baby, but they figured it out. Neither was also aware of the other's herculean efforts to make this moment a good and lasting memory—but they were each aware of their own.

For five minutes and fourteen seconds, the world and all its miseries and mysteries fell away, and, like birds, they were able to convince themselves that gravity wasn't the rule, it was merely an option.

# VOICES IN THE DARK

## 1

oh my god

Wh—

oh my god, Reid, wake up—

Jesus, what the fuck is that—

It's Charlie. Help me get up, hurry—

Why is she screaming like that?

I don't know. Watch your toes. We're coming, baby, we're coming! Ow—fucking doorway!

I got her. Hey, hey, Baby Bird, what's wrong, shhhh, shhhhh. Come here. It's okayyyy.

Reid, why is she—I've never heard her scream like this?!

I don't know. I don't know. Shhhhh. Shhhh. What upset you?

Is she wet? Is she—

Totally dry. And no fever. I don't know what's—

I've never heard—

I know. Baby, baby, it's okay.

Should we get to a hospital?

I don't—

Charlie! Please—quiet—WHAT DO YOU WANT?! JUST TELL US WHAT YOU FUCKING WANT!

Ana! Stop, you're making her more—

I'm sorry, I'm sorry, I'm just so tired, I'm sorry.

I . . . I think she's calming down . . . she's trembling so hard, though.

Jesus, me, too. My heart is going to explode. I'm sorry I yelled.

Can you get the light?

*Click.*

Everything looks normal.

I'm sorry I yelled. Reid? I'm sorry.

Yeah. It's okay. Does . . . does she feel warm to you?

No. Totally normal.

What time is it?

I don't know, like three? Shhh . . . shhh. . . . there you go, we're here, Daddy's here, Mommy's here . . .

Reid, what is *wrong* with her?

What do you mean?

I mean, what is wrong with her? Something is really wrong. This isn't normal.

The doctor said—

I know what the doctor said.

She's . . . she's just adjusting. That's all. We all are. She's fine.

God, I never want to hear her scream like that again.

I've got her, honey. Why don't you go back to bed?

Jesus, that noise.

Good thing the walls are thick, huh?

Yeah . . . Oh, look—

What?

It's snowing.

Yeah. Wow. We should probably close the window.

Yeah; or maybe leave it open just a crack? The heat is really strong here.

Right. Remind me to look for a humidifier.

I'll go get her a snack. Wait. Reid, did—

What?

Did *you* open that window earlier?

What do you mean?

I don't know, I just don't remember . . . Never mind, it doesn't matter.

I mean, one of us must've opened it.

Right. Okay, I'll be right back.

## A VERY BAD DAY

# 1

"Um. What the fuck is *that*?" Ana glared at the folded aluminum frame Georgia leaned against the living room wall. It looked suspiciously like a walker.

"Don't worry about it." Georgia spat her gum into a tissue. "Let's get crackin'."

They started with their usual stretches and exercises. Some in the chair, some on the floor. Then, around twenty-five minutes in, Georgia helped Ana back into her seat and said, "So, I've been thinking."

Normally, Ana would've made a joke—"That's so unlike you," or, "Did it hurt?"—but she was so fucking exhausted all she could do was stare. There'd been no more sleep last night, at least for the adults. Charlie had eventually settled down, but every time Ana and Reid attempted to close their eyes, the memory of those horrific shrieks came back, and they wound up staring at the ceiling until the sun came up.

Georgia continued. "Maybe I've been too gentle on you. Maybe one of the reasons you won't consider coming back to the clinic is because the work we do here is so comfortable. Too comfortable."

Already, anger rising. "Georgia . . . I won't consider coming back to the clinic because of *all the reasons I've told you*. The baby. The commute. The money. All of it, it's—"

"See, the thing is? I can help you figure all that out, and you know it. Are you aware there are clinical trials you could sign up for that would be totally free of charge? I looked up like three of them on the way here. It wasn't hard."

Ana breathed, trying her best not to let rage take over. Georgia took note of her silence and continued.

"You're one of the most stubborn people I know. And I bet if our positions were reversed, you'd be just as obsessed with finding ways to get *me* help. Am I right? So, then I'm left to figure there's a *reason* you're not doing it for yourself. I don't know what that reason is, but it's there."

A tidal wave of resentment. Because now even Georgia was treating her like she was broken. Like there was something wrong with her.

*But isn't there? Not with your legs but with your mind?*

"I tried the clinic for months, Georgia," Ana said through clenched teeth. "It didn't work. Sometimes people don't get better."

"You're totally right! And maybe you won't! That's okay! What's *not* okay is that you're not trying. Which means you're stuck in this *in-between* space. That space is awful . . . but it's also kinda comfy, right? The problem is, that place'll suck you dry if you let it. I think the reason you started crying yesterday wasn't because the exercises were hard. They *weren't* hard. They haven't been hard for a while. I think you're holding on to something too tight and—you gotta be like that stewardess, girl! I need you to stop giving me excuses and see where trying takes you! So!" She moved over to the walker and unfolded it. "This ain't an ideal setting, but we'll make it work. We're gonna stand you up with this bad boy, I'm gonna hold on to you, and we're gonna work on taking some steps. It's gonna suck. It's gonna be hard. You might fall. But if I can't bring you to the clinic, I'm gonna bring the clinic to you. If you hate it, well, you can always tell me to fuck off, but I don't think you wanna do that. Am I right?"

She held her hands out to Ana, waiting for Ana to roll her eyes, sigh, maybe lob a curse or two, and then put her hands in Georgia's to get started.

Instead, Ana started yelling. And once she started, it felt too good to stop.

## 2

*Okay,* Georgia thought as the door slammed in her face, *that could have gone better.*

Had that been a dumb thing to do?

She looked at the folded walker in her hands.

She'd actually had a lot more she'd wanted to say today. She was going to tell Ana about her brother, something she'd never told any other client before. Other than the cutesy jokes about her name, Georgia didn't like to reveal too much personal info. So much for that plan.

She gave Ana another minute to change her mind, then she hitched the heavy equipment bag up on her shoulder and began walking to the elevator.

After she pushed the bronze button that called the elevator up, and the mechanisms whirred and rattled, she looked back down the hall.

*Should I go back? Knock on her door and actually tell her what I'd meant to?*

It's not like it would take long. It was a quick story. About how her older brother, Michael, had been in a car accident at seventeen and had to have his left leg amputated. Georgia had watched a horrible depression take hold of him afterward. He began drinking heavily, abusing painkillers, receding from life, until eventually, whether by accident or on purpose, he'd been found dead at the bottom of an old bridge embankment just outside Odessa at twenty-two.

Georgia never told her clients this. She didn't want them thinking she was trying to compete with the difficulties they were experiencing. Also, it was just a sad damn story; she hated evoking that kind of an ending. But maybe Ana needed to know that Georgia came from a place of, if not understanding, then at least empathy.

Then again, maybe Ana just needed some time to cool off.

Georgia remembered talking with one of their mutual gym friends a few weeks ago. The friend had expressed surprise to hear that Ana, who'd always been such an athletic, body-connected person, wasn't more gung ho about PT. Georgia thought about everything Ana had been through—the fertility treatments, the pregnancy, the birth, the injury—and said, "Her body's gotta feel like a foreign country right now. Hell, a foreign planet. She'll step out of her spaceship when she's ready."

Which probably meant ambushing her with the walker had been a bad idea.

"Shit," Georgia muttered. "Good job, me."

She liked Ana. She hoped this wasn't the end. Her instructors had prepared her for the possibility that clients would have these sorts of outbursts from time to time. Hopefully, this would blow over. And if it didn't? Well. Goodbye, Deptford. Nice knowing you.

The elevator doors opened with a rattle, revealing the strange man who stood by the controls.

Seeing him this suddenly, Georgia realized what made this guy so unsettling. He somehow managed to blend into the elevator walls, yet once you knew he was there, he stuck out. He looked *of* the elevator, but your mind rejected that as impossible. She thought of parasites she'd seen online once, who bit off the tongues of fish and merged themselves into the fish's mouth: two creatures for the price of one.

Her own mouth dried up.

"Forget something?" he asked in his weird, glottal voice.

She regained herself. "You know what? I did. Sorry. Don't wait for me; I'll be a little while."

The man looked at her with a chillingly smug expression, hat shading his eyes, then reached over to his levers. The cage door rattled shut, then the proper doors, and she heard the elevator recede like an Adam's apple down an exceedingly long throat.

Georgia had decided on an alternate plan.

Once she was sure he was gone, she walked back down the hallway—first stealing a guilty look at Ana's apartment, half hoping the door would open and Ana would pop her head out, then continuing down the hall.

Georgia, like Ana, needed movement when she felt antsy. Since their session ended early, she had some time to kill. And hey, maybe Ana really was done with her and she'd never have a chance to be in this building again . . .

Georgia headed toward the beautiful, giant, marble-slick stairwell she'd noticed during her first visit. She might as well experience all she could of the Deptford while she was here.

## 3

Ana, for her part, felt terrible. Georgia hadn't deserved that. She'd never been anything but generous and considerate, and Ana had rewarded her with a scream-fest and a door in the face.

She fully intended to open the door, call for Georgia to come back. She'd apologize, invite her in, and then . . . maybe they could talk. Even though Ana was so tired she could barely think straight. Maybe talking would do her good. Maybe what she'd started with Mrs. Jacobs actually needed to continue with someone like Georgia.

Ana would've opened the door . . . but the yelling and the door slamming had woken up Charlie, and now Ana had to settle her down. As she did, Ana's thoughts moved on to wondering why the commotion hadn't caused any of those *other* babies in the other apartments to start wailing, too.

## 4

Georgia was also noticing how strangely quiet the building was. Worse, she had the unmistakable feeling that she was being followed.

It was hard to say when exactly that creeping, between-the-shoulder-blades feeling started. It snuck up on her gradually—and also, she didn't quite know what floor she was on anymore.

Some of the flights down the staircase were gigantic—obviously passing floors that were duplexes, maybe even triplexes, or apartments with massively high ceilings. Georgia knew from the elevator rides that Ana and Reid living on the "eighteenth floor" was a bit of a misnomer, but here on the staircase, the irregular spacing of flights made that number seem . . . irrational. They lived on the *pi* floor, the *infinity* floor, the *some-other-number-she-barely-could-remember-from-high-school-calculus-like-the-square-root-of-negative-gablinty* floor.

She still enjoyed herself, though. The building was beautiful. A marvel. She felt giddy, like she'd snuck off during a tour at the Met and discovered a private wing all to herself.

She stuck to the staircase—mostly. Occasionally, she would reach a landing, then take a few dozen curious steps into the hallway, just to see what it was like. Each floor was uniquely different. One had seas of silken paisley wallpaper stretching into eternity, with just the occasional wall sconce lighting the way. A couple of the floors had framed artwork, and one was full of photographs. She resisted the urge to look at the images for too long. She didn't want to get caught snooping.

But she *had* been caught, hadn't she? Even now she turned, expecting to see someone looking at her. That feeling just wouldn't go away.

Oh, well, what were they going to do? Yell at her? She wasn't hurting anybody. In fact, she was literally on her way out of the building. She just decided to take the scenic route, that's all. If they didn't want visitors to appreciate the staircase, why did they make it so . . . ornamental?

Come to think of it, Georgia realized, a scolding would be welcome. Because, for a huge building, it was silent as a tomb.

Where were the noises? The ambient sounds of life? TVs, arguments, music? It was eerie. Her footsteps, the rattle of the walker she carried, rang out way too loudly.

*Maybe that's why I feel like I'm being followed . . .*

She reached another landing and looked around. This floor was also wallpapered. Not paisley, though. No, the line drawings looked more purposeful than just paisley squiggles. They looked . . . No, that couldn't be right. They looked like faces. Human faces. Screaming. Swarmed by insects.

She hurried back to the staircase. The stairs felt safer. There was sunlight here.

Windows flanked the staircase wall, looking across the courtyard. Was that why she felt watched? Was someone across the way looking out at her?

She looked through the glass again. Then gave a startled gasp, jumping backward, hand under her throat, heart pounding.

A statue outside, on the wall, curved to look into the building. One of those weird little—what were they called? The word eluded her for a moment. All she could think of was the bad guy from the Smurfs. Oh, right. Gargoyles. Ugly fucking things. Ugly, but not a threat.

She laughed, embarrassed, and picked up her pace down the steps.

Why was it so fucking quiet?!

She tried to keep her mind occupied with thoughts of Ana. How she would apologize to her for pushing too hard. Maybe she'd call her tomorrow, tell her what she'd meant to tell her earlier. Hell, maybe she'd call her as soon as she was outside. Maybe if she'd told her when she had the chance, she wouldn't be here on the staircase, feeling hunted.

*How much pain is caused by hiding pain from others?*

*Wait, why the hell am I thinking I'm about to be in pain?!*

Then, suddenly, the staircase stopped.

No more steps.

Just a landing leading off down a long corridor.

She looked out the staircase window again. She definitely wasn't on the ground floor. She still had to look down to see the tops of the courtyard trees. But, as with all the other floors, no helpful signage whatsoever.

Fire protocol, she realized. Some buildings have a separate stair bank after a certain floor with fireproof stairs. She just had to find that stair bank to continue going down. Or, better yet, the elevator. That dreadful little man inside the elevator didn't seem so dreadful now—she might just kiss his face and greet him as her savior.

Her stomach dropped as she looked farther down the landing corridor and saw:

"Of course." She sighed. "Of course the lights are off."

An indefinite, dark tunnel stretched out before her.

What. The fuck. Was wrong. With this place? At this point, she didn't care if Ana asked her to come back for their next session. Georgia wasn't sure she ever wanted to come back here again.

She pulled out her phone, trying to ignore the fact that her hands shook a little, turned on the phone's flashlight, and shined it into the cavernous darkness.

Her pitiful light made the shadows around her look like they pulsed. Like the walls of the building were breathing.

*I should go back upstairs and find the elevator on another floor,* she thought. *One that has lights.* But that feeling of being watched, followed . . . she opted to keep moving forward.

Soon, the daylight from the stairwell windows felt very far away.

*When the elevator guy comes to get me here, he'll see the lights burned out in this hallway. He'll thank me. That's good.*

*But why haven't the rich jerkbags who live here complained enough to have this fixed already?*

She told herself to relax. Not just told—demanded. Turnabout was fair play. She'd just hurt Ana's feelings with some personal trainer tough love—she deserved nothing less herself. She was being weak. Stupid. Whiny. Scared.

*You're in a famous building in the middle of New York City, for Pete's sake. There's a crowd of tourists outside taking pictures of this place right now.*

Yet she couldn't make herself move farther into the black. Her guts crawled. Her groin tingled like she had to pee, and the walker, the bag of workout equipment on her shoulder, took on the density of sandbags.

The elevator had to be nearby.

*Move, dammit! Start with one set of ten steps. Come on! Motion is lotion!*

She started farther into the dark throat. One step. Another. Another.

Then a strange noise skittered across the ceiling. She stopped.

*Probably just someone's dog upstairs. One of those signs of life you were so desperate to hear. Shine your light upward and you'll see nothing but black, blank ceiling.*

She didn't dare look up. She ran. She didn't care how stupid she was being.

She ran past apartment doors, all shut, her cell phone light careening madly across them, desperate for a fire door or the elevator or—

She slammed into a wall. Unyielding and flat. It made her think of a body dropped off a bridge, crashing into the dirt below—

*No, no, no, no. No, this isn't right. Where's the elevator? Where's the fire door?* Her hands searched the smooth surface in front of her. There *did* seem to be a seam, but no knobs, no handles, no way to open what might be a door on this side of the wall.

Trapped.

*No!* She must have missed a hallway or something. Somewhere she could have turned. That's all. This was a residential cul-de-sac. *Keep looking! Ten more steps, bitch!*

She growled between clenched teeth, psyching herself up, and walked back into the darkness. One step. Another. Trying not to run. Casting her light about for the turnoff she must have missed. Not letting herself think this floor was a hunter's box.

*It's just a floor of apartments. Look, there are apartment doors to your left and doors to your right. Doors that cost probably ten thousand dollars a month to rent, and I'm sure there will be very angry rich people once they discover the lights to this hallway have burned out.*

She was breathing too heavily. She stopped for just a second, trying to slow things down, and that's when she finally heard something she'd been waiting for this entire ill-advised journey.

An apartment door behind her cracked the silence open like a tree snapping in half. Like a person screaming in church.

She turned around.

The open apartment was also dark, but something stepped out, just at the edge of the light from her phone.

Her mind wouldn't let her comprehend what she saw. At first, she thought it was a dog . . . but it looked . . . skinned alive? Like a goat hanging in a butcher shop window. Except a flayed animal wouldn't be able to walk.

And its joints bent . . . wrong.

It made a low, barely audible gibbering noise like an idling lawn mower engine.

The dog-thing exhaled a thick, luxurious sigh and began to walk slowly toward her. Georgia backed away, keeping distance.

Its nails clicked on the floor. Its skin was corrugated like brain matter, black rivulets of wet shadow running through its gray skin in skeins. As its face turned toward her, Georgia realized, no, it wasn't a dog, it was far more humanoid than that . . . and also eerily familiar.

All at once, she knew what she was looking at. It made no sense, but it was enough to break her paralysis.

She didn't waste breath screaming in terror. She threw her exercise equipment down and took a fighting stance, ready to catch the thing if it pounced. Then she let out a roar as powerful and intimidating as she could muster. It worked; the dog-thing shrank back a little.

Georgia took this as her cue. Confidence flooded her. She could do this. Her body was made for this. She'd sprint her way back to the sunlight, hell, all the way back to the top floor if she had to, and if this skinned monstrosity gave chase, she'd fight it off with her considerable strength.

That was her plan.

She turned to run, and the person—or thing—that had been following her enfolded her in its arms.

# A VERY BAD DAY (II)

## 1

No one was having a worse day than Reid. At least not in this office.

There comes a point with every prolonged sleep deprivation where one more night is finally one too many. Last night might've been that point.

He couldn't stop yawning. Every joint ached. His teeth wore a coat of slime—had he brushed this morning? The interior of his skull felt wrapped in cotton and lined with needles, and every noise pushed those needles in farther.

The Hasids had visited again this afternoon. As always, Reid turned down their offer to wrap him in tefillin or enlighten him on this week's Torah portion. As always, Reid welcomed their free challah. He tore off a hunk now, hoping a blast of carbs would help him think.

He had plenty to do—he was supposed to be working on one client's net worth statement and indexing a document production for another matter, and that didn't factor in the expectation that he drop everything to answer the phones now that Wanda, the office's longtime secretary, had retired rather than come back after the firm decided it was done with remote working. The lawyers at the firm also tended to turn to Reid first whenever they had computer trouble (which was often), or whenever there was a jam in the copier, or or or.

Instead of doing any of that, Reid pulled up a search page on his browser, and his fingers began to type:

Deptford Apartment New York Plummet

This was mostly what he did on the internet these days. Since the firm's firewalls didn't let him access social media, he would lose entire hours chasing down info on his new home, trying to corroborate and flesh out details he'd read in Preston Treadwell's book.

That damn book still remained *the* primary source of information on the Deptford. If he'd wanted to learn more about, say, the Dakota, the Ansonia, the San Remo, the Apthorp, he'd have a whole reading list. It made it that much easier to become a little obsessed. He hadn't felt this singularly dedicated to learning everything he could about a subject since he'd first picked up a guitar and just *had* to learn every chord, every pentatonic box, every bit of gear, every—

The office phone rang.

He closed his eyes. He hated this part of the job. When he started working at Tillistrand & Loeffler LLP, one of the few saving graces had been that he didn't need to deal with the phones. Like most people of his generation, he hated phones with a fiery intensity. Stopping whatever he was doing, breaking his concentration, to pick up the phone and play polite with some oblivious idiot, answer some pointless question, filled him with a red, swirling feeling that compounded on itself with every call.

*Riiiiing.*

And had Reid's salary grown alongside his newly expected tasks once Wanda realized she preferred staying home? As his mom used to say: "I'll give you three guesses and the first two don't count."

*Riii—*

He snatched up the receiver.

"What?" he snapped.

The caller seemed taken aback. Once they recovered, they asked to speak with one of the attorneys, who appeared to be on another line at the moment. Reid passed this information on, took the number, and hung up, perhaps a little too abruptly. Now Reid had to put the phone message in an email and send it to the appropriate lawyer—he'd do it in a second; first, he wanted to finish scouring this page of search results.

A half dozen articles on real estate prices plummeting. Several links to sites about, for some damn reason, Elizabethan playwright Christopher Marlowe. Apparently, there was something known as "Deptford archeological culture," stretching back from 800 BCE to 700 CE, and the Brooklyn Museum had an exhibit of Deptford plummets, a kind of weight used for plumbing purposes. Goddammit. Another yawn roared through him, long and deep. He clicked onto the next page of results.

He'd tried different word combinations, different search engines, all the internet tricks collected over the years. He still couldn't believe an event like the one described in the book would just disappear from the city's memory. Twenty people leapt to their deaths! From one location!

Christ, he was tired.

He turned around and pulled the book from his messenger bag. The book had started showing signs of wear.

He read the excerpt again.

From chapter 14, "Comings and Doings:"

> As the world struggled to recover from the Great War and ride out the subsequent Spanish Death, Mr. Janebridge's building was similarly not immune to tragedy. During the first half of the twentieth century, the Deptford was scene to many incidents that seemed to reflect the violent unrest being experienced

globally. From muggings and murders occurring just outside the building, to the highly bizarre incident that became known as "the Plummet." Even to this day, despite earning such a portentous sobriquet, not much is known about what appears to be either a horrific accident or perhaps a ritualistic suicide that claimed the lives of twenty individuals. News of the unusual incident didn't even make the front page of *The New York Times.* See inset for the bulletin the paper ran in the evening edition, where they describe the incident as simply—

The phone rang again. *Goddammit!*

"Yes?!" he demanded. Another pointless call. Another message to be delivered. Why was he expected to do this shit anyway—couldn't they just fucking email?

He slammed the phone down and seethed.

He wished he could shut himself in one of the conference rooms and read in peace.

There *was* one way to get a little privacy . . .

"Boss makes a dollar, I make a dime, that's why I poop on company time," he sang under his breath, and he pushed his chair away from his desk, the book stuffed under his arm.

## 2

When he came back out fifteen minutes later, there was a Post-it note on his monitor.

He saw red.

People loved to leave notes whenever he was away, no matter how long he was gone. One particularly egregious time, he was eating lunch at his desk (heaven forbid he get an actual lunch break) and he left to get a paper towel from the kitchen. When he got back, there was a Post-it on his monitor, asking him to check on the status of a particular document, and the pen with which it was written had been hastily discarded . . . into his food.

Ana and their friends had been horrified. He tried to explain that most of the lawyers who worked here were good people, but they lived in their heads, thinking of little else than their caseloads. This meant they constantly did things like that: they didn't always ruin his food, but they frequently left his desk a mess if they sat there off-hours, knocking things onto the floor, leaving dirty dishes or unfinished cans of soda, because they pulled an all-nighter and then simply got up and walked away when they were done. One of his many additional but unspoken tasks every day was closing all the cabinet doors that stood open because the lawyers had grabbed what they needed and disappeared.

For a while, he'd been able to write it off as just a quirk of the job: something for a funny Facebook post or to earn a sympathetic shoulder rub from Ana. As he edged into middle age, it stopped being quirky.

He'd been working at Tillistrand & Loeffler LLP for seven years now. He never thought he'd wind up becoming an office guy. His music schedule had always prevented it. Then about ten years ago, his mom's decline really stomped on the gas, and Reid found himself having to help out as much as he could. Finances had gotten hard, and a friend referred him to a small law firm looking for an extra hand with data entry. When *that* firm went under, Reid was recommended to *another* firm, passed off like secondhand office furniture. Before Reid knew it, what had once been a stopgap solution to save some cash had calcified into his actual life. He got used to the dependable income. His baseline had adjusted. It wasn't even *great* money, but compared to the living standards he used to have, this was downright civilized. He couldn't imagine going back to adding frozen vegetables to a packet of instant ramen and calling it dinner.

He could still play out occasionally, and he was finally able to buy gear for that eventual album he kept insisting to himself he'd record.

And there were streaming services to subscribe to.

And then they had gotten married.

And then they had tried to get pregnant.

And then they succeeded in getting pregnant.

And and and.

Adulthood was all about compromises, wasn't it? You decide what you need, what you want, and shift your priorities around until you find the least bad combination. Each compromise was a link in a chain, and if that chain dragged you down to the bottom of the East River? Well . . . at least you had Netflix and Spotify to distract you while you sank.

Now, approaching his desk, his anger quickly curdled into dismay.

On the monitor, he'd left his browser up, displaying all sorts of websites that had nothing to do with the job he was currently being paid to do.

The writing on the Post-it was rushed and angular. The chief partner's handwriting.

***SEE ME IN MY OFFICE, PLEASE.***

# 3

"So what's going on, Reid?"

Morgan Loeffler, Esq., bald and imposing, sat at his desk, arms folded across his chest, wearing a look of stony concern. It was the look he wore in a courtroom when his adversary began shoveling bullshit.

Another saying of Reid's mother: "I'm between two stools on this." It meant, as far as Reid had determined, "I'm caught between two feelings" or "two impulses." One of the interesting things about gradually losing a mother to dementia very early in life: Were the things she said inscrutable because they were adult or because they were already a little nonsensical? Either way, that phrase occurred to him now, and in the moment, it made sense. Reid was between two stools. Stool number one: fall on his sword, beg for forgiveness, be the good employee, and assure Boss Man it'll never happen again.

And over on stool number two . . .

"Nothing's going on." Reid shrugged, as apathetic as could be, even though the skin underneath his left eye began to twitch, an exhausted tic. "Everything okay with you?"

Reid's gaze drifted to his boss's wraparound window. This corner office, such a status symbol, and yet the view looked the same as the view Reid woke up to every day now.

Loeffler was unimpressed with Reid's insouciance. "Did Scott DeLisa call?"

Reid thought about it for a second. "Yeah, that sounds right."

"Did he leave a message?"

"Right. Yeah, sorry, I was going to send you an email, but I got distracted."

"I noticed."

Twitch twitch. "I'd appreciate it if you didn't look at my screen—that feels like an invasion of privacy."

"Does it?" Loeffler leaned back in his chair. "Would you like to debate the finer points of employment law with me?"

Reid felt himself growing hot. He aimed for sounding like an affable coworker. "Look. You've got me doing a net worth statement. Terence has me indexing a huge document production. I get requests from Ellen every five minutes to help her with her computer. I mean . . . how would *you* define my job here? Because it seems to me I'm expected to do *everything* for *everybody,* despite the fact that you *know* I've got a difficult situation at home, and now, apparently, I'm going to get reprimanded for occasionally looking at totally safe material that, for all you know, is related to something important?"

Holy crap. What was he doing? If he wasn't careful, he was about to spill everything he'd ever wanted to spill. Every grievance he'd ever mentally monologued.

Even Loeffler seemed taken a bit aback.

"No one's saying you can't—I wouldn't be talking to you right now if it was just one incident, Reid. We've been getting complaints from clients that you've become unpleasant on the phone. And you're taking longer and longer to complete tasks. I know we ask a lot of you, but—"

"Am I about to be offered a raise?" Twitch.

"Reid."

"Or maybe a paid vacation?" Twitch.

"I'm not going to reward you for declining performance, Reid. You know we're still bouncing back from the pandemic—a pandemic, I seem to recall, through which we paid your salary, uninterrupted and—"

"Sure, until you made me start coming back to the office while everyone else in the world was still working remotely. You *knew* I was actually needed at home, but I guess it was more important I put myself, my family, at risk just so someone's butt was warming the chair you were paying rent for. Right?"

"Reid—"

"That's what made it really special! My wife suffered at home, with a *newborn,* but, nope, I had to come here, even though there's nothing you need me to do at this job I couldn't do remotely—except, of course, answer the phones! Which didn't used to be my job!"

Reid was far too loud. Worse, Loeffler stopped responding. He seemed more interested in watching how far Reid would go than in defending himself. Fine. Let him. Reid continued, trying to rein in his tone if nothing else.

"Do you know how long I've been working here? Seven years! Do you know my birthday? My anniversary? Do you know *anything* about me? Do you know how my wife's doing with her injury? Do you know my baby's name? Do you know my mom died? Do you know she raised me and my brother on a part-time income in a two-bedroom apartment in Ames? I mean, this office is, like, six people—you should know *everything* about me! Maybe then you'd know why I was looking up the things I was looking up just now! Maybe you'd understand that I'm a human being with a context and, and needs that are sometimes a little more important than this rich people shit. Lemme capitalize that: Rich. People. Shit. And almost everything I do here is a waste of time. No one's gonna look at the index I write. No one's gonna double-check the numbers in that net worth statement. It's all. Just. Rich. People. Shit. And it's a waste of my goddamn time."

His under-eye vibrated.

Silence hung heavy in the air.

Reid's boss cleared his throat. "Are you finished?" he asked at last.

Reid smiled, heart pounding in his ears. He barely held back a visible trembling in his limbs, as if what was happening under his eye had spread.

"Yeah, I think I am."

And then he just stood there.

Of course, he was about to be fired. But he felt great. If this were a movie, Reid realized, the scene would cut here. Next, he'd be walking out of the building holding a banker's box full of his stuff, like a fern and a few framed photos—not that he had any of those things at his desk—and he'd laugh and hoot and maybe dance his way down the streets of New York to Katrina and the Waves.

Except this wasn't a movie. This was real life. Real life didn't have jump cuts. Real life made you live all the interstitial moments that, ultimately, cut you and bled you before any soundtrack could kick in.

His boss had spoken, and he'd missed it.

"Sorry," Reid said, swallowing, "can you repeat that?"

"I said I'm not going to fire you, Reid."

"You're not." Had he read his mind? Or was what should happen next just that painfully obvious?

"No," Loeffler said. His bald head was as dry as a freshly powdered stone. Nothing about this encounter had caused him to spring even a drop of sweat. "Here's the thing, Reid. I'm going to tell the other attorneys what you've said. As you've pointed out, it's a small office. I don't keep anything from them. They deserve to know how you feel. You *have* been working here a long time. And you're a very capable young man. I think they'll all agree: We've been too easy on you. We don't challenge you enough. So here's a challenge. I think it'd be better if you went back to an hourly wage, don't you? And since it's so hard to be here, maybe we'll cap the number of hours you're able to work? And, you know what? Maybe those hours should begin . . . oh, two hours earlier? Yeah, maybe we've been letting you roll in here just a bit too late in the day for the firm's convenience?"

Reid's eye stopped twitching, but all the moisture in his body had dried up. His throat was suddenly coated in peanut butter and cracker dust. "Wh-why won't you just fire me?"

"Well, if I fire you, you'll be eligible for unemployment, Reid. Frankly, I kinda feel like we've given you enough. So you either adapt to what we're asking you to do as your employer . . . or you tell us—and the New York Department of Labor—that you've decided to quit."

"This isn't fair," Reid squeaked. "I don't deserve—"

"You were right, Reid. You have been incredibly useful here. Losing you will make things very difficult for us and quite an inconvenience. Since you've made it abundantly clear there's no sentimentality on your end—which I respect—I don't see why I should make life any easier for you, either. You know what this kind of thinking is, Reid?"

Reid tried, and failed, to swallow. "What?"

"Rich. People. Shit," his boss said. "If you're still here in the next hour, I expect that net worth statement to be in my inbox, and I expect it to be perfect. Otherwise, we'll be looking at a pay dock. What can I say: times are tough."

Reid became weightless with resentment, with rage.

But didn't it feel so very much like plummeting.

# OLD HABITS

## 1

The next morning was a relatively warm and sunny Saturday. At the breakfast table, Reid abruptly declared he had to run some errands.

Ana, who had been vocal all week about how they needed to spend this weekend cleaning and prepping for Charlie's upcoming birthday party, was less than thrilled about this news. Reid stammered and assured her he wouldn't be gone long.

"I just have to run to Guitar Center and pick up some new strings and stuff," he said. "It's for a song I wrote. For Charlie's birthday."

Ana couldn't argue with that—she simply didn't have the energy.

"Ugh." She sighed. "You'll be quick?"

"Totally. In and out."

"Will you do me a favor, then?"

Reid was already throwing on his jacket.

"Home Depot. Yes. Totally."

Stepping outside into the sweet, crisp air, he tipped a wave to the unresponsive doormen of the Deptford and started walking at a clip away from the building.

It was all a lie, of course. He didn't need strings, and he hadn't written anything for Charlie's party. He'd just been feeling claustrophobic inside their apartment, heart pounding, close to panic. He needed to get out.

He still hadn't told Ana what happened at work. He couldn't. When he'd gotten home, she'd been too exhausted and stressed and he didn't want to add to it by telling her he was now unemployed—for either of their sakes. He knew what she'd say: what were the odds they'd move to this new, affordable apartment and then lose their main source of income, they must be cursed . . .

But, of course, the longer he waited, the harder it got to talk about.

He needed a little space, a little time, to think.

He figured he might as well go to Guitar Center anyway—he could always use strings, even if he didn't *need* them—and between that and Home Depot he'd probably bought himself an hour or two of away time.

He headed for the train and, when he stuck his hand in his jacket, he realized he'd brought his book on the Deptford with him. It had bounced around between this coat and his messenger bag over the past week.

It made him feel a little better, knowing it was with him.

He got to Guitar Center in good time, bought two sets of strings for his acoustic and one for his electric, then considered a quick circuit through the store. Browsing Guitar Center was always a ritual for him—he'd go to the non-guitar sections first, play a little piano, tap on a few drums, then wind up at the main event: the walls of electrics. He'd pick a few floor models up, noodle around.

He didn't do any of that this time. The panic hadn't ebbed. All he could think was how he shouldn't—*couldn't*—buy anything, how they were spending too much on food delivery, how they had no savings, how he needed a new job right away, one with health insurance, which probably meant this next job would be even more strict and time-consuming, he'd have less time than ever to play music . . . and now he'd promised Ana a new song for Charlie! Lies on top of lies. Disasters in slow motion. He walked out quickly and headed back to the train to go downtown to the Home Depot in Chelsea.

A train waited on the platform. He stumbled on and found a seat. In an effort to calm himself, he pulled out his book and flipped through it. It worked for the moment. He found himself lost in its pages, its scant black-and-white photos, its mysterious and gossipy anecdotes of scandal, death, and disappearance.

He didn't realize he'd not only missed his stop, he'd also gotten on the wrong damn train, until he looked up and saw he was in the process of going over the Manhattan Bridge. He was on his way into Brooklyn, a commute so ingrained in his body that it hadn't registered.

He'd gotten on his old train. Total force of habit. If he hadn't been reading, he would have noticed at the first stop and gotten off. Instead, he was stuck going over the river.

Sunlight winked off the buildings, off the placid water of the East River. He always loved going over the river. Even when the commute was long and miserable, the views from the aboveground stretch made him grateful to live in this difficult place.

He checked his phone. No urgent texts. He was making good time. He was on an express train that was, shockingly on a weekend, still going express.

*Screw it,* he thought. *Let's see how Brooklyn's doing without us.*

## 2

Twenty or so minutes later, he walked up the gritty, metal steps to emerge at their old subway stop in Brooklyn. All hail the conquering hero.

It was still early enough for morning crowds to thread the streets: people on their way to and from their various coffee and bacon, egg, and cheese runs.

Others filtered in and out of restaurants or snuggled up in the outdoor seating areas. For the homebound or hungover, dozens of scooters and bikes zipped up and down the streets to deliver goods. A few exercise freaks slalomed past, either jogging or biking. Others walked their dogs. It was a postcard-perfect Saturday morning in Brooklyn.

Reid started walking, letting his feet carry him wherever they may.

He felt in slightly better spirits. After deciding to stay on the train, he'd spent some time scrolling through old voice memos on his phone, looking for a good unfinished song he could turn into a suitable birthday present. He found one he liked—that song for Joni Mitchell he'd shelved for the time being—and now had something to focus his mind on: the search for a newer, better lyric.

Then he walked by a gaggle of young moms, four in total, each pushing a stroller with an infant inside, obviously on their way to either a park or a place to sit and chat over breakfast. Reid watched them and smiled. One of the moms stopped to adjust something in her kiddo's stroller, and they all laughed at an unheard joke . . . and then it was like someone squeezed Reid by the throat. He couldn't breathe. His eyes flooded with tears. His stomach lurched. Sweat broke out across his back and the nape of his neck. His ears rang.

He was going to puke.

Hate and terror and confusion swirled in his gut, and he had to stumble away, punch-drunk, before he threw up on his shoes.

*Fuck fuck fuck*

He didn't know where he was going, he just had to get far away from that fucking cruel pantomime of normalcy, that filthy blood-caked fist which had wrenched into his hair, rubbing his nose in a life that would never be his.

He was no stranger to panic attacks—they'd plagued him fairly frequently as a child—but it'd been a long time since he'd really had one like this . . . and his mom had been the one to most successfully talk him down from those humdingers. Where was she now? Rotting in a plain pine box in Cedar Rapids, a good ninety minutes away from where she'd lived but the closest Jewish cemetery they could find.

None of this was fair. Those happy, laughing, idiotic moms would never know how bad it could get. Their fucking husbands or boyfriends or partners or whatever didn't have to live those awful early days where Reid had to wipe his wife's *and* his newborn's asses. The agonized screams of the newly born and the newly paralyzed, the intense pain, emotional and physical, the begging to just die, please just let me die. None of them had to live through that one horrible night.

They probably all had jobs. Or money from their fucking parents.

They probably all still had sex lives.

They probably all had *help*.

That's why they laughed. Because they weren't so fucking alone.

He started punching his thighs as he walked. His heart lurched. He could feel a swell of tears burning against his eyes, his sinuses. Not just any tears—the ugly kind that came out in big, hitching wails. He walked like a drunk down the cluttered sidewalk, making mewling, glottal noises, hoping everyone was too ensconced in their conversations, their AirPods, to notice.

*No. No, I will not break down. She can, but I can't. I won't.* For all his defenses, he suspected if he ever did break down, there'd be no end to it.

That's when he realized where he was.

He'd walked to their former apartment. The second time today his body had followed old patterns. No, *third* time—because that's exactly what this panic attack had been, too. An automatic jaunt down a familiar road map.

He stared at the building that had held so many of his worst memories.

This fucking haunted house.

For a moment, he considered walking up and checking the mailbox—they likely had some wayward mail still ending up here. Instead, he opted for something a little less practical. He gathered his breath and, in a raspy wheeze, said:

"Fuck you!"

He pulled out two strong, almost throbbing, middle fingers and flashed them furiously at the building. This place of death and misery. No, not just the building—also at who they used to be, at the tragedies they'd experienced. His voice came stronger this time.

"FUCK! YOUUUU!"

He didn't care who heard. He realized, with delight, that he felt a little better. The storm started to disperse, the cramp in his chest let go.

Ana and Reid's apartment had been the first floor of this small, two-family duplex, with two entrances: one at the front of the building and one on the side. Reid had installed a ramp for Ana at the side entrance. A pretty lo-fi, rickety aluminum ramp that he'd secretly feared Ana would tip off of. Thankfully, that never happened. The ramp was still there, though, and it seemed like a monument.

"SUCK MY DIIICK!" Reid shouted jubilantly.

The side door opened, and Frank stumbled out of the apartment, shielding his eyes.

"Hey!" He sounded belligerent as always. "Who the frick—Reid? That you?"

Reid had just enough time to clock that Frank looked terrible, hair a mess, a stained wifebeater over his shapeless torso, one hand wrapped in a pretty heavy-duty bandage.

Then Reid booked ass out of there, running as fast as he could.

## 3

Laughter made him stop. He couldn't breathe he was laughing so hard.

He'd had no idea Frank was there. No idea he lobbed curses at their old landlord as well as their old apartment. It'd probably mean Frank's phone calls would continue—maybe even increase. Fine. It was worth it to see that stupid, enraged face.

Just in case Frank decided to follow him, Reid ducked behind some parked cars, waiting for the laughing fit to stop. It took a good five minutes, coming in waves. Tears streamed down his cheeks—joyous tears, not the ones that had threatened to overwhelm him in sadness.

As he crouched there, something occurred to him. A line he could use for his birthday song for Charlie—the theme, the hook. It was *perfect*.

He stood up, looked around to make sure no drunken, angry landlords lurked nearby, and hurried for the subway station.

The rhythmic roar of the train served as backbeat to the song Reid wrote. The lyrics came in a gush. It was amazing when that happened.

When he found a natural stopping point, he looked up from his notes app to see where he was. Perfect timing: only three stops away from his destination. That epic commute wasn't so epic when you were in the grip of inspiration.

He still had a few lines to figure out, maybe a middle eight to futz with, but once he set what he'd just written to the melody he'd already planned out, that was a good 85 percent of a song right there.

Look at that. Wound up being a productive trip after all.

The line that served as this new song's inspiration originated from his book on the Deptford. He pulled the book out now and flipped to the chapter where it came from. Waiting there in the text for him. Bashert.

It was a catchphrase from one of the Deptford's more famous residents in the 1970s. Winston Terry, a British musician and the lead singer of the semi-prominent band the Blue Danubes.

The book quoted him in one of its many tantalizing tangents. A *Rolling Stone* reporter had come to Winston's Deptford apartment for an in-depth interview (no photos allowed, of course). At one point, Winston mentioned that he tried never to think of his former bandmates, all of whom had died in a tragic bus accident a decade prior. "I don't get bogged down in the past, you know? All that matters to me is here. Now. Know your home, that's what I say."

The reporter had asked, "Could you repeat that?"

"Know your home. Where you belong, you know? This moment."

"And, sorry, just to confirm," the reporter asked, "is that 'your' possessive, or 'you are'? Know your home or know that you are home?"

"Is there really any difference?" Terry asked back. "Once you're there, you're there."

The book quoted that interview not just because it seemed to be a play on Winston's residency at the Deptford but it was Winston's last interview before completely disappearing from public life.

To make matters more mysterious, a few months after the interview ran, the reporter who'd conducted the interview also disappeared. According to Treadwell, she'd sent Jann Wenner a typed resignation letter reading, "I've decided to go exploring. Thanks for the memories. Maybe I'll come home with a story. Maybe I'm already there." She was never seen or heard from again. Her boyfriend insisted Winston had something to do with it—she'd said she was going back to the Deptford to conduct some sort of follow-up. Winston was briefly held as a person of interest, but because no crime could be seen to have been committed, nothing came of it.

Just another strange episode in the life of the Deptford.

*Know your home.*

*Know you're home.*

Morbid context or not, it was good advice. It also made the basis for a really good lyric. "Bird's Song," he was going to call it. Kind of generic, but he didn't mind.

Manhattan was colder, less sunny, more anonymous in its crowds, but as Reid exited the subway and headed toward the Deptford, his mood stayed buoyant.

In a strange way, he was grateful to his boss for finally forcing him to quit yesterday and giving him this clarifying morning of panic. He was free—in so many ways. He didn't need to tell Ana about his stupid job—something better was going to come along, and soon. The building would provide. He had faith.

It was Ana's job to heal. It was his job to make Ana and Charlie feel the way he already felt.

At home.

## 4

Ana didn't really notice Reid's change of attitude when he got back from his errands. She only clocked that he was smiling and that he was gonna lose that smile real quick.

She informed him with a shaking voice that she had to tell him something.

"*Now* what's wrong?" he asked, still grinning, as if *of course* there was something wrong, but it was no big deal.

It *was* a big deal.

"I . . . I think I figured out why Charlie's been so upset lately."

She took him to Charlie's room and showed him.

"Reid, I think we've got fucking bedbugs."

## THE BUGHOUSE

### 1

It had been two apartments ago: a lovely, spacious two-bedroom in a big building on Albemarle Road and Flatbush Ave., just off Prospect Park. Hands down, the nicest, roomiest apartment they'd ever lived in. Cheap, too. Suspiciously cheap.

A few weeks after they'd moved in, they shared the elevator with a handful of teenagers who lived a floor or two above them. When Ana and Reid got off on their floor and headed toward their apartment, the teenagers saw and called out, "Oh no! You live in the bughouse!" Another shouted as the elevator doors closed, "Yo, you'd better call Roscoe!"

Roscoe, Ana and Reid knew immediately, was the famous bedbug-sniffing dog from the commercials on NY1.

They looked at each other, panic beginning to rim their eyes. No, their apartment didn't have bedbugs. They would have been told before they moved in . . . right?

Wrong. A few days later, Ana found a string of red, closely spaced bites on her ankle. The next day, she found more on her thighs. Reid had a couple on his back. Then, hiding in the seams of their couch and mattress, they found the unmistakable bloated and bloody red bodies of the little fuckers themselves.

They later learned this was a legacy problem with this particular apartment. Their landlord had been so sure it had been fixed this time—he'd had the place fumigated twice before Ana and Reid moved in. The problem hadn't been fixed. It had only died down for a little bit.

Ana and Reid had to pull all their belongings into the center of every room. They had to keep all their clothes and soft goods in giant Tupperware bins. They had to change as soon as they got home and as soon as they planned on leaving the house. Then there was the revulsion. The itchiness.

Worst of all was the shame. Having bedbugs in New York City was the social equivalent of pulsing, oozing genital sores. They knew they weren't the only people who'd ever had them, or even had them *right now,* but the way people reacted at the mention of bedbugs? If you had bedbugs, nobody wanted to know you.

Ana and Reid didn't tell anyone until after they'd moved out of that apartment, packed up all of their belongings into a van, drove it to a sketchy warehouse in

Red Hook, and hired an off-the-books service to pump the van with insecticide overnight. It was the only effective solution they'd heard about (recommended by friends who, similarly, only mentioned previously having bedbugs in under-breath tones reserved for black market crimes).

It had been a nightmare. Maybe the worst thing the young couple had yet experienced.

And here they were again.

## 2

They stood over Charlie's crib, speaking quietly while the baby napped.

"S-so I was changing her and . . ." Ana lifted up Charlie's left leg. "There."

A row of red welts. Harder to tell for sure on the smaller, rounder surface area of the baby's thigh, but they looked evenly spaced. That telltale sign.

Reid bent down and looked closer. "Are you sure? It could be a rash or—"

"Reid. I *remember* what those bites look like."

She didn't need to mention how she'd gone nuts researching bedbugs, hoping against hope that maybe she'd been mistaken about the bites that had covered her body.

"This is a disaster," she moaned after they returned to the living room. "I mean, we have to cancel Charlie's birthday party; we can't have people over! And do we let the building know? Will they kick us out? Do we sneak an exterminator in, past the fucking elevator gremlin? And, ugh, you should let your job know! You might be bringing bugs into the office. And we've gotta go get bins and—"

"Okay. Okay." Reid put his hands on her shoulders. She stiffened under his touch. She loathed when people touched her like this, bending at the waist, looking down at her like a child. He sensed it and immediately let go. "Sorry. Let's just try to talk this through and come up with a plan."

"We know what to do! We—"

"No, we don't. Because we don't know what we're dealing with yet. One step at a time, okay? Breathe. Even if those are bug bites—which I'm not sure of—we don't know that she got them here. They could have been while we went on a walk or something."

"Reid—" She was about to remind him of their neighbor. How she, too, seemed to have been covered with red, angry welts; maybe those were bites after all—punctures circled in a corona of inflammation.

Instead, he asked, "Do *you* have any bites?"

That made her pause.

"No."

"Last time, you were covered in bites. Right? They *loved* you. And now—?"

Then she realized something. "Jesus, Reid, would I even know if I had bites on my legs?"

"Ha. Good point. I'll check you. Okay? And we'll check Charlie's mattress. And our mattress. And we'll just . . . stay calm."

He seemed completely unruffled. God help her, it almost reminded her of the nights when he jerked off in the bathroom before joining her in bed. He seemed just a little too relaxed . . . a little too privately satisfied.

*He's loose,* she thought wildly. *Like a Russian stewardess.*

It took effort, but she forced her panic down. It was like trying to stuff a helium-filled balloon inside a T-shirt.

"Okay," she said. "What do we do first?"

"Well . . . you said you wanted to clean the apartment this weekend anyway, right?"

## 3

They spent the next several hours cleaning and examining every inch of surface area of their apartment.

There were no telltale signs of bedbugs anywhere. The mattresses were all clean and clear. Even Charlie's. No bugs. No tiny bloodstains.

They also took the opportunity to finish unpacking and collapsing the remaining boxes, except the stack containing Reid's mom's stuff. This time, Reid indicated a willingness to just throw all those boxes away, and Ana, shocked, found herself having to defend the existence of that pile for a change.

"It's just *stuff,*" he said with a shrug, "but okay."

The only thing he was adamant about was they were *still going* to host Charlie's party in a couple of days.

"No way are we canceling," he said. "I want our friends to see this place."

"But—"

"Like their apartments are immaculate? Shit, I wouldn't be surprised if half of them already had bedbugs and never mentioned it."

She bit back the urge to ask him what his problem was today—and imagined her mother laughing at the idea that Ana thought of being calm as a problem.

Eventually, Reid got Ana to agree to monitor the situation another day or two before making any decision about canceling. If no new bites presented themselves, on Charlie or anyone else, maybe their apartment wasn't infested.

She had one condition. She sent him on another errand, fully expecting him to whine about having to go back outside. He *did* roll his eyes and say they didn't *need* it, but he went willingly enough.

While he was gone, she did an emergency load of laundry, washing all the sheets in as hot water as she could. They were tumbling in the dryer when he got back. He had two medium-sized bags in his arms, as well as the canvas tote he'd brought with him. To the unfamiliar eye, it might've looked like he was carrying potting soil or fertilizer bags.

"Uh-oh." He put them on the kitchen table. "Why are you itching yourself?"

"Psychosomatic," she said, scratching at her neck. "Don't worry. I know when it's fake." She inspected one of the bags. "Hello, old friends."

Diatomaceous earth. They got to know this stuff real well during their last brush with bedbugs. They'd been told all about it by the guy who ran the nearest hardware by Prospect, a guy named Sammy, who probably weighed close to three hundred pounds and wore parachute-sized superhero T-shirts tucked into khaki pants, and who, Ana noticed as he explained to them the wonders of diatomaceous earth, had only three fingers on his left hand.

"It's not actually dirt, you know," Sammy'd said. "It's ground up bits of skeleton. Little fossilized plants called diatoms. You wouldn't know it to feel it, but this stuff's razor sharp for the buggies. It gets all caught in their exoskeletons and slices 'em up something nasty. And, if that weren't enough, it sucks all the moisture outta them, too. Cuts 'em up and sucks 'em dry. What a way to go, huh? Can you believe some people eat this stuff?!"

Ana put the bag down. What they had was *not* food-grade; this was the serious stuff. Next, they'd need to sprinkle a line of it along their baseboards and also fill small paper bowls to stick under the posts of their beds. There was something almost ritualistic to the process. Tracing the borders of their domicile with enchanted powder. A warding off of a very specific urban spirit.

"Okay," she said, pulling out paper bowls from the tote, "let's get this over with and then, I dunno, order dinner?"

"The things I do for you," Reid said. He kissed the top of her head.

It was only after they started that she realized not only had he forgotten Home Depot once again, she'd forgotten to remind him.

*Where's my mind? And, for that matter . . . where's his?*

## 4

She lay in bed, hair still wet from her bath. Reid had gone over every inch of her. No bites, thank the Lord. And, she couldn't lie, the physical attention was . . . kinda nice. It had been a while since he'd bathed her.

He must have enjoyed it, too, since he'd just made one of his slightly longer-than-normal visits to the bathroom before getting into bed himself. She felt a flush of guilt and sadness at the thought of her perceived failures as a wife. She wished she could just will herself to be in the mood for physical intimacy.

*We should talk about this. We need to get better about talking about things.*

Not tonight. She was too wiped out. And who knew if Charlie was going to be up soon, fussing and crying.

*But if not tonight . . . ?*

She thought of Mrs. Jacobs. Was she lying awake, too? Itching? Dreading the demands of her own baby? Meanwhile, Ana scratched at herself. Random spots all over her body that pretended to be crawling with tiny legs.

She was just about to shake Reid's shoulder when she heard his soft snores and decided to let him sleep.

## 5

She woke up an indeterminate amount of time later, needing to pee. Her rest had been uneasy, skimming across the upper layer of sleep, never dipping beneath the surface. Phantom itches coursed up and down her body. Her mind itched, too, with a relentless thought: *Why can't the past just leave us alone?*

As she made her way through the still-somewhat-unfamiliar apartment—

*Ow, fuck, shoulder—*

She was aware the place felt just a tad cooler than it should. Not entirely unpleasant, but it was strange.

After she maneuvered herself onto the toilet, did her business, and maneuvered herself back into her chair, she made her way back to the bedroom and she had just managed to fit herself through the doorway when she heard a noise.

The hushed intake of air as the pressure changed . . .

It sounded like a window shutting.

A window inside their apartment.

She eased herself out of the doorway and turned around, half-convinced she'd imagined it . . . but the air did feel a tiny bit different now, didn't it? Except, who could be opening a window in this apartment? And where? And how?

Knowing it was laughable, impossible, totally stupid, she made her way to Charlie's room first.

The window was closed, but the curtains were open. That was normal; it gave the room a nice, ambient glow.

Charlie was awake, sitting up.

"Hey, Baby Bird," Ana said with a sigh. She went farther into the room, preparing to see whether there was a reason the baby was awake. "Don't mind me, I'm just losing my m—"

Her words caught in her throat.

Someone was pressing up against the glass of the window, looking in.

A face. Moon-pale and hungry against the blackness beyond.

It was such a shock that the impossibility of it didn't register until a few moments after.

Adrenaline and terror sizzled through her. She had to blink, squeeze her eyes shut for a second, just to test whether she really saw something, or whether maybe she was still asleep, next to her husband in the bed where sanity and her former life, the one she lived before this horrible vision, were.

When her eyes opened, the face was still there. Pressed so close to the glass that it was visible with horrid clarity. It was almost human. Almost. But with a puggish nose, flat and, and . . . *bat-like,* she thought feverishly.

The thing's lips quivered in a grin, revealing gnarled, dirty teeth. But something was wrong with its mouth. Its lips . . . rippled, moving the way the legs of a centipede move. Like its lips marched in place in an insectile circuit around the lower half of its face.

She could have sworn she heard its lips scratching against the glass with tiny little tickety-taps.

Automatic response took over. She turned and tried to speed out of the room as quickly as possible, a lunatic voice in her head shrieking, *Get away get away,* but a millisecond later, she remembered Charlie, she had to get Charlie out of there, too, and so she interrupted her turn, inadvertently rocking in her seat, spinning herself off her axis and pitching her forward and spilling her onto the ground.

The next thing she knew, Reid was by her side, frantic, asking her what was wrong.

Her own burning throat informed her that she'd been screaming herself hoarse.

She looked back at the window in Charlie's room so quickly she felt a muscle in her neck spasm.

Nothing but night through the opened curtains. Night, covering the courtyard and stretching out like an inky lake to the other side of the apartment building.

"A dream," Reid was saying. "It was a dream. You were sleepwalking or something. It was just a dream."

"I thought I saw . . ." But she had no voice to say it, and even if she did, there were no words. A face? A figure? Impossible. They were so many stories up. No one could be outside their window.

Ana noticed Charlie sitting up in her crib, staring at her, and guilt clutched her heart.

In the serene expression on Charlie's little face, Ana saw reproachment. Accusation.

It said, *You were going to leave me here. You were going to leave me with the monster.*

And the thing was . . . that wasn't wrong, was it?

In her head, Ana imagined her mother chuckling.

*You wanted a new problem, huh? Well, you got it.*

# A CITY INTERLUDE—FRANK

## 1

While Ana was wondering why the past couldn't rest, her former landlord also tossed and turned on the plastic-covered couch in the basement of the apartment building Ana and Reid had so recently vacated.

The basement was Frank's domain.

The whole building was his, of course, but the basement was his and his only. No one was allowed down here. It's where he kept his tools, his private things. His fireworks. His photos. It's where he could be alone, shut out from the rest of the frickin' morons and dirty scum populating this goddamn city. Decent, honest, thoughtful people like Frank were becoming the minority these days, just like Tucker said.

His hand throbbed underneath its bandage.

The wound was Reid's fault. So was Frank's insomnia.

That frickin' liar. That frickin' sneak. That frickin' cock-a-roach.

It had been bad enough how they'd left the place: in the dead of night, like vermin, and in *such* a state.

Holes in the wall. Skids and scuff marks across his beautiful floors—had Roller Bitch been drag racing in the living room or something?

They'd messed up the tile; they'd messed up the hardwood. They'd put shoddy ramps and rails in random places. There were stains Frank easily recognized as liquid that had been left to settle and soak into the wood. Maybe baby piss—who knew with these people?

It was enough to make you cry, what they did to this place. Frank's own father might've cried; he was weak like that. Much as it broke Frank's heart, though, he wouldn't cry. Instead, he twisted and wriggled on the squeaking plastic of his couch. Awake. Stewing.

He'd grown up in that apartment. He'd improved it with his sweat, his frickin' blood—blood he'd spilled yet again, trying to undo everything those no-good cock-a-roaches had done.

That bathroom rail for the cripple, for instance. (Shame about that wheelchair; she'd been real easy on the eyes before.) If Reid had just come to Frank to install it, it would've been done right. But no, Reid did it himself, resulting in powdery, ragged holes blasted into the tile that Frank had so carefully measured and laid and grouted himself. The remaining screws went in at ugly angles, stripped and almost impossible to get out.

Yesterday, Frank'd been crouched in the tub, trying to get that godforsaken railing out of the wall. Sure, he'd maybe had one or two highballs and was a little unsteady, but this should've been easy, so he had one hand on the wall, while the other hand held his DeWalt cordless, and he was trying to get the damn bit into the damn screwhead despite the awkward angle and then—godfrick*DAMNFUCK!*

The drill slipped and ate right into his other hand, right into the webbing between thumb and forefinger. And he'd pushed it in hard, all the way up past the drill bit.

The bit became gnarled in flesh. He couldn't just pull it out; he had to toggle the drill into reverse, pull the trigger, and ease the bit out with excruciating slowness.

The wound throbbed now, as if the memory of how it happened woke it up.

Frank got up from the couch and fixed himself another Jim Beam and 7UP. The ice from his tiny fridge felt good against his hand. The liquor felt good against his rage.

It'd bled like a sonofabitch. The human body was a big ol' bag of blood. Frank knew that from experience. Growing up in Brooklyn had been a real conveyor belt of examples of just how much people could bleed. Like when Vinnie Furnari got dared to walk across the I-beams at that construction site over in Bensonhurst and dropped seven stories onto the concrete. Like a garbage bag full of Karo syrup, he'd been; Frank never forgot that sight.

Blood.

Blood was important. Little cock-a-roaches like Reid and his brood only proved it. Blood was . . . what was the word he'd liked so much? He always tried to remember it, but sometimes words were slippery. Oh yeah, there it was. Blood was *determinative.* Blood made you who you are. Tucker was big on that—Tucker was a smart man.

Frank was not a hateful or bigoted person. Lefty faggots like Reid liked to throw words like *racist* around about some of the things Frank said or thought. But Frank knew plenty of good Blacks and good Mexicans and good Orientals. *And* Jews! If Frank had been given the choice between a Jew for an accountant and anyone else? He'd take the Jew seven days out of seven. They all had their purposes—was it racist to think a race was better at certain things? Nah, Frank didn't think so. That's a frickin' compliment. Hell, Frank had been okay with renting the apartment to Reid and his wife in the first place, hadn't he? He knew they were Jews, you could practically smell it, even before you saw some of the crap they hung on his walls. Frank figured they'd pay their rent on time and never have to beg him for an extra week or two to pay up the way some of his previous, darker tenants had.

Frank had great instincts. He read people. He was smarter than 95 percent of the other morons on the block, the idiots who drove values down, renting to anybody, making the city a frickin' hellhole again.

But he could be wrong from time to time, couldn't he? Not often, but it happened. He'd been wrong about Reid.

Bad enough what they did to the apartment, but Frank coulda gotten over that. It was seeing Reid this morning that *really* ate Frank up. They'd *lied.* They said they'd moved to a different state to be with Roller Bitch's mom. Now Frank *knew* Reid had been ducking his phone calls, only to come back, laughing, screaming taunts and curses, throwing two middle fingers at the building that Frank had spent his goddamn life's blood fixing and making a good home, even for ungrateful little Jew bastards like Reid and Miss Cripp-on-Wheels.

They thought they were better than Frank.

His rage throbbed and ached worse than the pulsing wound in his hand.

He would've run after Reid, but he didn't trust that janky ramp . . . and he'd already had a drink or two and didn't want to risk tripping over some broken sidewalk because the damn government spent too much money on pronoun parades and welfare for illegals instead of fixing things.

Jewboy and Roller Bitch were probably laughing about Frank right now.

They wouldn't be laughing long.

Let them underestimate Frank. They wouldn't be the first. Frank had ways. He was smart.

Bet those little cock-a-roaches didn't know that. Bet they thought they were so clever. Bet they didn't know, when they filled out their little mail forwarding change of address form, that if you were a landlord, all you had to do was send your tenants a letter at their previous address, *your* address, slap a first-class stamp on it, and write *Return Service Requested* on the envelope. The letter comes back, processed by the post office, with one of those yellow stickers on the front showing the *new* address. Easy peasy, pudding and pie.

He even had a buddy at the post office in Corona who owed him a favor and who could expedite the process.

Yeah.

He was going to find out where Reid was hiding now, where he'd rolled his wife and their screaming infant. Then maybe he'd go pay *them* a visit. Let 'em know they weren't so smart, they weren't so sneaky, so crafty. They had a lot to learn. And Francis Gardner Jr., was more than willing to teach them.

# PART THREE

## UPSTAIRS DOWNSTAIRS

# FROM THE DEPTHS

## 1

The next morning, Reid took the elevator down to pick up their Sunday morning breakfast order. He wasn't even bothered by the hassle anymore; it was pretty much expected by this point. And he was glad to step away from the apartment for a moment.

His newfound confidence that things were going to be all right wasn't *broken,* but the way Ana had screamed last night shook him up. It had also confirmed his instincts: he had to keep some truths from her. At least until she was in a better place, mentally.

For the first time in many months, he found himself wondering what would happen if it all got to be too much: the postpartum depression, the paraplegia depression, the regular depression, the anxiety, the sleep deprivation . . . *So many groups,* she'd said during that nighttime conversation when they'd first moved in. *I'm just so lucky.*

What would he do if she needed to spend some time . . . somewhere else? His own mom had to be committed briefly once, after a bad reaction to prescribed steroids—would he have to see the same thing happen to his wife? And would it be voluntary, or would the decision be left to him?

For a moment, he wished he had Georgia's number. He imagined calling or texting her, commiserating, coming up with a plan to help their girl. But Georgia never liked him, and as far as he knew, Ana and Georgia were still fighting.

Instead, he concentrated on humming the song he wrote for Charlie as he walked outside to pick up their breakfast and hummed it in the elevator back upstairs. The elevator gremlin didn't seem to mind.

When Reid got back to the apartment, Ana was on the floor. She'd spread out one of her yoga mats and was in the middle of what looked like an intense series of sit-ups and toe grabs. Charlie sat placidly in her activity station.

"Are you okay?" He asked, quickly putting the food down in case Ana needed him to do anything. Normally, she asked for his help during her exercise routines, but she went at it with such fervor it took him aback.

"I checked Charlie for more bites," Ana huffed in between reps. "No new ones. Just the old ones."

"That's good."

Reid would've sworn she did like five sit-ups in the time it took for him to say that.

"I'm fine," she said, grunting. "I just need to sweat it out."

"Your bad dream?"

"I'm *fine,*" she said again. She wasn't even looking at him.

"Okay. I believe you." He didn't—not entirely. But what else could he do? He unpacked their breakfast order, setting containers out, making sure the coffee cups hadn't spilled. He took a bite of his egg sandwich while he watched his wife rotate onto her side, adjusting her legs to bend at the knees, and then stretching her upward-facing arm toward her back, stretching her core. Charlie watched, too, and lifted her own arm in mimicry.

"We've really gotta stop doing this," he said, half to himself, looking at the food in his hand.

"Yeah," Ana said.

"Yeah," he repeated and took another bite.

While she continued her workout, Reid checked the diatomaceous earth for any critters. All seemed to be clear. Very encouraging.

"You sure you don't need any help?" he asked again. She'd made her way into her chair and started lifting hand weights. She'd worked up a mighty sweat, if that was her intention.

"I'm *fine,* Reid. Actually, if you want to be helpful, why don't you take all those boxes down to the basement? Bedbugs love cardboard." She indicated with her head the masses of collapsed, tied-up boxes scattered throughout the apartment.

"Sure." He moved her coffee within arm's reach for when she wanted it. Then he went to the kitchen and got her a glass of water, as well.

"Oh, and while you're at it—?" she began.

"Home Depot," he said. "Yes. Sorry, I didn't mean to forget yesterd—"

"Oh. Right, that, too. But I was going to say . . . while you're down in the basement, maybe see if you can find any evidence that the building has a bug problem?"

## 2

The boxes wouldn't fit down the trash chute, so he dragged them all out over several trips into the hallway and then another few trips to the elevator.

"Basement, my good man," he told the operator gremlin while he loaded the pallets into the car.

A few moments later, as they descended, Reid said, "Hey. Stupid question, but . . . is there an exterminator who comes to the building? Not that we have bugs or have seen bugs or anything, just . . . I'm thinking about when it gets warmer, you know. Just curious."

The gremlin tilted his head slightly. Reid wished he could see his face a little better, but the brim of his cap and the overhead light conspired to keep it shadowed.

"The super," the gremlin said with his gravelly, frog-like voice.

Reid started to ask a follow-up when the car gave a little lurch and rattle. They'd arrived in the basement.

## 3

Reid took the boxes to the trash area, a large, dark room directly off the main hallway of the basement. Several black, plastic garbage bins sat next to several blue ones, all honeycombed together in a large chain-link cage.

After he dropped the boxes off on the recycling side, he gave a cursory glance around the rest of the room. Looking for clues. Roach traps. Maybe other peoples' discarded bags of diatomaceous earth.

The room was surprisingly empty. Very little trash. Had it recently been garbage day? He realized he wasn't sure when the trash went out in this neighborhood—now that they lived in a large building, they didn't have to take care of things like putting the cans out to the curb.

Only one of the black bins had stuff in it. Reid poked around inside (a year of changing diapers had made him a lot less squeamish). No signs of another tenant's pest control in here. Only a few small, tied trash bags and some recently discarded workout equipment.

"Looks like somebody gave up on their resolutions early," he said to himself.

There was what looked like a folded-up walker wedged behind the garbage can, too. Reid momentarily considered rescuing the equipment for Ana—(*the building will provide*)—but then thought better. A) It was literally garbage, and B) she might be offended by the presumption.

Plus, he recognized the intensity with which she was working out. It was spite. She was trying to prove to herself that she didn't need any help after her fight with Georgia. Better to stay out of it and let trash be trash.

## 4

He was surprised to find how winding and disorienting the basement hallways could be. Dimly lit corridors looped and whorled like a roller coaster laid on its side. No wonder Vera didn't show this area off during the tour.

He chuckled, thinking of her twitchy face—what was *she* up to? Maybe she wandered the basement until the building had new tenants to show around. Heh.

He hoped he was going in the right direction. A person could get lost down here.

*No one goes in there,* that one delivery guy had said. *We all know better.* The smile on Reid's face faltered but didn't fall.

He let his fingers trace the concrete walls. They weren't actually wet, just shining with condensation, probably from the cold air outside and the warm, steady heat down here. The walls *were* warm. Almost organically so.

Eventually, he reached an intersection of corridors and found a simple, closed black door, set into one of the concrete walls. A surprisingly clean, almost gleamingly black-and-gold plaque hung on the door. SUPER.

Two other small signs, posted on either side of the door, indicated which wing of the building was which way. Reid oriented himself. He currently stood at the center of the building. Directly under the courtyard, he imagined. The super worked right in the heart of things. Seemed appropriate.

They hadn't met the super yet. That was kind of weird; Reid had never lived in a building where he hadn't at least known the super on sight. He raised a fist, intending to knock on the door and introduce himself . . . then stopped.

A strange noise, unplaceable in the echoing basement tunnels, but somewhere behind him. Almost omnipresent, low rumbling. Like a motor idling, or a tiger . . . or the sound of bones being slowly crushed under a tank.

Something was growling.

Heat pipes. That had to be it. Just the furnace.

He turned around. Three corridors offered themselves to him: the one he came down, one to the left of the super's door, and one to the right. He looked to the right-hand corridor. The fluorescent overheads had burned out farther down, plunging the hall into darkness.

No, don't bother the super . . . but maybe go exploring a bit more? There'd been no sign of bugs so far, but what other secrets might he find down here?

In his book, there'd been mention of a pool somewhere in the basement. For a brief period in the 1970s, the Deptford competed with Plato's Retreat as a destination bathhouse for scantily clad hedonists wanting an excuse to strip and squirm. As with many things involving the Deptford, it seemed, one day the pool room just mysteriously . . . stopped being open for business. Like it disappeared.

*Like it was a trap that had finally swung shut.*

That was a weird thought.

He imagined what the pool room must look like now, full of spiderwebs and dust—if it still existed. He could picture it clearly: himself opening a door, seeing the dry, empty pool that looked more like a glorified Jacuzzi than something you could do laps in, then stepping forward to peer into the basin of the pool and seeing hundreds of thousands—no, billions—of squirming insect bodies, the source of their infestation, only for that sight to disappear as the door to the room slammed shut behind him, trapping him in the dark with hungry, twittering things—

He stopped, suddenly realizing he'd taken several steps farther into the dark tunnel without even being aware.

The heat pipes continued to growl.

*Know your home,* he thought . . . and this time it felt like a warning.

An uneasy chuckle escaped his lips.

"Another time," he spoke to the walls. He patted the concrete like the hide of some beast. "We've got the rest of our lives together, right?"

He turned and walked back the way he was pretty sure he came. He felt a tickle at his back as if he were being watched, but he never ran. At some point, he noticed, the growling noise had stopped.

## 5

"Thank you kindly, good sir." He tipped an imaginary cap to the elevator gremlin as he stepped out into the lobby.

Before finally heading out to Home Depot, Reid figured maybe he should ask the concierge—Mr. Smiler—about the building's exterminator, too. Felt a little risky bringing it up, but he felt confident he could play it off. He approached the front desk, a reflexively wide smile stretching his face.

"Excuse me—" Reid began. Just then, the golden doors leading out to the front entrance burst open, and a man and a woman drunkenly stumbled into the lobby.

No, Reid realized, only the man was drunk—obliterated, looked like. The woman kept him standing.

Reid's entire body flushed.

She was the movie star lady he'd seen the other day. The one he'd meant to look up online.

She looked radiant.

A heavy coat, long and luxurious, more for a night at the opera than a Sunday morning stroll, draped her body. Her hair was hidden inside a turban-like wrap, and elegant sunglasses perched on her nose.

Her hammered companion wore a brown wool suit and tie. Strangely formal for a man whose beard was disheveled and whose hair was long and greasy. Hipster fashion was always so idiosyncratic. Dude probably spent more money on products to get his hair to look that grimy than Ana and Reid spent on groceries.

"Miss Varné!" the concierge exclaimed, leaving Reid immediately. "What are you doing out at this hour?"

"I know, I know." She had a soft, Eastern European accent Reid couldn't quite place—Polish? German? Russian?—but she spoke with the unmistakable, casual sass of a New Yorker. "I was starving; I couldn't help myself."

"But your condition—"

"You're sweet to care, *laleczko,* but a lady's gotta eat."

*A lady's gotta eat.* They must've gone out and had a few too many Bloody Marys at brunch.

Reid couldn't help himself. As she passed him, he said, "It'd be nice if we could just get food delivered up to our apartments, am I right?"

Miss Varné stopped. Looked him up and down. Even behind her sunglasses, her eyes felt like fingers on his skin. Gentle caresses both curious and provocative.

"It can be challenging sometimes," she said. "But why live in this city if you don't step out and say hello to it from time to time?"

With that, she made her way to the other lobby, shouldering her drunken companion. Reid watched them go. She had remarkable strength for a woman of her age.

When the concierge spoke to him, he jumped.

"Did you need something, Mr. Greene? It looked like you were about to speak."

Reid took a breath to respond when light glimmered on the floor.

"Oh, shit." Reid quickly stepped over to inspect the glittering object. An earring lay on the immaculate marble floor. A sparkling, dangly disco ball of jewels.

He practically leapt forward to retrieve it, then jogged to catch up with the woman.

"Excuse me, miss?"

She stopped and turned around.

Reid held out the earring to her. "This fell."

Her mouth formed a perfect O of surprise. She reached for her earlobe to confirm the bauble's absence.

"Raspberries," she said, accepting the earring from him. "Thank you!" She examined the hasp. "It must have slipped off."

*More like your space cowboy here probably knocked it off.* Just as Reid thought that, her companion began to sag. Reid, not knowing what to do, reached out and took hold of the strange man, trying to keep him at arm's distance.

"Raspberries!" she repeated, noticing Reid's new burden. "Suddenly, we are jugglers. Ugh. Would you mind terribly, my savior?"

"Mind?" he asked stupidly.

She disappeared, quickly stepping away to the front desk. Reid could hear her voice along with the concierge's in hushed conversation.

Meanwhile, Reid continued to hang on to Miss Varné's . . . date? Boy toy? Not his business. But the guy was dazed and confused, to say the least. Smelled strange, too. Not bad; almost antiseptic.

"My hero," the guy said, head rolling, eyes half-lidded. "Cap'n 'Merica."

"No problem," Reid replied.

A moment later, Miss Varné reappeared, sighing dramatically. "Broken. Alas the day."

"I'm so sorry, was it—?" Reid almost said *expensive.*

*You idiot, of* course *it was expensive.*

"Family heirloom." She spoke with genuine sadness. "Centuries old. Ugh. I'm having it sent out to be fixed."

Mr. Space Cadet made another incoherent mumble. Miss Varné shook her head. "Stop it. You're embarrassing yourself." She shot Reid a charming, if apologetic, grin. "I can take him back now if—"

"I don't mind," Reid said. "Do you need help getting him upstairs?"

She took off her sunglasses, and her intense, ocean-blue eyes almost made Reid's knees buckle. His heart began to pound.

"You sure?" she asked.

"Positive."

"Hero," the drunk wheezed.

Miss Varné ignored him, still staring at Reid. "Well then." She gestured toward the secret corridor. The secret elevator. "Follow me, my savior."

Despite everything—despite his fatigue, despite his wife's nightmare, despite the obnoxious space cadet he currently propped up—Reid suddenly had a feeling today was going to be a great day.

## NICKEL TOUR

### 1

Ana hadn't forgotten her nightmare. She remembered all too well that horrible face at the window. That awful skittering sound of its lips against the glass. And she would never forget the accusatory look of Charlie in her crib, as if somehow aware her mother had abandoned her to the monster, even for just a moment.

Was she losing her mind? On her way to becoming another Mrs. Jacobs? She didn't know. But she knew if she worked herself ragged, chances were better she'd sleep through the night and not be subject to all the questions waiting for her in the dark.

Once she was sure she couldn't possibly do another exercise, she put Charlie down for a nap and went to find something else to do.

### 2

While Ana cursed herself for lifting so many weights before needing to pick up her twenty-pound infant, Reid, a dozen floors below, bit back a grin. Now he knew what the second elevator was like: exactly the same as the first elevator. Down to the smallest detail. Even the second elevator op—*Gremlins 2,* he supposed—was so similar Reid almost burst out laughing. Had the Deptford purposefully hired twins?

How strange. How delightful. This building held so many mysteries—but for the first time, he truly felt like he'd be learning more—and soon.

The walk from the elevator was short, but as they reached her front door, Miss Varné mentioned, almost apologetically, that some of the nicer suites had direct elevator access.

"You don't think your apartment is nice?" Reid asked.

She gave a sly grin. "*Nicer* doesn't mean mine isn't nice."

She opened the door to her not-so-humble abode. Reid was so taken aback that his hold on Miss Varné's companion loosened slightly, and the guy sagged, then dropped onto his ass in the hallway with a heavy *whumph*!

"Oh, shit," Reid said. "Sorry! He just—"

"Pernicious anemia," she informed him, helping him get the man back to his feet. The man, for his part, didn't seem to mind. "And it gets worse when he drinks. It's so very sad. Here we go."

For a moment, Reid thought he saw something on the man's neck. Red, irritated skin. Was that a rash? Were there darker marks indicating some sort of . . . of bites?

Didn't matter. As soon as they stepped inside the apartment, Reid had to look around, and he quickly forgot whatever he had been thinking about.

## 3

"Would you like something to drink, my savior?"

This apartment was incredible. He wanted to take in every detail.

Bookshelves and closet doors lined a circular foyer. Miss Varné shrugged herself out of her large coat, opened up one of the closets, and Reid glimpsed an army of furs inside.

Next, she stepped out of her shoes and nudged them toward a brushed bronze rack full of colorful, elegant shoes whose simplicity belied their staggering expense.

Reid did the same to his own worn Adidas.

"Don't worry about his," Miss Varné said, indicating her companion's feet. "Let's just get him somewhere soft."

Corridors split off the foyer in three different places; Reid carried/dragged the guy down the corridor directly opposite the front door. It led to a room that made Reid's jaw drop almost as quickly as he dropped the guy onto a rich, brown leather settee.

The living room sported a massive set of windows looking out across Central Park and the narrowing view of the east side of the island. But that wasn't the kicker. The room was a duplex, and an exposed second floor landing lined with bookcases rose above and behind him.

And this was just *one* room.

Mr. Hipster muttered from his awkward position on the settee. Reid bent down to adjust him.

"Thanks, Cap'n." The guy's rotten, sickly sweet breath made Reid's eye's water. "She's a hell of a kisser . . . My guts, man . . ."

Miss Varné appeared, drink in hand.

"Would you like the nickel tour?"

# 4

There were movie posters everywhere. Hanging on the walls, artfully leaning against the baseboards. And not tatty, dorm-room reprints; these were old-school one-sheets, classy, mounted and framed. Reid couldn't help but notice a recurring face on most of them—and a name: Camilla Varné.

"This is my office. A mess. The less said about this room, the better."

They looked into a large room with a massive cherry desk in the corner covered in disorganized papers. But even this room was like a dream—like looking back in time through a photograph of some skyscraper office that smelled of cigarettes and whiskey and clever banter.

Unlike the living room, the rest of the apartment's windows had heavy leopard-print curtains draped over them. Rather than feeling gloomy, though, it gave everything an almost backstage vibe. You didn't need to see the city; you *were* the city.

"I do love the views," she said, almost reading his mind. "But it's so much more magnificent at night, don't you think?"

"I do," he said. He sipped at his drink. Strangely floral. Heavenly. His head briefly became a balloon.

The office contained more movie posters, including a stack in a corner apparently not important enough to be displayed. Framed photographs and golden, glass, and/or bronze statues Reid immediately recognized as awards crammed the bookcase.

"All these movie posters," he asked, "are they . . . ?"

She spread her arms. "Guilty. But they're not just movies. There's plenty of theater posters. I *love* the theater. I loved the pictures, too, but . . . more so during the studio years."

The studio years . . . Some of these posters, especially in the office, look like they dated back to the goddamn Second World War. One that appeared to have a stern Errol Flynn–looking guy in an army helmet, entitled *Tomorrow, Dover!* and, wait a second, Reid could make out the above-the-title lettering, that *was* Errol Flynn!

How old was this woman? She must have been in her nineties. She moved like she was in her sixties—and healthy sixties, at that.

"Do you still . . . work? On movie stuff, I mean? Sorry, that sounds—"

"Like I'm some sort of clock. 'Do you still work? Have your batteries died yet?'"

"I know they haven't!" he said hastily. "You're very . . ." He stopped himself from saying some god-awful word like *spry*.

She made a face. "I'll take that ellipsis as a compliment." Reid's cheeks heated. She continued, "But, no, not really. I've developed what the doctors call photodermatitis in my old age. Nasty word. It's an allergy, and it means caking on makeup and ointments to keep me presentable in bright light. It's exhausting and boring and thus, I am retired. Not that it stops my agent from emailing me with offers every damn day. Somedays I think emails are the very worst invention this damn species ever dreamed up."

Reid laughed. One of his many tasks at his job—his *former* job—had been organizing his bosses' inboxes once a week, filing every email into its appropriate client folder. One partner, now retired, even made Reid print out every email he received, just because he preferred reading a hard copy. That guy had been ancient . . . and probably young enough to be Camilla Varné's son . . .

Another poster caught Reid's eye. Glossy black, with jagged font and a cadre of twentysomethings gathered together in a clump, looking off in various directions with frightened expressions. It was jarringly modern, and the title, *I Was Your Murderer,* sounded familiar.

"Wait, I think I've seen that one," he said, pointing. "Were *you*—?" He stopped himself from making a face a second too late.

"Not a fan, huh?"

"No! I just meant—"

"It's okay, *golubchik*. That movie is garbage. You can agree—I'm not even in the damn thing."

"You're not? Then why—"

"My granddaughter is also an actress. Leonora. She does all sorts of those execrable little films, with the blood and the swearing, and the little bitty tank tops to show how pointy nipples can get when running through the woods. Probably because they usually film at night and she's afraid of becoming sun-allergic like me, the nasty little beast. I shouldn't complain too much. I'm her manager. Circle of life, right? Those that can't do, teach? Or something."

"Hey. Whatever keeps the lights on."

"I did a few scary movies in my day, too. And wouldn't you know: more emails. Fan emails. Convention invitation emails. Interview request emails. My god, I spend more time trying to answer emails than I ever did acting. I'll tell you, Reid, all I want to do to one day is throw that computer out the window and watch it smash on the pavement below. Maybe take out one of those tourists for good measure."

A wicked grin spread across her perfectly lined lips.

Reid felt a similar one on his own face. His name sounded like music in her mouth. He ignored the feeling that he hadn't told it to her yet; he must have, earlier. Nothing a little prolonged sleep deprivation couldn't explain.

"What next?" she mused. "I'd show you the bedroom, but . . . well, a lady must maintain some sense of mystery, wouldn't you agree?"

## 5

Reid and his host walked down the hallway. It felt like strolling through a private museum. More movie posters, as well as framed photos and occasional pieces of art. Originals, of course. He was admiring what appeared to be an original Jasper Johns when he felt a flush of guilt. He hadn't checked his phone in minutes. Usually, that meant a string of texts waiting for him, informing him about some new disaster or other at home. Here he was, hobnobbing like an asshole.

Then, an idea occurred to him. Something to allay his conscience.

"Have you lived here long?" he asked.

She nodded. "Oh yes. Very long. I can't imagine living anywhere else."

Reid tried to act as casually as possible. "It's such an amazing building. So historic. And so well maintained! Like, there's not even a bug problem, like I've heard about with older buildings this old. Right?"

She stared straight at him with steely suspicion. Like he'd asked her to describe her most recent gynecological exam.

*Nice, Reid. About as subtle as a hammer to the nose.*

Her silence went on for minutes, years, decades.

Finally, she reached out and patted his cheek with a soft palm. Her touch . . . electric.

"I wouldn't worry about bugs. Not here. Come, let's see the last room."

## 6

A large, ash-blond piano sat atop the middle of an ornamental rug next to a wire-mesh statue of a giraffe. So well polished, so immaculately kept, it practically glowed.

He'd never seen a piano that color before. It was like seeing the instrument for the very first time.

He couldn't help but gasp. "Whoa. Do you play?"

She shrugged. "Lessons when I was a girl. I never liked being told what to do. But for a few years, I was with Edgar Dellaritz, a very famous composer in his day. He moved this piano in and it fit so well, it just had to stay. Go ahead. It won't bite."

He sat at the bench, almost afraid to touch it, as if it were fragile. "How does someone even move a piano into a building like this?"

"One inch at a time."

He laughed. Before he could stop himself, his fingers brushed the keys.

They felt like silk. Like marble. Like cool water.

"I remember reading how they sourced some of the foundation of the Deptford from one specific village in Eastern Europe. And how they managed to add so many extra residential floors while still keeping the original roof intact. So, I guess getting a piano inside is a piece of cake, all things considered."

"You know about that?"

He gave a modest shrug. "I'm kind of obsessed with the building."

She regarded him again. Another penetrating stare, another quixotic smile. He suddenly felt very self-aware, almost embarrassed to be sitting in front of the keys like a child at a lesson.

"Tell me more about yourself, Reid. You have a wife and a . . . baby?"

"How do you know that?"

"Well, I saw your wedding ring, and I know I shouldn't assume it's a wife you have, but, sue me, I'm old and what's the point of aging if you can't bring a few assumptions along with you? I'd like to think that after a lifetime in the arts my, what is it, 'gay radar' is finely attuned. As for the baby, well . . . you're young and healthy and glowing and, honestly? You look exhausted."

"It's been a long couple of days. Moving has been . . . an adjustment."

She sighed wistfully. "Children are the hardest thing, aren't they?"

"Sure, but . . . I love being a dad . . ." His hands moved without thought, playing a quiet run of chords while his foot worked the sustain pedal. Nothing aggressive, just a couple of arpeggios of a few major sevenths. The keys were exquisitely weighted.

"You play very well. Very instinctual," she said. "Is this how you provide for your family? With your music?"

He stopped playing, self-conscious again. He didn't feel the need to bullshit her. He looked down at his hands. "No, uh . . . I have a day job. Or *had*. I just got fired the other day."

"Fired? That sounds spicy."

His fingers twisted into knots. "I . . . heh, I haven't even told my wife yet."

"Well, now we're getting somewhere! Tell me everything, Reid. I can't take the suspense!"

He turned to look at up her, eyes narrowing slightly. "Do you really want to know?"

"Of course I do." Her eyes . . . they sparkled the way her jewelry on the floor sparkled, the way this piano sparkled, a mad magpie glimmer that made it impossible to ignore. "I'm fascinated by other people's stories."

She patted his shoulder before sitting down next to him. Before he could stop himself, he started talking.

Eventually, as they spoke—he wasn't even aware when it happened—they made their way back to the library room. Or perhaps it was called a sitting room, since that's what her brown-suited companion was still doing: sitting.

The whole time, Miss Varné received Reid's story with those avid, hungry eyes. Her questions leading him to reveal more and more

As usual, Reid also threw in plenty of sarcastic, half-joking comments while he recounted their tales of woe. Miss Varné touched his upper arm.

"You don't have to make light of it, Reid."

That surprised him. "I'm not—"

"Yes, you are. You laugh, you make your little parentheticals. Believe me, I understand humor as a defense, but do you not think what you've gone through merits seriousness?"

"I . . . no, I'm, I just, it's absurd, right? To have that many bad things happen all at the same time like that?"

"So you're an absurdist? Like a Camus or a Beckett?" she asked this with a genuine curiosity, not any judgment, cataloging him in a mental index. "They, too, responded to a propitious amount of simultaneous suffering."

"Yeah, I guess so." He'd never put a label on it before.

She indicated the bookcases. "I'm a fan, of course. I did several productions of theirs, of Ionesco's, of Pirandello's. There's so much suffering in the world. So much pain. You get to be a certain age and you gain a collector's appreciation of it. But, my Reid, are you protecting yourself? Or are you protecting your misery?"

*My Reid.* He liked that.

Before he could respond, across the room, her companion pitched forward and fell straight off the couch, onto his face with a heavy *tumf.*

Miss Varné looked at Reid with an almost comical oopsie-daisy expression. "I should probably take care of him."

"Yeah, I'll . . ." Reid noticed the man tried, and failed, to get up. He hurried over to help.

Miasmic breath oozed from the guy. It smelled like he was rotting from the inside out.

"Cap'n 'Merica," the guy chuckled, "at it again."

"Yeah, congrats on finding the bottom of the bottomless mimosas, buddy. You sure you're okay?"

The guy belched: a wet, ripping noise. Reid turned his head away and noticed Miss Varné staring at him again. Long enough that he began to feel self-conscious.

"What?" he asked through a laugh, trying to play it cool.

"You're a very kind person, Reid. You take care of others."

"I guess I do. Something my mom taught me."

She walked—almost floated—over and offered Reid a hand. After Reid made sure El Drunko was sufficiently propped against the couch, he took that hand and stood. They made their way to the door, which she opened as he slipped his shoes back on.

"Be careful you don't get taken advantage of. One problem with absurdists is they don't always know when something stops being funny and starts being corrosive."

He was about to leave when he stopped. He thought of the doormen, of the elevator gremlin, of the concierge.

Fuck it.

"Hey," he said. "Have you ever considered hiring a personal assistant?"

"A personal assistant . . . ?"

"You know, just someone looking for a job, who could maybe come over a few hours during the day, Monday through Friday, do some of that administrative stuff you hate. Those nasty emails. Running errands in the sun. You know?"

She considered. "It *would* be nice to be able to catch up on some of my beauty rest."

"Maybe you could even find someone who lives close by? Like, someone who lives in the building?"

"Goodness. But the only person I could think of . . . I believe he was *fired* from his last job."

"I bet his rates are pretty reasonable, then."

# 7

Ana sat on the floor of the closet with her headphones pressed to her ear. So far, her plan was a bust; there were no sounds whatsoever coming from the Jacobses' apartment next door.

No movement, no footsteps, no baby—or adult—crying. Nothing.

She sighed, realizing she was being ridiculous. She'd come in here—once again, turning the living room into a disaster area by emptying out the closet's contents—to get some recording done while Charlie napped, but all she'd done so far is attempt to spy on Mrs. Jacobs.

Ana turned up the gain a little more, cringing in advance in case any incidental noise happened to occur and blow her eardrums out.

She didn't like doing this. It felt creepy and wrong. Then again, so did the absolute silence she heard beyond the ambient hiss of her mic.

Maybe the Jacobses had gone on a well-deserved vacation?

Possible . . . but she remembered just how frazzled and frantic Mrs. Jacobs had been. How broken (a word Ana hated, but how else to describe those laughs?). People don't usually get *that* bad if vacationing is ever an option.

Still. She had to admit this was going nowhere. Charlie would wake up soon, and then the day would be—

Someone giggled in her headphones.

Faint but unmistakable. A child's giggle.

Ana's body broke out in chills.

The Jacobses *were* home. Or at least the baby was. Maybe Mrs. Jacobs finally got away?

*But why would the baby be laughing? In otherwise complete silence?*

*Am I sure that's what I heard?*

She turned the volume up even further and listened for another few minutes.

No noises followed.

Although . . . there was something. Not human, but . . .

At first, she thought it was simply room tone—every room had its neutral sound no matter how dead—but it seemed to move in a regular fashion that made her curious. A soft conversation? A TV?

A memory of being on an examination table, shirt hiked up, freezing cold jelly smeared across her beautifully round belly as her ob-gyn ran a sonogram wand back and forth, came to mind.

Not exactly knowing why, Ana recorded a snippet of it to examine it later. Maybe if she fiddled with the EQ, she could isolate the source and hear what was being said. *This takes nosiness to a new level, Ana.*

No. Even more nosy was what she did next.

She worked her way out of the closet, ignoring the clutter strewn about the living room, got into her chair, and grabbed the key to the Jacobses' apartment.

However, once she got into the hallway, she stopped and really thought about what she was doing. What if Mrs. Jacobs was getting some much-needed rest? What if she was in better shape and a visit from Ana fucked her up again?

Worse, what if Mrs. Jacobs crouched by the door, waiting for someone to let her out so she could finish what she'd attempted last time?

*Plus what if the concierge comes back? What if he puts his hands on* you *this time, leads you into your own apartment . . . comes in and shuts the door behind him?*

Nope. This was a dumb idea. She wasn't going to bother the Jacobses.

Instead, she found herself doing something even more impulsive. She wheeled herself to the *next* neighbor's door and knocked on that. No real plan, other than introducing herself as the newest tenants. Maybe she'd be able to sneak a peek inside, see if there were, indeed, other babies in the other apartments.

Except there was no answer.

She wheeled herself to another door. Knocked. Waited. No answer.

Her heart began to pound. She moved on to another.

No answer.

Where was everybody? Was she alone up here—besides Mrs. Jacobs and her giggling baby, of course?

No, these were lottery apartments. They should never be empty. They should be the most competitive apartments in New York City.

*Maybe they were eaten by the face at the window . . .*

She tried another door. "Hello?!" No answer. Not even an angry fuckoffleavemealone.

*How quickly we become the crazy woman in the hallway,* her mother whispered. Ana tried not to let herself become upset, but this was just so eerie, so wrong.

And then suddenly she found herself at the top of the staircase. She'd made her way here without really noticing.

All thoughts ceased.

The staircase made an orderly, hypnotic path down into oblivion. It would be so easy to throw one's self down, tumbling like a marble in a chute. Do it fast enough and you might not even hear the snap.

*You're all alone here, Ana. You never should have come here. You don't belong in this building. You can't handle being in that chair. You're not strong; you're not inspiring. You were never meant to be a mother. It's okay, not every woman is. But you don't belong* here. *Do your family a favor. Stop being a burden.*

Blood chilled with certainty, she edged closer to the topmost step.

"Ana?"

She almost jumped out of her seat and tumbled down the steps accidentally.

Reid stood a few feet behind her.

She exhaled in a great, desperate gasp and pushed herself toward him, away from those awful steps. She stopped before she might run over his feet and bent forward to hug his hips.

"What's going on? What are you doing? Are you crying?"

"Nothing, I'm fine, I just—I don't know what just happened." She stopped. Sniffed him. "Have you been drinking?"

"No. What do you mean you don't know what just happened?"

"Nothing. I was just . . . lost in thought, doesn't matter."

"Oh. Okay . . ."

They made their way back to their apartment. He was in the middle of telling her that he'd gone to Home Depot and, wouldn't you know it, they were out of the parts she needed so he put in a special order that should be there in a few days, when they reached their door.

It was closed. Locked.

"Jesus, Ana," Reid said. "Did you bring keys?"

*Not for our apartment.* "No, I didn't realize . . . I guess I forgot to do the dead bolt thing."

"You left Charlie in a locked—?!"

"Just for a few minutes. She's napping, it's okay, I'm sorry." Shame burned through her, head to toe.

"Yeah." He quickly pulled his own keys out and unlocked their door. "Just. Please. You gotta remember to—"

"Obviously. Reid, I'm sorry. I just—"

"It's *okay.*" Convincing her? Or convincing himself? "She's safe here. We would've gotten help if we needed it."

He decided not to press the issue further. But she watched him fold it up and file it away behind his eyes all the same.

# MANTRAS

## 1

That night, a miracle occurred.

Charlie slept for ten hours.

And Ana, so exhausted from her exercises and the stress of the day, slept, too.

As all parents of an infant can attest, the world becomes a different place after some sleep. Get a couple of good nights in a row and, well, how you felt during the thick of it starts to feel like just a bad dream. Problems don't go away, of course, but they shrink. You can stick them in your back pocket.

During their pandemic pregnancy, Ana and Reid had attended several webinars and Zoom classes, one hosted by an NYU obstetrician with huge glasses and a severe case of white-lady locs. She made a show of informing the class that everyone would soon learn what she called "the Mantras of Parenthood"—little phrases you repeat over and over. One of them was "Everything looks better in the morning." Ana had turned to Reid and chuckled, "'I don't think she knows what the word *mantra* means," . . . before realizing their own Zoom hadn't been muted.

But for the next week, this so-called mantra held true. Everything *did* feel a little better. The days proceeded with a steady, pleasant pace.

Reid settled into his new job. Every morning, he left his own apartment at the normal time to head to the office, kissing his wife and baby daughter, then headed down to the lobby, where he traversed to the *other* elevator, tipping a wink or lifting a chin toward the concierge with an insider's acknowledgment . . . and, of course, receiving that unsettlingly wide grin in response.

Miss Varné—"Oh, please, *golubchik,* call me Camilla"—had explained to him that he wouldn't see much of her; she was serious about spending most of her days catching up on rest.

"I like to conserve my energies," she'd said, offering him a glittering smile that made Reid's heart flutter.

She was old enough to be his grandmother, for God's sake, but he could see why she had made it as an actress: she had an undeniable charm, a charisma. Ageless. He'd heard that people like George Clooney or even Bill Clinton had a unique skill that made you feel like you were the only person in the room, but Camilla . . . she made it feel like you were the only other person in on a secret with her. What that secret was he had no idea, it didn't matter; what mattered was she brought you into her confidence and made you feel that exclusivity. You might not be the only other person in the room, but you were the only other person in the room who *mattered.*

She set him up in her office. He perused the books and notebooks and old scripts that he'd noted earlier. Examined a few awards on the shelves. Photos of Camilla with . . . Jesus, was that Humphrey Bogart? John Friggin' Kennedy?! He really hoped that guy with the little mustache was Charlie Chaplin . . .

She hadn't exaggerated about her emails. Thousands of unopened correspondence clogged her inbox. Interview requests, script-read requests, solicitations from an agent who literally addressed her as "Miss Varné," which seemed to indicate a real lack of familiarity.

Then there was a second inbox (identical, like that second elevator)—this for correspondence regarding a woman named "Leonora Gish." Reid knew already that was Camilla's granddaughter, for whom she acted as a manager, but he couldn't help himself: he plugged the name into an incognito browser tab and did a quick search. She hadn't done many movies, but she was young—probably early twenties. He clicked on the images tab and thought, *She's gonna do just fine.* She was stunning, the spitting image of her grandmother. It was like someone had slapped a few de-aging filters on Camilla.

He had to stop his mind from wandering to inappropriate places. Imagining Camilla and Leonora entering, surprising him with gentle touches across his neck, his back, taking him by the hand to the pillowy couch across the room, laying him down, showing him how they were alike, how they were different—

He rubbed his eyes. Christ. He needed to get laid more often.

It was up to Reid as to when his workday was done. Camilla said he could leave whenever he felt he'd made enough headway. That first day, after several hours of answering emails and crossing off a few administrative tasks, he found himself at a loss. What next? Do too much extra work and be out of a job? He could explore her apartment, but that felt like an intrusion. However, if he went back to his own apartment he'd have to explain to Ana why he was home early.

He *should* do that. Charlie's birthday party was coming up in a matter of days and Reid could help with the prep. Not to mention . . . he really should come clean to Ana about his new work arrangement.

Why hadn't he yet? Why was he keeping this a secret? At first, he told himself it was just until he knew the money situation would be okay. But Camilla promised to be generous—overgenerous, really—so that wasn't an issue. Then he told himself he wanted to wait a little longer until he had his own plans figured out. This job was a stopgap. He'd need something more long term first. He wasn't a fast thinker—his mom called him "the Gristmill" whenever it came to making a decision. As soon as he had a plan, *then* he'd let Ana in on what had happened.

He knew that was bullshit, too. The real reason he hadn't said anything yet was he relished having his own space. His own little bubble. It had been so, so very long since he'd had something that was just his. He supposed it could be said that his day job had been that, but there'd never been any joy to be found there.

But at Camilla's apartment? He was *at work*. He couldn't be reached. It was *his*. Hell, he barely even had a boss.

Besides. It's not like he didn't help out literally every morning. Ana needed her own bonding time with the baby.

So, Reid developed his own little mantra: *This is* my *time.* After he finished at Camilla's, he would take the elevator down to the lobby—struck every time by the eerie similarity between the two elevator operators. Then he would stroll through the lobby and out the front doors for a long, luxurious walk in Central Park all by himself.

The second day of his afternoon My Time, as he exited the park on the east side, a man called out to him.

It took a second for Reid to recognize the guy: he was one of the Chabad Lubavitch Hasids who used to visit Reid's office. Reid's slowness at recognizing him was forgivable. Whenever the small cluster of Hasids would come by, this guy always hung toward the back. Some weeks he wasn't even there.

"That's your name, right?" he asked as Reid approached. "Reid?"

"That's me."

The guy was alone, smoking a cigarette. He exhaled a plume, tilting back to keep it away from Reid. "I thought so. I'll never forget you; that first time we went up to your office, you had the funniest answer."

Reid chuckled at the memory. A gang of black-suited Hasids had knocked on the office door and asked if there were any Jews working there. Reid's response had been: "Is that a trick question? Because real Jews know not to answer that whenever strangers are at the door. Especially ones in matching suits."

"Well," Reid said now, "I don't work there anymore, so. Thanks for all the free bread."

"Ah. Moving on to better things?"

"Much."

The cigarette looked good. Reid couldn't help himself. He asked for one. He'd just tell Ana it was a particularly stressful day and he bummed a smoke from a stranger. That was mostly true.

"Nasty habit," the guy said, handing one over.

"Habits are for nuns," Reid said.

"We're a tolerant religion," the guy replied. "Nuns are welcome."

They shared a chuckle, and Reid walked away, feeling cool and confident.

The next afternoon, Reid found a bench to sit on for a while, sipping a hot latte he picked up before slipping into the park. Hot drink on a chilly, sunny day: nothing better.

He idly scrolled through his phone, and when he looked up, he was surprised to find the same sandy-haired, black-hatted man a bench away, immersed in a paperback. Reid read the title: *'Salem's Lot.* A horror novel, if he remembered correctly.

"Meet any good nuns lately?" Reid called across the distance to the other bench.

The guy looked up.

"Hey!" he said, delighted at the coincidence. "Fancy meeting you here."

"Bashert," Reid said.

"Very good," he replied, impressed.

"You're not on challah duty today?"

"Sometimes I . . . take breaks from all that."

"I know the feeling." Reid stole a guilty glance to his phone's lock screen, where a picture of Ana and Charlie pointed up to the numbers of the phone's clock. He'd been so amazed and delighted when Charlie had mirrored Ana's gesture, he didn't think he would ever change the wallpaper.

"I don't have any cigarettes," the man said. "I ran out yesterday, and I'm trying not to buy a new pack until I absolutely have to."

"It's okay. I don't want my wife thinking I started up again." *I'm lying enough to her as it is.* "Speaking of, I should probably get back home. She could use my help." He stood, pocketing his phone.

"Yeah. Wives . . ." The guy gazed into space, with an expression of deep sadness.

Reid was tempted to ask if he was okay, then decided to leave him alone. "See you around," he called.

The guy gave him a distracted nod. "Bashert."

Reid walked away . . . then wandered the park for another two hours.

## 2

Ana's new mantra was simple: *No.*

She felt clearer than she had in weeks. Whenever the bad thoughts threatened to sneak back into her head, she simply repeated to herself:

*No.*

The urge to spy on—or even think about—Mrs. Jacobs?

*No.*

The urge to think about what she'd imagined outside the window?

*No.*

The urge to go back and look at that staircase?

*Definitely no.*

The incident in the hallway disturbed her more than she wanted to admit. The way Reid had looked at her. The desperation she'd felt, knocking on other people's doors, as if it weren't also totally normal for New Yorkers to ignore solicitation. Plus, she'd never been so tempted by self-harm before, even when things had been at their worst. It had just seemed such an . . . obvious solution. The kind that might come back.

She focused instead on all the positive developments.

The closet worked well enough for recording while she waited for the booth parts to arrive at Home Depot, and she started catching up on her audiobook deficit. This was especially good since she'd gotten some nervous emails from her authors, wondering about her progress.

Her new, intense workout regimen gave her some much-needed endorphins and made her feel more in control. She even sent Georgia a few texts—polite, no pressure, just checking in, sorry for being an asshole.

And there hadn't been a single new bite on Charlie, so, fingers crossed, their brush with infestation had been a false alarm. The humble party they planned for Charlie's first birthday could proceed.

As for Charlie herself? She was nowhere near as fussy or cry-y. She must finally be adjusting to their new—

(*You don't belong here.*)

(*No.*)

—home.

Even Reid seemed less cranky. He hadn't been acting like going to work was some unbearable imposition anymore. Maybe they'd all turned a corner, and just in the nick of time.

The only problem was . . . sometimes when Ana looked at Charlie, she started to wonder, *Is this* really *better? Is Charlie* too *calm?* Before the voice of her own mother could cut in and chide her for being impossible to please, Ana had to admit there *was* something strange about how Charlie was behaving now. She wasn't a miserable mess, but she also wasn't as giggly and delighted in the world as she used to be. She just kinda . . . sat there.

She didn't make her chirping noise anymore, either. Which, to Ana, meant she wasn't as interested in making her parents laugh.

*She's just growing up. That's what they do. They grow up, they become different, they stop doing the things you don't like, and they also stop doing the things you do like. It's all part of the gig.*

Was that another Mantra of Parenthood? She didn't know.

"Penny for your thoughts, Baby Bird," she said to Charlie, who sat in her activity station, unmoving, disinterestedly chewing on a toy she held in her hands.

Charlie looked back at her with unreadable eyes. The two of them stared at each other for a long, long time.

# THE COURTYARD

## 1

Hey, did BB seem weird to you at all this morning?

No?

She's been great lately. Why?

I don't know. Something feels off.

Now it's like I WISH she would cry a little, you know?

Honey

I know. I'm being ridiculous.

Maybe I'll take her outside. Fresh air.

Still haven't visited the courtyard yet

That's a great idea!

Hey, gotta go. Boss has big project I need to do. Important People coming to the office today and guess who has to straighten up the place, get food, et fucking c

Ugh why is that YOUR responsibility??!

🤷🏾‍♂️

All in a days work for this drone

## 2

"Everything okay, Mrs. Greene?" the concierge asked, jogging over to open the courtyard door for her, grinning his impossible grin.

Ana put on her own happy face. "Yep! All good. We're just going exploring."

"Be careful out there. It's a cold day. You don't want to stay out too long."

"I think we'll be okay."

It *was* cold. The air was brisk. After several days of bright, brittle winter sunshine, today looked like a thick layer of cotton had been pulled across the sky. But there was no snow on the ground and they were both bundled up.

The gigantic rectangle of the courtyard held a perimeter walkway, wrought iron table sets, even small tennis and bocce courts, wrapped around the centerpiece garden.

It was beautiful. She wondered why no one was out here, enjoying it. No one smoking a cigarette or going on a stroll. It made her think again of how no one answered her knocks, how empty the other apartments on her floor seemed to be. Except for that one giggle . . .

*No,* she thought resolutely, pushing all that away.

She sat at the outskirts of the courtyard, working up the nerve to go farther. The trees packed together tightly, making it dark and strangely intimidating. Like preparing to swim in the ocean in the middle of the night. Or standing at the top of a high, spiraling staircase.

But, of course, this was the inner courtyard of one of the most exclusive buildings in Manhattan. She probably didn't even have to worry about running into rats or a raccoon, unless they had a net worth of seven figures.

A small, unpaved footpath looked flat enough for her to wheel her way through. Once they reached the mini Central Park in the middle, Ana wanted to sit in the grass and play with her baby. She also brought her iPad, with a PDF of the next chapters she needed to record ready to be marked up.

"What do you think, Baby Bird?"

She waited for Charlie to give a hearty, enthusiastic chirp, but Charlie only briefly looked up at Ana from the front-facing chest harness and then back at the wall of trees. Charlie's head strained forward and she kicked her feet, as if trying to move them both herself.

"Okay, then," Ana said, a strange knot forming in her stomach.

As if to assure her that they were in the normal, rational world, a plane flew by overhead.

Ana wheeled them to the mouth of the trees, where darkness swallowed them.

## 3

"And when you're finished in here, why don't you come out and join us?" Camilla tipped Reid a wink before leaving him in her office, and suddenly, behind Reid's rib cage, it was the Fourth of goddamn July. Join them?! Did she not understand who she currently entertained in her living room?

Of course she understood. They were her friends and neighbors. It was no big deal to her, just another day when some pals stopped by to chew the fat.

Reid hadn't been lying in his text to Ana—well, not about this, at least. When he'd arrived at Camilla's apartment this morning, she'd informed him that it was a lovely, overcast day and so she would have a small group of friends over. Reid suspected it would be some of the building's other residents, but he could not prepare for who walked in.

He'd been in the living room, helping Camilla tidy, when the first guests entered. Now, in the office, he could hear the buzz of voices.

*Chill out, loser, it's not like Beyoncé, Brad Pitt, and Barack Obama are playing Twister out there.* Hell, there wasn't even a Paul McCartney in the bunch—one of those era-defining celebrities who would always be the most famous person in the room, even if they were no longer driving the zeitgeist.

No, Camilla's guests weren't Super Famous. But Reid knew why they filled him with giddiness. The book on the Deptford. Published in 1979, its last chapter was a who's who of its then current, famous tenants.

That chapter included Jackson Sterling, winner of two Pulitzers and two National Book Awards, revered for his brutally elegant Westerns; Dulcina Arvold, one of Britain's most highly regarded theater critics, known for her long-running feud with Laurence Olivier, rumored to have been the only woman John Gielgud actually ever slept with; former New York senator Teddy Wilcox—Republican? Democrat? Reid couldn't remember; Carl Reese, retired pitcher for the Yankees; and Poppy Loudon, silver-medal Olympic gymnast.

All of these people currently sat in Camilla's living room, gabbing while Reid hacked away at the overgrowth in Camilla's inbox.

There was one other guest out there, too. Camilla had a new boy toy. Reid had almost yelped in surprise, discovering the dude already sitting on the white leather couch.

"Morning," the guy said, staring into space, sounding only a little doped up. "Weird day, huh?"

For a moment, Reid thought it was the same guy from that day he first followed Camilla up here. He wore the same brown suit. But, no, this was clearly someone else. For starters, he had a shaved head and no beard—less hipster, more skinhead. Maybe he was the previous guy after some much-needed tidying? But when this guy reached up to tug a little at his tie, Reid noticed tattoos on his hands, which that previous guy definitely hadn't had. Both dudes wore the same dazed and disinterested expression, though. Camilla apparently had a type.

*None of my business,* Reid told himself. *Lifestyles of the rich and quasi-famous.* He focused on getting back to work so that he could join the fun.

## 4

Inside the trees, the silence was downright uncanny. It reminded Ana of her isolation booth, except for the rustle of leaves.

The path curved and wound, so rather than a quick, straight shot to the center, Ana had to navigate around bends slowly and carefully. That was fine; she didn't want to hurry—more than anything, she was determined today would be a good day. A happy memory. For both of them.

That said, she looked forward to finally getting to the center. Trees pressed in on all sides of the path, feeling *juuust* too close for comfort. What kind of trees were these anyway? Even though it was winter, the growth was impressively thick. *Hardy plants from the motherland,* Vera had said, right?

Perhaps because of the silence, or perhaps because she felt rested and cogent enough to finally articulate something, she found herself speaking to Charlie while she maneuvered them down the path.

"Hey, I'm . . . really sorry for everything, Baby Bird."

Charlie was silent. The leaves rustled around them.

"I really want to be a good mom to you. And more than that . . . I want you to have a good life. I hope you know that." She pushed them forward. "I know things have been rough lately. For both of us. It really, really sucks. And I'm sorry."

Not even the sound of real birds. And was the ground getting rougher? Her arms, already sore from her recent workouts, strained with the effort to roll over the terrain. "I didn't have a good mom myself, so . . . I don't think I know what I'm doing a lot of the time. And I know most moms feel that way, but . . . well, in my case it's true."

There was so much more she wanted to say—so much she wanted to *hear* herself say to her daughter—about how she'd had complicated feelings about being a mom even before they blew their savings on fertility treatments, but how it had also been important to her to try, and she knew she and Charlie would grow closer together in time, become best friends . . .

. . . but that's when she noticed the path had disappeared. The ground had become uneven and soft. It took more and more effort to roll her wheels through the terrain.

She looked around. She must have made a wrong turn somehow.

"Where'd—? What the hell?"

There wasn't even a path behind them. How long had she been off-roading without noticing?

She closed her eyes. Breathed. Determined to not get upset. To not get scared. Of course, anyone not in a chair could simply backtrack or push forward through the trees and get wherever they wanted, but she tried not to think of that.

What was really unnerving was the feeling inside her wheels. She'd been using this chair long enough that she was familiar with various vibrations in the metal. The feeling of a subway train underneath her; asphalt versus concrete.

Something about this ground felt . . . different.

"You know what? I think we've explored enough. Maybe let's fight our way through Au Bon Pain instead."

She turned in her seat. She couldn't get her bearings. How was this possible? The courtyard wasn't *that* big.

Fighting feelings of anger, of fear, of humiliation, she worked on turning her chair around in the mud. It wasn't easy. Then she backtracked.

Where was the path? She was positive she'd come this way, but she didn't recognize a goddamn thing.

*Stay calm.*

"Did we . . . get lost, Baby Bird? That's impressive."

Ana pushed forward, now no longer sure what "forward" even meant. For one horrific moment, her chair snagged on something—a branch? The ground?—and she almost started yelling, but she was able to get her wheels free with a jerk.

This was so unfair. She just wanted to have a nice day. After all they'd been through, she thought they deserved that, but, no. Just another friendly reminder that everything had changed and nothing could be easy.

The ground became even more difficult to wheel over. She panted with the effort. Finally, it became so frustrating she yelled out to the too-silent forest:

"I. Hate. This. FUCKING. *CHAIR!*"

As if in response, something reached out and grabbed one of her wheels, dumping her and Charlie out of their seat. Ana only registered they were falling once she landed in the dirt.

# GOOD COMPANY

## 1

"Well, I was *hoping* you'd join us!"

Camilla sat in her living room, the duplex with its massive library stretching out along the upper level, in one of her immensely comfortable brown leather seats. The heavy curtains stood open to the cloud-covered day. Flanking her, forming a horseshoe with the couch, love seat, and two other chairs, were her guests.

Reid had psyched himself up to meet them, but now he found himself frozen. One other person, one Reid hadn't seen come in, was here.

Winston Terry, the famous and famously reclusive musician. The main inspiration for the lyrics to the song he was writing for Charlie, which ran on a loop in his head even now.

They all stared at Reid.

"You *are* joining us, aren't you?" Camilla asked, bemused. "Or are you just going to stand there and pose?"

"Oh god," the woman Reid knew to be the former Olympian said, her expression all elegantly sleek lines under her black hair aerodynamically pulled back into a flawless bun, "should we call Dogan over? Maybe he'd like to do a quick sketch?"

Dogan, no last name, a famous artist Reid also recognized from his book on the Deptford.

Jackson Sterling, the writer of cosmically depressing Westerns, snorted. "Can't remember the last time Dogan joined us for one of our bull sessions." He had a gravelly voice wrapped in a perpetual sneer. It complemented his round, weathered face, intermittently speckled with grayish plaques Reid tried not to stare at.

"He's coming tonight, you know," the theater critic said in her high, proper British accent.

The former politician grunted. "Course he is. When there's an actual *event,* he's gotta be seen, right?"

Reid, smiling stupidly, asked, "What's tonight?" He didn't think it was possible, but he blushed even harder.

The group shared a chuckle.

"Co-op meeting," the politician said, and Reid nodded like, cool, totally, been there.

Camilla urged him to grab a drink and sit down. Reid forced himself to act chill, act *normal,* and complied. In his head, he kept repeating:

*Know your home.*

*Know you're home.*

And here he was, staring at the originator of that phrase.

"Nice to meet everybody," Reid said after pouring himself a modest glass of brown liquor (*Jesus, is ice always this loud?*) and sitting down on an open corner of the couch.

Next to him sat Camilla's new brown-suited boy toy, staring off into space. Reid was determined not to be as useless a presence in this room. He put on a charming grin and was in the process of opening his mouth to ask about the topic of conversation when Winston raised his far-less-moderately-filled glass and said:

"Right, Reid. Tell us all about yourself."

## 2

Reid thought he did pretty well. He made eye contact. He didn't stammer. He didn't apologize. He didn't crack any self-deprecating jokes. He acted—and almost believed—like he belonged in this room.

They were particularly excited when he began talking about Charlie.

"A year old *tomorrow*?" Dulcina Arvold clasped her hands in between her ample breasts. "Oh, what a special time! I remember my own at that age like it was yesterday."

"Very special," Poppy Loudon agreed. She had a much harsher Eastern European accent than Camilla's. "Being a year old is when you really start *listening,* don't you think? When you begin hearing the music all around you."

"Good lord," Sterling groaned, pouring himself another drink, "that's twee."

The gymnast waved him away. "You always act like sentimentality is some mortal sin. There's nothing wrong with twee!"

"Said the diabetic about the jar of sweets."

"*Now* who's being precious?" Arvold, ever the critic, chimed in.

"Jackson loves his similes almost as much as he loathes using quotation marks," Camilla said to Reid, and Sterling raised a glass to her.

"That was a metaphor, sweetheart, not a simile."

The gleeful barbs came almost as frequently as the follow-up questions about Charlie. What she was like, how she acted. Their youthful energy impressed

Reid, despite the fact that the youngest among them—Reid guessed Carl Reese, the ballplayer—had to at least be in his mid-to late-sixties.

It was Reese who threw in, "That must be so hard with your wife in a wheelchair."

Reid flinched at that. He didn't remember telling them about Ana's injury, but he must have, and now he felt terrified he'd gotten too comfortable and might start repeating himself like an idiot.

After a few more minutes of conversation, Teddy Wilcox slapped his hands on his rather substantial thighs and stood up. "Camilla, I'm starving. Think I might head to the pantry."

"Oh," Poppy said excitedly, "I'll join you."

Camilla's toy also shot to his feet as if he were expected to go along with them. Camilla stopped him with a casual hand and spoke to her guests.

"You'll do no such thing. Stay. We've got plenty of *măruntaie*. It comes from Christopher himself." On the coffee table was a spread of artisanal-looking crackers encircling a ramekin full of a brownish dip. "Don't go all the way to the pantry. Besides, you need to save room for tonight, you pigs."

Christopher—so that was this companion's name—sat back down, disinterested as paint. Reid couldn't imagine how good his snacks must be. On the other hand, maybe he was a really talented chef? Maybe that's what had earned his place here? Maybe that explained his passive-yet-cocky smirk?

Reid found himself looking at that smirk. Something about Christopher's mouth . . .

Winston reached forward and scooped some of the dip onto one of the crackers. "No complaints from me," he said, munching on his snack. "This is delicious, Cammy."

"Thank you," Camilla replied proudly.

Almost automatically, Reid picked up a cracker, as well. He pierced the jellied spread with the knife provided and smeared it onto the cracker. He felt eyes on him. They were curious what he'd think.

He, on the other hand, had a hard time not staring at Christopher's mouth. There was a rash or something around the guy's lips. Irritated skin from shaving? Did he recently get rid of a goatee? That must be it, although the shape of the angry skin looked more like the guy had made out with a vacuum hose.

The taste in Reid's mouth obliterated his thoughts.

He forced his face to stay neutral. He remembered a catered event he'd been dragged to as a kid—Rosh Hashanah dinner or maybe a funeral—where his mom had kvelled over some chopped liver. He'd tried it, and it was the most disgusting thing he'd ever had. Eventually, when he got older, he found a taste for it and was just as likely to kvell when given the opportunity. This dip, whatever Camilla called it, was appalling . . . but he suspected one day he'd also be capable of liking it. His palate just needed to grow.

"Whoa," he said, "that's . . . that's interesting."

The room abounded with delighted noises.

"So there's a separate pantry floor?" he asked before anyone could get him to comment further on what he'd just eaten. "It's just, like, food storage? I didn't know that."

"There's a lot you don't know about the Deptford, pallie," Teddy said and gave Reid a wink.

"A building should always have secrets," Poppy Loudon said, "don't you think?"

Camilla informed the rest of the group that Reid "is *incredibly* interested in the Deptford. In fact, he's practically memorized Preston Treadwell."

Sterling made a gagging noise. "Christ. *That* book, huh?"

"I love it," Reid said. "I know it's out of print, but I thought it was—"

"Rubbish," Dulcina Arvold said. "All of it."

Reid deflated. "All of it?"

"He made a lot of enemies with that book," Senator Wilcox said.

"He got what was coming to him," Sterling said.

"Wait, what happened to him?" It never occurred to Reid to find out what happened to the author.

Wilcox drew a finger across his bullfrog neck and made a sound reminiscent of Donald Duck getting caught under the wheels of a semi.

Arvold waved a disapproving hand at the boys. The twinkle in her eyes said otherwise, though. "Oh, that was totally unrelated. A tabloid rag-wringer like him makes enemies everywhere."

"Jeez," Reid said. He suddenly felt lost, the rug pulled out from under him. Was the book he had been relying on inaccurate? Was he back to being a total outsider?

Sterling noticed. "Look at him. He looks like we just told him Santa wasn't real."

Reid brought his eyes up to meet the writer's. "Actually, Mr. Sterling," he said with some steel in his voice, "I never thought Santa was real."

Before Sterling could respond, the retired baseball player spoke.

"They're just giving you shit, Reid. Don't let them get to you."

"Besides," Camilla added with velvet confidence, "the actual history of the building is far more interesting than Treadwell's schoolyard gossip. Darker, too. Dark enough that much of its history will never make it to print."

Reid turned to her. Her companion, Christopher, sat between them, staring off into space, so Reid leaned forward. "What kind of history? Why haven't there been more books written about this place? I dig around online *all the time,* and I barely ever find anything! I keep searching and searching but . . ." He laughed, embarrassed by his unguarded hunger.

They all exchanged looks.

"What is it about the Deptford you like so much, Reid?"

Winston asked that. He'd been silent for much of this, just watching the conversation play out. Reid had almost forgotten he was there. Now, he looked at him.

A thousand politic answers flitted through his mind.

Then he thought, *Screw it,* and went with what he felt.

"I love how this building was a big Fuck You."

He felt them all perk up at this unexpected answer. He continued, still looking at the only other musician in the room.

"Maybe there's a lot of gossip in the Treadwell book, but I think he got the historical stuff right. What life was like when this place was first built. The Astors and the Four Hundred and all that. Snooty people in white ties going to the opera to socialize and excluding people for sport. I didn't know people looked down on living in an apartment then or how this area of Manhattan was literally a wasteland! Like, a full-on shantytown, just tents and lean-tos and poor people everywhere. But then Thomas Emile Janebridge comes along and is like, 'Fuck that. *These* people deserve some beauty to look at, too! Those Edith Wharton assholes think living in an apartment is so gauche? Well, here's an apartment building that might as well be a mansion!' Not only that, the Deptford opened its doors to artists and immigrants, people the Astor scene wouldn't have been caught dead associating with. People who didn't exist as far as the rest of the world was concerned. Sure, other buildings started to follow suit, the Dakota, the Ansonia, the Bramford, and the Upper West Side became the Upper West Side. But only the Deptford remembers its roots. It *always* keeps a floor open for the poorest people they can find. It always makes sure that, no matter how rich and fancy most of its tenants might be—no offense—there's always affordable housing for the people who still don't exist to the rest of the city." Reid laughed. "I mean, who the hell am I, right? Nobody. And I live in the Deptford! That's amazing! It *still* feels like this big middle finger to the rest of Manhattan. To the rest of *everything.*"

"You make it sound so noble," Wilcox said. It was unclear if he sounded sarcastic or impressed.

"But of course," Arvold added, "you know its history isn't so sterling, though, right?"

"Isn't so *what*?" Sterling smirked.

"You shut up." Arvold turned back to Reid. "A lot of horrible things have happened here. One could argue more than most other buildings. That doesn't bother you?"

"There are things this building has seen that'll make your toes curl," Wilcox said, scooping up another handful of crackers and dip. "Stories your Treadwell never caught in his trawling expeditions."

"Did you know this building used to be used as a sort of drop house for all sorts of illicit activities?" Sterling asked. "Including body disposal?"

"Yes!" Reid was so excited he almost spilled his drink—which was how he noticed someone had refilled it. "I mean, I don't know any of the details, I just . . . like I said, I did a lot of googling and found an old front page from the *Tribune,* and there was an article about a missing bootlegger and the authorities thought he'd been disposed of at the Deptford. They called it a, what was it, some Italian term . . ."

"*Lupara bianca,*" Sterling said. "A hit with no discoverable body. A lot of nasties lived here, so they had an arrangement. Entire apartments used just for dismemberments. Others for bootlegging. But it wasn't just, say, rival booze-slingers who disappeared here. The entirety of the city's underworld understood that you could bring a body to the Deptford and, for a price, they would make it disappear. Gangsters, bootleggers—"

"Annoying politicians," Wilcox added.

"Athletes who didn't cooperate with certain outcomes," said Carl.

Poppy pitched her voice low, her sharp accent contributing to her ghost story whisper. "Some say that the criminals who lived here buried their victims' bodies inside these very walls and that, if the city were ever quiet enough, you would hear their very bones shifting, trying to become whole again."

"Then again," Arvold said, "some people read too much Poe."

"Any Poe is too much Poe." Sterling snorted.

"What about the Plummet?" Reid asked abruptly.

"The Plummet." Camilla didn't ask it like a question; she spoke it like a noir cliché about a name she hadn't heard in years.

"Yeah," Reid said. "In 1919. That's the one I'm kind of obsessed with. I can't find any other details about it. Was that . . . just gossip? Did it not actually happen?"

"No, it happened," Camilla said.

"What was it? A mob hit?"

Everyone exchanged looks.

Finally, Sterling spoke.

"I don't think anyone knows what it was, Reid. Sometimes, bad things just *happen.*"

"But—"

"The blood on the sidewalk, though . . . I often imagine it must have been truly humbling that day. When a body falls from a high height you might think it ruptures or bursts—to an extent, it does—but there are already all sorts of holes and egresses, so really what happens is everything gets *ejected.* A great turning-out of the pockets. You become a yard sale for all you really own."

He dipped a cracker into the viscous paste and tipped Reid an inscrutable wink as he ate it.

A momentary hush fell over the room. Then Camilla said, "Well, on that note. Reid, why don't you head home? I have a feeling we're about to move on to other things, and I could certainly use some rest before tonight."

The workday was barely half over; Reid still had a lot of time to kill. He should just head home and help Ana prep for the party tomorrow, but . . .

"You sure there's nothing more I can do around here? I can help clean up or—"

"That is so very sweet of you, *golubchik*. I don't want you to think we're chasing you away. This has been an extraordinary pleasure. It's been so long since any of us have met someone so interested in our humble little home."

"Be it ever so," Wilcox said.

"And—oh!" Camilla's eyes lit up. "While I'm thinking of it, we never set a proper payday!"

She moved to a desk and Reid knew straightaway she was about to give him money. He felt immediately uncomfortable. All these eyes watching. It was like being pantsed on a cold day.

"That's okay," he stammered, "we can figure that out later, no rush—"

"Oh, don't worry about it," she said, and she presented him a heavy wad of cash. "You've been so helpful the past few days; I can't tell you how much I've appreciated it."

Reid looked at the money that was now in his hands. "But . . . but this is more than we agreed—"

"You're the breadwinner, yes? You must provide for your young! Consider some of it a birthday present for your precious little one tomorrow."

"Don't sniff at it, mate," Winston chimed in. He'd poured himself another drink and was now standing at the window, looking out at the city. "Camilla's wealthier than sin and never learned what to do with her money."

"Because I live within my means, Winston Terry," Camilla said. "I don't spend all my money on instruments like some people."

Reid couldn't help himself.

"What kind of instruments?"

Winston turned and looked at him.

"Wanna see?"

Down in the courtyard, Ana had begun to scream.

## 3

Reid followed Winston to another duplex apartment a few floors beneath Camilla's.

He kept telling himself, *Remember this. Remember this moment.* But as soon as he saw Winston's digs, he knew his mind would never be able to grab the experience. It was total overload.

Records on the wall. Things Winston had produced or played on. Gold. Platinum.

Photographs. Camilla's were impressive, but these were downright mind-blowing.

Chuck Berry. Bruce Springsteen. Led Zeppelin. Paul McCartney. Fucking Elvis. "That's me and my group when we shared a bill with the Rolling Stones and the Animals."

Then he saw the music room. Like Camilla's two-tiered library/sitting room, except instruments filled the walls. Guitars, basses, mandolins, dulcimers, banjos, ukes, zithers, things he'd never even seen before. On the floor were drums, cajons, bongos, congas, theremins, two pianos (one upright), a mellotron, a few keyboards off their stands and leaning against a wall, and more, more, more. Beyond beautiful. *Worn.* Played. Loved.

Reid's mouth literally watered.

Winston told Reid to try whatever called to him. Reid approached the wall of guitars and picked up an acoustic guitar with a cherry sunburst finish and a pickguard decorated with trumpet vine flowers. A Gibson Hummingbird.

"That's a rare one," Winston said proudly. "The back and sides are maple instead of mahogany. Nineteen sixty-four."

It sounded immaculate. Bright, clean. The fretboard and neck provided the most exquisite action. Reid played a few basic chord sequences, and suddenly, Winston had a guitar in his own hands. He began noodling over what Reid played. His fingers were impossibly fast and dexterous.

"I would love to hear one of your songs, Reid," Camilla said from the doorway. Reid didn't realize she had followed them. In fact, the whole party had moved here, and Reid had been too captivated to notice.

They all echoed Camilla's sentiments. Reid protested at first, but his heart overruled his brain, and he started playing the song he'd just written for Charlie.

And it wasn't bad.

And they all applauded afterward. Even Sterling.

"I like that chorus, brother," Winston said with a knowing smirk. Reid began to apologize, and Winston waved a hand. "Don't even think of it. It fucking *works*. That's all that matters."

"It's a lovely song, Reid," Arvold said.

Reid glowed. "Thank you."

Camilla hugged him. He thought of her body against his. He thought of her granddaughter. She leaned her mouth toward his ear.

"I thought of one more favor to ask of you today," she whispered. "If you don't mind."

Next thing he knew, he floated back down to the lobby, a smile almost stretching from ear to ear on his face. This was one of the best days he'd had in years. Among the best in his life. Maybe *the* best when you considered the sorts of days he had lately.

Camilla's request was simple: the jeweler had called to say her earring was repaired and ready to be picked up; would he mind running down to pick it up before they closed for the day? Reid realized, not without some shame, that he would've done anything she'd asked, really.

He was making his way through the lobby to the front doors when someone shouted his name.

# COMMITMENT

## 1

She'd fallen on her side, thank God. Charlie was okay.

Ana sat up, checking them both for injuries, just to be sure. She slipped Charlie out of the chest harness and sat her on her butt in the dirt. Charlie, for her part, found all this delightful. Finally animated, she put her hands in the soil and cooed.

"Glad you're having a good time," Ana said. "Just . . . wait here."

Ana crawled to her chair. Unlike her daughter, she hated how strange and unpleasant the ground felt. It was warm. Sickeningly warm.

*It's like we're lying on the side of some massive beast.*

"Oh, my fucking GOD, stop!" she reprimanded herself.

When she reached the chair, she noticed two things. First, she'd been wrong; nothing had reached out and grabbed them. The wheel was just caught in some branches. She worked on untangling them from her spokes.

That's when she noticed the second thing. She'd cut herself in the fall. Another branch had poked its way through her coat sleeve and into her forearm. Not too deep—although it hurt like a motherfuck as she pulled it out.

Blood dripped down from the tip of the branch and into the dirt. Feverish imagination working overtime, she watched as the ground appeared to open up and accept her blood. Like a mouth in the dirt.

*Jesus Christ, Ana,* focus.

She threw the stick away and went back to trying to free her wheel.

It took a few more moments to notice the spiders.

At first, just one or two caught her attention. Little, semitranslucent arachnids in the mud. Unpleasant but not enough to cause a panic.

Then their number increased, and Ana realized they were coming from the narrow gash in the ground she'd imagined had opened up. It no longer reminded her of a mouth. The word her brain went to was *vaginal.*

This wasn't the work of an overactive imagination. This was very real.

The trickle became a flood. A cataract of dozens upon dozens of bent and angular arthropods emerged from the hole. They moved with a nauseating liquidity, tumbling over each other as they reached the top.

Ana threw herself backward and scooted away as quickly as she could, all too aware that any number of those loathsome creatures could be making their way toward her in the dirt and grass. She moaned, slapping away at the feeling of little segmented legs on her skin, and the only thing that made her stop was when she realized Charlie was gone.

## 2

"Charlie?! Oh god, Charlie?!!"

Nothing but the rustle of leaves. She listened so hard she even forgot the spiders swarming through the dirt and grass around her.

*"Charlie?!"*

She yelled as loud as she could, as if her baby could respond. Why wasn't anyone rushing over to help her?

She tried to still her imagination. Please. Just for a moment.

The whisper of leaves continued. Began to form words.

*Shhh. Shhh.*

The words became clearer. The shape of a voice coming through. Recognizable and unexpected. It almost sounded like Georgia's voice.

*You're here now.*

*Don't resist.*

Yes, Ana really thought it might be.

From far, far away—and yet as sure as if she were whispering in Ana's ear.

*Wait here. They'll come for you. You're right where you need to be.*

It was as seductive as the call of the staircase. *Throw yourself down. Be free of all these responsibilities, all this pain. Shut* us *up. Shut your mother up. Shut the baby up. Shut your memories up.*

Images flashed through her brain, quick as thought, beyond understanding.

Horrible things. Ancient things. Writhing, insectile bodies.

She saw her own skeleton, rotted and picked away. Lying on these courtyard grounds, forever in overcast gloom, ragged bits of flesh waving like flags, the victory of myriad sets of teeth stripping her meat away. Next to her, a smaller skeleton, similarly stripped, except for two shriveled eyes, loose in their sockets but pointed back at her.

But there was no fear, no pain, no panic. If she stood on the staircase now, she'd throw herself down, no question. The peace and quiet seemed so nice.

Then, unmistakable, behind the trees to her right, a sound she hadn't heard in days:

Charlie's delighted, fluty chirp.

Ana didn't give herself a moment to doubt. She pulled herself forward, using her elbows like a soldier in basic training, until she came to a thick wall of green. Could Charlie have crawled through here somehow? Only one way to find out.

Ana forced her way through dirt and bramble until she found herself in a huge clearing with mowed and cultivated grass. A few gray granite picnic tables guarded the periphery. The day was still overcast, but compared to the thick foliage, here it felt as bright as a beach in August.

And there, in the middle of the field, cozy in her puffy little red winter onesie, sitting on her diapered butt, was Charlie. She was chewing on something, but when she saw her mother, she clapped her hands and chirped again. Was that a clear leg squirming out of her mouth? Ana didn't care. She called her name, crying, crawling toward her.

"I've got you. I've got you." Once Charlie was back in her arms, she couldn't stop repeating it. "I've got you."

They were in the little Central Park. Charlie had found it.

*Or maybe it opened up around her, just for her. You don't belong here. But Charlie does. She's—*

"Shut up shut up shut up," Ana begged herself in a whisper. She made her breath steady itself, smelling the good, pure baby-smell of her daughter. Soon it began to work, and she calmed a little.

She focused on the nearest picnic table a few feet away. Picnic tables existed only in normal, sane places where people—normal, sane, able-fucking-bodied people—went to *fucking picnic.* They were okay.

There was a clear path leading to this area from inside the courtyard park, over there on her nine o'clock. Somehow, she'd just lost it.

And, in fact, on her right, she could even see through the trees to the inner walls of the Deptford. The tree cover wasn't so thick here. Insane to imagine the difference between this and where she had been.

She quickly scanned herself and Charlie for any of those translucent, awful, spidery things. Nothing. Just dirt and a scrape on her arm.

She supposed she could go back and get her chair, then sit here with Charlie and enjoy the afternoon as planned—she probably hadn't even lost that much time, now that she really thought about it—

No. She could see her way out, and she wasn't going to risk losing that even for a moment. She held Charlie in the crook of her arm and scooted herself out of the courtyard.

Something like five minutes later, they emerged.

Ana kept scooting herself away from the trees. She couldn't get far enough. Finally, she rested against the wall of the Deptford.

She stared back at the trees that made the courtyard park. So small. So compact.

Sweat dried on her skin, under her hair, and the winter air made her shiver. The clamminess of her skin made her feel wet all over, and that made sense, because looking at those trees now she felt as if she'd just escaped a giant mouth, one that had sampled her, swished her around, and then allowed her to be spat gently out.

As if he'd been waiting for this moment, the concierge suddenly appeared, asking her what was wrong, was she okay, sounding almost like he meant it—almost, but not quite.

She told him her chair got stuck and she couldn't get it out. He snapped his fingers and another doorman arrived.

She watched the doorman disappear into the trees.

Barely a minute later, she heard the familiar rattle of metal slowly getting louder. The doorman had found her chair. He'd freed it and walked right out of there. Easy as pie. Of course. He probably could've danced his way out.

She hugged Charlie close.

"I won't let anything bad happen to you, Baby Bird," she said.

Then she remembered the way Charlie giggled in the meadow and had to wonder: Had Charlie really thought it was so bad?

## 3

"Reid!"

He turned around. For a split second, he didn't recognize the woman in the wheelchair yelling his name across the lobby.

It was Ana. She was there, with Charlie, talking to the concierge by the doors leading to the courtyard.

"What—" Reid stammered, blinking, coming back to reality. "What's going on? Everything okay?"

But everything was very clearly not okay. Ana seemed incapable of responding. She looked awful. Tear-streaked. Filthy. Mud all over her clothes. Leaves in her hair. Blood running down one arm and staining her lap.

Charlie, on the other hand, seemed completely unbothered.

"Everyone's present and accounted for, Mr. Greene," the concierge said through his ear-to-ear smile. "Unless you need anything further, I'll leave you to tend to your wife."

He walked back to the desk.

Reid looked at Ana.

"What happened? What's—?"

She squeezed his hand. Hard. "I . . . I got stuck in the fucking, the courtyard thing, I got all turned around and I fell out of my chair and, and, it fucking sucked, it was awful."

"Honey." He sighed. He took Charlie from her.

"Thank you. I'm okay, it was just . . . wait, what are you doing home so early?"

"No, yeah, I left early. I wanted to help clean up and stuff for tomorrow. Boss said I could leave after the guests arrived, so."

"But were you coming from the elevator?"

"Yeah, I went upstairs first. You weren't there, so I came back down."

"Got it." She sounded relieved, uninterested in having any more mysteries for the day. "Can we go back home?"

"Absolutely," he said. "Want me to drive?"

"Yes, please."

She looked so small, so filthy, so broken. For a moment—less than a split second—she disgusted him.

He handed Charlie back to her, casting one furtive eye to the front door and hoping Camilla wouldn't mind that her earring would have to wait another day. Then he got behind Ana's chair and took his family upstairs.

That night, after Ana was bathed, bandaged, and put in bed, he shut himself in the bathroom and searched "NYS involuntary committal" on his phone. He scrolled for a while before guiltily x-ing out of the window.

They were a family. He wasn't going to give up that easily.

# A CITY INTERLUDE—BIZZIE

## 1

Bizzie mainly remembered his time at Rikers like one of those ball dispensers they used for bingo and other church events when he was a kid. Each ball was a sensation. The rattle of the bus on the way there. The stench of shit, of metal, concrete, bleach. The cold, hard floor for a bed. Too many men in a tiny room. Someone coughing. Worries about getting sick. The rattle of the bus on the way back.

Only two constants threaded their way through this staccato jumble.

The first was his desperate need for a fix. That feeling of *pop* as needle punctured skin and everything got quiet. God, he wanted that so bad.

The second was his determination to never fix again.

## 2

The day he was released, he was brought into a little room and an official-looking guy handed him a letter. The letter had already been opened, and it informed Bizzie that his dad had just died of a heart attack. The guy wanted to know if this would affect Bizzie's release—did he have a place to go, would he start fixing again, all those kinds of questions. Bizzie had said no, he wasn't going to fix again. As for a place to go . . .

The guy told Bizzie he could start a new job tonight. It'd be good for him to have something regular and dependable. A schedule, a paycheck.

"What kind of job?"

The guy shrugged. "We have a little placement program with this apartment building off the park. It's cushy. You might even wear a suit, you believe that? *You*?"

## 3

He didn't really even think about the job until he arrived at the Deptford. What was going to be expected of him? The parole guy hadn't said, and Bizzie had forgotten to ask.

He eyed the doormen as he passed. Weird robotic fuckers. Except for the guy behind the desk; he had a Halloween mask smile and was creepy as hell.

Bizzie was directed to an elevator—not the visible one off the main lobby but another one kind of tucked away in a second lobby.

He wasn't told what floor to go to, just that the elevator op would know where to take him. After a quick ride, the elevator lurched to a stop, and the doors opened on a floor.

An old man wearing a silk robe over black silk pants met him in front of the elevator.

"Hello," the man said. "My name is Dogan."

And Bizzie realized what this arrangement might be.

## 4

Bizzie had done sex stuff before. It was fine as long as it was consensual. This would be consensual. Provided it didn't get too weird.

But then, as he helped Bizzie into soft, stretchy designer jeans and a button-down shirt, the old man said, "Don't worry, you're not going to have to do any . . . *sex stuff*."

"I'm not? Then what—?"

The old man laughed. Bizzie couldn't tell how old he was. Sometimes he looked ninety. Sometimes he looked fifty. "I'm a painter! You're going to be one of my subjects, that's all. Nothing scary."

"Oh."

"But first, you're going to be my guest tonight. We're going to a soirée. Do you know what a soirée is?"

"Like a party."

"Precisely!"

"What's the party for?"

The old man's eyes lit up. "It might be somebody's birthday tomorrow."

*Might?* Bizzie almost asked but didn't.

## 5

They took stairs up to another floor, another apartment. A large, luxurious space, but almost completely unfurnished other than the bare necessities. No real furniture other than a random couch and some chairs. The only light came from a few dim lamps and the moonlight coming from windows overlooking the courtyard. Throw some spray paint onto the wall, some trash on the floor, and it'd be no different from any dozen other flats and lofts Bizzie'd partied in.

God, he wanted a fix.

But he wouldn't. Even if it was offered. And he hoped against hope that it wasn't offered. Not in a place like this. A place like this, it was hard to say no.

The old man spoke up from his side. "We call this the pantry."

## 6

Bizzie didn't expect to see someone he recognized.

He saw him across the room. Apparently, Bizzie wasn't the only person with this kind of arrangement: everyone here was either old and rich, or . . . well, like Bizzie. That second group included the guy Bizzie recognized. Shit, what was his name?

He wore a brown suit and hung off the arm of some attractive old woman who almost looked like she coulda been a movie star. What was his name?

It had been a long time since they'd seen each other, but they'd hung out, shot up next to each other on numerous occasions.

Remembering that, the craving came on strong. That puncture. That *pop*. Most people hated needles—hell, even a lot of junkies hated needles—but not Bizzie. For Bizzie, every needle felt like a new line separating the past from the present.

His friend—the fuck was his name?—sat on a couch in the corner of the room. Bizzie's old man talked with some fellow oldsters, so Bizzie wandered over to the couch and sat.

"Shit is weird, huh?" Bizzie asked. There was no answer. He turned to look at his friend. "Do you remember me? I like your suit."

Still no answer. Guy was clearly high on something. Oh well.

Bizzie watched the crowd mingling and chatting. He found himself looking at a dazed young woman with sandy-blond hair pulled into a ponytail. At first, she seemed like the exception—she didn't look like Bizzie or any of his friends. She looked like a fitness freak. Super tall, broad-shouldered, like an Amazon. But the way she was swaying on her feet, the heaviness of her eyelids, she looked just as cracked out as Bizzie's friend.

He turned back to the guy.

"Do you remember me?" No response.

Then, like a bolt from the blue, Bizzie remembered the guy's name.

"Christopher! Right? You were friends with Sussman, yeah?"

Christopher's dull eyes brightened a little at hearing his name. Bizzie brightened, too. Maybe he *did* recognize Bizzie. Maybe the two of them could be actual friends, form a little support unit, help each other out. Bizzie felt the oppressive weight of loneliness he hadn't even really clocked lighten a little. Christopher.

His name was Christopher. And if he didn't want to be friends, maybe he at least knew where Bizzie could find—

Christopher leaned forward, opened his mouth, and emitted a long, thick stream of dark red liquid. It came out in a chunky spurt, like soup from a hose. The gunk splatted onto the hardwood floor, black in the low light.

Bizzie stared at it. That didn't look like normal puke. And it stank like a hot fridge.

Before Bizzie could call for help, someone was already there. That glamorous old woman.

In a flash of movement too fast for Bizzie to comprehend, she dropped to her hands and knees and began drinking the puddle of vomit up from the floor. She made greedy, delighted noises.

"Mmm. Mmm. Mmmm."

Meanwhile, Christopher emitted a weak wheeze, thick and odorous red still dripping from his chin.

Bizzie scrambled up and ran.

## 7

The old man he'd come with, Dogan, his host, his employer, his whatever the fuck, caught him.

"What's wrong? What is it?"

Bizzie couldn't put words together. He was too freaked out. He couldn't stop seeing that woman lapping up that puddle of Christopher from the floor, he couldn't stop hearing those delighted, wet noises.

And then the old lady was *here,* next to them, laughing, wiping at her mouth with a handkerchief.

"Couldn't help myself," she was saying to the old man currently holding on to Bizzie's arms.

"Any good?" the old man asked.

"Nah. Just about rotten. Still. Had to try, right?" She smacked her lips.

The old man chuckled. "Well, I'll get the new one started up." He patted Bizzie's arm in an almost absent-minded gesture of fraternity. "In case you want something fresher."

"What are you waiting for?" the old woman asked. "An invitation?"

"Wh-what are you guys talking about?" Bizzie asked.

Music played from invisible speakers, ambient jazz. Harmless, innocuous shit. Now it sounded loud and lunatic. Insects on fire.

"Hey." The old man turned Bizzie's head to face him. Bizzie jumped at the feeling of fingers on his chin. A smile creased the old man's wide, wrinkled face. "Have you ever seen a Pulitzer Prize? Come. You can see some of my paintings, too. How 'bout that?"

Bizzie was walked into another room. That was fine, as long as it was far away from the music, the blood-smeared woman, the puddle of Christopher.

This room was quieter and empty save for a bed and a bunch of bookcases. Bizzie knew this kind of room. The room of shhhs and whispered pleas and promises to not tell anyone.

The mattress was huge and empty, but the fitted sheet looked clean and soft.

There were trophies on the shelves. The old man stood next to one such display, grinning hugely.

Bizzie couldn't help himself. He got closer. He recognized some of the shapes . . . Could they be the real deal? He was looking at a couple Oscars. Some Emmys. A fucking Grammy.

"We keep some trophies here for people to look at," the old man said. "People enjoy trophies. I won this one." He pointed proudly to a giant, novelty-sized coin with some old-timey dude's face in profile.

Bizzie leaned forward, reading.

"But this is from, like, a hundred years ago."

Hands were on Bizzie's shoulders now, turning him around, facing the old man.

"Relax." The old man leaned forward and kissed Bizzie on the mouth. Bizzie felt relief flood him. Not desire, far from it; but finally, something he understood.

Then the old man's tongue kept going. And going.

Down Bizzie's throat.

It wasn't a tongue, it was a finger. It wasn't a finger, it was a hose. A ventilator tube. A gastric pump.

Then a horrible sensation: pulsing, spewing, something was coming out of that tube and flooding, coating, Bizzie's insides with heat. Thick, awful fluid pumped from the old man into Bizzie.

Bizzie tried to pull away, but—*Oh god!*—the old man's lips were somehow holding on to Bizzie's. Like Velcro. No, stronger. He felt the skin of his lips tugged with resistance from the old man's. A word flashed across his mind: *adhesion.*

Bizzie pulled harder. In his panic, he barely felt the tearing, barely heard the ripping noises as the skin around his own mouth gave way.

He tore his lips off.

There was very little pain. Only that churning, thick liquid in his guts. Like he'd just drunk a gallon of Pepto. He stumbled backward, feeling light-headed, and his legs hit the bed, making him fall, making him realize this wasn't a bed for sleeping.

The old man whispered with soft, purring care into his ear:

"You're so strong. Stop fighting." The old man leaned over him, trailing a light finger over Bizzie's abdomen, a mockery of seduction. "See . . . your innards are starting to liquefy. Just a little for now. But you'll live longer if you don't fight it. You want to live longer, right? It doesn't hurt. It just feels . . . sloshy. Right?"

It did. Sloshy and dizzying and not entirely unpleasant. But his lips burned, the air buzzing against open wounds and raw skin. Had he been doped?

He looked at the old man's face—although he wasn't an old man after all, was he? He was a monster. An obscene host of prickly hairs circled the monster's maw. The monster's tongue came out and collected what remained of Bizzie's lips from those hairs, then the monster spat it to the ground with all the thought of a man spitting watermelon seeds.

"I'm just going to take a little sip, okay? It won't hurt. That's one thing we promise. It will never hurt. You just sit back and relax, and we'll go back out into the party. Then later, I'll paint you."

The old man opened his mouth and a fleshy black tube eased out, veined, segmented as an insect's leg, with a hole at the end like another mouth—

No. Not a mouth.

Like the lumen at the tip of a syringe.

His dear old syringe. Come for him at last.

Bizzie opened wide and the tube entered him with slick ease.

He thought of that puncture. *Pop.*

His eyes rolled away and drifted to the ceiling.

A mural, stretched almost wall to wall. Dark, made of browns and tans and blacks and red, so it took a little while to really see.

It was of a knot of flesh: naked men and women, tangled together. Like an orgy but without any sense of eroticism. No sexual energy, only a sense of rapture. Worship.

A massive tick-like creature loomed over the horizon, its great mouth open to the sky. From its maw emerged dozens upon dozens of appendages, each entering a throat of a member of the naked horde.

Bizzie closed his eyes and thought of nice things. Like drinking sodas on the boardwalk.

The last remaining lottery balls of his life rattled and bounced inside their cage and Bizzie's ruined lips formed a smile around the straw.

# PART FOUR

## BIRTHDAY

PARTY

# 1

All things considered, Ana thought she was doing a great job welcoming people into her apartment, pretending like things were normal.

She knew about pain fog and sleep-deprivation fog, but the fog through which she moved today was entirely new. It was *unreality* fog. Nothing felt real.

How was this all happening after yesterday's events? Who were these people anyway?

With one exception, they were all Brooklyn playground parents. Though technically that meant they were Reid, Ana, and Charlie's friends, *really* they were Reid and Charlie's, because Ana had rarely joined them at the playground or other social events. To them, she was just Charlie's mom or Reid's wife or, worse, their one "friend in a wheelchair."

The phone—a golden-and-ivory landline receiver in the kitchen they often forgot existed—alerted them of their guests whenever they checked in downstairs. Kacey and Steve arrived first, with three-year-old Eliot and thirteen-month-old Donna in tow. Then came Matthew and Brian (with a bottle of moderately priced scotch and tales of a babysitter because Marlena was too cranky). Then Felix and Audra (with four-year-old Lissa). Mark and Jessica (with two-year-old Ezra). Derek (whose wife, Erin, couldn't be there, but whose fifteen-month-old, Gemma, was along for the festivities). Bethany (whose wife, Xanthe, couldn't be there, but whose six-month-old, Liam, could be).

The one exception was 470-month-old Emma Bradley, author of the *Blood Rink* series. In her most recent email apologizing for her slow progress, Ana had found herself inviting Emma to the party, even though Emma was, to put it mildly, awkward as fuck.

Ana had considered inviting other friends from her non-mom life. Dance friends, gym friends. She'd texted Georgia several times now, with no response. She took Georgia's silence as a sign that she'd been right not to reach out to anyone else—they'd all moved on. Probably for the best. Especially given how unreal Ana felt.

Only one moment seemed to honor the strangeness of her experiences lately. When little Eliot first burst through the door, demanding to "see birthday baby" he stopped, tilted his head to the side, and said, "Mama, I don't like this music." Kacey ignored him, working on his jacket zipper, but Ana noticed.

No music was playing.

Ana filed that away as worth remembering.

The rest of the party quickly became a blur of loud adults and louder children, and that's why Ana allowed herself to have that first beer.

## 2

She'd stopped drinking while they were trying to get pregnant, then continued not drinking during the pregnancy, and after her injury she couldn't drink because of various medications. It had been years since she'd had a beer.

She took her time nursing it, and for the first hour, it helped with that pervasive feeling of unreality. It wasn't just that she was still shocked from the courtyard; she was also realizing how unsocialized she'd been. It had been so long since she'd been around so many humans at once.

People seemed to treat her in two different ways, and maybe it was a mark of the books she read to Charlie that she thought of them, irrespective of gender, as Mama Bears and Papa Bears. The Mama Bears were too soft, either ignoring Ana, looking past her, over her, trying desperately to avoid mentioning the apparently contagious fact that she was in a wheelchair, or treating her like a child herself. "Oh, let me get that for you, Ana." "Here, I'll do it, Ana." The Papa Bears were too hard. "You are so fucking brave, Ana. You're just such a badass." "I bet PT really sucks, huh? My grandma had to go through that after she broke her hip. Brutal stuff." "Do you mind if I just scooch your chair over so I can get by? No, it's okay, I'll just push it real quick. There we go."

Ana swallowed it all. The beer was useful lubricant. That's why it was there, right? As every third person at the party joked, first birthday parties were really for the parents, after all.

She even allowed herself to crack open a second.

Eventually, Ana noticed she was sitting amongst a knot of all the other mothers. *Funny how every party always winds up segregating itself by gender,* she thought.

The conversation turned to momstuff.

First, they began cataloging their children's various developmental milestones. Ana kept mostly quiet because she didn't want to offer how Charlie had developed from being miserable to being a zombie since they moved here.

Then came the gleeful discussion of births and birth recoveries, spoken in low tones like delicious secrets kept through the ages. Ana, just buzzed enough now, couldn't stop herself from contributing.

When Bethany mentioned how annoying her post-birth hemorrhoids still were, Ana laughed and said just be glad your husband didn't have to wipe your ass for weeks before you could handle the logistics.

When Kacey complained about how boring breastfeeding could be, Ana interjected with a grin, "I know, it's like you're stuck sitting in the same spot forever, right?"

Kacey went ashen, and Ana assured her she was just joking. Then she confessed she hadn't had the option to breastfeed because of the medications she'd had to take, but, if you thought breastfeeding is boring, just be glad you didn't have to read up on ways to avoid pressure sores from sitting too long. Weird how the mommy blogs left that out, huh?

Maybe she was being cruel, but it came from a genuine attempt to lighten the mood. She spared them the worst details. What it was like spending most of those postpartum months in either shrieking agony or numb misery, sobbing, begging for answers from an indifferent universe.

Also, she was surprised to find, every time she made things awkward, she began to feel a little more real again. She remembered who she was, what she'd survived. Even the incident in the courtyard (whenever it snuck into her mind) took on an air of triumph. She found herself tasting pride for the first time in a year.

That said, she suspected none of the other moms minded when eventually Emma stole Ana away to breathlessly monologue about her ideas for the next installment of *Blood Rink*.

## 3

A little later, a hand fell on Ana's shoulder, and she almost yelped.

Brian leaned down to whisper: "Reid's in the kitchen."

For a moment, Ana didn't know why that was important. Then she remembered.

She handed Charlie off to the nearest set of eager hands and then made her way through the guests.

Reid stood before the cake, holding matches. It was a chocolate-frosted yellow sponge cake festooned with baby birds. Ana had put the finishing touches on it this morning.

"You wanna do the honors, or should I?" he asked.

"It's all you," she said, surprised at the smile spreading across her face.

He lit the match, then touched it to the big waxy *1* stuck in the middle.

Reid's eyes glistened. "That smell always makes me think of my mom, you know? That match smell. All those damn holidays with candles. I wish she was here to celebrate."

She took his hand.

"Me, too."

He looked at her. "We've been through a fucking lot, Ana."

"Yes, we have."

A moment passed between them. They basked in the candle's glow, breathing together, two mountain climbers finding a place to rest against the howling winds of impossible heights. For that moment, all the secrets they kept from each other didn't matter. Love made everything make sense again.

They brought out the cake. Charlie sat in Matthew's lap by the dining room table, being pestered by little Eliot. She'd spent the entire party uninterested and distant, but when the lights were turned off and the cake came out of the kitchen, glowing in the darkness, held aloft by her mom, guided by her father, Charlie's eyes lit up.

She ate her piece with gusto, smashing her little hands against her face trying to cram more buttercream richness into her mouth. She'd been a little zombie for days, but whatever was going on couldn't compete with the awesome power of sugar.

Next, Reid brought out his guitar and offered to the group his present for the baby of the hour.

"I've been trying to think of a clever title," he said, blushing in that way he often did the moments before losing himself in a performance, "but every title I came up with, I just didn't like as much as what I was calling this song as I was writing it. So, whatever, here it is. It's called 'Bird's Song.'"

And it was good.

Really good.

It brought tears to Ana's eyes. With its lyrical refrain of "Know you're home" (or was it "Know your home"?). Love for Reid burned in her chest.

Reid also knew he had written something special (although, in a way, he thought the song had already had its premiere). It was a song he knew he would play for Charlie at every step of her life, delighting in her embarrassment at her corny old dad with his cheesy guitar.

It was a song that promised a future full of memories.

## 4

It was Kacey's idea to go up on the roof.

Little Eliot, excited by Reid's song, had declared over the din of adults and children than he wanted to do a birthday dance for Charlie. The adults all stopped to watch as Eliot spasmed and gyrated like a tiny pagan currying favor with an easily pleased deity. Behind the performance, the curtains stood open, revealing the city beyond.

Eventually—after pouring her fourth plastic cup of white wine—Kacey scooted Eliot away. "That's enough, bud." Then, as if noticing it for the first time, she gestured toward the window. "Ugh! This view! My god, you guys are so lucky!"

Felix, overseeing the knot of children, chimed in. "This building really *is* awesome, you guys."

Kacey's eyes glimmered with chardonnay. "When do we get the full tour?"

Ana expected Reid to jump at the opportunity, but he seemed to shrink.

"Oh, I don't know," he said, opening his own beer. "It's not that exciting. I don't want us tromping around, upsetting the one-percenters, you know?"

A chorus of disappointed *aww*s rose in response.

"Trust me," Reid said, indicating the window, "the view is the best part."

What was this about? Ana wondered. Why was he suddenly so shy?

"The view kicks ass." Derek picked up Gemma and joined Kacey at the window.

"Yeah," Gemma said excitedly. "Ass."

Steve concurred through a mouthful of brie. "The city just looks so . . . spread out from here. Like it's all yours."

"Yeah," Reid said. He walked over to where Charlie sat quietly among the scrum of infants. He picked her up and popped her on his hip so he could keep drinking his beer. "Back in the day, when you stood on the roof, you would get a three-sixty view of the whole damn island."

Kacey gasped and almost choked on her drink. "Wait, is there roof access? Can we go up there?!"

"I want to see!" Audra chimed in.

"Also," Jessica said in a stage whisper, "I'd *kill* to smoke a cigarette."

"Oh my god, me, too," Kacey said, no pretense of lowering her voice. "Ana, don't you want a smoke?"

Ana's face caught fire, blood boiling like magma.

Reid answered for her: "Oh, um, it's actually a staircase to get up to the roof, so."

"So you need working legs to get there," Ana said, hoping she sounded breezy and fun and not at all bitter.

After another excruciating pause, Kacey threw an arm up in the air.

"Who cares! We could carry you up! Two on each side, like a queen!"

"Yeah!" Audra added.

Ana smiled in spite of herself at the unexpectedly tempting offer. "No, no, seriously, that's okay. Seriously. And someone needs to stay with the kids—we don't wanna take *them* up to the roof, right?"

Derek, who'd just put Gemma back down with the squealing, squirming kids, protested. "We don't want to leave you alone!"

"It's okay. I gotta start picking things up and making sure the birthday girl is ready for her sugar crash—"

The parents continued their performative protest. Then a meek, awkward voice cut through the chatter: "I'll stay here with her."

Emma.

She didn't like heights, she explained. They made her think scary thoughts.

"Great," Ana said.

The crowd of adults disappeared with comic swiftness. Reid left last, exchanging a look with Ana that said, *This wasn't my idea.*

She stuck her tongue out at him. *Don't act like you don't love it.*

"Where's Momma and Dadda going?" little Lissa asked, a mixture of terror and confusion on her face.

Ana gave her a reassuring smile. "They're just running upstairs for a sec. They'll be right back. Hey, how's about we play with—"

Emma materialized next to her. "What did you think about Diabolique's conversion to Roman Catholicism and vampire hunting? I feel like it's going to open things up to be even sexier between her and Mathilde, but I hope it's not too controversial. I mean, I want it to push some buttons, but not make people *mad,* you know? Also? I've been doing a lot of reading lately about women's basketball leagues and, I don't know, maybe Claudia needs to fall into a new sport or . . ."

Ana tried to smile while she chugged the rest of her beer.

A minute or so later, her bladder announced, without any warning, that it was ready to burst.

*You don't own beer, you rent it.* Some boyfriend or other had said that in college. She hadn't thought of it in ages, but yikes did it prove to be true.

"Sorry, Emma, I gotta pee, can you watch them real quick? I'll be right back."

"Sure," Emma said. Then something in her face changed. "You don't . . . need help, do you? Because . . . I'll help you if you want. Or need."

Unexpectedly, Ana found herself grinning at that. At Emma's sincere weirdness (or was it weird sincerity?). Emma had been the first person at this party to just *ask* what Ana would like. Ana had no doubt Emma would have helped if—and only if—Ana had said yes. She might have been an odd duck, but at least she wasn't putting on an act. As far as Emma was concerned, Ana's paraplegia was no weirder than the hundred other weird things bouncing around in her brain.

"Nah," Ana said. "I got this."

She quickly wheeled herself out of the room and soon sat on the toilet, in blissful silence, alone.

She realized she was humming Reid's song. She truly loved it. She'd be sure to tell him that when he got back.

This felt real. This felt like a life she'd known.

When the screams began in the other room, Ana's immediate thought was: *This does, too.*

# ROOFTOP

## 1

Ana had been right: Reid *didn't* want to show everyone around the building. Now that he worked for Camilla, he found his almost childlike glee about the place had been replaced with a sense of stewardship. Acting as a sort of tour guide felt crass, cheap.

Like Ana, Reid had also been gripped by a strong sense of unreality this morning. As they finished setting up the apartment—which included him surreptitiously dumping their remaining bags of diatomaceous earth down the garbage chute—he thought, *What are we doing? Can Ana handle this? Why do we care about these people anyway?*

However, as Reid and his guests scaled the staircase leading to the rooftop entrance, some of that giddy thrill returned. He hadn't been up here yet. It felt like today was *his* birthday and he was opening up a present. *This is my home. This is mine.*

*Know you're home.*

They stepped out into the bright winter sun, and everyone gave a very satisfying gasp.

## 2

The roof of the Deptford was almost as lovely as the view itself. There were intermittent peaks from the gables, and a wrought iron waist-high railing stretched around the perimeter. A decorative combination of slate and concrete sparkled in the sunlight and showed no evidence of age.

At one point, there had been a small farm up here, with a chicken coop and a vegetable garden. Nowadays the roof was decorative, with benches and small trellised huts that reminded Reid of sukkahs. In a few spots, wildflowers grew in wooden troughs.

Lampposts, of the same period and design as those throughout Central Park, also dotted the rooftop landscape. It was eminently relaxing. All around them: New York City lay hazy under the bright blue sky. The sounds of traffic and city life played like an homage at their feet.

Kacey, who seemed to have become more drunk with the barely elevated atmosphere, shrieked, "We should have barbecues up here!"

Her husband, Steve, turned to Brian. "You kidding? We could have football games up here! This is huge!"

Brian rolled his eyes. "Yeah, except for that giant fucking hole in the center. But, look, Matthew!" Brian got close to the inner edge of the roof and looked down. "Wow, the courtyard kinda looks like Central Park from up here!"

"I can't believe there's so much green in the winter!" Matthew responded.

"Reid." Audra pulled out a yellow box of American Spirits and lit up. "This is *insane.* Like, where's the infinity pool?"

"Oh my god," Jessica said. "You know what you should do? Set up an Instagram account for this place! Document the inside for us peasants!"

Reid's stomach cramped in disgust.

"Look at those gargoyles!" someone else yelled, peering down on the street side. "They look like they're ready to eat everyone on the sidewalk from up here!"

"Whoa, don't get too close," Reid cautioned, a bit more urgency in his voice than he'd intended. "People have fallen off this thing. It's happened before." They all turned to look at him, suddenly children on a field trip, eager eyes and gaping mouths. Reid smiled. "It's true. In fact . . . you guys ever heard of the Plummet of 1919? It's pretty infamous."

They oohed and chattered, excited for a story.

Rather than tell them, Reid surprised them by shoving Brian over the edge first.

Then Steve. Then Kacey. Then Matthew. He pushed each in turn, splat, splat spl—

He shook his head. Jesus, where did *that* fantasy come from?

His guests were still staring at him, expectantly. He laughed, a bit disturbed—"Sorry, um . . ."—but before he could continue, something caught his eye elsewhere on the roof.

Someone stood on the roof inside one of the shaded huts, out of the sun, looking out at the city. A ripple of gooseflesh sped across him as he recognized who it was.

"Just a sec," he told the group, and jogged over.

"Hello there," Winston Terry said as Reid approached. "Nice day for some roof time."

"We're allowed to be up here, right?"

Long pause.

"Course you are, brother. You live here, too. Hey, today's the big day, huh? How's the old baby doing?"

"Great! I . . . I played her my song. I think she really liked it."

"Well, that's the whole game right there, innit."

"I just wanted to say thanks again. For, y'know, the inspiration."

"Anytime, mate . . . anytime . . ."

Winston stared past Reid to the cityscape beyond.

The darkness in the little hut was thicker than Reid would have thought. He couldn't see the back of it, like it was a drainpipe leading back into the building or something. Yet another of the Deptford's many mysteries.

"Birthdays always make *me* a bit blue," Winston said. "Time passing, yeah? It's merciless."

Before Reid could respond to that, his eyes adjusted enough to the gloom of the hut and he noticed Winston wasn't alone.

Camilla stood just behind him, floating up to the surface of the darkness like a drowned body in a midnight lake.

"*Golubchik.*"

Reid actually jumped a little. "Oh, god, hi, sorry, I didn't see you there!"

She and Winston both stared past Reid at the city beyond.

"Is everything . . . okay?" Reid asked.

"Late night last night, *golubchik.*"

Even in the shadows, neither of them looked tired, though. Their eyes looked brighter. Refreshed. Avid. Almost . . . younger.

Then Kacey and Audra staggered up to Reid, gibbering excitedly.

"Reeeeid!" they intoned together, dissonant and insane.

"You didn't finish your story!" Audra whined. "About the Plumbing or something."

Reid spun to face them, then glanced back at the shaded hut to confirm he hadn't hallucinated Camilla. With an uncanny, almost mechanical smoothness, Winston receded into the shadows behind her.

"Hope you're having fun," Camilla said. Was she about to disappear, too?

"Oh, um, it's—" Reid turned to look at his friends, then back at Camilla, disoriented.

Steve jogged up to them. "Hey, Reid, can we take pictures? I want to get a close-up of one of those gargoyles!"

"Can you take us to any other floors?" Kacey begged. "We wanna see more inside!"

"Just a fucking second!" Reid heard himself snap, shrugging Kacey's hands off his shoulders. "Stop acting like fucking tourists! Jesus Christ! You're embarrassing!"

A beat of silence. Steve stopped few feet away, stranded in an awkward no-man's-land.

"Okay . . ." Kacey said, eyes wide and hurt.

Reid gave a high, winded laugh. "Come on, I'm joking! Um. Hey! This is Camilla Varné. She lives here! She's actually my boss now! Maybe she looks familiar? She's a movie star, you know."

Camilla floated up a little closer from the shadows, as if beckoned. She offered a polite and patient smile.

Kacey, Audra, and Steve looked at Reid skeptically.

"You . . . work for her?" Steve said, joining his wife.

"I thought you worked for those lawyers," Kacey said.

A fake smile stretched Reid's skin. "Nah, I quit that shitty job. I'm Miss Varné's personal assistant now."

"It's true." Camilla's velvety voice sounded as smooth as the shadows that draped her. "He's very helpful."

"Oh," Kacey said. It was clear Reid's brusqueness still stung. "Well . . . congrats."

Reid shook his head. "Sorry, Camilla, I should get back to—"

"Of course. Lovely to meet you," Camilla said, then retreated into the darkness.

"I'll look you up on IMDb!" Kacey proclaimed.

Reid escorted them back to the group, face burning.

"Seriously," he said as they walked, "I was just playing before. Sorry. It sounded funnier in my head."

"When did you quit your job?" Audra asked.

"Doesn't matter. Hey, you guys wanted to see the building, right? I can totally make that happen!"

Now they were back with the rest of the group. Only Kacey, Steve, and Audra knew of his little outburst, so he played it cool. Hopefully, Steve and Audra weren't too offended, and Kacey seemed drunk enough that she'd get distracted by another emotion soon enough.

He didn't want to take everybody on a tour, but maybe the offer would dissipate any remaining tension. He could take them down the staircase to a couple of floors just to give them a taste, then back up to their apartment and wrap things up.

*Or take them down to the basement, see if the building lets them find their way back to the elevator.*

He started to ask them to follow him when the door to the roof burst open.

It was Emma what's-her-face, Ana's weird author friend, pale and sweating.

"Come help!" she gasped. "Hurry!"

# 3

The apartment was a cyclone of crying children, each feeding off the others' distress. But as far as Ana was concerned, *she* had the most reason to be losing her mind right now.

*Did I really see that?*

She had Charlie in her lap. Charlie was the one kid not freaking out. She might've even been grinning.

The other kids—Donna, Eliot, Lissa, Ezra, Gemma, and Liam—squalled on the floor near her wheels.

*Did I really just see Charlie—*

Now the rest of the party entered the apartment. The adults began freaking out, too; the cyclone grew. Ana retreated farther, becoming as detached as the daughter on her lap.

"What happened?! What's going on?" a parent asked, scooping up a child. All the children were being scooped up. It had gone from party to crime scene in an instant.

"It's okay," Ana said distantly. "Everything's okay. Charlie just . . ."

*Say it.*

*No, it's impossible, there's no way—*

"She just what?!"

"Charlie just . . . bit Eliot. That's all. It's okay. Just a little excitement. Too much sugar."

*Only, it wasn't just a bite, was it?*

"Oh my god!" Kacey exclaimed, inspecting the wound on her toddler's neck. Eliot clung to his mother, wailing.

"That's a *bite*?!" Steve gagged.

"Yeah, I . . ." Ana trailed off. Kacey sobbed over her baby, demanding a bandage, disinfectant, anything, everything. Reid rushed to provide it.

The wound on Eliot's neck looked more like a cigarette burn than a bite. A round, rough, raw circle of outraged flesh—only, with a dark, seeping hole of a puncture wound in the center.

"Oh, baby," Kacey cooed over Eliot's wails. "Oh, sweetie, *how did this happen*?!"

Ana could have answered that. She knew how it happened, no matter how her brain tried to keep the image away.

In fact, she'd helped cause the injury.

She'd pulled Charlie's face off Eliot's neck and ripped that ragged wheel of skin along with it.

## 4

The party cleared out quickly. As soon as the last guest left, Ana wheeled for her still-filthy coat.

"We need to take her to the doctor," Ana said. "Now."

Reid held Charlie in his hands as if Ana had handed him some inscrutable work of art.

"Why'd you do it, Baby Bird?" he asked Charlie. Charlie stared back at him with her dull, disinterested eyes.

"Reid!" Ana snapped.

"Yeah, yeah," he said. "I just don't understand what happened. She bit that kid? Like, she just went up and bit him?"

Ana went through it again. She'd heard screaming while she was in the bathroom. She came out to find Charlie, her face buried in Eliot's upper shoulder, Eliot shrieking, the other kids shrieking, Emma shrieking. Ana thought it had been a fight, that maybe Charlie had gone a little sugar-mad. But then she pulled Charlie away and . . .

"She's not acting normal. *It* wasn't normal." That was the only way Ana could conclude her story.

"Do you think they can see us for an appointment?"

"They'd fucking better."

She held Charlie while Reid got into his own winter gear.

"Do you want to carry her downstairs?" he asked. "Or should I?"

"You do it," she said, eager to have Charlie away from her. "I'll call the doctor while . . ." Then she remembered—amazing how she could forget sometimes, even a year in—that she couldn't wheel herself and hold a phone to her face at the same time.

Thankfully, Reid didn't miss a beat. "I'll call, it's okay."

"Thanks."

*I just don't want to feel her body against mine,* she didn't say.

There were a lot of things she didn't say.

Like how she could have sworn, when she pulled Charlie off Eliot, that Charlie's lips latched onto his skin like Velcro.

Or like how Ana was almost entirely sure something had been coming out of Charlie's mouth and into the wound she'd made, something lightning fast and almost . . . insectile.

# PRECIPICE

## 1

Miracle of miracles, Dr. Bronson could squeeze Charlie in. He even moved their already-scheduled first-year exam up. "Not much of a birthday present," he said, "but you caught me on a slow day."

Miracle of miracles.

Unfortunately, Bronson wasn't much help.

Sure, Charlie's temperature was a little low, but they'd just rushed in from the cold. Sure, it was a little weird she's becoming a picky eater, but it happens and it's just a phase. And, yes, she definitely seemed out of it, but she also experienced her first real sugar crash—and before you point out, again, that she's been like this for a week, Mrs. Greene, I've made a note. It could still just be the stress of the move. Or teething. Or any number of other culprits. We'll simply have to continue to monitor; nothing seems *empirically* wrong. In fact, look at how she didn't even flinch when we gave her her shots! This is one tough kid!

Ana knew she sounded lunatic—like one of Those Parents—but she didn't care. She begged Bronson to keep looking in her mouth for anything strange, palpate her chest, feel for something foreign. She stopped just short of demanding x-rays or an ultrasound because she saw how Reid was looking at her.

Of course, she refused to say exactly *what* she wanted Bronson to find.

So, after all that rushing, all that panic:

"Deep breaths. You've got yourself a healthy one-year-old. Happy birthday, Charlie. And happy birthday, Mom and Dad. I mean, the first birthday really is for you guys, when you think about it."

## 2

The late-afternoon sun hung above the highest buildings of the skyline, blasting orange light into the cab's back seat and giving Reid a headache. Christ, what an exhausting day this turned out to be.

Charlie, in her car carrier at Reid's feet, stared at nothing, wearing an expression far too mature for her face.

*What's going on, Baby Bird?* he wondered. For some reason, her stoic reception of her one-year inoculations unnerved him. He had been dreading that.

A cell phone rang, snapping him out of his thoughts.

Ana pulled hers out of her jacket pocket. When she saw who it was she made a sound, half sigh, half sob.

"Fuck. It's Kacey."

"Oh god, don't answer—"

But she did.

Reid could hear the angry voice on the other end. He could imagine what was being said: the same words he'd probably be shouting if his own kid had been bitten at a birthday party.

Ana tried to cut in. "I'm . . . I know, I'm so— . . . I'm sorry— . . . We're—"

She suddenly became pale. "Oh my god . . ."

"What is it?" Reid asked, stomach in a slow nosedive.

Ana waved her hand to say, *Not yet, Reid.*

"Look, stop, stop," she urged into the phone. "Just a second. We're coming from the doctor's right now. He said Charlie was fine, so I don't think— . . . No, but maybe it's unrelat—"

"Is something wrong with Eliot?"

Ana opened her mouth to respond to Reid, but the voice in her ear caught her attention first.

"Yeah, that was Reid. Like I said, we're in a car coming back from the d— . . . What is *that* supposed to mean? He—?"

She stabbed Reid with her eyes. His stomach sank faster. He felt himself grow suddenly hot.

"Look," Ana said into the phone, "I know you're upset, but you don't have t—"

She listened. Anger hardened her face. No, not anger. Rage. It actually made Reid a little giddy seeing her get so furious.

"Just take care of your kid, and we'll take care of ours. Okay? Leave my fucking husband out of it. Thanks."

She hung up.

They sat in one of those plastic chunks of time that might have been a few seconds, might have been a few months. Finally, Reid asked:

"What's . . . ?"

"Eliot's sick," Ana said sharply. "He's got a really sudden high fever. Says he's in a lot of pain. Kacey's saying it's Charlie's fault, that Charlie did something to him."

Ana stared straight ahead. They headed up Broadway, only a few minutes away from the Deptford. Mostly stop-and-start traffic at this point.

Charlie made a noise, and their eyes whipped to her, like they thought a bomb was about to go off. Nothing happened; Charlie continued to just stare at nothing.

Reid swallowed. He'd have to ask sooner or later. Might as well just do it now.

"What else did she say?"

Ana breathed a slow, steady stream out of her nose. Made a show of putting her phone back in her jacket pocket.

"She also said you were a dick to her on the roof."

"What?"

"She said, 'He was a real dick to us today. Just because he quit his job to work for movie stars doesn't mean he can treat the rest of us like shit.'"

*Oh, that fucking wine-drunk cunt.*

He gave a wheezy, unconvincing laugh.

"That's . . . Jesus, what is she . . . even talking about . . . ?"

"I'm wondering the same thing."

She looked at him, cold and flat. Reid couldn't take it and looked away, his face burning. He met the eyes of the driver watching the drama in the rearview mirror.

"You wanna pay attention to the fucking road?"

## 3

"So you've been lying to me for how long?"

She didn't sound upset. Which, of course, made it worse.

They sat around their kitchen table. Charlie had some untouched mac and cheese in front of her, which had been prepared in silence after they got back. Besides pulling answers from Reid, Ana tried to get Charlie to take a bite—she hadn't had anything since her cake a million years ago.

After enough silence had spooled out, Reid told her everything. He debated keeping the lie going, was in fact convinced he could, but decided it was more effort than it was worth.

"Like a week. Last Friday."

"A week."

"I didn't plan on it! It just . . . I knew you'd be upset."

"If you knew I'd be upset, that means you knew you were doing something I'd be upset about."

He blinked, no response. That was pure Wife Logic: unsparing, withering . . . airtight.

"And why won't you fucking eat?!" she suddenly snapped at Charlie.

"Hey, hey." Reid took over with the spoon, having equally little luck.

Ana moved away from the table. She ran her hands through her hair. "Look. Reid. I'm happy you quit, okay? You hated that job. And I love your music, you know that. That song you played today was beautiful. I have always told you I'd support it if you wanted to pursue your music full-time." For the briefest of seconds, he thought that'd be it. "But—"

"I knew there'd be a 'but.'"

"Of *course* there's a fucking but! You lied to me! You didn't let me in on a huge decision!"

"There wasn't a decision, it just happened!"

"There was absolutely a *decision* when you *decided* not to tell me. And, like, what do we do about money now? My audio stuff alone won't—"

"I'm getting paid, Ana. Jesus, it's fine! We're gonna be fine!"

"Great. And how much are you getting paid? How often? Are taxes being taken out? Are there benefits? I'm not making enough to get SAG health insurance yet. Did you forget you were getting health insurance from the firm? Are we on COBRA now? What about our savings? School for Charlie?"

"I—*we* will figure all that out! Jesus!" He felt overheated. He suddenly understood that hack comedian pantomime of tugging on your collar when you're in trouble.

"Maybe I could take on a few more audiobooks, but I can't even count on you to fix my fucking booth, so we're gonna have to call someone to come and repair it—"

"I will fix your booth! I'll call Home Depot right now!"

"Do you not understand how quickly money disappears? We barely have any savings left and things happen. Emergencies. Moving expenses—"

Reid had joked about record-scratch moments in the past: where the needle suddenly skips the groove and everything screeches into silence. This was one such moment, but there was nothing funny about it.

"Moving expenses? What are you talking about?"

Now it was her turn to squirm. "We . . . we can't live here forever, Reid."

"What do you mean?"

"Charlie's going to grow up, remember? Like, physically get bigger and need more space?"

"There's plenty of room here, Ana."

"And, I don't know . . ." She dropped her voice to an almost whisper. "Can't you feel how weird things are here?"

"Weird."

"I don't like this place, Reid. I . . . I feel like I'm losing my mind here. It's awful."

She bit back the urge to tell him about the courtyard. Her dreams.

Meanwhile, he flashed on the basement. The rooftop.

Charlie sat in her chair, staring into space.

Then Reid dropped the spoon onto the kitchen table harder than it needed. It gave an outraged clatter. He got up and moved around the kitchen with manic aimlessness.

"See, *that's* what this really comes down to. That's why I didn't say anything."

Now it was her turn to ask him what he meant by that.

"I really don't want to say it, Ana."

"Say it. What are you talking about?"

It was a dare. He stopped himself. Took a deep breath.

"Look," he said slowly. "We're both stressed. Our sleep schedules have been fucked. You know how you get when things are bad."

"How do I 'get'?"

"Ana."

"Jesus, Reid! Fucking say it—!"

He kept his voice infuriatingly calm. "Do you have any idea what you were like at the doctor's? Or in the hallway the other day? Or after the courtyard? It's like, every day I come home from work and, *What new disaster is waiting for me?*"

"That's really rich considering *you haven't even been fucking coming home from work*."

"Okay, great, act like I'm the problem here. Let's just keep pretending like things don't get really fucking scary when *you* get pushed too far. Like that one night didn't hap—"

He stopped himself.

But there it was.

They stared at each other, waiting to see who was brave enough to finally drag that conversation into the light.

Before that could happen, there was a knock on their front door.

"Ignore it," Ana said, eyes filling with frustrated tears. "Please."

Another knock.

Reid straightened his spine and said, almost cheerily, "No."

He moved past her and opened the front door.

Ana stayed where she was. She heard an unfamiliar, vaguely Eastern European voice come from just beyond their threshold.

"Reid, *golubchik,* I'm *so sorry* to bother. I hope the birthday girl is doing well."

## 4

Camilla left a moment later, but in that short time, both Reid and Ana realized they stood at the edge of something. The sort of night where the wrong thing is said and everything changes.

Reid shrugged on his jacket.

"I'll be back in like an hour," he said. "Then we can keep talking."

Ana hadn't moved from the kitchen. "So this is how it's going to be? She's just gonna come down at all hours to give you tasks, and you'll jump to it?"

"Which is it, Ana, do you want me to have paid work or not?"

"*Is* it paid? Have you even gotten a paycheck? I mean, what kind of arrangement do you have with this woman?"

"Jesus. Are you jealous?"

"I'm curious about your fucking job. I'm your wife!"

"I don't know what to tell you, Ana. You've got all the information you need. I have to run down to the jeweler's and pick up an earring for her. Okay?"

"But why now? Why does she need it *now*?"

"Did you hear me? Do you want me to invite her back in? She said she was sorry to ask, so . . . !" He spread his hands out and then let them slap against his thighs. "If you hadn't gotten lost in the fucking courtyard, I could've done this yesterday." He stopped. Reassessed. "I'm sorry. That was shitty of me."

She looked at her hands. "Kacey was right, you *are* a dick."

That was bait. Reid decided not to take it.

"I will be right back. I need a fucking breather anyway."

He headed for the door before he could stop himself.

As he rode the elevator down, the day replayed over and over in his head. How unfair Ana was being. How unfair Charlie was being. How perfect the timing had been for Camilla to give him an excuse to take a break. This was all so fucked up. He stepped out of the building and onto the sidewalk, deep in thought. He was about to head toward Columbus when—

"Ey! Reid!"

A familiar voice, slurred and strident, sent a palpable chill through him.

No, couldn't be . . .

"Yeah, I see you, you frickin' sneak!"

There in the usual small crowd of tourists and picture takers, pointing right at him . . . was Frank.

# PUSHOVER

## 1

Frank wasn't much of a beer drinker—highballs and wine, sure, the sweeter the better—but today, he was. It felt appropriate. His dad had liked beer, and Frank had always wanted to kill his dad. So today, Frank spent most of the day perched at the bar of O'Donoghue's Pub on Seventy-Second and Broadway, downing pint after pint.

Frank's buddy from the post office had gotten back to him last night. When Frank learned where Mr. and Mrs. Fancyass, he of the eminently punchable face, she of the wheelchair and the tight body that was undoubtedly plumping up at rapid speed, lived now—not in Iowa or wherever they said, but the *frickin' Deptford*!—Frank fumed all night, and then, bright and early this morning, stormed outta his house and onto a train. He didn't know what he was going to do, just that he was going to confront those lying, lease-breaking frickin' scumbags.

When he got to the luxury building, he looked up, up, up, feeling the eyes of the gargoyles looking down. He looked at the strange doormen waiting outside the black wrought iron gates. Frank was an old-school New Yorker who'd worked in construction, so he knew a bit about the history of this building, how people had tended to disappear back in the day. Maybe that was why he felt a nervous rumble in his gut being here.

Or maybe it was something even simpler. This goddamn frickin' building made him feel small. He hated feeling small. His pops had been small. A pushover.

Then Frank noticed people about Ana and Reid's age going into the building, bringing kids about the same age as that little maggot who'd pissed on his floors.

They *were* here. Had to be. Probably throwing some sort of fancyass party. Inviting fancyass friends to ooh and ahh, this place is so much better than your last place, where your disgusting landlord made everything so working-class, so *Brooklyn*.

Frank decided he was going to go get a drink and come up with a plan. He walked over to Broadway, found a bar not crawling with other fancyasses having fancyass brunches, ordered some brews, and nursed his aggrievements.

It was an impressive list. After Marla had taken her cottage cheese ass and left him, his resentment at the world grew. Tucker knew. Tucker spoke for men like him, men who the world was trying to break down, make weak and apologetic for existing.

They day grew late. One more beer. Frank swallowed it with a grimace, pushed himself off his barstool, left just enough cash to cover the beers—didn't need a frickin' tip to pour—and stumbled back to the Deptford. He didn't know what he was gonna do next, but he knew someone was gonna get hurt.

And, would you look at that? Just as he approached the Deptford, Mr. Fancy-ass himself was walking out.

Sometimes the universe played ball.

Frank felt his hands curl up into fists.

Time to frickin' push back.

## 2

"Hey, Frank." Reid sighed, annoyed, as if he'd expected to run into him. "Can't really talk."

He tried to keep walking, but Frank got in his way.

"So you're a rich-ass fancy-pants now, huh? Well, you owe me frickin' money."

That stopped Reid in his tracks.

"Excuse me?"

"You owe me frickin' money! For repairs! For what you did! To my building!"

Spittle flew from his lips. Spittle and the warm barn-stench of beer. Christ, he was blitzed out of his walnut-sized brain.

Reid had to hide a laugh at how pathetic this was. Frank had found out where they'd moved, gotten on a train, and then had to drink up some courage to come yell at him. "Fuck you, Frank." He stepped off the curb and tried to cross the street, but Frank juked into his way.

"Yeah, fuck me. You done messed up my floors! You frickin' moron! I laid that wood by hand! You know how many nails that took? I don't use no glue. That's *nails,* you understand?" Frank swayed on his feet, staring at Reid with half-lidded intensity. "And the tile in the bathroom. What'd you do to the tile? You shoulda called me to do it, I coulda taught you! That's the problem with people like you, you think you know everything and now look at my hand—" He held up a bandaged paw. "Look at what happens when you—"

"Oh my gooooodddddd, shut the fuck up!" Reid shouted at the top of his lungs. "You unbelievably annoying piece of shit!"

It was like the whole world stammered to silence. Frank's mouth opened. Closed. Opened. Like a fish trying out the air.

People were watching now. Reid didn't care. He threw his arms open dramatically.

"I know, Frank! You're smarter than everyone else! You know more about houses and construction and politics and world affairs than anyone else. Has it ever occurred to you that maybe you think you're smart because people have learned it's completely pointless to try to correct you?"

Frank blinked, trying to process this. Then he puffed his chest. "I don't *need* correctin'—"

"Because arguing with you is like arguing with a goat getting its dick electrocuted! You're just, *Naaaah! Naaaah!* You just make noise! You're not smart. You're just—*Naaahh! Naaaaaaah!*"

Frank was too drunk to be quick or articulate—he wasn't those things even in the best of times—so he spoke slowly and deliberately, squeezing his eyes shut like a little kid trying to recite Latin.

"You listen to me and you listen good."

"Oh, goody! What new lesson shall I learn today?"

"You—you listen to me. Nobody talks that way to you. I mean, *me.* Nobody."

"No, they wait for you to be gone, Frank. *Then* they talk about you this way. Everybody hates you, my guy!"

"Maybe everybody hates *you*! Ever thought about *that*?"

"Great point, Frank. We done here?" Reid patted Frank on the shoulder and tried to finally move past him. It had been fun for a minute, but now—

"You listen to me, you kike sonofabitch." It shot out of Frank's mouth with the muscle memory of someone not unpracticed in saying such things. "You don't know how lucky you had it. I let you live under my roof. You and your slimy frickin' family. I gave you a good home. You don't get to disrespect me."

Reid turned around to face him. He had never before become so instantly, tremblingly furious. "What did you call me?"

"Yeah, see? You think I don't know? I *know.* I know your little rituals. You and your frickin' kike wife. And, hey, whatever happened to *her*? She used to be hot, but now she's like a frickin' shopping cart, right? How do you even look at that thing? Seriously. Man to man. Can she even feel anything anymore? Or was that always a problem with your little yid prick, huh? Your little frickin' kosher sausage?"

Reid's fist connected with Frank's jowled chin. He felt Frank's teeth scrape against his knuckles, and somewhere, angels sang.

Frank staggered back, his gummy eyes bright with shock. There was definitely a crowd now. People probably taking pictures. *Let them,* Reid thought and immediately on the heels of that: *Oh shit, I'm gonna go viral as the guy who beat up an old man.*

Or maybe not. Frank seemed to be recovering. Raising both his fists. Honest to God preparing for a bare-knuckle brawl.

"That's how you wanna be, college boy?" Frank blinked a few times and spat blood onto the sidewalk. "Okay, let's go."

Reid heard himself hissing curses back at Frank. It made him think of when Ana made fun of him for putting on some sort of fake, tough-guy Noo Yawk accent. Was this authentic enough? This street brawl in the gutters of Eighty-Second Street?

Reid raised his own fists, elated at the idea of finally venting some fury, when a calm, velveteen voice piped up beside them.

"Gentlemen, please."

No real urgency in the voice. Might as well have been strolling up to someone at an office party, asking about the dip.

Frank jumped all the same. "What the frick?!"

The concierge stood there, flanked by two imposing doormen. "This is more of a scene than we're comfortable with outside the building. If you could please—"

"I ain't gonna please nothing for nobody," Frank spat—figuratively and literally. "This goddamn Jew bastard owes me money."

The concierge, turned to Reid. "Mr. Greene, I do apologize for this, but—"

"What're you apologizing to him for? I'm the one getting robbed! And lookit my hand! Lookit what he did to my hand! How'm I supposed to—"

Smiler grabbed Frank's arm. Suddenly, but gently. Then he leaned toward Frank and began whispering something into his ear.

Reid couldn't make out what was said.

All he could hear was a low, harsh buzzing coming from Smiler's lips.

All he could feel was the pain in his fist.

All he could see was how Frank's expression changed from his usual beleaguered, half-lidded sneer . . . to wide-eyed, open-mouthed disgust. Or was it terror?

The front of Frank's pants darkened. His bladder had let go. It puddled around his right foot.

Smiler let him go and took a small step away. When Frank could find his voice again, he began to whisper:

"You're . . . you're . . . frickin' crazy. You're all frickin' crazy! I . . . I ain't gonna, I ain't gonna . . ."

Frank didn't finish his threat. He backed away and bolted down the street in a loping, bowlegged trot, like some primate not quite used to moving on two legs.

Just like that, the adrenaline turned off, and Reid began to shiver. The air must have dropped ten degrees in an instant. It was dusk already. That awful, winter dusk that comes on way too early, when it should still be a bright and sunny afternoon—

"Mr. Greene. Are you all right?"

Smiler turned to him. Reid wanted nothing more than to keep his distance.

"I'm fine. He just . . . started harassing me." He made a weak gesture toward the tiny crowd that watched the proceedings. "Anyone here can back me up, I bet—"

"I witnessed the encounter myself," the concierge said, smiling.

"I didn't want to hit him. But he called my wife—"

"I understand. Absolutely."

"My hand hurts."

"I expect it does."

"I . . . I should go back inside and tell Ana. Get some ice." He suddenly felt embarrassed. Vulnerable. He wanted to be with his family and process what had happened. He wanted to be far away from this strange man who could make a belligerent drunk piss himself in fear with a whisper.

Smiler stopped him with a low, raised hand.

"But I believe Miss Varné requested you complete an errand for her, yes?"

"Huh? How did you—?"

"I'm sure she would appreciate this task being completed before the evening gets too late. The store might close."

"Right. Yeah."

"Everything is fine, Mr. Greene. You did nothing wrong. Just a mild interruption."

Reid looked up at the building, craning his neck as if he could somehow see his apartment, his wife and daughter. They suddenly felt impossibly far away.

"Yeah. Right. I got interrupted."

He had a sudden urge to make a break for it. Run past the concierge and the two doormen . . . and then the *other* doormen standing sentinel by the gate who just stared.

"Everything is fine," the concierge repeated as if reading Reid's thoughts. "We'll all be here when you get back."

# MEETINGS

## 1

Isobel was meeting Claudia on the ice tonight. A culmination of two hundred years of flirtations, betrayals, misunderstandings, and near misses. Within minutes, old feuds would be forgotten, shirts would be torn, and Claudia would trace her tongue around Isobel's erect nipple. Isobel's fangs would lengthen in ecstasy, in concert with the sensitive skin.

*"Did you know that when blood hits the ice . . . it bounces?"* Claudia asked in an erotically charged whisper that filled the otherwise empty hockey rink.

*"We are creatures of forever, old friend. But that does not mean like we must act as if we have all the time in the world,"* Isobel responded, snapping her hockey stick in two and coyly threatening Claudia's heart with the sharpened wood.

The blunt end of that stick would be put to different use later in the scene, but for now, Claudia arched in aching instigation. *"I want to taste so much of you tonight that my tongue will never forget, even if I rip open a sousand sroats—"*

"No. Fuck."

Ana tried that sentence again.

"*'Even if I rip open a sou—'* Goddammit!" She overenunciated the words to get them comfortable in her mouth. "'A. Thousand. Throats.' Why is that so hard?"

She scrolled ahead on her iPad to see how much longer this chapter went on. She'd gotten another couple of pages of text down. Slow going, but at least it was progress, and it took her mind off Reid.

That fucking liar.

She was recording in her broken booth. She'd debated going into the closet, but the thought of pulling everything out again exhausted her. Not to mention the temptation for spying on Mrs. Jacobs . . . or thinking about the staircase . . . or any other thing that might make Reid think she was crazy . . .

God, she couldn't concentrate.

Charlie played quietly in her crib—or, really, sat and stared at nothing. Ana had given up trying to feed her. The only thing Charlie would accept was more birthday cake, so Ana gave her a little and then stuck her in her room, because she was a terrible and hopeless mother, but who gave a shit?

Her recording felt similarly hopeless; she'd have to do it all over again whenever / if ever she repaired the booth. At the moment, though, it was action and it sufficed. *Motion is lotion. (Where'd you go, Georgia?)*

She played back what she'd recorded so far, and it wasn't as awful as she thought it'd be. She might be able to stitch it onto the stuff she'd already recorded. She'd have to run it through a noise filter first, so it wouldn't be a perfect match, but people weren't listening to these books for her audio quality.

Something about the ambient hiss of the room tone, though . . .

She raised the gain on the file, listened again. Something was there. A distinct, rhythmic noise buried in the hiss of the room. Faint, moving enough to be noticeable. Like a snake under a blanket.

Then she remembered that last time she'd tried to spy on Mrs. Jacobs. After that giggle. She'd heard something similar then, hadn't she?

She pulled up the file she'd recorded and played it.

It was the same sound.

But wait . . . did it come from the Jacobses' apartment or from her own?

She decided to set the microphone up in the middle of the living room as an experiment. If Reid walked in on her, fuck it: it's not like he could think she was any more insane.

As she worked, she didn't notice the sun nestling itself behind the skyline. Another winter evening, come to claim everything too soon.

## 2

Reid still thrummed with so much nervous energy that when he arrived at the jewelry store, he didn't notice the door was *pull* not *push* and bounced off the glass and steel. He laughed and tried again.

Nothing could ruin his mood. His knuckles ached where they'd collided with Frank's face . . . but his own face wouldn't stop smirking. He'd finally punched that fucking asshole. What a *treat.*

He kept flexing and closing his hand, relishing the dull throb. While the jeweler retrieved Camilla's repaired earring. Reid moved on to imagining punching certain politicians, certain celebrities, hell, his erstwhile boss.

"I've got to say," the jeweler announced, coming from the back room, "it was an honor to work on a piece this vintage." He was a chubby little man, with gold, wire-rimmed glasses, one of the titular sons of Rosemund & Sons Jewelers, Established 1972.

Reid snapped out of his thoughts. "Yeah?" He didn't know why he feigned surprise—of course Camilla would have been wearing something remarkable.

"If I were looking at this with my appraiser's hat on, I'd say this was at least a hundred and fifty years old."

"Whoa."

Harry Rosemund, who dreamed of selling this godforsaken store and retiring to somewhere—anywhere—smaller and quieter than New York City, where he could raise goats and chickens instead of dealing with the meshuggeneh clientele, had even looked up how much an earring like this went for. He'd never stolen from a customer before, but when he saw the price . . . his eyeballs nearly smacked into the lenses of his gold-rimmed glasses.

Of course, he would never do something like that. If he was being totally honest, there was something about this particular piece of jewelry that felt . . . wrong. Unsavory. He'd be glad to be rid of it.

"Truly an honor," Harry Rosemund repeated.

Reid's suddenly went pale. "Oh, um, does this need to be paid for now, or . . . ?"

"No, no." Rosemund smiled. "Someone, I'm assuming your employer, called ahead, and it's been invoiced. She warned me a young, handsome man would pick it up. I don't normally allow such a thing, but she was very charming."

"She is," Reid replied. "Would you mind putting this in some sort of box or—?"

The jeweler gently took the earring and gave Reid a wink. "Say no more." He took the earring into the back room again for a moment.

Reid watched him go, and a curious thought occurred to him.

*Camilla doesn't really need a personal assistant, does she?*

*Just like she didn't* really *need me to pick this up right now.*

*But then why was she so adamant about getting me out of the apartment?*

Before he could pursue that line of thinking, another customer entered and leaned on the counter next to him.

"Well, well, well," the newcomer said. "Bashert, huh?"

It was his Hasidic friend from all his recent park walks.

"Hey," Reid laughed politely, not in much mood for small talk. "Just picking something up."

The jeweler came back and handed Reid a box in a tiny, clear plastic bag.

"'*Something,*' he says," Rosemund told to the Hasid. "An exquisite piece." Then he turned to Reid. "Please, thank your employer again."

"I will."

Reid went to the door but held back, just for a moment. He watched as his Hasidic friend emptied a small bag of jewelry onto the counter. "Isaac." Rosemund sighed. "Are you sure you don't want to keep at least some of this? What if she comes back?"

Reid took that as his cue that this was no longer any of his business. He left, hearing only the spitting noises the Hasid—Isaac—made, knowing they meant she, whoever she was, wouldn't be welcome even if she *did* come back.

## 3

Ana fiddled with the EQ until she isolated the noise. It was a mixture of high and low frequencies—she had to turn the EQ meter into something resembling two mountain peaks, or bunny ears. Or a pair of upside-down fangs, she thought and shivered.

As she listened, not-so-distant memories fired off in her brain.

The distracted way Charlie looked those first few days in the apartment.

One of the things poor Mrs. Jacobs had said in her nonsensical ramblings. *It's like music . . . It's in the air, I think.*

Eliot's complaint to his mommy: *I don't like this music.*

The noise Ana had isolated . . . She might not have thought of it as *music,* but it did have some sort of tonic center and a rhythm. The low end throbbed and hummed. The high end moved around like ceramic plates rubbing together.

Was someone playing music elsewhere in the building?

She supposed that was possible—but the same music, days later?

Maybe there was some sort of ambient noise in the building? Like a power line hum? That might possibly sound musical if you didn't know what you were hearing.

Another memory: this one, years old. From her and Reid's early days.

Nearly every guy she'd ever dated always had a subject they desperately wanted to share with girls. They'd breathlessly monologue like a seven-year-old at show-and-tell. With Reid, it had been the Beatles.

Ana hadn't been super familiar with them, beyond the songs pretty much everyone knows. When she'd told him she'd never listened to *Sgt. Pepper,* he balked and made her sit through it. During the fade-out of that final piano chord in "A Day in the Life," he told her that at the very end of the album, the band, as a practical joke, stuck a high-tone frequency specifically designed to make a person's dog go nuts.

When he was a kid, Reid said, he'd always been able to hear that frequency, too. Then one day, he just couldn't hear it anymore.

Children can hear frequencies adult ears can't.

Was that what little Eliot heard?

Or Charlie?

Were they picking up this strange, phantom noise?

*I don't like this music.*

She turned the microphone's volume up . . . up . . . up . . . With these EQ settings, she couldn't *not* hear it.

*I don't like this music.*

Thoughts of cancer-causing microwaves or other paranoid, half-formed ideas crossed her mind. Was this building dangerous for young children? What if it affected adults, too? Was that why Mrs. Jacobs was fucked up? Was that why she saw strange things? Were they being manipulated? Brainwashed?

She raised the volume.

Reid needed to listen to this, too. Maybe his musically adept ears would have a better idea what it could be. She'd have to warn him about how high she set the microphone gain, though. Otherwise—

*EEEEEEEEEEEEeeeee!!*

A shriek pealed through the apartment, splitting Ana's ears like an arrow.

Ana screamed along with it, throwing her headphones off her head.

Her ears rang in agony, but there was no time to waste.

That shriek had come from Charlie's room.

## 4

It was just like her nightmare.

A face, floating outside Charlie's bedroom window.

A hideous, white, leering face.

Except, despite the dreamlike cast Ana's still-ringing ears gave to everything, this wasn't a nightmare. This was real. The pain in her head, the dry, metallic taste in her mouth, all of it.

Cold air sighed into the room and Ana realized the creature outside had raised Charlie's window. *Oh god.*

This time, she didn't hesitate. She pushed herself forward as quickly as she could, grabbed her baby, stuffed her into the lap carrier, and hightailed it out.

Tried to, at least.

*Wham!* Her fucking wheel caught on the doorframe, preventing her escape.

Moving at what felt like a snail's pace—*no, not a snail, an injured gazelle*—she backed up, toward whatever horror just slid into the room, then pointed herself more accurately through the doorway.

She knew she shouldn't, but she threw a glance over her shoulder.

Under the window crouched a humanoid thing with a flat, hideous face. It looked at her . . . and smiled. A clear, gooey substance dribbled from its upturned mouth.

Ana turned back and pushed herself through the doorway as the thing began to rise.

She slammed the door shut. A split second later, a heavy thud, then scrabbling against the other side of the wood. That creature had opened the window; could it open a door?

No time to think about that. She had to move.

Charlie made another shrieking noise. Ana realized with horror, it wasn't a shriek. It was her noise. Her happy chirp. Only it somehow had more tones—as if she had more than one set of vocal cords.

*Nope, deal with that later. First, safety.*

Charlie twisted and squirmed against the lap strap, seemingly trying to escape while also making grabby motions at the bedroom door. Reaching *for* the thing in her bedroom. Ana's fevered mind told her: *Summoning, she's summoning that thing.*

The thing in the bedroom hit the door again.

Then the sound of claws scratching against the doorknob.

*"Fuck!"*

She heard a gagging noise and looked down to see Charlie spitting up onto her lap. Except . . .

*That's not regular spit-up. That's the same clear, sticky shit that monster was spewing—*

*No time! No time!*

Ana did the first thing she could think of, realizing it was insane and risky.

First, she snatched up the mic and wire in the middle of the living room floor and threw them into the booth. The coil of wires formed a nest and she put Charlie on top of it. She pushed the nest under the shelf inside the booth where her laptop sat, closed the door, and slid one of her hand weights against it. The setup inside the booth was probably dangerous for a one-year-old, but one crisis at a time; she'd just have to trust her baby not to kill herself.

Charlie's chirps disappeared. The booth swallowed the sounds up.

Next, Ana raced to the front door. She pulled a sweatshirt off the pegs by the door and bundled it in her arms.

She yanked the front door to the apartment closed just as the bedroom door swung open.

## 5

An old man stood in the hallway. Ana almost ran him over.

"Whoa," he said, hands up. "Slow down, slow down!"

"Please," Ana begged, pushing herself away from her door, moving through sand. "Please, you've got to help me."

"It's okay," the old man said. He had kindly eyes and wore a red smoking jacket made of luxurious velvet. Obviously, one of the tenants from downstairs. How appropriate; he sounded as blithe as a man at a cocktail party, strolling through a garden. "You're okay. You've had a very stressful day and you just need to relax."

*"What?"* She gulped between breaths.

"Go back inside and relax. What happens next is painless. For everybody. It's all part of the big day."

She backed away from him.

"You . . . You're . . . What *is* this?"

The apartment door opened, and the thing emerged. It hadn't found Charlie.

Ana remembered the sweatshirt bundle in her arms and clung to it protectively. She could back herself up only one wheel at a time now, moving in fits and spurts, but at the moment, no one gave chase. It was a standoff.

The old man reached out a hand, palm up. She could see he had long nails, loathsomely and luxuriously long. "We're not going to hurt anyone. On the contrary. We have a present for baby. Give her to me."

He took a step forward.

"Don't fucking come near me." She put the bundle on her lap and pushed herself backward with a mighty shove. As she rolled, she pulled out her phone. "Leave us alone or I'll call the police." She dialed 9 . . . 1 . . .

"Oh?" He seemed genuinely interested. "What are you going to tell them?" He continued to advance. "We're prepared for the police, dear. We've been around a long time."

*Vampires,* she thought feverishly, remembering faces at the window. *They're vampires. Hahaha. Of course. Ancient bloodsuckers who want to drain us dry.*

She heard a rustle of fabric above her, as well as an insane clatter her mind did not want to comprehend. She looked up to see someone crawling on the ceiling.

The newcomer dropped and landed next to the old man. An old woman, resplendent, well coiffed. The expensive necklaces draped around the woman's neck rattled as they settled around her neck.

"Have I missed anything?" the old woman asked in a posh British accent. She sounded a little winded.

The old man turned to her. "She won't give the baby."

From the doorway of the apartment, the dog-bat-man-thing gave a muted grunt. More clear goo dropped from its too-human mouth.

The old woman made a sad face, her lined lips pulling down in a baby-doll pout. "Oh, darling. It's fine. She's ready. She's been preparing for this for weeks now."

Preparing? Charlie had been *preparing*?

"What did you do to my baby?" Tears pricked Ana's eyes.

"She's not your baby anymore," the old man said, advancing.

"STAY THE FUCK BACK!" Ana screamed.

Her mind moved a mile a second. They were right; calling the police was useless. She knew that after her little chat with Detective Hauck.

So what could she do? Call for an ambulance? A fire truck? Would those protect her in any way? Wouldn't the slimy concierge be able to turn them away, false alarm, no need to go upstairs? She needed something specific to her, something they wouldn't be able to grease over.

Her mind went to the first thing she could think of. The thing she'd always wanted to do when she was growing up.

She pressed the third *1* and, when she heard the distant mumblebuzz of the operator coming from the phone, she yelled, "Help! My name is Ana Greene, I live on the top floor of the Deptford Apartment Building, and . . . and my mother is here!"

The richies paused. They weren't expecting that. Good.

Ana continued to back up, distancing herself. The phone was in her lap, next to her fake Charlie.

"Her name is Cathy Stillson. She came all the way from Connecticut, and she's trying to hurt me and my baby! Please, you've got to come quick—she's abusive, and I'm in a wheelchair! PLEASE HURRY!" She glared at the old couple. "They're on their way. You hear me? They said they're on their—"

Ana was trying to pay attention to too many things. She'd lost her internal map and realized too late: the old man had been purposefully backing her this way. To the stairwell.

Her chair dropped over the first step, spilling her out, hurtling her down the stairs. Her head slammed into marble, then blackness.

This time, the sirens outside wailed for her.

## RUNNING

### 1

Reid ambled back to the apartment, enjoying the cold, early-winter darkness.

Then his phone rang.

The call was brief.

Before it was over, he'd broken into a run.

### 2

They directed him to a room on the second floor. That was good, he hoped—she wasn't in such bad shape that they had to keep her near the entrance.

Ana shared her room with another person, and Reid could make out brief little snores coming from the other side of the thin white curtain dividing the space. Or maybe they were moans.

Ana was barely conscious.

They'd loaded her up on painkillers and wrapped her neck in a thick, foam collar the color of old bones. They told him—whoever they were, doctors, nurses, receptionists, Reid hadn't thought to ask—she was okay, just a little banged up, all this was precautionary because a fall like that could create a lot of hidden injuries that too much movement could exacerbate.

What the fuck had happened? And what was going to happen next? Was she going to be in worse shape, emotionally, physically, after all this? What if she was further paralyzed? The unfairness of it all hit Reid again, and a scream threatened to tear out of his throat.

He fought it back. As always.

He took her hand, and it, surprisingly, flexed around his own.

Ana's eyes fluttered open.

"Hi!" he exclaimed in a whisper. "Hi, baby."

"Reid . . . ?"

"I'm here. I'm right here. What happened? How did you fall?"

"I . . . fell . . ."

He couldn't tell if that was a question for confirmation, or a decent attempt at sarcasm.

"You fell," he repeated. "Down the stairs. What happened? Did you slip?

They told me there were cops in the area, so they got there right away, and they found you on the staircase."

As if not quite listening to him, she gave a wheezy little laugh and said, "Back in the hosp'al again. Wheee."

"Oh, honey." He was about to ask her one more time how it happened when she blinked herself further into consciousness and squeezed his hand in a death grip.

"Vampires," she said.

"What?"

"Gotta be vampires. '*We are creatures of forever, old friend*' . . . hahaha . . ."

"Who—"

"The Deadford. They 'tacked . . ." She blinked, squeezing her eyes shut, opening them wider, trying to rouse herself from the drug-induced stupor. "'Tacked me. On the ceiling. The window. Wanted her."

"You gotta slow down, baby. I can barely understand you. Just slow down and tell me."

"Nighttime, sun's down, vampires, gotta be . . . haha, it's all in the book . . ." Her lids drooped, losing the fight with unconsciousness.

Reid shook her hand like a service bell. "They attacked you? Through the window? That's impossible, honey. What are you trying to say? What—Wait a minute." He looked around. Panic flooded him in a white, electric rush. He'd been so consumed with making sure Ana was okay that somehow, impossibly, he hadn't thought to ask this first.

"Oh my god. Where's Charlie?"

## 3

There was a cop waiting inside the apartment.

Reid stood before him, bent at the waist, panting for breath. He'd run all the way from the hospital. His lungs burned. A stitch ate into his side. He didn't think he'd ever run so much in his life.

The cop—a uniformed guy who barely looked to be out of his teens—explained the situation. Ana had called to report her mother had shown up, trying to steal their baby. Ana had fallen down the stairs. Now there was no sign of baby or grandma.

The words swirled around Reid like tracers during a bad acid trip. The only thing he could focus on was: Charlie wasn't here; she was missing. Everything seemed tilted off axis. *Cathy? Cathy left her assisted living facility to come here and—?*

Kindergarten Cop was in the middle of asking Reid if they had Cathy's number and if they'd like to press charges, when Reid noticed the door to Ana's VO booth was closed.

Wait a second. When had she fixed the door?

Then he noticed the hand weight. One of her ten pounders. Easy to miss because Ana liked to use the darker-colored weights. She'd always said, and rightly so, that it was bullshit for companies to genderize everything, from razor blades to mechanical pencils. "Maybe someone using weights for physical therapy after childbirth paralyzed her doesn't want a dumbbell the color of a fucking Lisa Frank notebook," she'd grumbled.

He moved the weight and the door swung open.

At first, he didn't see anything. Then, from under the desk space, he heard a raspy little chirp. Baby Bird had blown her little voice out, but there she was, dazed and confused but no worse for wear as far as he could tell. She was wet and coated in something sticky and awful, but he didn't care. He covered her in kisses, holding her close, telling her over and over again that he was here, that she was safe. He repeated Ana's phrase without knowing it: "It's okay, it's okay."

"Holy shit," the cop said in amazement. Reid almost forgot the guy was there. "I—I didn't think to look—I didn't hear anything—"

"Great police work, dude. Really. A-plus." Reid held Charlie so close he had to remind himself not to crush her. "It's a voice-over booth. It kills sound."

The cop gaped. "I—it just looked like part of the—"

He gave up. He called in to report the new development—conveniently leaving out the fact that he'd been in this apartment for God knows how long *with* the baby they were looking for and hadn't thought to fucking poke around.

Dispatch gave him the okay to come back, and the cop muttered into his walkie, "Good. This place gives me the creeps."

*"Hey."* Reid growled. His eyes burned. For a half second, he hated the guy more for his judgment of the Deptford than for his negligence. Then it passed.

Reid said they wouldn't be pressing charges, that everything was okay, and he got a card to use in case the situation changed at all.

After the guy left, Reid's legs turned to rubber, suddenly remembering how much they'd run in a short amount of time. God, had it even been five hours since their lovely little birthday party?

He considered going back to the hospital to visit Ana, but she'd been so out of it. He wanted her to rest.

Instead, he cleaned Charlie up and changed her. A puddle of something inexplicable oozed under her bedroom window, but he decided that was a later problem. The window was open just a crack—

(*They 'tacked me . . . the window . . .* )

—but definitely not wide enough for someone—

(*vampires*)

—to slip through.

He grabbed a bottle of formula and some of Charlie's favorite snacks and sat with her on the couch. She must be starving . . . but once again, she wasn't interested in anything he had to offer.

He turned on the TV to help soothe her—really him—but failed to choose a show.

Midway through singing to her and trying to get her to eat an Apple Apple pouch, he fell asleep without realizing it.

## 4

He woke up an hour later. The word *Roku* ping-ponged across the television screen with dumb insistence.

Charlie was gone again.

He bolted to his feet, head whipsawing with cartoonish speed. How? Where?

He must have spoken out loud because a voice came from the kitchen.

"It's okay. I've got her."

Camilla emerged, bouncing Charlie on one hip, a smile on her lips. Charlie had one hand in Camilla's hair. Charlie smiled, too.

# ROOFTOP (II)

## 1

His first question was the most absurd one.

"Did you get her to eat?"

"She's picky," Camilla replied, "isn't she?"

"She didn't use to be. How did you get in here?"

"I used the door, silly."

"Not the window?"

Charlie blew a raspberry and continued playing with Camilla's hair.

Camilla smiled. "Birthdays are so special, aren't they? It's really just another day, and yet they change our perception of everything. They redefine—"

"WHAT THE FUCK IS GOING ON?!" Spittle flew from his lips. He began to shake.

Camilla's cultivated eyebrows rose over half-lidded eyes. Her smile never left her lips.

"I guess I deserve a shouting-at. You must be so confused."

"Yeah. Right." He picked up the remote, turned off the TV, threw the remote back down. A real impressive display of force. Then he stood. "Give her back."

"Of course." As if it were no big thing. As if he'd asked her to pass the fucking breadsticks.

She walked into the living room and handed the baby over. Charlie immediately began to squirm and reach for Camilla. Reid tried to turn Charlie around, get her to focus on him, but no matter what position he put her in, she kept straining for Camilla. He had to keep her from falling, she was trying so hard to escape. Also she felt . . . wrong. Not as baby-warm, not as baby-soft.

"What did you do to her?"

"Me, personally?" Camilla looked downright tickled. "Not a thing."

"Then what—? Why—?"

"There's something I need you to appreciate before we have this conversation, Reid." Camilla leaned against the wall, unperturbed.

*"What did you do to her?"*

"Because the sheer fact that we're having a conversation sets you apart from most people in your position. It's not something we're in the habit of doing. It's why we didn't tear your apartment apart, looking for Charlie after your wife invited the police in. Everything is happening this way because we're *allowing* it to happen. We're allowing it to happen because . . . well . . ."

He was about to ask for—demand—more clarity, less smug bullshit, when Charlie wrapped her mouth around the flesh between his right thumb and index finger. She didn't bite. Instead there was a ripping sensation. Like someone coated his skin in adhesive and then yanked it away. He hissed in pain, and when he looked down, there was a ragged circle of abraded red.

"Fuck!"

Distracted by the pain, sharp and confusing, he barely noticed as Camilla scooped Charlie back into her arms. Charlie stopped squirming and settled contentedly in the older woman's hold.

"I swear to god," Reid hissed, "today has been too fucking much, and if I don't get some answers, I'm—"

"The day is over, Reid. It's nighttime now." He looked up at her, boiling. She still had the same bemused smile. "Come to the roof with me and I'll explain everything."

She floated toward the door, leaving him to scramble for his coat and follow.

## 2

He had to hustle to catch up. No matter how fast he moved, she stayed ahead of him, even up the stairs to the roof. If she hadn't eventually stopped and waited, he might never have caught up.

"It's too cold for her up here," he said, finally coming up alongside her. He looked at Charlie, who wore only a thin cotton shirt with a bright yellow Tweety Bird on it, and purple pull-up pants.

Charlie didn't seem bothered, though. She nuzzled contentedly against Camilla's chest. Again, Reid remembered the feel of her in his arms. Like food left out just a little too long. Not cold but definitely not hot.

Wind whipped at them. Shroud-colored clouds oozed across the starless night sky where the only source of light not drowned out by the city was the moon, casting lunatic blue light onto the roof. He had no idea what time it was. Traffic honked below, but it was a midnight darkness. A lonely darkness.

"I don't like this."

"You know that's not true, Reid. You like it very much." He could hear her voice so clearly, despite the wind and the city noise.

"No, something's wrong."

"I think all your life, you've been looking to belong somewhere. Somewhere *special.* Where you could lay down your resentments and be special, too. Are you listening?"

"Yes."

He was. He had just been distracted by a scraping sound. Concrete on concrete. A giant grinding its teeth.

"I'm going to show you something. Then we'll go back down and talk some more."

"I need to get back to my wife. I need to show her Charlie's okay and—"

"Oh, darling," Camilla sighed. She looked lovingly at the baby in her arms, then back at Reid. Her hair, her skin, glowed in the moonlight. She didn't look *younger,* she looked as if youth itself were a joke and this age a perfection. "Charlie isn't okay."

"What do you mean?" Reid asked, trembling. Cold. Terrified. His heart thudded. His balls drew into his torso. His stomach churned acid.

"You've been chosen, Reid." She turned back to Charlie. Kissed her on the head. "But choice requires sacrifice, doesn't it? Time to say bye-bye."

Then she turned Charlie around so she was facing out toward the city, and in a graceful underhand, she threw Charlie off the roof of the Deptford.

For a feverish instant, Reid thought, *Fly. She's going to fly.*

But Charlie didn't fly. Reid watched his baby plummet over the railing and the world filled with his screams.

# PART FIVE

## BIRD'S NEST

# "VAMPIRES"

## 1

"You're going to want to scream when you open your eyes."

Reid stirred, dimly aware he lay on an unfamiliar surface. Firm, yet cushioned. A little scratchy in a fine-napped way, like a pool table. No, not a pool table. The inside of one of those velvet boxes that engagement rings come in. The kind with a hinge so taut they snap shut like little jaws. They can

(*vampires*)

bite.

His eyes opened.

He was on a settee, or was it a chaise, and it took him a moment to realize he recognized it from Camilla's apartment. Leopard print. Maybe actual leopard skin.

Took him another moment to remember what he heard Camilla say while he swam up from unconsciousness.

*You're going to want to scream when you open your eyes.*

Took him yet another moment to understand why.

Reid wouldn't have thought he had any more screams in him.

He was wrong.

## 2

He tried to scramble up and away from the settee, the chaise, whatever the fuck it was. He had to get the hell away from the monstrosity staring at him. Some hideous, four-legged, wrinkled thing. Garishly white and gray. Inhuman. And yet . . . a human face. Resting on an impossibly bent neck. With inquisitive, watchful eyes.

"I warned you," Camilla said with the faintest chuckle. "You're okay. He won't hurt you."

All Reid could do was pant out syllables. "Wha. Who. Whe."

Looking at the thing made Reid want to throw up, but he couldn't tear his eyes away.

It took a few steps toward him, claws clicking against the hardwood in a distressingly solid way. Nightmares didn't click against the floor.

Its legs joints were . . . wrong, like a human figure that had been shrunken and stooped and twisted. Its back legs bunched up to accommodate its four-limbed gait. And that face . . . that strangely human face . . . its nose, its mouth, were wet with very real, very organic-looking mucus.

For a moment, he had the utterly insane notion that it looked familiar—when would he have ever seen a monstrosity like this?

The realization came quickly. He'd stared at the building's gargoyles often enough. Not to mention the photos of them in his book.

No. No, impossible. Those gargoyles had been documented and photographed for decades. If they'd moved or disappeared, someone would have noticed.

*Noticed the way they noticed when a tiny baby was thrown off the roof?*

The more he stared, though, the more he realized this creature wasn't *exactly* like the gargoyles outside. More like what you might get if you morphed a normal human figure *with* one of those statues, then pressed Pause somewhere in between.

"I'm gonna throw up," Reid moaned.

"Oh, please don't. That chaise was gifted to me by David O. Selznick. It's very hard to clean."

Reid waved a weak hand toward the creature. "Just . . . just get it away from me. *Please.*"

Camilla gave it a gentle nudge, and it retreated into a corner of the room where the lamplight didn't quite reach. It wasn't much better knowing that it was there, hell, that it existed anywhere on this entire blue planet, but the distance helped.

That's when he registered who was in Camilla's arms. Smiling. Content. Not a care in the world. Not exploded on the pavement hundreds of feet below.

"Charlie," he wheezed.

Baby Bird gave a delighted chirp. Baby Bird, who had just been thrown off a goddamn roof and who had somehow—

It all came flooding back to him. Everything.

Camilla had thrown Charlie over the side of the building. Reid had screamed so loud and so long, he felt like all his blood vessels would burst: *No no NO.* He'd tried to run to the edge to see the horror waiting on the sidewalk below, but Camilla held him back with one impossibly strong arm. He cursed her. He moaned and howled and sobbed, and then Camilla put a manicured finger to her lips and hushed him.

"Do you hear it?" she'd asked him, her eyes sparkling with moonlight.

He listened. Cars. Whistling wind. Blood in his ears—*Blood on the pavement my baby oh god my baby*—not hearing anything, not hearing . . . Then he'd realized he also wasn't hearing screams, the screech of traffic, the wail of sirens because a fucking baby had fallen from the . . .

"Careful," Camilla cautioned.

He'd moved on unsteady legs toward the edge. Sank to his knees like a man in prayer. Leaned over the wrought iron railing to peer below.

Charlie clung to the side of the building a few yards beneath him. Her pudgy little hands gripped the stones with absent-minded confidence like tiny spiders. As if this were the most natural thing in the world.

"Charlie isn't okay," Camilla had repeated. "She's *perfect*."

Charlie looked up and gave him a gleeful chirp. *Hi, Daddy.*

Then she giggled, open-mouthed, allowing Reid to see her four teeth, and that's when he fainted.

He felt like he might faint again. He gripped the settee with both hands to steady himself and felt fresh tears running down his cheeks. "What . . . is *happening* . . ." he tried to whisper, but it stretched into a long, keening noise. The sound of a mind close to breaking.

His eyes shot to the corner where the man-thing sat, watching. Reid began to hyperventilate. He focused harder on controlling his breath than on anything he'd ever done before.

Just when it seemed like he had gotten himself under control again, Camilla pulled him to his feet with her one free hand. Her strength . . .

"Let's go for a walk," she said, then turned to the man-thing. "You stay here, *dziadu*."

## 3

She took Reid to the kitchen, where tall stools flanked an immense marble island. She sat him down, then pulled out a heavy-looking tray from the fridge. Charcuterie.

"Don't worry, it's perfectly normal. And quite expensive." Next, she pulled out a tub of ice cream from the freezer. "The birthday girl, however, needs sugar. Loads of it."

Camilla dipped her finger in the tub and offered it to Charlie. Charlie grabbed the finger and greedily sucked the ice cream off.

Reid accepted all this in a daze. He kept seeing Charlie clinging to the side of the building. The impossible creature in the other room, just sitting there, obeying Camilla's command.

He felt like he'd been coldcocked with a cinder block. Like when he'd been told his mother had died, or when they'd received Ana's prognosis. His entire world had been turned upside down and shaken; he could do nothing but wait for it to settle.

He grabbed a slice of cheese with a numb and shaking hand and stuffed it in his mouth. He had no appetite, but the way the soft, fatty goodness melted in his mouth . . . He was hungrier than he'd thought. Having a little nourishment helped settle the static in his brain.

Camilla ran a perfectly manicured hand over the soft hair on Charlie's head. "Were you able to get my earring back, by the way?"

Reid blinked. "Oh. Uh. I . . ." He pulled the earring out of his pocket, almost surprised, as if it had been planted by a magician. He put it on the counter.

"I hope you weren't given any trouble about having it invoiced."

"No . . ." He couldn't stop staring at Charlie. Charlie, who stared back with her bright, inquisitive eyes, her chubby cheeks working as she sucked on more ice cream. Then he remembered what else had happened tonight. "Did you send me to pick up that earring because you knew something was going to happen to Ana?"

"Have a little more to eat, and then I'll tell you everything, okay?"

Reid picked up some cheese. Stared at it.

"She . . . she thinks you're all vampires."

"Hm."

"Is she right?"

Camilla laughed.

Tears spilled out of Reid's eyes. He squeezed the cheese in his hand. Made it ooze through his fingers. "It's not funny."

Camilla clucked her tongue. "Reid, I think I mentioned that cheese is very expens—"

*"Is she right?"* He picked up another piece of cheese and squeezed it, tossed the mush on the counter. "This building is full of . . . of vampires?"

She stared at him for a long moment.

"What do you think, Reid?" she asked at last. "Have I *fed* on you? All those days together, did I ever try to *bite* you or—"

Reid suddenly launched himself backward, his stool making an outraged rasp against the floor. "Bites." He pointed at Charlie. "Oh my god, she, she, she had bites, and now . . ." He was crying again, his voice sliding higher and higher as hysteria took him. "Change her back! Change her back!"

"Reid, I really do want to explain, but this is all very embarrassing."

*"I'll fucking kill you."* He grabbed the cheese knife and pointed the blade at her.

"And then what?"

"I'll . . . I'll fix her. Make her normal again."

"How will you do that if you kill me, Reid? You don't know *anything*."

Reid let loose a frustrated growl and grabbed a fork off the counter, too. He held both pieces of silverware together in a cross shape and pushed the makeshift crucifix toward her.

"Oh, *golubchik* . . ." She looked at him with such pity. "Here."

Suddenly, Charlie was in his arms. He held her tight, but Charlie immediately began to squirm again, wanting to be back with Camilla. Meanwhile, Camilla grabbed a bottle of that sweet, floral liquor she'd given to him what felt like months ago. Reid watched as she poured him a glass, trying to still Charlie as best he could. As soon as Camilla set the glass down, he took it up greedily. The liquor would help steady him.

Before it could hit his tongue—

Charlie was out of his arms and back in Camilla's. One moment, she was there, the next, she was giggling and back to playing with Camilla's hair. Reid almost choked in surprise.

"I'm moving to the living room," she said. "Come join me when you're ready to listen."

Once again, she left him behind, and he was struck how she seemed to float when she wanted to, moving with such fluid grace that it seemed like her upper body didn't move. She was so beautiful it was terrifying.

He had to do something. Fight back, get the upper hand. But how? He didn't even know what he was fighting against.

On the heels of that thought, a larval plan began to form.

He stood to leave the room . . . then refilled his glass and grabbed a few slices of cheese. If he was going to defeat some monsters tonight, he'd need his strength.

## 4

Camilla stood by the window in the living room, Charlie propped on her hip.

The open drapes exposed the cityscape beyond. A sea of earthbound stars. Camilla looked out at them. Her reflection—and she had a reflection—looked back at Reid.

"Thomas Emile Janebridge loved this city. Even in its infancy, he could see what it would become. When our tiny family left its home in Europe, we knew we wanted to settle here, in the heart of things. We recognized this place, this city, the way like recognizes like. The way, I think, *you* recognized this city when *you* first moved here. A place holding a mirror up to your dreams. Am I correct?"

He didn't know what to say. Even as his plan began to form in his mind, he suddenly felt ridiculous, his hands loaded up with party snacks.

"Do you know what the city reminded Janebridge of? When he first saw it? Was that mentioned in your book?"

"No."

"He was struck by how *organic* it was. By which I mean actual organs. *Organisch* was his word; translates from the Dutch as, essentially, made of living tissue. The city was much smaller compared to what it is now, but even then, it was massive. Congested. Compact. Like the secret jewels inside a torso. Each separate part fulfilling a unique function. Each separate part comprised of its own component parts. Each separate part as important, as fundamental, to the body as the next."

Reid tried to speak. "What does this have to do with—"

She turned around. Her eyes flashed as bright as the lights of the West Side. Charlie's eyes, too. Reid's knees trembled. "Viscera upsets us. Our own biology is monstrous to us. When all it wants to accomplish is life for the greater organism. Life for *the body.* The *system.*"

She walked over to the brace of couches and sat down. She sat Charlie next to her. Reid had a momentary impulse to tell her not to do that—Charlie could topple over the side—but then he remembered the rooftop. *Stick to the plan,* he told himself. *It's your only hope.*

"'Vampires.'" She chuckled. Did she sound contemptuous? Pitying? He couldn't tell. "Need I remind you, *golubchik*: I've made *movies.* I show up on film. I don't have fangs. I don't burn up in the sun. Still, you're not the first to use that childish term. We're 'vampires' the way a woman with bad PMS is a werewolf, I suppose. Inspiration. I've met authors and poets over the years, inspired to create little fantasy tales after crossing our paths. But, of course, we predate those silly bedtime stories. Just as we predate your curses and your crosses, and, honestly, Reid, I thought you said you were Jewish."

His face flushed at her mocking tone. But she was talking. That was good. Terrifying but good.

"Okay, then . . . what are you?" he asked.

"Would a name really give you comfort? We are a family. We are eusocial. *Organisch.* Each of us has our function, and we contribute to our greater whole."

His eyes passed to Charlie, sitting there, staring at him. His throat suddenly became very tight.

"I want to know what you did to my daughter." His voice choked with tears.

In another freakish flash, Camilla stood in front of him again. It was a wonder his bladder didn't let go with the shock.

"Now we're getting somewhere." She took his glass with silky, feminine grace and stole a sip. Fine hairs around her lips emerged and rippled against the glass. His stomach knotted. "You see . . . breeding for us is very . . . complicated. Allow me to tell you a bit about the birds and the bees."

# 5

He listened, surprised to find his mind also casting backward to when he and Ana first tried to conceive. They, too, had been shocked at how complicated conception could be. They remarked at the time that it was a wonder anyone *ever* had a baby.

It was nowhere near as complicated as what Camilla described, though.

"Our kind," she explained, "does not *produce* children. They have to be made."

She described a rather disorienting process. Nowhere near as simple as biting a neck or swapping blood. He tried to follow it, but he kept getting distracted: by memories, by the liquor in his system, by the look of Charlie on the couch, staring back at him like a doll.

The process involved a series of steps. "Introductions to the body," she called them. She didn't explain what exactly these introductions were—"But we do occasionally take samples to see how the process is going. That might have looked like little bites to you." She smiled. Charlie did, too. Was she following the conversation?

"Now, I'm going to give you some very exclusive information, Reid." He was appalled to find himself the tiniest bit titillated. "The top floor of this building . . . is what we call our nursery. It's where we cultivate candidates. We choose them from families who, forgive me, probably won't be missed."

"'Cultivate candidates'?"

"Age is the most important factor. We've learned over our long history that the highest success rate occurs when a candidate is on the cusp of one year. Not younger. Not older. Even at the perfect target age, there's no guarantee the changes will take. Most of our attempts are unsuccessful. Another lottery, if you will."

"You're talking about . . . dead babies?"

"Yes."

"Jesus."

"I don't know what to tell you, Reid; nature is cruel. But that wasn't the case with your Charlie. She's taken to the process *extraordinarily* well. Isn't that right, Charlie?"

Charlie looked at Camilla, and again, Reid thought Charlie was listening along. No, impossible.

*This is all impossible, Reid.*

"Has . . . has it ever been attempted with adults? The . . . process?" Camilla giggled behind a hand. "What's so funny?"

"Of course it's been attempted, *golubchik*. Many times. I believe you read about one such example."

"What?"

"It wasn't so long ago when a not-so-nice mobster with whom the building had been associating for business purposes discovered the truth of our situation and tried to force us to 'transform' him and his closest friends. About twenty of them. We warned him it wouldn't work, but he insisted. They realized pretty quickly we'd been telling the truth. Splat."

Reid blinked. "The Plummet?"

She touched her nose. Bingo.

His head swirled with questions, each one prompting a dozen others.

"How many of you are there?"

"Not many. If I said, 'Not enough,' that would sound greedy, wouldn't it? But who wouldn't want more family, am I right?"

"Is everyone who's famous . . . like you?"

That got an actual laugh out of her. A high, fluty guffaw, almost an adult version of Charlie's chirps. "Good Lord, no! Most everyone who's famous is just the child of someone else who's famous!"

Reid felt chastened by all her laughter. He blushed and looked down. Then something occurred to him. "Wait, what about your granddaughter?! If you can't have kids, then—"

When he looked up, a twentysomething woman stood there. Radiant and ethereal and so young. He stammered to silence.

"I think you'll find," the young woman said, "most of the residents here have 'grandchildren' in our respective fields. Successful . . . but not too successful."

The illusion only lasted a moment or two. Then with a sickening sound reminiscent of dry foliage being crushed, Camilla stood once again in her place. Still radiant and ethereal. Charlie blew a raspberry and clapped appreciatively. "That's getting harder and harder to maintain, which is why poor Leonora doesn't work much anymore. I'm getting too old." She sat down on the couch next to Charlie.

"You get old?"

"Why do you think we are concerned with reproduction? Why do you think your storybook 'vampires' make no sense? To be immortal *and* breed would be the ultimate moot point. Eventually, we would overrun the place."

"I guess I never thought of that."

"No, why would you?" She looked introspective. "Yes, we get old, Reid. We age. We even die. Birth and death are inextricable, Reid; one cannot exist without the other. I will die, same as you. Only I will live a very, very long time. I do not burn up like flash paper in the sun—but the sun does speed up the process. My joints and bones will shrink, my posture will stoop. My skeleton will warp and twist. My skin will go gray and stony. I will become like my friend in the other room. Like the rest of our elderly. I will do my part in tending to the newest youngsters at the top floor for as long as I am able. Then, if I'm lucky, I'll enjoy a nice, long retirement on the building, looking out over the city I love, before I'm finally frozen in place. I can't complain. I've had an incredibly long life, full of experiences you could only dream of. This is our gift, you see. Do you understand what I mean about systems? About organs?"

He did, he supposed. The points started to connect, insane though they were.

"So, those . . . statues outside, the gargoyles, are they—?"

"They are the ones who came before us. Our ancestors. In fact, one of them is Janebridge himself. His body, now part of this structure he loved and cultivated and nourished."

He had so many more questions, but one in particular burned in his mind.

"Why are you telling me all of this?"

"Because, Reid. Your Charlie is special. I am of the opinion that you're special, too. So I would like to make you an offer."

He downed the rest of his drink, hoping it would give him the strength to hear whatever she said next.

"We would like you to join us. How's that for simple?"

## 6

It amazed him how silent and still things became. He felt suspended. Breathless.

"What does that mean, join you? I thought you said your process doesn't work on adults."

Camilla leaned back, crossing her legs. "It doesn't. You won't live like Charlie will or like I do. You'll have a normal life span. But you'll still be a part of us. An integral part. We have room for people like you. You'll help us keep the building going. You'll help us raise your little one. You'll be part of our family."

*You'll finally belong, in other words.* No more fear. Of alienation, of exclusion. No more insecurity, economic or cultural. Hell, they might even be able to help his career along.

What stopped him from immediately saying yes was Ana.

*Stick to the plan.* But already the plan was changing.

Reid licked his lips. He swallowed. Despite the liquor, his throat was incredibly dry.

"What if I have conditions?" he said at last.

"Conditions?" She looked intrigued. Or perhaps condescending? "And what, pray tell, makes you think you're in a position to negotiate, *golubchik*?"

That made him think of his boss, that shitty, smug smile. That awful feeling when he realized he'd been checkmated.

*Shouldn't have done that, Camilla.* He swallowed a marble, hoping he wasn't about to fuck things up for everybody.

"Because. You might not have to worry about crosses or holy water or whatever, but I do know one thing scares you."

Her expression faltered the tiniest bit. "What's that?"

He reached into his pocket.

"Exposure," he said, and pulled out his phone.

His voice memo function was open and recording. This entire conversation. This entire insane conversation.

She scoffed. "You . . . you think anyone would believe this was a real conversation?"

But there was something in her eyes. Maybe not fear but at least uncertainty. This development was unexpected.

"And before you think of taking this phone from me," he cautioned, "you should know I'm a musician, and I'm paranoid. All my recordings automatically back up to my cloud. And Ana has access to it, too. If something happens to me, she'll listen to it; she'll know."

"And then what?"

He had to be honest. "I don't know. But I *do* know one thing about the Deptford: there's a reason only one book was written about this place. There's a reason no one ever films here or takes photos. You all *really* like your privacy. And we could start a process you'd really want to avoid."

She stared at him for a long time. He felt sweat prickle the back of his neck.

"So what is it *you* want? You've given yourself leverage. What will you use it for?"

"Two things," he said. "First. I want one more night with Charlie. To think about things."

Camilla opened her mouth to say something and then stopped, reconsidered. "That seems fair. And the second?"

"I want you to fix Ana."

# 7

He took Camilla's silence as encouragement. He felt light-headed and reminded himself to breathe. "You *can* fix her, right?" He hated how small he sounded. He also knew Ana loathed the implication that she was broken . . . but she wasn't here right now, was she?

"I assume by 'fix her,' you mean her legs, yes?" Camilla asked at last.

"Yes."

"Reid. Of course we could fix that. We could ensure that her legs never give her trouble again. You have no idea the things we can do."

A relief he'd never known washed through him. "Then, would you extend the same offer to her? Let her work *with* me? Helping the building, taking care of Charlie? I know you weren't including her in your plans—don't lie and say that's not true. You wanted her alone tonight. But I could talk to her. Please. She's so strong. You'd be so lucky to have her."

Camilla sighed as if Reid had asked her to pick him up from the airport. Finally, she slapped her hands against her thighs and stood up.

"You're lucky I like you so much, Reid. Very lucky. But keep in mind, if you decide to keep that recording . . . I'm not the only one who lives here. Do you understand?"

"Of course." He was sweating now. He hoped it wasn't obvious.

"Take your daughter with you. Enjoy your time together."

He went to Charlie and picked her up. The baby, who had been serene this entire time, suddenly got fussy and upset again. Camilla made an inhuman clicking noise that came from deep inside her throat; Charlie tried—and failed—to copy the noise, then stilled.

Then something occurred to him. "Oh, shit, um . . . Charlie bit a kid this morning, and he's gotten kinda sick. Is he gonna be okay?"

Camilla made a face that seemed to indicate a real uh-oh. Then she covered it with a shrug. "Probably nothing to worry about. She's just a baby. I'm sure he'll be fine."

Reid made a mental note to check in on Eliot. "Now," she said, "I'm going to snack on something and rest. I, too, am exhausted." She seemed fresh and unruffled, not exhausted at all. Reid couldn't tell if he'd upset her with the little power play he'd just pulled.

She started walking away from him, then stopped.

"Would you like to see how we eat? Have a sense of who you're trying to threaten?"

Again, flashes of his boss, that devastatingly embarrassing final day. He stiffened his spine.

"I want to know everything." Dictating terms.

She led him to her bedroom. The one room in her apartment he hadn't yet seen.

When she opened the door, she revealed a room without windows. Utter blackness inside—he couldn't even see a bed. But the light thrown by the hallway bulbs enabled him to see a figure inside. Lying on the floor, propped up on one elbow. Confused.

Reid could make out the silhouette of a suit. The muted color, recognizable even in the dark.

Another of her companions.

Reid swallowed. "Why do they always wear that suit? Is it special or . . . ?"

Camilla snorted. "No, *golubchik*." She patted his arm, and he jumped slightly. "I just like to be seen with a certain class of person, that's all."

"Oh."

"He was a bad man. Remember that. We only choose bad people."

She smiled, and as she stepped out of her slip-on shoes and began to remove some of her jewelry, little hairs sprouted from her mouth. They rippled, reminding him of millipede legs. She began to make a soft choking noise. Retching.

Reid thought she was about to puke right in front of him.

Charlie babbled delightedly.

Drool began to course down Camilla's jaw. Her eyes rolled back in ecstasy.

Her smile remained.

She crouched into the darkened room. The dazed man on the floor made another dreamlike noise, not quite understanding what was happening.

In the wrapping shadows, Reid saw something emerge from Camilla's mouth. Something long and fingerlike.

Before he could see what happened next, Reid ran.

# COUNSEL

## 1

First thing he did when he got back to his apartment was put Charlie in her activity station.

Second thing he did was dry heave into the toilet. He couldn't stop shaking.

As he staggered back into the living room, he gave a weak chuckle and asked his daughter, "Betcha didn't know your dad was that good an actor, huh?" Then he regretted saying anything—what if they could hear him *through* her?

No. No, that was insane.

*Insane as everything else that's happened?* Charlie gripping the wall of the Deptford. Whatever it was that came out of Camilla's mouth. That entire fucking conversation.

His eyes locked onto Charlie's. His, panicked and terrified. Hers, unreadable.

He *had* been acting with Camilla. He'd lied about everything—the recording, his conditions, all of it. He'd *never* work for monsters, nor was he willing to hand his daughter over to them. He'd just wanted to buy some time.

But time for what?

"I'm going to save you, Baby Bird. It's not too late, I know it."

He started frantically tearing through the kitchen.

Garlic. The few cloves they had left over from a rare night of making pasta instead of ordering in. Cursing himself—*Stupid, stupid*—he approached Charlie and pressed the clove to her face.

She blinked and stared at him.

"Okay," he exhaled. Did that prove anything? He didn't know. He knew only loathing, a horror for those *things* that had corrupted his family.

Next, he pulled their cheap little tool kit from under the sink and hammered the cloves to the side of the door like a mezuzah. Maybe that would keep them from coming into the apartment? *Stupid, stupid.*

What else could he do, what else? Sunlight. Stakes. Silver. None of that seemed to apply. What other vampire lore might hold a possible solution?

"Don't invite them in," he muttered. Another shudder racked his body, this one small and tight as an electric shock. How does that rule work when you live inside *their* house?

*I can't be in a vampire story,* he thought wildly. *I'm Jewish! I don't belong h—!*

Then his eyes fell on the boxes of his mom's things, and he remembered something Camilla had said.

*"We predate your crosses."*

He pulled the boxes away from the wall and tore through them, ignoring that voice telling him how stupid he was being. If these creatures predated Christianity, maybe something else that predated Christianity held answers? Maybe he wasn't in the wrong story after all? Maybe?

He knew the odds were slim he'd find anything, but his mom had been a volunteer at her synagogue for a long time, so she'd held on to a fair amount of Judaica among her personal effects.

He was about to give up when, in the second box, hidden under some siddurs, something called to him: an oddly shaped lump wrapped in an old washcloth. He pulled it out and unwrapped it with great care—not just out of reverence but because nearly every member of his family had cut the hell out of themselves on this particular object. Had it not been of immense sentimental value, it would have been chucked in the trash with a vengeance at least a hundred times over the years.

It was an old bronze paperweight in the shape of a chai—the Jewish word for *life,* a combination of two letters that Reid always thought looked vaguely cow-shaped. It was big and heavy, about seven inches in each direction. The story went that it was made from candlesticks that had been secreted out of the synagogue in Reszel, the village where Reid's grandmother had been born and from where she'd fled. Dull, clumpy seams marked where the metal had been merged together, like scar tissue.

Remembering his mom's reprimands to be careful every time he or his brother got remotely close to it sent a pang of sadness through the cloud of panic. Damn, grief was impressively persistent. He wished he could call her up, ask her advice, even about these insane, impossible developments.

He sat down on the couch, looking at the chai, holding it by the one safe side along the top side of the letter *chet.* Even if it didn't cause a single monster to recoil, he felt safer having it near him.

"We're gonna figure this out," he said absently to Charlie. "We're gonna make this right."

Charlie looked at him as if to say, *How? What could you possibly do about this?*

"First step, we're gonna get out of here. Today. Get a hotel. Never come back."

*What about Mommy? They can fix Mommy.*

That made him pause.

*And what about me? What if I can't live anywhere else? What if I can't survive—?*

"I don't know! But—we'll figure this out, we'll—"

*You can't win, Daddy. But you* can *lose everything.*

He shook his head, trying to banish these awful, tempting thoughts.

The booze, the exhaustion, the emotions swirled through him. He sat there, staring at the chai for an indeterminate amount of time. When he finally came back to himself, he noticed dawn had not only broken, it was well into morning. A new day.

That might have given him another flush of panic, but as he sat there, a potential solution had occurred to him—someone he *could* talk to. Maybe even get some answers.

Then, with a jolt, he realized he'd just left Charlie in her activity station for hours.

She hadn't screamed or cried or made a ruckus of any kind.

From all he could tell, she'd just sat there.

Staring at him.

"Come on, Baby Bird," he said, getting them ready to go outside. They just had to act normal one more time to leave the building. Then, after this errand, they'd head to the hospital to be with Ana. Fill her in on everything. Plan their next move. But first: "We're gonna go get some counsel."

## 2

Isaac had a headache—an unpleasant, but no longer unfamiliar, way to start the day.

The other Lubavitchers knew this, and so Isaac's one big task this morning was getting coffee for anyone else working the Mitzvah Tank who wanted some. Only Akiva put in a request, so as Isaac trudged back to the Tank, a repurposed minibus currently parked at Madison and Fifty-Seventh, he carried a tray with only two cups: one for Akiva and one for himself. Coffee didn't help the headache . . . but what he'd add to the coffee usually did. For a little while, at least.

It was a gloomy day. Cold, intermittent cloud cover. Maybe a snowstorm on the horizon. Isaac took his time walking back; he liked gloominess these days.

When he saw a stranger standing by the Tank and talking with old Mendy, though, Isaac had a moment to wonder how long he'd taken—they never had visitors this early. (They rarely had visitors at all; most people ran away from them or pretended they were invisible.)

He got closer and realized this wasn't just any stranger. It was Reid, that Reform Jew he'd been running into again and again lately. *Bashert,* he thought, and for some reason shivered.

The huge face of Rebbe Schneerson smiled back at Isaac from his giant picture plastered across the side of the Tank as Isaac approached.

"Ah. Here he is," Mendy said. They'd been talking about him.

"Hey," Reid said, sounding relieved and looking like death. A baby was strapped to his chest. Isaac thought momentarily of Benjamin, and for a moment, his heart crystalized and shattered the way it always did.

He felt something else, too. A sense of momentousness. Heavy. Foreboding. Not a *good* feeling at all. It mixed with his headache like snake venom mixed with blood.

"Can I talk to you for a few minutes?" Reid asked. "In private?"

Isaac made a valiant attempt at sounding jovial. "Of course! Walk with me to the park?"

Isaac took his cup of coffee and handed the tray over to Mendy to pass on to Akiva, and then he and Reid made their way to the nearest park entrance.

They walked in silence. That foreboding dread didn't go away. Maybe it had something to do with the fact that Reid's baby kept staring at him? The eyes . . . No baby's eyes should be so . . . cold.

Once they reached the park, Isaac was about to crack a joke about the scintillating conversation so far, but then Reid finally spoke. Isaac was surprised—perhaps even a little grateful—that it took only one sentence to capture Isaac's full attention.

"So . . ." Reid said, distinctly not making eye contact. His voice caught; he cleared his throat and tried again. "What can you tell me about vampires?"

It was 8:37 a.m.

# TERRA FIRMA

## 1

Her mother leaned over the crib in the baby's room.

Wet sounds. Contented humming. The distant sound of traffic, hundreds of feet below.

Ana walked over to the crib on nervous legs.

Her mother looked up.

Blood slathered and smeared her face.

She held one of Charlie's chubby legs like a drumstick, shiny cream-colored gristle dangling from where it had been pried loose from its socket, and before she took a big bite, she looked at Ana and—

## 2

Ana didn't so much wake up as bob to the surface.

She blinked, trying to remember where she was. An unfamiliar bed. A bright, white room.

A hospital.

As if waiting for that realization, her head began to throb distantly.

She looked around. To her right: a larger, older woman with a shock of orange hair in another bed, deeply invested in a magazine.

To her left: her wheelchair folded neatly next to a tiny nightstand.

No visitors.

No Reid. No Charlie.

Ana sat up. She wasn't connected to anything, which was a relief. Just a pulse meter on her finger. Also a foam collar that left her skin damp and cold after she took it off. A few bends and twists told her her neck was okay. Or, at least, okay enough to ignore for now.

She worked at lowering the gate on the side of the bed. Once it was down, her roommate muttered without looking up:

"They're not gonna like that."

"Yeah," Ana said, "well . . ."

She moved her legs over the edge of the bed.

For a moment, she flashed on the morning she discovered her paralysis. The first time she'd had to move her legs like that. How she'd thought walking to the bathroom would make the strange, painful tingle go away, only to drop to the floor like a stone.

That would have been a year ago today, wouldn't it? The day after Charlie was born?

*Is that today? How long have I been unconscious? And where* are *they?*

That horrible night a few months later also began the same way: Ana sitting at the edge of the bed, just like this, forgetting for a split second that her legs no longer obeyed her and plummeting to the ground.

Those two awful moments, worse than any other experiences she'd ever had, when she had to feel that betrayal and that implacable yank of gravity.

Not this time. This time, at the very least, she knew what she was in for.

She reached forward and grabbed her chair, then lowered herself into its seat.

She asked her roommate what time it was.

It was almost noon.

## 3

She'd been at a low level of panic since waking up.

Where were Reid and Charlie? Why weren't they here?

Would Reid have even known where Charlie was?

Had *they* gotten her? As soon as she got into her chair, she retrieved her clothes and her effects from the flimsy purple wardrobe in a corner of the room. She tried Reid's cell, but he didn't answer. She tried the landline. Nothing.

A nurse came in to check on her as she got herself situated out of the bed.

"Well, look at you," the nurse cooed. "How'd you get in that chair all by yourself?"

Ana barely listened; she'd been too focused sending another frantic text to her husband.

That same nurse brought in covered trays to be placed bedside—"You woke up just in time for lunch!"—before attending to Ana's roommate. The roommate put her magazine down and made staccato, pained moans while attempting to sit up farther.

Ana waited for the nurse to be particularly occupied and then wheeled into the room's bathroom to change into her street clothes.

"You okay in there, hon?" the nurse called out distractedly. Ana called back that everything was fine.

Once she was dressed, she tried Reid and the landline one more time—

*What if Charlie's still in the booth, starving, and Reid never thought to look in there?*

*What if he went to the police to file a missing baby report?*

*What if the booth is empty and Reid is dead, his throat ripped open?*

*What if I just leave now, just leave them to deal with this insanity and go somewhere far, far away?*

—and then she slipped out of the bathroom.

The nurse was busy holding the lunch tray closer to the woman's chest. Now was as good a time as any.

As quietly as she could, Ana simply wheeled herself out of the room.

She made it a few feet before the nurse noticed. "Hey. Hey!"

Ana moved faster.

The nurse popped out of the room.

Ana moved even faster.

"You can't—hey! You can't just leave!"

Another nurse leaned over a reception desk.

"Ma'am! You need someone to come and pick you up!"

Ana had to laugh at that.

"Pretty sure I can handle a wheelchair all by myself," she called back, expertly avoiding the other people in her path.

## 4

No one stopped her.

She supposed they had her info, so it's not like they wouldn't be billing her. She guessed that meant her injuries weren't grievous enough to make restraining her a priority. She was just one of probably a myriad of difficult patients who refused to listen. Good riddance, good luck, pay your bills on time, and come back soon.

As for the cops, she had no idea. Maybe her gambit worked and the building had backed off a little? Maybe she'd bought her and Reid enough time to escape? Since he wasn't answering, she had no idea, but she had to find out.

*Maybe they're interrogating Cathy right now . . .* That actually made her laugh a little.

It took ten minutes to find a yellow cab equipped for her. Probably should have just used an app, but cabs kept whizzing by, and she foolishly thought the old-fashioned way would be faster. If she *had* used the app, it'd probably take ten minutes for her driver to show up, at which point a fleet of hundreds of accessible yellows would parade past and—

*Stop it. Stay loose. Get home.*

She listened. She breathed. Panic banged and scratched inside her, but there was nothing she could do except move as quickly as she could.

## 5

When she finally reached the Deptford, she could feel the building's gargoyles staring down at her. Beyond them, clouds hung heavy in a slate gray sky.

The doormen were also staring at her. More so than normal.

The one at the front gate. The pair at the front door. One standing like a coatrack in the front lobby. And of course, the damn concierge.

She felt the elevator gremlin's beady eyes burning into her from under his shady hat brim. Her whole body tingled unpleasantly under his gaze.

The elevator reached the top floor and came to a halt with a sound like a bomb blast. Was the building always this quiet? Did it always feel like it was holding its breath?

Ana supposed it did.

She wheeled herself away from the elevator as quickly as she could, hating having her back to the man inside. She felt relief when she heard it recede down to the lobby.

She sped down the hall, past all her unseen neighbors' front doors, past Mrs. Jacobs's apartment, until she reached her own.

## 6

She'd successfully avoided panicking up to this point.

When she discovered that Reid and Charlie weren't here either, panic finally won its tug-of-war.

Heart jackhammering, breath whistling, she looked in the bedroom, in Charlie's room, the living room.

The booth door was open—but by whom?!—and she looked in there, too.

Nothing. Nowhere.

No note.

No blood, no real sign of struggle, that was good, except—

It was only after her initial circuit through the apartment that she really began to notice what she'd been seeing.

Reid's mother's things were out. That giant bronze chai paperweight.

There was garlic on the wall.

A memory emerged, dull and shapeless. She'd told him at the hospital.

"Vampires," she said out loud now, in a quiet, almost disbelieving voice.

He'd believed her.

*Oh, Reid.*

She felt sick with love, with terror. Where were they?! Fuck!

*Okay. Okay, let's game this through.* Maybe he had taken the threat seriously enough that he'd gone to stay in a hotel or something. But why hadn't he come by the hospital to tell her? Why hadn't he at the very least left a note?

The panic blotted out everything, and she didn't notice the phone was ringing until the third ring.

The landline.

Who would call the landline?

On the heels of that thought, like thick poison sliding into her guts: only the building called this phone.

Unless it was Reid . . . but why wouldn't he call her cell?

She imagined the concierge downstairs, his wet lips pulled upward in his fishhook grin, disgustingly thin hands wrapped around the phone against his cheek, waiting unctuously for Ana to answer.

*Don't do it. Whatever they're calling for, it's not good. You're not expecting guests or anything, so—*

"But they know I'm here," she whispered.

The phone continued to ring.

*Let them think you're taking a shit or something. Who cares?!*

If it was the building calling, she had to know. What did they want? What did they have?

Her hands, slick with sweat, could barely hold the ivory-colored receiver.

"H-hello?"

An unfamiliar voice responded.

"Can I speak with Reid, please? This is Isaac. From the Mitzvah Tank?"

## 7

"*Wh-who* is this?"

"Do I have the right number? This is Reid's residence? Or did he give me a fake number?"

"Who. Is."

"This is Isaac Blau; I met with Reid—well, I've met with Reid several times by accident, but this morning on purpose. Is this Mrs. Reid?"

It was like she was hearing some other language. It didn't help that the man's voice slurred with what she thought was the practiced deniability of a day drinker. "You met with him—today?"

"This morning, yes. It didn't go *great,* but—"

"Was Charlie with him? Our baby?"

A beat. "Oh yes. Your very—*ahem*—well-behaved baby girl."

"This morning."

"This morning. Is there something wrong with our connecti—"

"What did he say? What did he talk to you about?" She tried to keep her voice calm and steady, and found herself looking around the apartment again as if this conversation would help her realize she'd overlooked something obvious.

A laugh. When he spoke a moment later, it sounded as if he'd just taken a sip of something. "Well, it might seem a little odd, but—"

*"What did he talk to you about?!"*

A pause. Ana could feel the man on the other end weigh his options: talk with the crazy woman or invent a reason to end the call.

"Vampires," he said at last. "We spoke of vampires. For the book he's writing?"

"The book he's writing." *Oh, Reid.*

"He wanted to know . . . well, he wanted to know if they existed in Jewish lore. How a Jew might fight them. Hypothetically, of course. Luckily for Reid, I love this stuff. He's seen me reading scary novels before, so I guess, bashert, right? Anyway, I told him I'd have to dig around. That was before things got a little tense between us. He was eager to hear what I learned as soon as possible, so he gave me all his numbers. He hasn't been answering his cell. Is he—"

"Did he tell you where he was going next?"

"No, but—"

"Then I've gotta go—"

"Wait, wait, wait," he said jovially. "Can I tell you what I learned, so you can pass it on to him? He said it was urgent."

She almost hung up anyway, then forced herself to wait. "Yes. Please, I'll . . . I'll give him the message."

"Wonderful." Papers shuffled. The man cleared his throat, then another audible swallow of something liquid. "Well, of course, first there's Lilith. Good old Lilith, Adam's first wife. Great-grandmother to all sorts of supernatural nasties. There's the Alukah, and the Motetz Dam . . ."

Ana listened as he rattled off a brief list of names that meant nothing to her. It took hardly more than a minute or two—but it felt interminable. Finally, she snapped.

"But how do you kill the damn things?!"

Another appraising pause. "Most of what I've found so far is your garden-variety 'cut off the head, bury the body upside down' sort of stuff. But I know Reid wanted something interesting, something really historical. So! I kept digging."

*"And?"* She kept herself from yelling.

"I found something while reading up on estries—I mentioned estries earlier, yes? I was skimming through the Sefer Hasidim and came across some detailed descriptions. How estries are undeterred by religious iconography, how they can stroll into a temple or a church and not bat an eye. Heh, no pun intended with the bat part."

Ana squeezed the phone.

"Anyway, there was one particularly novel method of killing an estrie. Surprisingly simple. Ready? *You stuff earth into their mouth.* Isn't that interesting?"

"Earth?" Again, like a language she didn't know, yet spoke.

"In fact, two things seem to be consistent among most ancient vampiric creatures. One is a shared aversion to earth and dirt, which I think is why later vampires like, say, Dracula, need to sleep in a coffin full of their own, special soil. The other thing is a particular hunger for babies. They crave babies. Spooky, huh?" She thought of Charlie and didn't answer. Isaac didn't notice her silence; he was too energized by the topic. "I thought that earth detail might be appropriate for Reid's story, considering what else we talked about."

"What else did you talk about?"

"Why, the relationship between Jews and vampires! Jews *are* vampires, Mrs. Reid! At least, according to those who hate us! Foreign interlopers who don't belong, who use good Christian blood to maintain their longevity, who hypnotize and pull strings from the darkness? Heh, who wear dark clothes and have vaguely Eastern European accents and are insidiously interested in real estate? We're meant to be fundamentally homeless parasites, aren't we? Of *course* native soil would be a weapon against our analogue! Reid found this all very interesting."

She was desperate to hang up the phone, but had to ask. "Did you say things got tense between you?"

"Well, I can be a little self-indulgent sometimes." His voice became sad and lugubrious again. "Speaking of, would you maybe mind telling him one other thing?"

"I really need to go, Mr.—"

"Yes, yes. Just tell him . . . *maybe* he's right. About surviving. It would be nice to believe he's right."

## 8

Her mind whirled.

Earth.

Babies.

Vampires.

Reid had gone to—was that a rabbi?—and asked about vampires. With Charlie. *But where were they now?!* The rabbi had been no help there.

Maybe Reid had gone to get more supplies? Like what? Graveyard dirt?

But, no, Reid didn't have that information yet. Why wasn't Reid answering his cell? Did this have something to do with their argument? *Maybe he's right. About suffering.*

A faint thump came from the closet, and all her thoughts evaporated.

She stared at the closed closet door.

Had something moved in there?

Was something in the apartment with her?

Her mouth went very dry.

She suddenly realized what she'd done, coming back here. All this wondering what Reid might have done . . . but what if something had been done *to* him?

The closet door appeared to bulge and breathe. Her fevered mind playing tricks.

Was someone here? Some*thing*?

She looked around for the most immediate weapon she could grab. Her eyes fell on the large, bronze paperweight on the couch. Sharp as hell. Basically, bronze knuckles, right?

She picked it up, careful of the razor edges.

"Hello?" she asked.

*Stupid. Stupid, Ana. No one's in there . . . and, if there were, you just gave them a big heads-up that you're onto them.*

She pushed forward . . . forward . . . close to the closet door, the sharp chai in her lap.

Without warning, she grabbed the knob and threw the door open.

It was full of clothes. Coats, jackets, outerwear. No gibbering, four-legged, backward-limbed monster flew out at her.

If she really wanted to know if something hid in the dark depths of the closet, she would have to wade in. But why? If some monster wanted to leap out, now was its chance . . .

Suddenly exhausted, she moved out of the way of the door and shut it again.

She looked at the bronze chai in her hand and was hit by sudden, heartbreaking nostalgia. She missed Reid's mom. She missed feeling like she had at least one family member they could go to for help—or even a sympathetic ear. They were so alone.

Then her eyes fell on the put-all next to the front door.

No. They weren't entirely alone.

Reid had gone to seek advice; it was finally time for Ana to do the same.

# NEIGHBORS (II)

## 1

Each time Ana knocked, she looked nervously down the hall toward the elevator, waiting for the concierge to suddenly appear and tell her she needed to go home and lie down. She refused to look toward the staircase.

She knocked three times before using the key. She half expected the locks to have been changed, but the handle turned smoothly in her grip.

Mrs. Jacobs's apartment was silent as a tomb.

Some instinct stopped Ana from calling out after she slipped inside. The same instinct made her engage the dead bolt, keeping the door from fully closing behind her.

She sat in the darkened front hallway.

She inhaled and exhaled slowly.

The apartment had a strange, meaty smell.

Then, ever so faintly, a noise. Ana recognized it, although she tried to tell herself she was wrong. She'd heard it recently—in her dream, when her mother stood over Charlie's crib, a tattered leg in her hand.

It was the wet sound of eating.

## 2

At first, Ana wondered if maybe the Jacobses had a cat—maybe a pet was eating some food and that explained the soft, smacking sounds in the otherwise silent apartment.

When Ana reached the living room, it took her brain an entire minute to fully process what she saw. She sat in the shadows of the hallway, blinking. Mouth agape. Not even breathing her calming breaths.

Mrs. Jacobs wouldn't be answering any of Ana's questions after all.

Two small mountains sat in the living room, against the farthest wall.

*The couch. They must be sitting on the couch.*

The couch wasn't visible anymore, though; only two large piles of clear, curdled substance, tapering from a wide base as they rose several feet, like a pair of second-grade science fair volcanoes made out of rubber cement. Two humans emerged neck-deep from the top.

Mr. and Mrs. Jacobs. Their faces tilted up to the ceiling, mouths open wide. Like baby birds waiting to be fed.

More gunk splattered the walls behind them and the floor, like they'd been shot at with a spray gun. It had dried and cemented them in place, Ana understood.

The only light in the room came through the closed drapes, so it took Ana longer to see the source of the noises.

Mrs. Jacobs was closer to Ana. The second pile, between Mrs. Jacobs and the wall, was her husband. A small, shadowy shape, often made invisible by the low light and the natural shadows of the corner, crawled over him.

*I don't want to see this. I don't want to see this.*

The shape skittered over Mr. Jacobs like an insect, never pausing to think or plan. It knew what it was doing. Then it stopped, puked a little more goo onto the pile, skittered some more. After a moment, Mr. Jacobs made a wheezing, plaintive noise—still alive!—and the shape crawled up and began vomiting into Mr. Jacobs's mouth.

Rather than gag or even fight back, Mr. Jacobs appeared to accept it gratefully.

Whatever substance kept Mr. and Mrs. Jacobs glued in place, it also appeared to be keeping them alive.

But why? What was the purpose of all this?

*You know, Ana. You know what that shape is; you're just refusing to think it—*

No—

*That's their baby. And that's what Charlie's become, too, unless you—*

NO.

Ana caught a glimpse of light. Shining off Mrs. Jacobs's face.

Her eye.

Her eye was moving.

Mrs. Jacobs was alive, too, and she looked at Ana, making a low moaning noise.

Ana felt her heart leap into her throat.

That wet, pleading eye. *Help me,* it begged. *Do something.*

But what could she do? Ana supposed she could go back to her own apartment, find something sharp to cut Mr. and Mrs. Jacobs free, but what could be done about—

*Say it—*

The baby. What could she do about that?

Isaac's voice recurred to her. *They crave babies.* But maybe not to *eat*.

Wait.

The spider shape was gone.

The baby was gone.

*Fuck.*

The air suddenly got thin and hard to breathe. Ana's heart thudded in her chest. Her mouth tasted metallic and rancid.

With one more helpless glance at Mrs. Jacobs, whose moans began to grow, she eased her chair backward, scanning the room, concentrating on being as quiet and imperceptible as possible.

Maybe the little creature had just moved behind Mr. Jacobs and was out of her field of vision. That's all. Maybe—

A noise above her. With what felt like torturous slowness, she tilted her head and looked up.

The Jacobs' baby clung to the ceiling, a few yards away and moving with astonishing speed. She felt herself lock in fright. She couldn't tear herself from the spot as she watched the tiny figure speed its way across the ceiling toward her.

A second later, it dropped with a hiss onto Ana's lap.

That broke her trance. The baby gave an unbearable, alien shriek and tried to latch its hideously adhesive lips onto her. Ana picked it up and held it out. It felt like a knapsack full of wet cement, so solid, so loathsome, so . . . *wrong.* Kicking and squirming, it opened its mouth, and a long, fleshy appendage emerged from the depths of the baby's throat.

Ana screamed in outrage, in terror. As long as she held this creature, she was stuck, she couldn't get out, so she did the only thing she could. She threw the baby across the room.

As soon as her hands were free, they were on her wheels, spinning herself backward, turning around to face the hallway, slamming unheeded into walls, and then racing to the door.

But she didn't hear the creature land. No thud. No crash.

Only a skitter along the wall a few feet behind her. Behind . . . and then above. This time, it would land on her back, stick its mouth onto the nape of her neck, rip skin away, incapacitate her just enough so that it could entomb her in more of that awful stuff and—

If she hadn't left the front door to the apartment slightly open, that would have been it. She would have slammed into the wood, fumbled with the lock, and that thing, that creature, would have been on her.

As it was, she reached the door, noticed the tiny sliver of light around one side of its frame, and yanked it open with all her might. Undoing the dead bolt as she did so, she burst out into the main hallway of the floor, then spun around and slammed the door shut.

She hoped the door stopped her pursuer cold. She hoped it smashed its monstrous face into the wood and died on impact.

Instead, after the reverberation of the slam rippled away, all was silent . . . and then a soft, curious scraping arose from behind the door.

Could it turn the knob?

No. It wasn't strong enough to do that yet . . . was it?

She had her answer momentarily.

The scraping sound moved lower and lower down the door.

Through the thin crack between the door and the threshold, a tiny brown-and-red nub appeared. It forced its way through with what appeared to be some effort.

It was the tip of whatever had come out of the baby's mouth.

Searching for her. Reaching for her. A prehensile straw. Viscous fluid dribbling from the tip.

With sick relief, Ana realized the baby was still too young to think of things like opening doors. It was just hungry, full of need.

It was just an infant.

She shivered, like she'd moved through spiderwebs. She wiped herself of the sensation of crawling with spindly legs, and with trembling hands and arms, made her way back into her own apartment.

Then she promptly headed for the bathroom and threw up.

## 3

The toilet flushed, and her head rang from the effort of dumping her guts out through her mouth.

*The way the baby vomited on its parents.*

Her feverish brain whirled, piecing together what she'd seen. The baby-thing incapacitated its parents and kept them alive so it could, what . . . use its mouth-thing to . . . to drink their insides? Punch holes in their bodies and . . . Did it drink blood? Something more visceral? Maybe whatever it used to feed its victims also turned their insides into something a little more . . . drinkable? Didn't certain snakes and spiders do something similar? Predigest their meals on the outside?

The adhesive mouth, that must have been to keep it latched onto its prey. Like a leech.

A horrible image came to her. The fleshy appendage-thing was a straw. The parents, with their upturned mouths, were juice boxes.

She almost puked again. She wanted to scream, scream, and never stop screaming.

When she heard crying elsewhere in her own apartment, Ana figured she was hallucinating, but the sound didn't go away. She froze and listened.

Not just any crying.

A parent knows.

It could be a crowded restaurant, a playground full of dozens of other kids crying in the same way . . . or an impossibly empty apartment.

That wasn't just any cry.

It was Charlie.

Ana sped back into the living room, slamming one shoulder against a doorframe as she careened into the room.

The door to her recording booth was open. The cries came from inside.

No. No, that was impossible. She'd checked!

She looked inside again, but it appeared empty. And the cries had an odd quality. Muffled.

It came from a pile of blankets in the corner of the booth. Who had put those there?

"Charlie? Is that you, Baby Bird?"

She couldn't quite reach them from where she sat, so she locked the wheels of her chair and transferred herself to the chair inside the booth.

"Charlie? What's wrong, baby?"

Every sense in her head shrieked that this was wrong, this was a trap, but she couldn't fathom what kind of trap it would be, or why, or how someone would trap her in her own apartment. Numbed and disoriented by everything—the birthday party, the attack, the hospital, the empty apartment, the neighbor—she just wanted to see why her baby was back in the booth, crying in a strange and distorted way.

That's why when she lifted up the blanket and revealed the baby monitor, vibrating ever so slightly with the sounds of Charlie crying, she didn't immediately flee. She was just confused.

When the door to the voice-over booth clicked shut, firmly and irrevocably, her first thought was simply, *Oh. Reid finally fixed my booth.*

## 4

She reached for the handle, but it wouldn't budge. It was locked.

That was also wrong. It shouldn't lock from the outside.

But this handle was new. It had just been replaced. And reversed.

Reid stood on the other side of the glass. He held the other baby monitor and his cell phone in his hand. The cell phone on which he'd recorded Charlie's cries for the doctor another lifetime ago. He pressed Stop on the phone; the cries ceased.

Ana still felt confused. She rattled the knob. It remained locked.

She wasn't mad until Reid's voice came over the baby monitor.

"Ana. Just stop for a second. I have to tell you something. A lot of things."

She wasn't mad until he said those fateful words.

"Just hear me out . . . and try not to get mad."

# MAD

## 1

Hiding in the closet had been a top ten stupid idea. She'd almost caught him when she peeked in.

But then . . . she hadn't caught him. Something distracted her, and he'd remained undetected.

As Reid crouched behind the coats, he found himself thinking about fate versus coincidence. How certain events seemed to be happening exactly how they needed to.

Tumblers in a lock, falling into place. *Bashert.*

His conversation with Isaac had been like that, too. At first, Isaac had seemed the exact right person to speak to. He just so happened to have many opinions on the myths of vampires and their historical association with anti-Semitic tropes. He was shockingly well versed in horror pop culture. Books. Movies. "I'm drawn to dark stories," he'd said. "Especially lately. You're meeting me during a very strange time in my life, Reid. I suppose that's true for everyone these days."

That should've been Reid's first clue.

Isaac had bought Reid's lie—inspired in the moment by remembering the book Ana was currently narrating—that he was writing a vampire novel from the Jewish perspective, with a Jewish hero who wanted to use tactics "predating the cross" to fight ancient evils. Despite having a list of other novels Reid should check out, Isaac said he'd have to check on more historical texts for the kind of information Reid seemed to be so desperately craving. They exchanged numbers. Reid gave him the landline, too, to make sure he got the info as soon as possible.

"It's really urgent," Reid told him. "Deadlines."

Perhaps if the meeting had ended there, things would have gone differently. But it hadn't.

In the closet now, Reid heard Ana leave the apartment. He wasted no time, springing into action. He laid the baby monitor inside the voice-over booth, then hurried back into the closet, waiting to see what Ana did next.

His mind returned to Isaac.

That whole time, Isaac wouldn't stop staring at Charlie. Unable to ignore it any longer, Reid had finally asked:

"Do you . . . have kids?"

Isaac nodded, still staring at Charlie. "A little boy. Five years old. Although . . ." A small bottle came out of Isaac's jacket. Svedka vodka. The bottle's contents went into Isaac's coffee cup. "He's dead."

Reid stammered an apology. Isaac shrugged, putting the lid back on his coffee cup.

"He had asthma. Then he caught that damned virus. What can you do? When your number comes up, it comes up."

Reid reached for the phrase everyone lobbed at him when his mom died. "May his memory be a blessing."

Isaac laughed—a short, humorless sound. "Such a weird saying, isn't it? When you've lost something, don't you think memory is more of a curse?"

Reid remembered Isaac dumping jewelry on the counter of Rosemund & Sons. *What if she comes back?* His wife, must be.

"Would you mind terribly if I held her?" Isaac asked abruptly, indicating Charlie. "It's been so long."

"Oh. Um." A sudden image of Camilla's *appendage* coming out of Charlie's mouth, plucking out one of Isaac's eyes, slurping it down like boba. "I don't think that's a good idea. She's not great with strangers."

"Ah." Isaac took a long sip of his coffee and looked off, sadly. Somewhere in the park, a woman shrieked in joy or madness. "I think it's very funny you're writing about a Jewish vampire hunter, Reid."

"Why's that?"

"Because. No matter what answers I might find for you . . . your hero is fucked."

Reid blinked. "I'm sorry?"

"He's fucked. If you truly want it to be a Jewish story, he can't defeat the monsters. Not really. He'll become food for them in the end. That is the true lesson of Judaism."

"Jesus, dude."

"Jesus is just another Jew who can attest to what I'm saying, Reid." He took a deep swig of his spiked coffee, then added some more vodka.

Reid stared at him. So did Charlie.

"When we speak of creatures like the vampire," Isaac continued, "we speak of metaphors. We give them little Achilles' heels so we can feel better, but tell me: What vulnerabilities does grief have? How would a hero defeat *that* monster? He can't, can he?" His welling eyes latched on Charlie again. "I could've saved my boy, you know. A simple vaccination might have done it. Or maybe not. Maybe it's just our lot to suffer. That's what our people are 'chosen' to do. Our birthright. Our curse."

"No," Reid said, defensively covering Charlie's shoulders with his hands. "No, you're wrong."

"Am I?" An ironic grin. "I think I'm a little more well versed in Judaism than—"

"The lesson of Judaism is we *survive.* We're survivors."

"But why do we always have to survive *so much,* Reid?" Isaac leapt to his feet. "Is that really survival? Running from one set of jaws to another? What did we do to deserve the Shoah? Or bondage in Egypt? The destructions of our Temple? The pogroms? The ghettos? Why do we need armed guards at our synagogues now, *today*? What did I do to deserve my son's death? What did you do to deserve your own sorrows? 'Happy is the person You discipline, Adonai!' Why are we so damned disciplined? I know you agree with me! What was it you said when we first met? When you were asked if you were Jewish?"

*Real Jews know not to answer that whenever strangers are at the door.* "That was a joke." But Reid burned with the embarrassment of recognition.

Isaac laughed poisonously. "No, Reid. That was *memory.* And that's why heroic stories of fighting monsters with symbols of some glowing Messiah's godhood aren't for us. They're for *them.*" He indicated the other people in the park. "Hey, but don't let that keep you from whatever you're writing, huh? *We deserve our own silly fantasies, too, dammit!*" He shouted this at the passersby. Most ignored him. He chuckled, pleased with himself.

*This man is a vampire,* Reid realized. *He's not a monster, but he thrives on misery. He needs to drink from my cup of sorrows to digest his own.*

Reid wanted to tell the guy off, wanted to let him know just how pathetic he sounded. He wanted to argue, say, *Maybe suffering* is *a birthright, but maybe you just didn't do everything you could to protect your kid.*

Instead, Reid stood and took a step back. Then another.

"Where are you going, Reid? Am I scaring you? Is this a horror your hero cannot face?"

"Thanks for your help." Reid continued walking away. Isaac sat down, raising his voice as if addressing the world.

"Why do *you* think we must suffer so? Why does HaShem test his chosen people? Is there even a God at all?"

Reid reached for one of his favorite old songs, the one he'd only half-jokingly described as the most profound lyrics ever written. "A womp-bob-a-loo-bop, a womp-bam-boom."

With that, Reid left Isaac to his coffee, mind swirling.

Obviously, Isaac was just one damaged human being, but . . . was he right?

Reid had expressed similar sentiments himself, but now, hearing them like that, he felt a loathing for them. More disturbing, Isaac's fatalism reminded him of someone else. Ana.

*"Our curse."* The same word Ana had used when they'd first won the Deptford lottery.

Something fundamental was shifting inside of him.

He'd had half a mind to go back to continue arguing with Isaac, to try to articulate how he was feeling—after all, argument was a central tenet of Judaism, right? He'd even stopped in his tracks in the park, ready to head back to that bench—but then, *again* with perfect timing, a tiny voice came from under his chin.

"Dadda?" Charlie had said.

Reid looked down in astonishment. She'd never said that before.

She looked up at him from the chest carrier. Her eyes were clear. So beautifully, perfectly clear. His heart began to gallop.

"Dadda. Ess go home," she said. *Let's go home.* Her first sentence.

Just like that.

He'd been overthinking everything. The answer was so simple. Charlie. Always Charlie. Doing what was best for Charlie. Giving her the best life possible. Why was he running? They were being offered safety and security and he'd just been too unprepared by life to recognize it. That confrontation with Isaac was *exactly* what he needed to avoid a catastrophic mistake. What were the odds?

A new plan, then.

Before heading back to the Deptford, Reid made one additional stop: that long-promised visit to Home Depot.

And did the store have exactly what Reid needed? And had Ana chosen that exact moment to begin calling his cell, telling him she was awake and ready to bust out of the hospital, giving him no chance for second guesses?

*Bashert.* Tumblers in a lock.

Now he just needed to make Ana understand.

## 2

"Just, please. Listen," he urged her through the baby monitor. "Stop and just listen. I didn't want to do this."

Ana stopped for a moment . . . then resumed her yelling and cursing. Her face, warped in a fury he'd never seen before. Her voice, audible but indistinct through the heavy glass, like she yelled at him from underwater.

Guilt and panic surged through him. He should let her out. This was stupid. This was cruel. This was—

The only way. She was too sensitive, too upset, too convinced their luck and lives would always be bad. Too much like Isaac.

He shut his eyes and held the baby monitor against his forehead for a moment. He dreaded what he had to do next to get her to be quiet. He thought of the things he wanted to say to Isaac. The things he wanted to say to himself.

Deep breath, for volume as well as strength. Then:

*"Shut the fuck up, Ana! Jesus fucking Christ! You're going to ruin everything, you idiot! For once in your fucking life, stop overreacting and listen!"*

He'd never spoken to her like that before. Her wide eyes confirmed as much.

He hated to hurt her . . . but the words he said weren't untrue. She *could* ruin everything. She needed to listen.

She needed to hear the truth.

It would feel good to speak the truth.

So that's what he did.

## 3

She listened, horrified.

His spiel—god, it sounded like a sales pitch, like he'd signed them up for a time-share—was brief yet interminable. The Deptford's residents were special; they'd offered to make Charlie special; and they were willing to let Reid and Ana live here as part of the family. They'd even be able to help Ana get out of her chair.

It was so simple. So easy. Which was how Ana knew:

They'd lied to him.

They'd lied to him, and he wanted to believe it.

If she had any doubts what was really in store for them, she just had to go next door and visit the Jacobses.

She didn't realize she screamed this out loud. She didn't realize she sobbed and begged Reid—*he* was the one who needed to listen!

She didn't realize this, because it made no difference. Reid just kept patiently explaining, again and again, that she was overreacting. That he'd made a *deal.* That *Everything* would be okay.

She rattled the door, desperately hoping it would break and swing open. Or that *he* would break and let her out.

Neither happened. Her mother's infuriatingly snotty voice spoke up.

*He's not budging, Ana. And you're going to burn yourself out. You need to calm down and think. You need to save your energies.*

For what?

*For finding Charlie and getting the fuck out of this building.*

## 4

He was relieved she'd calmed down. She'd finally stopped yelling and rattling the door. She was quiet. Receptive.

He reiterated everything he'd been saying, now with as much sincerity and love in his voice as he could convey. He knew she wasn't going to hug him and thank him—not yet, at least—but maybe now he could hope she'd at least not despise him. Maybe in time, she'd even forgive him.

He hated this. He hated being the bad guy. He just wanted what was best for her and Charlie. Even more than what was best for him, he wanted to provide for his girls.

He tried, again, to explain it all.

Ana bowed her head.

She really was listening! Good! Except . . .

When she continued holding that pose after he'd finished speaking, he and his sinking gut realized . . . she was looking for something. What was she looking for?

She picked up the microphone in its little desktop stand. Nothing in Reid's brain could put together what she was doing. Was she tidying up? Was she going to try to use the microphone to speak to him?

It wasn't until she turned the microphone stand around and started slamming the wide, heavy metal base against the glass of the door that he understood. At which point there was nothing he could do to stop her.

## 5

The thick glass took several swings, and it didn't break neatly the way windows do in the movies. Once she'd managed to punch a hole through, there were all sorts of crags and jagged edges that needed to be swept away from the frame.

"Are you going to make me crawl out, or do I have to use this on your hands?" she asked Reid as she used the mic stand to clear all the broken glass.

Reid stepped back.

"Ana. Come on, what are you doing? This is insane!"

"Yeah, *I'm* the crazy one," she said. She reached through and, after a short struggle, opened the door from the outside, drawing shallow wounds across her arm but miraculously avoiding any serious cuts.

That done, she crawled out of the booth and made her way toward her wheelchair.

Reid moved it away. "Did you not listen to a thing I said?"

Blood pounded in her ears. "I listened, Reid. You definitely made sure I had to listen."

"And—?"

"And you wanna see what your new friends have in store for us? For Charlie? Go next door and take a look. Give me my fucking chair back." He'd never done something like this before, so egregiously violated the unspoken rules of wheelchair etiquette. It infuriated her almost more than him locking her in the booth.

Reid was too busy whining to respond, though. "You didn't *listen*! You don't understand. They said Charlie's *special*. We're *special*. We won't be like *them*!" He indicated the wall, the next-door neighbors, the poor unwashed masses that they'd somehow risen above.

"Reid." She kept her voice calm and even. "Give me. My fucking. Chair. Now."

"Not until you talk to me about—"

"Then I'm sorry." She sighed, and she swung the mic stand onto his foot. He screamed in surprise and agony. She probably broke a toe or two, but she didn't care. He let go of the chair. She pulled it toward herself and scrambled into it.

He seethed, bending down to hold his injured foot.

For a moment, neither spoke. They simply stared at each other, each aware that suddenly, something had irrevocably changed between them. An invisible seal in every relationship: physical violence. They'd never used it before, and they couldn't turn back now.

After appearing to summon almost superhuman strength and dignity, Reid said, "I am trying to help us."

Ana fought the urge to spit on him. She'd never been so furious in her life. "Try better," she said, and wheeled her way to the door.

He grabbed her handles, keeping her from moving.

"Let me go," she said.

"No. We're going to talk about this."

She turned in her seat, brandishing the mic stand. "I will break every finger in your fucking hands if you don't let me go."

He chuckled, and it sent a feverish chill through her body. "They can heal me," he said. "It won't matter what you do to me, they can make it better. They could heal you, too, if you weren't such a fucking—"

She swung the mic stand at his hands, hoping to reduce the bones in his precious guitar-playing fingers to a fine powder.

Unfortunately, her angle was awkward and her arms were tired. He grabbed the stand before it did any damage.

Before he could do anything with it—*He might smash my head in,* her thoughts whirred; *No, Reid would never do that*—she let go and reached blindly for the next object she could use to defend herself. Her hands found purchase on an item that had been left by the door.

The bronze chai that had belonged to Reid's mom.

Ana grabbed it, aware it sliced into her palm, and slashed blindly behind herself. She felt it eat into flesh—probably his arm or his shoulder. He howled in outrage.

He also backed away. Those monsters might have promised to heal him, but pain still scared him. He wasn't as friendly with it as she was.

"Ana," he said cautiously through heavy breaths.

She pulled open the front door and then stopped.

Charlie's chest carrier hung on a hook by the door. Ana grabbed it, stuffed it under her legs, and left the apartment for the last time.

## 6

She stopped halfway to the elevator. What was she doing? If what Reid said was true about the tenants of this building—and, of course it was, she'd seen too much to doubt it—would she really be safe in the elevator? Trapped in a tiny box operated by one of them?

What choice did she have?

Every fear she'd ever had about moving to the top floor began singing at once, a hellish and exultant choir. In a way, she almost longed for a fire, a power outage, a gas leak, something normal and definitive that kept her trapped up here, instead of this desperate uncertainty.

She heard Reid's voice echoing her thoughts.

"Ana," he said with pity. "Where are you going to go?"

He didn't shout, but his voice carried down the hallway in a resonant rumble.

She turned to look at him. He stood just outside their apartment door, yards away but too close by half. One hand was clutching his shoulder.

"Stay away!" she shouted, holding the chai up as a warning.

He took a step forward, limping on his smashed foot. He put both hands up in a placating gesture, giving Ana a better look at his slashed shoulder. His palm was smeared with blood.

"If you're going for the elevator," he said, "it won't come. They're not going to just let you leave."

"Why not? Why the fuck should they care about me?"

"Because *I* care about you." He sounded genuine. His voice choked with tears. That made it all the worse. "And because . . ."

"Because what?"

"Because I think they know you'll try something stupid if I don't convince you not to."

*Something stupid, like try to rescue our daughter from the monsters you just fucking gave her to . . . ?!*

"So then why don't they just kill me? Take me out as a variable? Stay. The *FUCK*. Back."

He'd taken two more hesitant steps forward. Now he stopped.

"They had a late night the other night. They usually rest during the day." He gave a soft, breathy laugh and a tiny shrug. Trying for charming. Then his face became serious. "Look. They're not *evil,* Ana. Please. If you won't believe me, can't you at least believe that I love our daughter? That I want what's best for her?"

"Where is she?"

He swallowed. "Downstairs. With the super."

"The super?" She almost gagged on the word. This was all so fucked.

"She's safe. Better than safe. She's—"

"Help! Help!" Ana screamed, knowing it was pointless. Knowing they were surrounded by empty apartments—no, only some were empty; some would open to reveal the scuttle of tiny legs . . . and soft slurping noises.

"Ana," Reid said, and it was clear he was losing patience. "Baby. *I'm* helping."

"You were played, Reid."

"No, I fucking *wasn't*!" He actually stamped his foot, his uninjured one, like a toddler.

She had hurt him physically. Now she wanted to hurt him emotionally. She wanted him to feel crippled. She didn't shout; she kept her voice just loud enough to carry down the hall.

"You were played because you've wanted to feel special all your life. And now you're lying to yourself because you're desperate. You *know* you're lying, Reid, and that's why—"

"Lying?" His voice met hers, equally calm, equally even-toned. "You want to talk about lying? Why are you pretending to care what happens to Charlie, Ana? It's not like you even love her."

Something about the deadly calm with which they spoke drove it home all the harder. They each wanted to hurt the other, yes, but with the only weapon left—truth.

"What?" she gasped as if he'd physically punched her.

"You never wanted her. I had to beg you to continue the treatments. You regretted having her. But do you really hate her *this* much? That you would take her away from love, from security, and curse her with a mother who ruins her life? *Why,* Ana?" His voice broke with tears she knew were actually genuine. "Just because it happened to you? You hate her so much, you want to turn her into you? Bitter and resentful and, and . . ." He threw his hands up in defeat.

She had never heard him like this before, and she realized he had never truly been honest with her. He hadn't *lied* to her, not directly. But for years, he had always held this back.

Hearing the words coming out of his mouth seemed to have an effect on Reid, as well. He lost his calm, making himself angry again.

"*Well, I'm not going to let that happen.* She can have a better life—we can all have a better life, which is all I've ever wanted to provide! I've been carrying both of you! *Me!* By *myself*! While you stew in your goddamn weak, selfish shit! And now I *finally* have some help! Besides, you wanna talk about evil? Remember what *you* almost did?! That night?! That fucking night you tried to kill our daughter?!"

She always thought the moment Reid finally threw that evening in her face would be one of the worst moments of her life. For a split second, it was. For a split second, and for the millionth time, she remembered that night with crystal clarity—it crushed her—and she had the urge to give up, slink away and leave them both.

Then she heard her mother's voice. Cathy, Queen of Judgment. The mother Ana had fought so hard not to become.

She said, *He's right.*

Which confirmed all Ana needed to know: he was wrong. Because he was doing what Cathy always tried to do.

Ana stiffened her spine and said, "I'm not going to let you turn Charlie into something she's not."

She headed for the stairs.

## 7

She expected him to reach out and grab her as she wheeled past. Instead, he started laughing, a high, lunatic laugh.

"Oh my god, what are you gonna do," he asked, now behind her, "*crawl down*? Are you serious?"

"Guess so," she said over her shoulder. "Where's the super? Down in the basement, right?"

"See?" He cackled, every inch a schoolyard bully. "You don't know *anything*!"

She reached the top of the stairs and applied her brakes. As she clipped on the chest carrier and prepared to lower herself down to the first step, Reid's laughter stopped.

"Okay, stop. Ana. Stop. This has gone on far enough. This is too pathetic even for you."

Suddenly, he was behind her, holding the handles of her chair. He tried to pull her backward, but the brakes held firm.

She'd almost forgotten how strong he could be. Reid wasn't an athletic guy, but he had impressive upper-body strength for someone of his size and build, and he rarely had occasion to show it off. He always said playing guitar was "good for the guns."

The wheels gave an agonized shriek as Reid forced her to turn around and face the other direction.

It was stunning. It was abrupt. It was violent and terrifying to be so manhandled.

They stood there, panting at each other. Two strangers, scanning the other's face for anything recognizable. The high-pitched, rubber scream of the wheels echoed down the hallway.

Then Reid said, "We're going back to the apartment." Firm. Resolute. Nostrils flaring.

"No."

"I will pull you out of that fucking chair if you don't come back into the apartment with me so we can talk about this."

"No—"

He reached out and grabbed at her arm. It was such an ugly violation that she could only give a little cry and squirm her arm out of his grasp. She managed to slip out, but she knew she wouldn't be so lucky the next time. This was a wrestling match she couldn't win.

"*Now,* Ana." Nothing but pure hatred in his voice.

Her heart hammered in her throat. Her eyes bulged out of her skull.

"Stop," she panted. "Please."

As she'd predicted, he grabbed her again and caught her arm. He didn't tug, but he didn't let go, either. His touch was revolting, unfamiliar. She looped her other arm around the armrest of her chair, to anchor herself, but that wouldn't hold her for long.

"I'm not going to ask you again, Ana. I'll drag you if I have to."

"Okay! Stop! I'll come with you, just stop. Let me go!" Then she changed her tone abruptly. No longer desperate, but calm. Firm. "Reid? I'm serious. *Stop now.*"

It was her mom-voice. It said playtime was over. And it worked. He let her go.

He loomed over her, waiting to see what she would do.

"Thank you," she said. She caught her breath, then shut her eyes and said something else. She kept her voice at a low mumble, just audible enough to hear, not loud enough to understand.

"What?" he asked.

She mumbled it again.

"Goddammit, Ana. *What?!*" He slapped his hands on his thighs, leaning down to her, the way so many strangers did, bending to talk to her like she was a child. In that split second, more than the violence and the hate and the words that could never be unsaid, everything was decided.

"I said, 'It's time to get loose.'"

She unlocked the brakes, grabbed his shirt, and leaned backward.

## 8

The chair tumbled them both down the stairs.

It was a clumsy, ugly fall, with Reid fighting to stay upright until the moment gravity took over. Because of his weight, it wasn't a true tipping over like she'd imagined. Instead, when she began to tip, he managed to prevent that from happening, only to then stumble forward a step, accidentally pushing her wheels over the edge, and lurching himself in an awkward, slow fall over her.

Ana, for her part, slid out of her chair, scraping her head against a few steps before stopping herself with her elbows.

Her chair clattered all the way down to the first landing, making a loud, outraged racket.

Not loud enough to mask the noise she heard a few steps below her head, though.

A sickening crack.

Ana was upside down, looking at the ceiling. She managed to reorient herself onto her stomach and palms to see what had broken.

Reid lay on the steps below her, contorted in a sickeningly unnatural position.

For a moment, she thought he was dead. As she crawled down toward him, she noticed him blinking, moving his mouth with a horrible, drowning-fish sort of gasp.

His eyes widened as she approached, reminding her of the way Mrs. Jacobs had stared from her cocoon.

"Reid . . ." she whispered.

She wanted to sob, to beg for forgiveness. She choked back the urge; thinking of Mrs. Jacobs reminded her what he'd wanted for them.

Reid wheezed. "I can't . . . I can't . . ."

When Ana finally pulled up even with him on the steps, she was close enough to hear what he said.

"I can't move."

She didn't stop to comfort him.

Instead, she thought with morbid fascination, *My god, what are the odds?* and continued to pull herself down the stairs.

# THE CRAWL

## 1

Ana made her way down the slick marble steps, one by one.

Eventually, Reid found his voice and screamed after her, demanding she come back, begging she help. She left him where he lay. Would he ever get up again? No time to care. She had to get Charlie. Her name pulsed in Ana's ears.

*Charlie. Charlie. Charlie.*

She moved slowly, sore from the fight, the broken glass, the receding adrenaline. Sweat poured into her eyes. Hair plastered to her face. Her palms hurt. Her muscles shrieked. She quickly discovered the safest, most controllable way to move was by arranging her legs forward and then dropping her butt onto each next step, and all that constant thudding gave her a dull throb in her lower hips. She almost had to laugh: *Wow, I can feel my ass for the first time in forever.*

She'd folded up her chair, and dragging it with her slowed her down even further. Worse, it was so atrociously *loud.* It gave her location away like a clarion.

*Oh well. Keep moving. Charlie. Charlie.*

At least she could be thankful she'd never upgraded from the cheap, light, no-frills wheelchair; this one folded up neatly, bounced easily, and put up less of a fight than a more solid, expensive one would have.

She'd found the bronze chai further down on the steps and tucked it inside the baby carrier. Her only weapon. As she moved and twisted, she felt its sharp edges occasionally nip at her skin.

After what felt like an eternity, she made it to the next floor. She gave herself a moment to catch her breath.

*"Anaaaaa,"* Reid's ghostly voice wailed. *"Pleeeeeease."*

A quick, nervous glance down the hallway, just to make sure no one—no *thing*—was about to pop out of one of those closed apartment doors and rush at her.

Then she army-crawled across the landing to the next flight of steps. Reach, reach, pull. Bump, bump, bump. Clang, clang, clang.

Eventually, Reid's voice became a faint, incoherent echo.

All that remained:

*Charlie.*

*Charlie.*

*Charlie.*

# 2

By midafternoon, the sun began to dip, and Ana lost count of how many flights she'd descended.

*Thank God I've been working out my arms lately.*

That made her chuckle a little.

More than all the physical discomfort was knowledge, a howling storm rattling the windows of her sanity, of just how many more floors there were to go. How many more stairs. How many more inches. She'd never really had a fear of heights, but this was its unexpected cousin—she crawled, but she felt dizzy with displacement.

Only giving birth came close. From the moment labor began, a dark and yawning tunnel had opened up, a tunnel of variables, of uncertainty. *How hard will this be? What will the pain be like? How long will it last? Will I be one of those women who get to say it was over before I knew it? Will I be in labor for entire days and think it'll never end? Or will I join the tragic sisterhood of women killed in childbirth?*

You can count on the mind-cleansing adrenaline to take care of the initial few hours. It's all so new, you become reactive . . . but after a while, the novelty wears off and you find yourself beginning to process that this could very well be the rest of your life—and you're just along for the ride.

*At least during labor I didn't have to worry about any fucking monsters falling on my head.*

"Whatever," she whispered, like an affirmation. *Stay loose.*

Her grunts and short falls echoed in the stairway. The clatter of her chair announced her progress.

She knew she was being watched, too. The same way she knew the sweat drying on her skin: she could *feel* it.

Why they didn't descend on her en masse, she didn't know. Curiosity maybe. Waiting. Perhaps there was a trap.

Or perhaps they were scared.

*Right. Scared of you,* her mother's voice whispered in her head. *The cripple literally butt-skipping down the stairs at the rate of one flight an hour. Real intimidating.*

No, Reid had said in his backhanded way that maybe they were still sleeping. That they'd had a late night and implying she wasn't enough of a threat to be worth waking up for.

Unless other things scared them. Like the sunlight streaming through the windows.

But Reid had insisted that they *weren't* vampires. If they *were* vampires, why would they allow for windows in the first place?

*Hubris,* another voice whispered in her head. *They've never had to worry before.*

Then, an unbidden thought: *Reid would know.*

Not the Reid who locked her in a booth or hurled insults to prevent her from rescuing their baby. The Reid who had been her best friend, her partner, her lover, her caretaker. The one who wrote songs for her and sang them in bed. The one who asked her to marry him outside the Beacon Theatre after a Steely Dan concert. The one who held her while she wailed in despair and told her things would be okay.

*Her* Reid.

A grief so sharp it didn't even hurt slid into her chest. She couldn't breathe. Air came into her lungs in short, hitching gasps.

She let herself feel it, then let it pass.

She had no time for grief, not yet. The sun was still out and she was, impossibly, somehow safe for the moment. She just had to keep moving.

Thump, thump, thump she went down the steps. Clatter, clatter, clatter.

*Charlie. Charlie.*

The sun continued to descend, flooding the stairway in rich yellow light. Like a blessing. Like confirmation.

*I just might make it. I just might—*

The sunlight faded as a thick cover of clouds rolled over it. Dimly, she remembered a snowstorm had been forecast for some point this week. Had it saved this exact moment to begin?

That was bad enough, but the next thing was worse.

Much worse.

In the unnaturally silent building, she heard the unmistakable sound of apartment doors creaking open.

## 3

The first attack came ten minutes later. It dropped from the ceiling onto Ana's lap as she lowered herself to the bottom step of the flight she was currently descending.

Dense and heavy, the creature probably would've hurt like hell the way it landed on her upper thighs. As it was, she felt the reverberation in her fillings.

She shrieked in horror and outrage and, in a flash, shoved the thing off her.

It tumbled down a few steps of the next flight and then righted itself with the agility and speed of a cat. Its mad, human-ish face leered up at her. In the soft, snowy dusk, Ana could see tufts of white hair above its gnarled ears.

Someone's kindly grandparent, twisted into a monstrous caricature. Its skin corrugated like the surface of a brain, spotted with pink and red and ashy gray.

It stank, too. A hot, wet, subway smell, poorly masked by something nauseatingly like cologne. She could still smell it on her as the creature crept up the stairs toward her.

It pounced.

At the same moment, Ana used all her strength to swing her folded chair forward. She barely managed to get it in front of her as a shield the moment the monster slammed into her.

Jaws snapped. Swampy, fetid breath caressed her skin. The steps bit into her back as the thing forced her down.

She didn't realize she'd shut her eyes, and when she opened them, the hideous face, its bulging, wet eyes, its pug nose, pressed toward her from the other side of the chair's wheels, inches away.

It opened its mouth, and a sharp-ended tube wormed out from up its throat. Ana shrieked and tried to push it away. She'd never be able to push it far enough to escape that probing appendage. It threaded itself through the spokes of the wheel and made its way straight for her face.

Ana clutched the sides of the wheel and turned.

The monster gave a high-pitched scream as the spokes crushed the tube in a crimped, painful kink. It tried to pull back, to retract, but it couldn't.

Ana wasn't strong enough to keep turning the wheel and slice the thing in chunks, but she'd at least trapped it enough to reach down, grab her chai, and slice at the fleshy, puckering tube-thing barely an inch from her eyes. She worked the serrated edges back and forth until a good portion of the appendage dropped into her lap, puckering and pouting and twitching. Gouts of dark blood followed it.

The creature scuttled back, retching and whining. Blood sprayed from its wound, splashing the immaculate white marble, Ana's chair, her face and arms.

It retreated up one of the walls. As she watched it crawl alongside the staircase window, Ana realized another creature, already on that wall, watched them. The injured one mewled and sulked, and its friend watched Ana warily.

Ana tried to keep an eye on both as she dragged herself and her chair across the landing and began to descend the next set of stairs.

That's when she noticed, after this flight, the staircase came to an end.

The landing below continued down a long hallway with no obvious exit. There must be a separate fire stairwell or something on the floor.

Not good; she'd have to take focus away from keeping the monsters at bay to figure out where to go next.

*Can't worry about that yet. Gotta get down there first.* She was still halfway down this final flight of steps. At least once she made it to the landing, she'd be able to use her chair and move much—

A creature emerged from the hallway below. A pincer attack.

*"Fuck all the way off!"* she screamed, brandishing the bloody chai.

The creature hissed, its disgusting mouth tube reaching out ahead of its face, and it began to crawl up the steps toward her.

Ana cast a quick look behind her at the other two monstrosities. They hugged the wall like insects, one still bleeding profusely from its mouth, spattering the floor with audible drips.

Gripped by mania or nihilism or just sweet adrenaline, Ana resumed her journey downward.

The third creature paused, surprised. *Good.* Ana kept lowering herself down the stairs. No plan. Just moving.

Suddenly, outside, a cloud shifted, and a sharp blast of sunlight shot through the window. Barely over the horizon, the sun blazed with magic-hour intensity, throwing a spotlight onto the creature on the steps.

It didn't shriek or sizzle or smoke.

It blinked at the intense brightness and threw an arm across its face in a bizarrely human gesture. From her close vantage, Ana could see how the crenulated flesh on the creature's arm began to turn grayer in the sunlight. The skin, drying.

Ever so subtly turning to stone.

That told her everything. She understood at once how these creatures were, and weren't, vampires. How her attackers were, and weren't, the same as the gargoyles adorning the building. *What did Isaac call them? Estries?*

The sunlight succeeded where her threats did not. The creature on the steps begrudgingly retreated to the nearest wall and scuttled onto the ceiling, out of the invading glare. There was a strange lack of urgency to it, but Ana didn't question the opportunity. She moved down the steps as quickly as she could, dragging her chair, trying to keep all the monsters in view while watching where she was going and staying aware of any newcomers.

She reached the landing, unfolded her chair, and seated herself. The next staircase had to be somewhere beyond in the yawning, increasingly dark hallway.

Just as she unlocked her wheels, the sunlight disappeared behind another cloud. The stairwell, the landing, the hallway beyond, plunged into a wintery gloom. Ana put her arms to work.

The floor was blessedly flat and smooth. For a moment, giddiness overwhelmed her. Her chair still worked—worked magnificently—and she felt a thrill bordering on love. No, fuck that, it was love. Love for her chair, for movement, for herself. She remembered hearing someone in a support group once complaining about a monument for a dead kid they'd seen on the internet. The kid had used a wheelchair his whole life, and when he died, some well-meaning fuckwits had built a statue depicting the kid finally flying away from his chair, as if that signified a sort of blissful freedom.

"Fuck that," the furious person had said. "I *love* my chair. My chair *is* freedom."

As Ana rocketed down the hall after her interminable stairwell crawl, covered in a monster's blood and pursued by its companions, moving at a speed that matched a high sprint, she understood that love, that gratitude. It was bliss.

Then the hallway came to a dead end. Ana barely prevented herself from crashing into a featureless wall.

Her hands—shaking with fear and severe muscle fatigue—pulled out her cell phone and turned on the flashlight app. She scanned the wall. No door, no elevator, no exit. Nothing.

"No, no, no," she moaned—had she missed a turn?

No.

No, this was a trap. *This* was why they were in no real rush to stop her.

It was over.

She turned herself around to face down the hall.

The glow of her phone's flashlight disappeared into the long, hungry darkness. But she saw, farther down, the darkness coming alive with squirming, swarming bodies.

Tears spilled from her eyes at the unfairness of this end. She'd tried, but she had nowhere else to go.

*Charlie.*

*Charlie.*

*I'm sorry.*

Then she gripped the serrated chai and held her head high. At least, she would go down swinging.

# UTILITY

## 1

Across the river, around the time was Ana discovering the horror feeding inside her neighbor's apartment, Frank sat on the plastic-wrapped couch in his basement, holding an ice pack to his jaw. Stewing.

He also had one word on repeat in his mind. That word was:

*Nobody.*

Nobody frickin' messed with Francis Gardner Jr. like that. Nobody. Frickin' *nobody.*

His face still hurt from where that frickin' piece of rat shit socked him. His teeth had cut into his cheeks. It'd been a cheap shot. Nobody should get away with cheap shots.

Nobody.

He stood up and marched to his worktable, to his rust-red metal toolbox.

He had other toolboxes, bigger, more organized. This one contained the tools he used the most frequently: screwdrivers, Allen wrenches, staple gun . . . and, of course, the hammer. Old Faithful.

He pulled her out.

Next, he went to a closet and found, buried in the back, an old ConEd jumper he'd worn as a joke for a Halloween party. It was authentic; he'd won it in a poker game back when that mongrel Dinkins was letting Brooklyn burn and leaving a mess for dear old Rudy to clean up.

Add his favorite tool belt and he looked downright convincing.

He slid the hammer into its holster on the belt.

This country was going to shit, and people like Reid made it happen; the puppet masters bringing in the unwashed, diseased, illegal hordes—hell, it was probably their fault there'd been a damn pandemic in the first place. And Frank had given that Christ-killing sonofabitch a place to roost and breed? It made his skin feel creepy-crawly to think about.

Well. He'd learned his lesson. Never again. And now he was obliged to pay that lesson forward. Him and Old Faithful.

Like Frank always said: he was here to educate.

# 2

He bounded up the steps of the subway station, stopping at the top of the stairs to dial his friend Carlo at Con Edison.

Carlo answered on the second ring. Frank wasn't interested in niceties, so he cut straight to the chase.

"Carlo. Who does electric over at Eighty-Second and CPW?"

"Jeez, Frank, what's doing? How's—"

"I'm talkin' about that big, ugly piece-of-crap apartment building, the Deptford. Who handles electric over there? I know landmarks get their own point man; I want this guy's name."

"What are you doing over at the Deptford?"

*"Gimme his frickin' name, you moron!"*

Frank walked, not caring who he bumped out of the way.

"Okay, Frank, jeez." Carlo looked up the info. "A guy named Paul Russell. But, seriously, Frank, if you're thinkin' about taking a job in that building, trust me, buddy. I've heard chatter. You don't wanna get involved with that place if you—"

"Don't tell me what I want. Lemme worry about what I want."

Frank hung up and reached the building ten minutes later.

He marched straight up to one of the two doormen standing outside.

"Where's your service entrance?"

The doorman blinked at him. Frank snapped fingers in his face.

"Hey. I'm talking to you, ramrod. Your service entrance! I'm with Paulie Russell. I got sent straight over here. You've got an emergency with your wires."

The doorman looked at his partner, who gave a slight shrug.

"Don't think of telling me I ain't got no appointment. You know who also don't make an appointment? An electrical fire. You know who else don't make an appointment? City inspectors."

The doormen led Frank around to the back of the building. Frank muttered the entire time, a low and rancid monologue about how he didn't want to be here, how Paulie always sprang this last-minute crap on him, how this had better be a quick job.

He was proud of himself for committing so well to the act. Especially since, in the back of his head, all he was doing was a gleeful mental jig: *I'm gonna scare him good. Gonna let Jewboy and Roller Bitch know I can get to them whenever I want.*

They arrived at an inconspicuous metal door set into the side of the building. Practically invisible, the way it blended it. Frank didn't see a key or a number pad, but somehow the doorman opened it, and Frank had the sudden, inexplicable feeling that he was sneaking into some massive, living organism—giving a dinosaur a colonoscopy or something. He shook it off.

The doorman took Frank through a short hallway, down some gray concrete stairs, to the basement.

"Yeah, yeah." He abruptly waved the doorman away. "I got it from here, thanks. I'm not a moron."

The doorman stared at him for a beat, perplexed and dumb.

"Don't you have work to do? I know I do. Your mannequin ass breathing down my neck ain't gonna make it go any faster."

The doorman didn't inquire further—or maybe he couldn't; the guy's lips were pressed so tight maybe they didn't even separate. He turned and left Frank, going back in the direction from which they'd come.

*So this is the frickin' Deptford,* Frank thought as he looked around. *Just like any other basement. Nothing special.*

He knew which floor Reid lived on from the changed address. Frank could probably find an elevator, but that felt like cheating and might compromise his element of surprise.

Besides, his dander was up—full of piss and vinegar, his dad would've said.

After a few more minutes, when he was sure that Ken doll doorman would be back at his post outside, Frank doubled back to the service stair.

*Jeez, Frankie boy,* a voice like his father's intoned, *you seriously going to walk?*

"Naw," he muttered sarcastically to the voice in his head. "I'm gonna crawl. Frickin' moron."

He started up.

## 3

Frank knew there'd be a transfer floor soon enough—city ordinances required a certain number of flights for fireproof stairwells, and then you could go hog wild on top of that.

The more he marched upstairs, the angrier he got. Sure, it'd been his idea to walk instead of taking an elevator. But the fact he *had* to make this decision made him hate Reid all the more. He'd held Old Faithful in his hands since around the third flight. Now he throttled the hammer's handle like a throat, imagining all the things he was going to do—smash Reid's kneecaps, smash his teeth, maybe even try a few swings against the wife's legs just to see if they could still feel stuff.

Eventually, he reached a door with a crash bar: the top of the service stairs. He banged it open and found himself looking into a pool of impenetrable dark. The hell?

He stood at the open doorway, confused, waiting for his eyes to adjust. A voice slightly below him screamed, "Don't let that door close!"

Frank almost let it close out of spite—nobody barked at him like that. He looked down and saw a small figure about a foot away from where the door had opened.

"Huh?" he belched. "The frick is going on here?"

His eyes began to adjust to see the figure—a woman—staring at him in astonishment. Not just any woman. This one had wheels.

*"Frank?"* she asked in complete shock.

He was kinda shocked, too. "Roller Bitch?"

## 4

He thought about bringing the hammer down on her head right then and there. A quick little *boop* and *squish,* and she'd probably thank him for putting her out of her misery.

As his eyes adjusted to the gloom down the hallway, he saw several hunched, dark figures, squatting and blinking back at him. They had human faces, but those faces were grotesque, exaggerated, hideous.

Disgust roiled his gut. He knew what he'd walked in on.

*Of frickin' course. Some frickin' ritual or something, in the dark. Blood-drinking, Christ-killing, baby-eating, Adrenochrome-sipping psychopaths. Goddamn mongrels. Makes all the sense in the world.*

Forgetting Roller Bitch, he stepped forward. He didn't notice that the door didn't close behind him, that the woman in the wheelchair had leaned over and caught it, and was now pulling herself through the doorway with all her might.

"Where the frick do you ugly-ass cock-a-roaches even come from, huh?" he demanded of the shadowy figures. "What mongrel country did you crawl out of, before you came here and tried to take over? *Huh?*"

The figures inched forward. On all fours, like the beasts they were.

"You frickin' parasites! What kinda sick shit are you all gettin' up to in the dark, here?"

"Frank," Roller Bitch whispered from the doorway. He whipped his head over to where she sat, halfway between the door and the security stairs. Her eyes were huge. *"Run."*

"Don't like me ragging on your friends, huh?" Frank scoffed. "Don't like that I got it all figured out, huh?" He twirled the hammer in his hand. "I'll take Old Faithful here to George frickin' Soros himself!"

Roller Bitch's eyes darted to something behind him and became even bigger with dumb shock.

Frank made an interrogatory noise—"Whuh?"—and turned around to see, by the light thrown from the open security door, what she was looking at.

On the ceiling, on the walls, several small shapes skittered with lightning speed from the upper stairs to join the creatures on the floor. Christ, they looked like . . . like little kids. Various ages. One or two even looked like toddlers.

"The hell . . . ?" Frank managed to ask before the smaller creatures fell on him.

He felt little lamprey mouths latching. When he threw them off, chunks of his flesh went with them, leaving raw, seeping wounds that pulsed fire. They came from all sides. Left, right, top, bottom. The jolting pain, so scattershot, sent bursts of white across his vision. He wasn't even aware when Roller Bitch disappeared down the service steps, closing the door and trapping him in almost total darkness.

He was too concerned with the gibbering, filthy creatures crawling all over him. The larger ones had decided to join the fun.

Frank brought his hammer up, but he never got the chance to bring it down.

The rest of his existence was only pain and horror. But for all that, on some dim, inchoate level, he was also elated.

Because he'd been right. No matter what those oh-so-enlightened frickin' morons liked to pretend, no matter how horrified they might have been at the things Frank often said, he'd been right. The hordes were here. And they were hungry.

*Wait 'til Tucker finds out about this,* Frank thought as his lips were pried open and a hot, fleshy tube tore down his throat.

# LIGHT AT THE END

## 1

She moved with astonishing speed. These stairs were brutally hard: concrete and steel with shallow steps, too, so the thudding and dropping became hypnotically regular.

The nearness of her goal wiped everything clean. All she knew was the rattle in her teeth and joints as she crawled down the steps as fast as she could. She didn't let herself stop; she didn't let herself count. She just moved. Nothing came after her. After the door had clicked shut, she'd heard Frank's choking screams, then silence. Only the sound of her breath, her chair, her progress.

Before she knew it, she'd reached a door with a sign: 1ST FLOOR.

More stairs continued to the basement . . . but there *was* a door *here.*

This was her last chance. She could leave now. She could hop into her chair and head straight for the street and never look back. She'd have to get past the doormen and the concierge, but they probably wouldn't bother her if she left them Charlie.

She looked at that door for a moment. A heartbeat.

*Charlie.*

She continued down the final flight.

## 2

Once again, being in her chair felt like a blessing.

The chair moved with noticeable cants and lurches now—the wheels had been abused a bit too much—but she could still move forward, and that's all that mattered.

Ana made her way down the winding basement hallways. Instinct guided her. She'd never been down here, but she had a feeling where the super's office would be. It just felt . . . obvious.

She stopped only once, when she passed the room where the trash chutes spat out their contents into the waiting bins below.

An item caught her eye and made her remember something. She recognized it immediately. It had tumbled down one of the chutes but had missed its target—probably because it was so heavy and lumpy. It lay a few feet from the bins. Another lucky break. Would it do the trick? Who knew. But she moved her weapon to underneath her leg, retrieving the item and slipping it into the baby carrier against her chest.

It fit perfectly.

*What are the odds . . . ?*

Ana made her way back to the basement hallway. The corridors wound, but she never lost faith in her sense of direction. She was headed to the center. And soon enough, there it was. The door to the super's office.

She knew it wouldn't be locked. They were waiting for her.

She was right.

She made her way into the room.

## 3

Ana blinked.

She blinked again and again.

Nothing could make her brain make sense of what she was looking at.

The door had opened on a large, square office lit by a single round fluorescent in the center of the ceiling. The fluorescent light buzzed patiently.

Halfway across, the room was bisected by a wall.

A wall of flesh.

An enormous, bloated mass of skin—not stretched taut like a canvas but thick, full of organs and blood and life. An organic mass. A *comfortable* mass.

Tendrils of flesh reached up and out, into the walls, like pipes. There *were* regular pipes, too. Pipes that had brought her own apartment water, no doubt. But the distinction between the organic and the mundane components for the apartment complex ceased to exist. This thing, this creature, this monstrosity . . . *was* the building. Or part of it, at least. The beating heart.

Ana could make out veins and other markers of life on its surface. The indentations of what must be, or have once been, a face marked the center, its mouth skinned over, but still identifiable. Eyes stared out, two dull marbles packed deeply into similarly colored clay.

Slits festooned the surface. Ana recognized them from her experience in the courtyard—those almost-vaginal openings she'd seen in the dirt. She remembered the courtyard ground's impossible warmth, how it expanded and contracted.

As if on cue, a small but noticeable stream of clear spiders secreted themselves from one of the small openings and skittered around the surface of the skin. The same bugs she'd seen before.

"Parasites," Ana whispered, one part awe, two parts horror.

"They feed off her and keep her clean," a voice said to her right.

Ana didn't whip around. She was too deeply in shock. She turned dumbly to the person who had joined her in the room and stood by her side.

It was Vera.

# MOTHER'S GIFTS

## 1

"If you look closely," the broker-not-broker continued, "you'll see that they're not all the same. Some of them . . . Ooh, look, there's one."

She pointed excitedly to a stream of insects crawling over the great fleshy expanse. At first, Ana couldn't tell what Vera was talking about, but then she saw—not every spider-thing was clear. Some were pinkish. Others bright yellow. One was a golden brown with dark spots and, at least from this distance, fewer legs. They crawled from one slit to another, running their own inscrutable errands.

"The golden ones are very special. You don't often see them out in the open like that. Wow."

Vera's voice was tinged with rapture. Ana might have expected it to sound crazy, but in the presence of this thing, this impossible thing, awe seemed as sensible a reaction as any other.

"What do the golden ones do?"

Vera looked at her.

"Would you believe me if I told you?"

Ana let out a short, surprised laugh. She was about to admit that was a good question when, hearing her own laugh, she realized she was crying. Tears streamed down her cheeks and clogged her voice.

Vera gave a patient, almost empathetic, smile. "The small clear ones clean her. There are others who massage her—she doesn't move much, so she gets aches and pains without a little help. Others help her eat. She's her own ecosystem, you see. Each of those miraculous little critters serves a purpose. Just like each of us."

"Oh." *Sure. Why not?*

Ana's eyes traced the creature again. The way it—she—made up the entirety of the wall, then branched up and into the shadows of the ceiling.

"Is . . ." Ana cleared her throat a little. "Is she the building?"

She spoke in a hushed whisper. It couldn't be helped.

"No, no," Vera replied. "She is what makes the building special. What makes you stop and stare when you pass it on the street. What makes it . . . sing. A building is just a house. She is *home*."

That ghost of a face stared back at them placidly. Could this creature hear them? Could she recognize speech?

"Where did she come from? She looks like she used to be . . ."

"She used to be one of them. The chosen ones."

*The vampires,* Ana almost said. *The estries.*

Vera continued, "They all have their roles, too. She was chosen among them for greater things by the one who made her. The way a queen bee one day births another queen. A lottery, if you will."

Ana let that comment go. Instead, she said, "Them. You keep saying 'them.' Aren't you . . . ?"

"Oh, Anna, I'm a regular person. Just like you. I'm not lucky enough to be one of the chosen. But, I *am* lucky enough to be a witness. To their beauty, their power. I help them however I can, along with the other people like me, who know the truth. Like I said—"

"'We all have roles to play.'"

"Exactly."

There was a faint, almost-metallic scraping noise—a soft *shhhhhwwwshhing*—as a chute in the ceiling swung open. The scraping noise increased, louder and louder, and then, with a pop that sounded like a cork from a bottle, the chute spat something heavy onto the concrete floor. It landed with a sickening thud.

Frank.

His body seemed different now, though. Hollower. Deflated. Not just because of death but like . . .

*. . . like he'd been emptied.*

Ana could make out what appeared to be puncture wounds all over his skin. A second later, his hammer followed down the chute and landed near his body with an impotent clatter.

*I guess Old Faithful wasn't much help.*

"What did they do to him?"

Vera smiled. "They fed. And now . . . watch this."

Several of the creature's slits dilated, and larger, almost crab-like creatures scuttled out. They swarmed over Frank and began dragging the body toward the flesh wall.

"Now she feeds, too."

Muscles beneath the skin worked, and the lower edge lifted like a heavy curtain. Tiny legs underneath the edge ushered Frank's body in and the curtain descended over it.

Ana fought the urge to throw up. Mostly because she imagined if she did puke, some special form of arachnid would shimmy out of some yonic gash and slurp it up, and that sort of thing might be the last little snip her sanity needed to become completely untethered.

"What does *she* do?" Ana asked, indicating the fleshy wall that was currently rippling in slow, chewing-like motions. "For them. For the chosen ones. What does she do that they feed her like this?"

Vera gave a small eye roll. "You mean, besides get rid of evidence? She is their *mother.* Their queen. She—"

"She makes more of us."

This time, Ana did whip around in her seat.

Behind her, standing in the doorway and in the basement hallway, crawling on the walls and ceilings like roaches, like bedbugs—the residents of the Deptford.

## 2

Ana reacted by pushing herself away from the intruders. With an unconscious grace, she spun her chair around and retreated closer to the thing Vera had called their queen.

She stopped herself just in time, inches away. The thought of colliding with the flesh wall, falling into it and potentially being overrun by those crabby spider things, almost made her bolt.

So far, the queen seemed unperturbed by her proximity.

The hallway filled with bodies. Ana recognized the old man, the one who'd made her fall down the steps, at the front of the pack. He smiled. they all did. They looked . . . opulent was the only word she could think of, a horde of mostly elderly opera patrons gathering during an intermission.

"Stay away," Ana warned, though exhaustion left little threat to her words. She pulled the chai out from under her legs and held it up like a talisman. "Stay back."

The old man smiled magnanimously. "I take it your husband didn't do a very good job convincing you? Oh well." He stepped into the room, flanked by a few of his brethren. They didn't enter very far: less out of hesitation, Ana sensed, and more to keep the room from overcrowding.

An older woman with a French accent and a chin made of wattles spoke. "That icon you're holding does nothing, little one. That's for children's ghost stories."

"Stories we helped create, over the centuries," said another with a British accent.

A gruffer voice farther into the crowd: "Careful, though, that thing is sharp as shit. She cut the hell out of Montgomery. He might never feed again."

"Oh, how awful," the Brit said.

Tsks of pity—for her? For the one she maimed? Ana couldn't tell. It gave her flashbacks of people talking about her in the hospital, of brokenhearted looks and hushed conversations, just behind her back or above her head.

Still, they kept a little distance. For now.

"I'll cut the hell out of all of you. So stay back."

"What is it you want, love?" the Brit asked. "What can we do for you?"

Ana stared at them, mind racing.

"Talk to them, Anna," Vera stage-whispered. Even in this situation, Ana seethed internally whenever someone continued to mispronounce her name. "They're *good.* They'll be so good to you."

"You want out of that chair?" The old man in front took another step forward. "We can make that happen."

Ana moved before she could think. She swiveled her arm and pressed the brass chai against the queen. The flesh rippled as if trying to move away from the sharp point. A low rumble made its way through the room.

Panic changed the faces of every creature staring at her. It was delicious.

"Hey, hold on," the old man cautioned, freezing in place.

Vera held her hands out. "Anna, Anna—*stop.*"

There was a moment of silence, brief but heavy. As she waited, Ana braced herself for something hideous to ooze out of the nearest vaginal opening and scurry up her arms, mutant spiders filled with poison or equipped with razor beaks.

Nothing came out. The queen didn't have any natural defenses.

Then, in a half-formed realization, Ana realized that's what the richies must be. *They* were the defense. They really were all an ecosystem. The problem must have been *these* richies were old and soft. They'd gotten lazy, the way richies always did, and so Ana had gotten the drop on them.

"We have been very patient," the old man said, his face becoming a mask of stern, paternal anger, "but do not test us. We prefer to do things without violence, but that's only a preference—"

"Oh, come on. We all know what she wants."

Another of the vampires—a woman's voice. Heads, including Ana's, turned to look at the speaker. The woman made her way through the crowd to the front.

Ana recognized her immediately. It was the old woman Reid had apparently begun to work for. The movie star. She was draped in a sparkling wrap, and in her arms, curled peacefully . . . was Charlie.

If she could have, Ana would have bolted from her seat and charged them.

"She wants her baby back," Camilla finished.

The old man in front protested, "But—"

Camilla waved him away. "I know."

Ana found her voice again. "Give her back. Give her back *now* or I'll slice this freak bitch open and—"

"Okay, Ana," Camilla said. "I understand. Here." She held Charlie out.

Ana almost didn't believe it. "You—?"

Camilla indicated the queen. "Just, please, don't hurt her."

Ana didn't want to lower her weapon for any sort of handoff. "Give Charlie to Vera and then give her to me. Vera, so help me, if you try anything—".

Vera twitched. "Don't do anything crazy, Anna. Please just don't—"

"It's *Ana,* you fucking asshole! And I swear to God—"

"It's okay," Camilla repeated. "Vera? It's okay. Let's not make this difficult. Here, take her. Gentle."

Camilla handed Charlie over to Vera. Charlie looked happy enough to be transferred . . .

Until she was placed on Ana's lap.

As soon as Vera stepped tentatively away, leaving Charlie with her real mother, Charlie started to scream.

Shriek.

Wail.

The sort of crying an infant does when handed over to a total stranger.

*She doesn't recognize me.*

Ice-cold needles stabbed into Ana's heart.

*No,* Ana told herself. *Not now. We'll deal with this later.*

She held squirming Charlie tightly with the arm not holding the weapon.

"Now," Ana said, speaking loudly over the wails, "back off and let us out. I mean it. No one follows us. No one tries anything. Just let us go, and we'll be gone forever. I won't say anything about—anything."

She had no idea how she'd maintain her leverage of threatening the queen while she escaped, but that was Future Ana's problem.

"We need to talk first, Ana," Camilla said. "There are things you need to know. You can't just take her."

"Fuck you I can't."

"If you take her, she'll die, goddammit!" That gruff old man, brusque and weather-beaten, looking like something of a cowboy or a rancher, spoke up. Gray splotches mottled his skin. "That what you want? Rescuing her only for her to die?"

Ana addressed all of them. "I don't believe you. You're all liars. You just want to keep her so you can do whatever it is you do, turn her into one of you, and I'm not going to let that—"

*"Ana,"* Camilla said—raising her voice over Charlie, her pity unmistakable. "You're too late. We already did it."

Charlie continued to scream and cry, but it was like the whole world went silent.

*You're too late.*

"What?" Ana gasped.

"She's one of us now," Camilla said, and fuck if it didn't seem like she was genuinely sorry to break the news.

"No. No, she's not, she's . . ." Ana looked at her crying baby. She looked so normal, so very much like Charlie—but her desperation to be back with these creatures was clear.

*Too late.*

Ana had survived all of that—endured all of that—done that to Reid—just to be too late?

*No, no, no.* They were lying again, they had to be—

But the way Charlie was screaming now . . .

"Do you want to know what the golden ones do?" Vera asked. It took Ana a moment to remember Vera meant the spiders crawling in and out of the monolithic queen. "I told you that some act as her hands. Some clean her. Some massage her. The golden ones . . . are Mother's gift. They go inside a body and, if that body is lucky, they merge, they grow *together.* Another ecosystem, Anna—*Ana.* Another partnership. Symbiosis. The golden ones make a person *chosen.*"

"That is how we are made," the Frenchwoman said.

It made sense to Ana, and yet it sounded completely incoherent. "You put . . . one of those things in her? You put one of those fucking things in my baby, in—"

"More than one, dearie," the Brit said. "It's an intricate process. But she took to it brilliantly!"

"More than brilliantly!" said the unctuous old man. "She even took over the process herself!"

Ana's stomach dropped. *"What?"*

"That day you explored the courtyard? She found the heart. She fed *herself* some of Mother's gifts!"

Charlie in the courtyard; Charlie putting something in her mouth; Ana being too relieved to care . . .

"No . . ."

Camilla took over. "No child has survived so many gifts in generations. Your Charlie was so amazingly receptive. It speaks to how strong *you* are, Ana."

"And do you know what that means?" Vera added, practically bouncing in her toes. "She could be the next queen!"

Camilla ignored Vera and focused on Ana. Her eyes shimmered with compassion. "She'll have her own children. Generations will spring from her. Revere her. She'll be loved and protected for centuries upon centuries. She'll never want for anything. Don't you want that for her? Isn't that all parenting *is* in the end?"

"She's so *lucky,*" Vera rhapsodized.

Charlie, the lucky marvel, wailed as if she'd been stuck with a hot poker. She tried desperately to escape her mother's grip.

*Too late. I'm too late.*

Ana was crying, too. Huge, painful tears. She didn't notice that she'd dropped the arm holding her weapon. She'd stopped threatening the queen. She couldn't do anything but swallow great, convulsive sobs.

"I don't know what to do," she said through tears. "I never know what to do. Baby Bird . . ." She tried to look at her baby, face-to-face, but Charlie refused; she kept turning back to the vampires in the doorway. "I can't think when you cry like this."

*Too late.*

Camilla said, "If you take her from us, where she can't feed, where she can't grow, it *will* kill her."

"And she'll probably kill you first," the cowboy added.

"Like you saw with Mrs. Jacobs," the old man said. "She'll have no choice."

"Please stop crying, Baby Bird, please. I can't . . ."

Then, abruptly, Charlie did stop. She perked up her ears and listened to something Ana couldn't hear. Her face even broke out into a sunny, chubby smile.

Ana was baffled. "What happened? What's . . . ?"

Vera beamed. "The queen. She's singing."

"I don't hear anything," Ana said. She stole a glance. The wall of flesh vibrated ever so slightly.

Then Camilla began to sing, too. One by one, the rest of the vampires joined in, softly, respectfully.

Ana recognized it: the same alien melody she'd heard when she'd adjusted the EQ in her recording booth. It was the ambient sound that ran through the building.

The same sound, Ana realized, that Charlie must have heard when they first moved into the building. Back then, it upset her. Back when she was *her* baby. Now . . .

Charlie listened and delighted in the music.

She cooed and giggled and stopped straining.

She looked at the singing throng of creatures in the doorway and hallway, and her face lit up with pure, unadulterated love.

## 3

*What does it mean to be a mother?*

The pain in Ana's chest was excruciating. The pain of drowning lungs and shattered bones. Keener than any she'd ever experienced before, despite considering herself an expert. God, she couldn't breathe, couldn't think. It was too much. Too hard. Too unfair.

*Too late.*

She wanted to take it all back, every dark moment she'd ever wished for the life she'd lived before, the life before Charlie. She had no one now, not even Reid, and she was only in this agonizing moment feeling how full her life had been. Too late.

*What does it mean to be a mother?*

An impossible choice. Take Charlie and both die . . . or give Charlie to these monsters.

Then she looked at Charlie—really looked at her.

Charlie beamed at the song being sung for her.

Charlie radiated.

And Ana began to realize—

*No. No, please, don't realize this—*

But she did.

Charlie was happy. Truly, perfectly happy.

It didn't matter that it was unfair. It didn't matter that forces had intervened and stolen her from Ana. None of that mattered now. Ana had been willing to risk her own safety . . . but she couldn't deny Charlie a life where she smiled like this.

*What does it mean to be a mother?*

*This,* she realized in agony.

"Okay." It fell out of her mouth like a final breath. In her head, the word echoed as *No, please, no.*

"What?" Camilla asked, even though the room was quiet.

"Okay," Ana repeated. Firmer this time.

She relaxed the arm holding Charlie a little.

If Ana had any doubt she'd made the right choice, it evaporated when

Camilla quickly stepped forward to retrieve the baby. The monster held Charlie close with an intensity Ana recognized as purely maternal.

Even so, Ana regretted it immediately. She wanted Charlie back. No, she wanted Charlie to *want* to come back. But Charlie didn't.

"Please just keep her safe," Ana begged. "Please just keep her happy."

"We will. I promise you. She will be *so* happy." Camilla brought the baby to the rest of the Deptford residents. They all gathered around her, and Charlie gave a little chirp of delight.

That noise.

It entered Ana's heart like a fishhook, then pulled it, still beating, from her chest. With it came the rest of her insides, a chain of viscera, each link a future memory that would now never come true. A first sentence. A first day of school. A temper tantrum in a grocery store. A school project. A dance. A heartbreak. College. Jobs. Arguments. Slammed doors. Curses. Embraces. Tears. Sharing a drink. Laughing at how hard things used to be. Becoming a friend. A confidante. Rewriting painful definitions of mothers and daughters at long last. All of these: promises that are made, tacitly or not, when a child enters your life and you believe, perhaps against better judgment, that the world will let you have them as payment for those first years of pain and confusion.

She would never get these moments.

But that couldn't matter. Because Charlie still might. Some version of them anyway.

*I got her where she was meant to be*, Ana thought. *I did the job. Mother's gift.*

Her darkest fears had always been that she didn't have what it took to be a parent. That conception had been a fluke. That Cathy had been right: Ana was too stupid, too broken, too selfish to even do the piss-poor job *she'd* done.

*What does it mean to be a mother?*

But that was the trick. There was no one meaning.

Motherhood was her, was Cathy, was Reid's mom, was this monstrosity in the bowels of a Manhattan skyscraper. Motherhood was joy, was pain, was standing over the crib with a knife, was standing over the crib with a lullaby. Motherhood was breakage, was expansion, was depletion, was fulfillment, was creation, and an endless series of goodbyes. Motherhood was contradiction. That was its beauty. That was its horror. And if it drove you mad trying to square its inconsistencies, well, tough luck, because motherhood cared nothing about what happened inside of you. Motherhood had already taken what it needed from inside of you and had given it to the world. Anything else was up to you and fate. *Bashert.*

All these thoughts, in a pregnant instant. And Ana was left hollowed out, abject in her misery, wishing it could be any other way.

She looked at the happy family. One day, maybe this pain would be a memory. One day, her heart would agree with her brain that she'd done the right thing.

A voice spoke up inside.

*But you don't have to make it* this *easy for them, do you?*

Was that her voice? Or Cathy's? Funny how they could be indistinguishable sometimes.

It made a good point, though.

They'd all forgotten about her for the time being. No one paid her any attention.

And Ana was still her mother's daughter enough to know that sometimes spite was the last dish on the menu . . . but it could fill you up.

Ana pulled out what she'd brought with her in the baby carrier.

Once it was freed and in her lap, she spoke up:

"But first you're all gonna have to start from scratch. Just like me."

## 4

She didn't think what Isaac said on the phone really meant anything. These creatures weren't some mythical folktale inventions that could be dispatched with the right ingredient.

All she knew was that this wasn't food-grade diatomaceous earth. This was the kind that killed things.

*I'm sorry, Baby Bird. I hope this doesn't hurt too badly.* But she also hoped it did. Charlie was a baby and would forget—Ana wanted the rest of them to remember.

This would mean her own death, too, but at the moment, she felt she had nothing left to live for, so what better time to try?

With a swift brutality, Ana used the chai to slash at the face of the fleshy queen, where the mouth appeared to be.

The huge, diagonal slash revealed a gaping hole full of bony stumps that must have once been teeth before the creature developed whatever other hole it used to digest its food.

As soon as the vestigial mouth opened, the room filled with a bellowing tone. An instant later, it was matched by agonized shrieks. The vampires. Outraged at what Ana had done? Or from the force of Mother's now-uninhibited voice?

Not wasting a moment to ponder, Ana poured the bag of diatomaceous earth into the queen's face.

*Stuff earth into their mouths,* said Isaac.

*Cuts 'em up and sucks 'em dry,* Sammy from the hardware store had said, and, hey, maybe the old texts were onto something.

The queen's monstrous bellow continued, but an inhuman gagging noise joined it. The queen's skin quickly turned a sallow, sick color. Muscles contracted and pulsed. Veins bulged, and a greasy kind of sweat oozed from gigantic pores. With slippery, nauseating sibilance, crabs and spiders of all shapes and colors began pouring out of every opening and falling to the ground. Those that didn't land on their backs, in the telltale posture of dead insects, skittered blindly across the concrete, desperate for salvation.

Ana waited for reprisal, for her swift, violent death. Nothing came. The monsters were all still incapacitated by shock, by the overwhelming noise that tore through them.

This was her chance to escape. She thought of saying something pithy first. "Now you know how I feel," or the like.

She didn't get a chance. Suddenly, Vera's hands were wrapped around Ana's throat, and there was no more air to speak.

Vera loomed over her, squeezing, shaking her, eyes full of a zealot's fury. She screamed curses, but Ana couldn't catch them. The world began to gray.

Vera shook so hard that Ana's chair tipped over, spilling them both to the floor. Vera's hands released Ana's throat in the fall, and Ana gulped at the air.

Then Vera recovered, came for her again, face warped with rage. Ana reached blindly for something to defend herself, and it wasn't until the hammer crashed into Vera's skull that Ana even realized what her hand had found. Old Faithful.

Vera staggered backward. A moment later, blood dripped, then cascaded down her face. Her furious eyes became glassy and confused.

Ana took her moment. She righted her chair, put herself back in place, and wheeled to the exit.

Keening, thrashing bodies clogged the doorway. Ana met little resistance, literally pushing them out of the way, sometimes making them fall to the ground. She probably ran over some toes or arms, but no one noticed.

Perhaps she'd seen too many action movies in her life; she kept expecting the building to start collapsing. It didn't.

She also expected someone to stop her. To attack, punish, kill her. Doormen came down from upstairs to see what the matter was, but they ignored her. She left behind an orgy of confusion, mourning, and chaos.

Before she wheeled herself to the stairs and prepared for one final, shorter stair crawl, she looked back at the super's office.

Vera, not dead after all, gibbered and mewled, trying to force herself into the queen's gashed-open mouth. "Take me, feed on me, use my *life*!"

And there in the crowd was Camilla. Camilla sensed Ana's gaze and turned around. On her tear-streaked face was a look of utter hate, but also desperate confusion. It begged: How did this happen? What do we do now?

Ana didn't care what they did now. All that mattered was, in turning, Camilla had also given Ana one last look at Charlie.

Charlie sobbed in agony. Again, that impulse—it would never go away—to hurry back and try to comfort her, shield her, damn the consequences. Ana fought it. She forced herself to see how Charlie was wrapped tightly in protecting arms. Safe. As shielded as anyone could be in this cruel world.

For entirely different reasons, Ana sobbed her entire way out of the building.

## 5

Manny Langan had been a doorman at the Keene Apartments for twelve years, and he loved the job. Fresh air, human interaction, a sense of helping people? Nothing better. New Yorkers had a reputation for being unfriendly and brusque, but that was bullshit. New Yorkers were the friendliest people in the world, always ready to help a fellow human out . . . provided they weren't too busy.

Manny always made sure he was never too busy.

Plus, working at Keene meant he got to look across the street at the Deptford every day.

He loved that damn building . . . even if he didn't like the guys who worked the doors.

They weren't like any other doormen Manny knew—and he knew a lot, both in and out of the union. The Deptford crew never socialized, never offered to take photos or provide trivia about their famous building to the small but steady gaggle of tourists who gathered outside its gates. Hell, they never even smiled.

Frankly, Manny thought they gave doormen a bad name. They made it easy for the kind of people who looked through doormen (or doorwomen, or doorwhateveryoumightbe), to keep that snobby attitude going.

That wasn't the case now, though. Something appeared to be happening inside the Deptford. As Manny helped Mrs. Engstrom juggle her dog, Sweetie, and an Amazon delivery into the Keene, he heard the usually stoic Deptford doormen break into a run, clamoring back into their building, leaving the front gate open.

"What the . . . ?"

Something about the Deptford had changed, too, but, if you'd asked him what, he wouldn't have been able to say.

The Deptford just looked . . . different now. It seemed to sag. Droop. But not *physically*. Like seeing a face that looks young and healthy, but then the lighting shifts and suddenly it becomes haggard and powdery. Nothing had changed, but everything had changed.

The Deptford looked . . . old. Dead.

A building and nothing more.

Then a woman in a wheelchair blasted through the front door, sobbing. Covered in what might be blood. *What the hell is going on?!*

Manny took off running, careful not to slip in the light dusting of fresh snow, and reached the woman seconds later. Before he could ask if she was okay, a guy in a concierge uniform with the craziest smile Manny had ever seen tore out of the Deptford lobby after her. Manny still had no idea what was going on, but there was no mistaking the look on that guy's face. He meant *bad* business.

Manny put himself between the concierge and the handles of the wheelchair. *What is with that guy's smile?* He held the guy at arm's length, trying to calm him down, trying to give the woman in the wheelchair time to get some distance. *What am I doing?* he kept asking himself. *What did I just shove myself into?*

Suddenly, the crazy smiler's face darkened—physically, like a cloud passed over him. Manny had the wherewithal to let the guy go and step back.

The guy was in the middle of shouting, "DO YOU REALIZE WHAT YOU'VE—" when the shadow darkening his face materialized into a huge chunk of stone, obliterating his head like a boot stomping on a cherry pie.

"What were the odds?" Manny would later ask his wife that night. "Poor guy. That was like winning the lottery from hell."

For now, though, all Manny could do was grab the lady's chair, screaming, and run for cover as the sky began to fall all around them.

# 6

From *The New York Times*:

**HISTORIC APARTMENT BUILDING SITE OF BIZARRE COLLAPSE; TWO INJURED, ONE KILLED**

**By Stephanie Hartmann**

Known for its postcolonial architecture and its grotesque statues, the Deptford Apartment Building has been a frequent stop for Manhattan sightseeing tours. However, yesterday evening, the 144-year-old building suffered a series of infrastructure failures, resulting in two injuries and one fatality.

Twenty-five of the building's gargoyles, the entirety of the building's ornamentation, fell to the sidewalks below in what appeared to be a synchronized drop.

"It's an incredible tragedy," Lucy Nguyen, spokesperson for the NYPD, attests. "This kind of failure cannot be allowed to occur, no matter how old or historic a building might be."

Ruth Carville of Knoxville, Kentucky, remains at Weill-Cornell in unconscious but stable condition after being struck by debris. Another bystander, name withheld, reportedly lost an arm. A Deptford employee, name also withheld, was struck and killed.

No explanation has been provided on the cause of the incident, the most recent in a storied, if not frequently mysterious, history for the Deptford. Lt. Clayton Harrison, another officer on the scene, claimed: "As we secured the scene, I touched one of the statues. I expected it to be solid stone, but when I touched it, it just crumbled into dust. How is that possible? If they were that old, why didn't they become dust when they hit?"

When asked about the city's liability, a representative of the mayor's office replied . . .

## A CITY INTERLUDE—ANA

### 1

She moves quickly down the sidewalk. She's not late for her appointment, but she's not as early as she wants to be. It's a beautiful spring day, and she's smiling.

It's a beautiful smile. Radiant for its simplicity. Anyone looking at her might notice a certain, intangible gratitude hanging off it. Her life has been hard . . . but these days, her smiles come more easily.

She still cries a lot. Even though it's been almost five years.

Sometimes she replays the difficult conversations she had to have the day after she crawled down the stairwell of the Deptford.

She kept the group of people she personally informed small—Reid's brother and two of his closest friends—and she kept the story simple. They had been fighting, and Reid was bitter over having to be a caretaker. He said he wanted time to focus on his music, and he disappeared with no forwarding information whatsoever.

Most galling had been how unsurprised one of Reid's friends had been. Had Reid been fantasizing about just this sort of event?

Then again, hadn't she?

The time might come, she knows, when she'll have to declare Reid dead, or at least legally missing. There's insurance, there's Social Security, hell, maybe one day she'll meet someone else and decide she's willing to give marriage another shot. Stranger things have happened.

It had been harder to lie about Charlie.

She could have put together a simple story about a sudden illness, a heartbreaking death. It would have been less to remember.

But she hadn't told that story.

First, she knew if she did that she would have been assaulted with concern, and condolence. Sympathy-besotted friends and acquaintances would attend her night and day. *How tragic: first her legs, then her husband and baby. Let's start a GoFundMe, let's organize a concert, let's let's let's.*

She didn't want anyone to feel bad for her ever again.

Instead, she made up a different story. She said the pressures of her new life, Reid leaving her, were so great that she simply gave custody of Charlie to her own mother. They'd repaired their relationship, and now Cathy was Charlie's legal guardian. Ana knew her postpartum had nothing to do with her own mother—that it was a natural phenomenon that affects people no matter their relationships with motherhood—but she found this apocryphal detail oddly cathartic. It reminded her of her epiphany in the Deptford's basement. Motherhood had so many meanings.

Surprisingly, Ana discovered this story took care of the sympathy she'd been worried about. In fact, people treated her *distinctly* cooler—as if personally offended by her admission that she couldn't be the mother Charlie needed. She regularly attends support groups now and recognizes this distaste. Her fellow group participants describe similar experiences whenever they stick up for themselves or don't act like the Ideal, Inspirational Disabled Angel. Such realness, such wholeness, makes people uncomfortable.

It's fine. She'd wanted distance from her previous life. She'd wanted a fresh start.

She also didn't want to lie about Charlie being dead.

Because Charlie wasn't dead.

It would feel strange to carry that story around with her when she knows very well where her daughter is and how she's thriving.

That's why she's hurrying today. That's why she's maybe going to be late for her appointment.

She doesn't care. It's a beautiful spring day, and beautiful spring days in Manhattan are made for diversions.

## 2

She first saw the building while on one of her walks. (Not actual *walks,* of course, but she gets a kick out of how inefficient language can be.)

The building, like so many others, had been vacant since the middle of 2020. Even years later, Manhattan still has plenty of paper-covered windows and signs on doors.

Then, one day, this particular building wasn't vacant anymore.

Recently, with astonishing speed, it opened up to tenants. A sign out front proclaimed: LUXURY APARTMENTS. AFFORDABLE OPTIONS.

Ana wheels herself past that sign now.

Two doormen stand outside. They don't seem to notice her. One stands in a conspicuously stilted manner, ramrod straight, as if he can't move his neck. As if he'd been paralyzed in a fall but had somehow been given the ability to move again in a limited, puppetlike capacity.

It reminds her of those old Batman movies where they forgot to build mobility into the cowl. Ana and this man had watched those movies together. They'd laughed about that very detail. Her heart aches to think about him, even now. Even after everything.

She recognized him immediately the first time she passed him. Others who knew him might or might not do the same—and on the unlikely chance that they happen upon him, he wouldn't talk to them even if they try. He's too focused on his job.

Ana doesn't try to talk to him. She moves past the front entrance and around the corner. On the other side of the block, she's able to approach the building from the rear. There's no entrance, so no doormen here.

It's not a historic building. It's not architecturally striking. It's actually rather modest. But there *is* something about it. It glimmers and sings the way the most remarkable buildings in New York City do. It happens all the time. For whatever reason, a building will catch your eye and you'll stop and say, *Wow. I love this fucking city.*

Ana approaches the building and puts her hand on the wall.

She feels it. Minuscule, barely perceptible movements. Breath. Pulse.

*Is it really her?*

Ana doesn't know . . . but she thinks so.

She has adapted, just as Ana knew she would.

She is growing and taking care of her own family.

Ana is adapting, too.

She can occasionally use a walker now. Just a few steps, but significant progress. All the same, she prefers her chair. She loves her chair. It saved her life and gave her freedom. She doesn't really care if she ever walks again—but she relishes the effort.

Her experiences at the Deptford didn't make her think she could do *anything.* On the contrary, it made her realize how much she needed others. And how much others needed her. She no longer sees her disability as a limitation, just as a new way of living; and she works at a foundation that helps with spinal cord injuries, where it's her honor to help hasten that realization in others.

She doesn't keep her feelings inside anymore, either; in fact, she's something of a loudmouth. She doesn't think twice about speaking up or pointing out when things aren't more accessible. And, sure, she's sometimes resentful and frustrated, and the depression comes back and visits from time to time. But she knows none of those things define her. They're simply part of her. They're all just . . . well, buildings in the greater skyline that is her inner life. Some contain worse memories than others, but some are breathtakingly beautiful.

Speaking of.

She keeps her hand on this building's wall for a while. Something new and intangible has grown inside of her. A feeling. One she hasn't felt in a long time. Call it *peace.* As good a name as any.

Eventually, she knows she has to move on or someone will come and shoo her away.

Tears stinging her eyes, she lets go.

She whispers to the walls: "Love you, Baby Bird."

Nearby, almost as if in answer, an actual bird gives flight, singing. The timing is almost too perfect.

Ana looks up, smiling, and watches the bird against the sky.

She bears the bird no jealousy. She knows that feeling of flight. It's all the same. A flap of wings. A step. A push of a wheel. A blink of an eye. A breath.

Movement is movement, no matter how small or how achieved.

She points herself forward and moves.

# AUTHOR'S NOTE AND ACKNOWLEDGMENTS:
## ON GRIEF, WHYS, AND TWENTY FUCKING TWENTY-ONE

I hadn't intended on writing this part.

Readers of my previous novel, *Mary: An Awakening of Terror,* will know I wrote a pretty thorough foreword *and* afterword for that book, explaining where it came from and what I was trying to do with the story. I'm quite proud of what I wrote there; and that wraparound material wound up being really well-received (there might even be a few readers who liked the foreword and afterword better than the novel-stuff in between).

Writing an afterword for *Mary*'s follow-up seemed like an exercise in, at best, repetition, and, at worst, diminishing returns.

However, the deeper I got into the writing of *Nestlings* (which for a while was subtitled, *We Don't Belong Here*), the more unshakable the feeling became that I *needed* to do it again. There was something I needed to articulate.

But I'd be lying if I didn't say the prospect filled me with dread.

Lemme back up.

*Mary*'s foreword was, in effect, a eulogy for my mom, who died while I was working on the final draft of that novel in early 2021. Because that book was dedicated to her—and frankly because it had enough words already—I didn't go into further details about what *else* was happening that year. But as 2021 rolled on . . . well, here are the highlights:

In January (on the sixth, in fact, a few hours before the insurrection went down at the Capitol), my wife's mom died. Thirteen days later, my mom died. Two months later, one of my wife's best friends died. Then in September (the weekend before my fortieth birthday), our beloved cat died. The very next day, our beloved dog died. A few weeks after that, a potentially life- (or at least career-) changing professional opportunity fell apart after a year's worth of development. Then, like a hellish buzzer-beater, before December could end, my dad died of a sudden, aggressive cancer.

That's a lot for one year, right?

*But wait! There's more!* the mad, cosmic Pitchman of Bad Times shrieks with glee. In a way, those losses were the simplest part. Because on top of everything, this *whole time,* my wife was essentially bedridden, laid up by a mysterious chronic pain that made it impossible to move some days without unbearable agony. She saw close to forty doctors—none of them knew what was happening.

Meanwhile, up until the weekend they died, both our pets required intensive amounts of care. Our dog, in particular, had canine dementia, kidney problems, splenic cancer, seizure disorders, and who knows what else. As long as she ate and appeared to enjoy life, there was no way we were going to put her down prematurely, but taking care of her meant constant attention and medication and walks and cleanup from when she woke me up (around 4:00 a.m.) to when her sundown scaries dissipated and she finally fell asleep (around midnight). And since my wife couldn't, y'know, *move,* the bulk of this caretaking was up to me.

From March 2020 through September 2021, our little family was in this excruciating holding pattern: my wife, in agony; and me, under prolonged and extreme sleep deprivation, running on about four hours a night for eighteen months. (Our pets, it should be said, probably had an amazing time. Food, constant attention, the humans around 24/7? Living the dream.)

Along the way, my wife and I had to reconcile with further news that we almost definitely weren't going to be able to have biological kids of our own. Also, the less said about our living situation, the better. We had a landlord who was . . . well, I'm sure you can intuit after reading this book. Oh, and hey, did I mention this was all while an existentially terrifying, once-in-a-century pandemic was still raging, and more than half of our income had disappeared because our industry (film / TV / commercial acting) ground to a halt? On *that* front, I'm sure everyone reading this went through something similar, so that all just goes without saying.

Twenty Twenty-One was fucking brutal. I'd call it our annus horribilis if that phrase didn't make me titter.

But here's the thing. Even now, as I summarize those events, I find myself thinking, "Okay, *and*?" It's one thing to use a book to memorialize the death of a single person . . . but all this? What's my *point*? And here comes that dread again . . .

Isn't it funny how, in life, tragedies and traumas can just pile up, willy-nilly, but as soon as we decide to set it all down in writing, there's gotta be a point? A "why?" Some sort of thesis or payoff or grand unified theory. Otherwise, it's just *gratuitous.*

Being raised Jewish (don't let the name "Cassidy" fool you), you become pretty comfortable with "Why?" It's our holiest question—we're always asking it. Even if, most of the time, it only leads to either another "Why?" or to the universe finally smacking you with, "Well, why the fuck not?"

I suppose one major reason I needed to include all this is because, frankly, to me, this book would feel incomplete without it. This book *is* 2021 to me; that year imbues every moment of the story.

Unlike *Mary,* this wasn't a story I'd been carrying around with me since I was a kid. This was a relatively recent idea that, initially, just seemed like a hoot to write: "*Rosemary's Baby* meets *'Salem's Lot*"—count me in.

But as 2021 rolled its destructive, table-clearing way onward, writing this book became something far more intense.

I knew it'd be a New York story, but suddenly, I found myself able to try to capture the incredibly strange period of time we were living through in 2021 (and '22). Nowhere near as "post-pandemic" as we wanted to pretend, but also nothing like the nightmare we'd experienced in 2020. A nebulous time. Vacant buildings. Anxious interactions. An uncomfortable, unresolved feeling in the air I can only describe as . . . *We don't belong here.*

I'd also known this would be an explicitly Jewish take on vampire mythology, but as I worked on the manuscript, the volume of anti-Semitic incidents and statements swirling around became unignorable. Those constant cultural reminders (as well as that push and pull of assimilation) I think anyone from a nonhegemonic group recognizes . . . *We don't belong here.*

And, more than anything, this story allowed me to unpack the sudden disability my wife was experiencing, as well as my own surprise at finding myself as a caretaker. Not to mention what it was like to begin the year with parents *and* child surrogates *and* plans for future children . . . only to end the year with none of those things. Again, that feeling: *We don't belong here.*

But life didn't care, because here we were. "Why?" "Well, why the fuck not?"

This book is my attempt at articulating something happening in real time—a certain emotional homelessness. It's lecture notes written during a crash course on grief. Every character, including the city itself, is in an uncomfortable period of transition. Even our vampires-not-vampires are just stalling for time before they become statues to be gawked at.

It's a book about change. And it's a book about grief—essentially, change's hangover.

It's a book of liminal spaces. Because, as 2021 taught me, that's what grief is.

Grief is the space between two states of being: who you were and who you are.

It's an excruciatingly long, unlit hallway.

A staircase you have to crawl down, one interminable flight at a time.

I finished the first draft of this book on December 31, 2021. It was important to me that I not let that year end without some sort of victory. That said, it's not like on January 1, 2022, I hung up my mourner's clothes and hot-stepped into a new year. As the character of Frank exists to remind, oftentimes, it's when you think you're moving on that the past decides to rear its ugly mug. Trauma's like a bomb blast: there's the initial impact . . . and the shockwaves afterward.

I don't have some grand, unifying thesis for everything that happened. There's no punch line.

But at least I have this book to remind me that I got through the first part.

I also have this afterword—the one I hadn't planned on, and which has been making me ask "why" this whole time I've been writing it.

"Why" is a holy question. And writing is a holy act; sometimes it can lead to an epiphany. Suddenly I'm realizing *exactly* why I needed to include this damn thing. Look at that: bashert.

If this book is 2021, then I need to quickly tell you a little about 2022.

By 2022, we'd moved into a new apartment, and, most important . . . my wife was out of bed. Thanks to new doctors—and a heroic physical therapist—she *finally* had a diagnosis and a treatment plan.

In fact, a few months ago, I watched her perform the lead role in a play—a live performance! In a theater full of other people! Not only did being in an audience again feel like a miracle, it was an intensely physical role for her. She was playing an arctic scientist, climbing all over a stage decked out with expressionistic icebergs everywhere. This person who, barely a few months beforehand, couldn't even get out of bed without agony.

It was a lovely play, but I'm pretty sure no one else in that audience was crying like I was.

She still experiences occasional flare-ups of pain, but rarely like before. And we both know we're only at the beginning of processing the losses we incurred over Twenty Fucking Twenty-One. Somedays our house is like a Kübler-Ross theme park. I think Healing begins when you finally recognize there *is* no moving on. Only moving forward. You don't actually leave anything behind. You carry it with you. That's why the process of healing can feel so slow: you're carrying more weight now.

But I'm gonna wrap this up now, because I have a feeling you know this.

I'm willing to bet you've had your own Twenty Fucking Twenty-One.

I'm willing to bet you've also worn change like an ill-fitting garment that was *clearly* meant for someone else, not for you.

Hell, I'm willing to bet many of you reading this have had a year—or years—that make my Twenty Fucking Twenty-One look like a pizza party on ecstasy. Full of traumas and tragedies that don't have a payoff or a thesis or a punch line and fill you with dread to talk about.

And if you haven't *yet,* well . . . I hate to say it but Twenty Fucking Twenty-One has room for all of us.

I hope this book is scary. I hope this book is entertaining. But I also hope maybe its existence can also stand as a little confirmation for you (and for me), that bad years *do* end.

I hope that you're in a better place as you read these words. I hope you're climbing expressionistic icebergs.

And, if not, then, in the somewhat bastardized words of a Jewish prayer: maybe next year, wherever you find yourself.

I'm indebted to a number of people who made this book possible.

First and foremost, my wife. For everything.

Secondly, my editor, Jen—not just for making me a better writer (however much I kick and scream), but for her generous and frank insights into both childbirth and postpartum.

Early readers who made this book so much better with their insights and questions: Stephanie Willing, Brian Silliman, Matthew Trumbull, Rachel Harrison, Clay McCleod Chapman, Anna O'Donoghue, Kim-Mei Kirtland, Marguerite Turley, and Katlin McGrath.

Other massive thanks go to Jessi Gotta, Becky Comtois, and Patrick Shearer, for the inspiration. My reps, past and present (Daniela Gonzales, Lawrence Mattis, Casey Minella, Samantha Starr, Harris Spylios), as well as their intrepid assistants (Sarah Flores, Jack Clayman), for their patience as I put projects on hold to work on drafts of this book.

To Liz Garbus, Dan Balgoyan, Michael Sheen, Rich Gold, Jenna Santoianni, Andrew Miano, Britta Rowings, for their belief in that *other* project, which kept me going through a lot of 2021.

To everyone at Tor Nightfire, for all their tremendous work and for patiently fielding all my anxious emails, especially Libby Collins and Isa Caban. All hail the Coven.

To my agent, Alec Shane, and lawyer, Joe Dapello.

To the Chabad-Lubavitchers who always bring me challah at my office.

To John Darnielle, for the permission to use his lyrics as this book's epigraph (and his lawyer Ryan Matteson for handling my correspondence).

To Craig "muMs" Grant. We miss you.

To my dad, Barry Cassidy. There's so much more I want to say. Hopefully with the next book.

Speaking of books, in earlier drafts of this one, the conversation between Reid and Isaac about vampire fiction was much, much longer, and I got to name-check some of my favorite vampire/vampire-adjacent books. Those would include: *'Salem's Lot* (Stephen King), *The Keep* (F. Paul Wilson), *Black*

*Ambrosia* (Elizabeth Engstrom), *The Vampire Tapestry* (Suzy McKee Charnas), *The Hunger* (Whitley Strieber), *30 Days of Night* (Steve Niles, Ben Templesmith), *In the Valley of the Sun* (Andy Davidson), *Fledgling* (Octavia E. Butler), *Certain Dark Things* (Silvia Moreno-Garcia), *The Southern Book Club's Guide to Slaying Vampires* (Grady Hendrix), *Anno Dracula* (Kim Newman), *The Passage* (Justin Cronin), the African Immortals series (Tananarive Due), the Vampire Chronicles (Anne Rice), *Dracula* (Bram Stoker), *Varney the Vampire* (James Malcolm Rymer, Thomas Peckett Prest), and "The Vampyre" (John Polidori).

I'm also indebted to novels about parenthood and pregnancy, such as *Nightbitch* (Rachel Yoder), *Baby Teeth* (Zoje Stage), *Good Neighbors* (Sarah Langan), *The Changeling* (Victor LaValle), *Rosemary's Baby* (Ira Levin), *Such Sharp Teeth* (Rachel Harrison), *Full Immersion* (Gemma Amor), and *The Shining* (Stephen King).

And special shout-out to Bari Wood's *The Tribe,* the first unapologetically Jewish horror novel I ever read (and still one of the only).

Lastly, this book depicts physical disability, and I wanted to acknowledge something more than just names here.

Horror is full of examples where physical disabilities are used as a cheap and easy way to either scare the nondisabled reader with the promise of punishment or wring some cheap sympathy out of an already-disabled, vulnerable character. As with *Mary,* I found myself very aware that I was writing about a lived experience I myself hadn't actually gone through firsthand. Also, as with *Mary,* I did what I could as far as research, interviews, and consulting with sensitivity readers went. But I also wanted Ana to be imperfect, a "bad" disabled character, someone who's uncomfortable, cranky, depressed, confused, stubborn, in mourning for her life before—so that her story could ultimately, hopefully, be an empowering one. One of the prayers we say during Yom Kippur is the Al Chet, a sort of call-and-response communal apology. It's based, in part, on an archery term, and when we recite it, we atone for the times we "missed the mark." I've always liked that phrase, how it implies goodness is a target, not some ephemeral state of being. I hope, if *you* have dealt with a disability like Ana's, you find that at least some aspects of Ana's journey feel authentic. I hope I haven't missed the mark too badly with you. And I am so grateful to everyone who fielded my questions about paraplegia, nerve damage, and (very, very!) rare complications that could hypothetically arise during childbirth—especially Dr. Demetrios Karides and Dr. Allison Snyder.

I am also grateful for those who helped me understand what life can be like when you rely on a wheelchair, including the YouTube channels of Wheelsnoheels, Pro Tips for Paras, and Paralyzed Living; and those who helped me check the text for any unintentional ableism, particularly Tessa Villanueva.

And most of all, the invaluable Christopher and Dana Reeve Foundation, for all their resources for the newly paralyzed. And especially one amazing person at that foundation, Donna Lowich, who not only put up with all my questions but also with my erratic schedule, and who never flinched when she received that first email from a total stranger which essentially began, "So, I'm a horror writer and I have some questions . . ."

May we all be so fearless.

NAT CASSIDY
November 2022
New York City

## ABOUT THE AUTHOR

Kent Meister

NAT CASSIDY writes horror for the page, stage, and screen. His critically acclaimed, award-winning horror plays have been produced across the United States, as well as Off- and Off-Off-Broadway. He won the New York Innovative Theatre Award for Outstanding Solo Performance for his one-man show about H. P. Lovecraft and was commissioned by the Kennedy Center to write a libretto for a short opera (about the end of the world, of course). As an established actor on stage, audio, and television (usually playing monsters and villains on shows such as *Blue Bloods, Bull, Quantico, FBI,* and *Law & Order: SVU*), Cassidy also authored the novelization of the hit podcast *Steal the Stars,* which was published by Tor Books and named one of the best books of 2017 by NPR. His Nightfire debut, *Mary: An Awakening of Terror,* was published in 2022 and was named one of the best horror novels of the year by *Esquire, Paste, Harper's Bazaar, CrimeReads,* and *The Lineup.* He lives in New York with his wife, the actor Kelley Rae O'Donnell.

natcassidy.com
Twitter: @natcassidy